Apollo reached ou **fingers around Ell** **hands still. "What** **he asked, his voice**

She looked up at him soft, sassy pink lips shaped into a perfect O. Her Color flooded her face.

"If you were thinking you were going to take my shirt off, either stop now and walk out that door, or keep going and realize that I will have you flat on your back and screaming my name in a *very* different way before you can protest."

Her color deepened…her eyes grew even wider. He thought she would run. Because Elle was a *good* girl. And she was stone-cold, aloof, and fancied herself far above him.

It had made him want to destroy that façade from the first. He hadn't. Because he knew that she was innocent. Knew that she was nothing more than a cosseted rich girl who would be completely out of her depth with a man like him. A man who had grown up on the streets in Athens—who had learned the hard truths about life early on. About loss. About the true nature of people.

He had known that if he ever touched her it would violate the trust he had built with her father.

But if she was going to touch *him* now, if she was going to remove the barrier that had always loomed between them, then he wasn't going to put a stop to it.

One Night With Consequences

When one night…leads to pregnancy!

When succumbing to a night of unbridled desire
it's impossible to think past the morning after!

But, with the sheets barely settled, that little blue line
appears on the pregnancy test and it doesn't take long
to realise that one night of white-hot passion
has turned into a lifetime of consequences!

Only one question remains:

How do you tell a man you've just met
that you're about to share more than just his bed?

Find out in:

Look for more *One Night With Consequences*
coming soon!

THE GREEK'S NINE-MONTH REDEMPTION

BY
MAISEY YATES

First Published in Great Britain 2016
By Mills & Boon, an imprint of HarperCollins*Publishers*
1 London Bridge Street, London, SE1 9GF

© 2016 Maisey Yates

ISBN: 978-0-263-92116-8

Our policy is to use papers that are natural, renewable and recyclable
products and made from wood grown in sustainable forests. The logging
and manufacturing processes conform to the legal environmental
regulations of the country of origin.

Printed and bound in Spain
by CPI, Barcelona

Maisey Yates is a *USA TODAY* bestselling author of more than thirty romance novels. She has a coffee habit she has no interest in kicking, and a slight Pinterest addiction. She lives with her husband and children in the Pacific Northwest. When Maisey isn't writing she can be found singing in the grocery store, shopping for shoes online and probably not doing dishes. Check out her website: maiseyyates.com.

Visit the Author Profile page at millsandboon.co.uk for more titles.

To Jackie, Megan and Nicole for listening to me say,
'This is weird. I'm not doing it right.
I don't think this is good enough!'
every time I work on a book, and helping me through it.
Every time.

CHAPTER ONE

SOMETIMES ELLE ST. JAMES imagined taking a pen and stabbing it straight through Apollo Savas's chest. Not to kill him of course. He didn't have a heart so the wound would hardly be fatal. Just to hurt him.

Still, other times she fantasized about crossing the boardroom, wrenching free the knot on his tie and tearing the front of his shirt open, scraping her fingernails down his heated skin and feeling all those hard muscles beneath her hands. Finally. After nine long years of resisting him, resisting the heat that roared through her body every time their eyes met.

That one was *way* more disturbing than the stabbing thing.

It was also far too frequent.

They were sitting in a crowded meeting and she should be paying attention. But all she could think about was what she would do to him if she had five minutes with him, alone, behind a locked door.

It would either be violent or naked.

He was talking about budgets and cuts. And she hated those words. It would mean scaling down her team again. As had been the story of the past twelve months, ever since he'd bought her out from her father's holding company. A company that had since sunk into bankruptcy.

Just another moment in a long line of Apollo undermining her. Finally, her father had been forced to give her responsibility. Since his stepson had finally proven to be a viper in the nest, so to speak.

She'd been installed as CEO. Then Apollo had come down like a hammer.

It was his fault. At least in part. And nothing would convince her otherwise.

She had a plan. A plan he seemed intent on thwarting at every turn. She knew she could rescue Matte without all of these sweeping staff changes, but he wouldn't give her a chance.

Because—just as he'd always done—he was making it his mission to undermine her. To prove he was better even now.

But that didn't stop her eyes from following his hands as he gestured broadly, from wondering what those hands might feel like on her skin.

She could write what she knew about sex on a napkin. The sad thing was, it would be two words.

Apollo Savas.

He'd been sex to her from the moment she'd understood what the word *sex* meant. From the moment she'd understood why men and women were different, and why it was such a wonderful thing.

The dark-haired, dark-eyed son of the woman her father had married when Elle was fourteen. He had been fascinating. So different from her. Rough around the edges, a product of his upbringing in a class of society Elle herself had had no contact with. His mother had been a maid prior to her marriage to Elle's father. The culture shock had been intense. And very, very interesting.

Of course, since then he'd grown into a dark-hearted

man who'd betrayed her family and put her under his boot heel.

Still, she wanted him.

The Big Bad Wolf of the business world, huffing and puffing and blowing your dreams down.

"Don't you agree, Ms. St. James?"

She looked up, her eyes locking with Apollo's, her heart thudding a dull rhythm. The last thing she needed was to admit she'd missed what he was saying. She would rather admit to having fantasies of killing him than the alternative.

"You'll have to repeat the question, Mr. Savas. My attention span for repetition isn't infinite. This is the same song you've been singing for months, and it isn't any more effective or logical than it was last time."

He stood, his movements liquid silk. She could see from the black glitter in his eyes that she was going to pay for her words. The thought sent a shiver down her spine. Fear mingled with unaccountable lust.

"I am sorry you find me boring. I shall endeavor to make myself more interesting. You see, I was speaking of the fact that for a company to be successful it must be sleek. Well oiled. Each cog functioning at top capacity. Extraneous cogs are unnecessary. Sluggish cogs are unnecessary. I was attempting to be delicate with my metaphor." He began to walk down the length of the boardroom table, the postures of each person he moved behind straightening as he did. "Perhaps I would have held your attention a bit better if I would have simply said that if I identify a portion of your company functioning at less than optimum capacity I will start slashing and burning your employees like they were dry brush."

Her entire face felt like it was on fire, her heart pounding harder now. She clenched her shaking hands into fists. "Everyone in this company—"

"I'm sure your speech is about to be inspiring and truly emotional, but since this is not a feel-good underdog sports movie, you should perhaps save your breath, Ms. St. James. You can say what you will, but I have seen the numbers. Conviction doesn't equal profits. I will be reviewing everything closely and making cuts at my discretion. With that, I think the meeting is adjourned. Ms. St. James has a very low tolerance for my droning, I hear. If it is the same for the rest of you, you should be pleased to be sent on your way."

The collective surge of bodies making their way out of the room reminded Elle of a herd of wildebeests fleeing a lion.

A big, bored lion who wanted nothing more than to scare them by flashing his teeth. He wasn't going to give chase. Not now.

No, now his focus had turned to her.

"You are in rare form today, Elle."

"I am in exactly the appropriate form, *Apollo*," she said, reverting to the use of his first name.

They were *family*, after all.

Not that she'd ever seen him as a brother. A sexual fantasy she didn't want. Her biggest competitor. Her darkest enemy. He was all of those things, but not a brother.

"I own your company," he said. "I own *you*." Oh, dammit all, why did those words make her...ache? "You never seem to show me the proper amount of fear."

"Real leaders don't rule with an iron fist," she hissed. "They understand that intimidation isn't the way to gain respect."

She shouldn't be talking back to him, but she could never control her tongue around him. They'd known each other for too long. Had spent too many years in the same household.

And she had spent too many years tearing strips off him when she'd felt like she had the upper hand. When she was the blood daughter of her father, the one who held a rightful place in their upstate mansion.

Things changed. Oh, how things changed.

"Says the woman who is no longer in a true position of leadership." He smiled. Showing his teeth.

She wouldn't scatter. She would not. She was not a wildebeest.

"Oh, but I am. As long as Matte is an independently operating entity beneath your large corporate umbrella, I am here to run it as best as I can. I am here to stand in the gap for my employees and give you the information black-and-white printouts can't."

"You're being ridiculous. Everything is electronic now. I'm not wasting resources on printouts."

He turned and started to walk out of the office. "You know what I mean. A flat, two-dimensional report reducing everything to statistics and cold numbers is hardly the be-all and end-all."

"That's where you're wrong," he said, taking long strides down the hall.

Elle had to take two steps to his one, her high heels clicking loudly on the marble floor as she hurried after him. "I am not wrong. It doesn't offer the whole picture. You can't possibly know how the company is really functioning. How each worker impacts the creative process. Matte isn't just a magazine. It's a line of cosmetics, a fashion brand. We have books and—"

"Yes," he said, stepping into an elevator, "thank you, I am very familiar with how my assets function."

"Then you should be aware of the fact that I have strategies in place that require all of the manpower I possess. Initiatives that take time to launch but will catapult this brand into worldwide recognition."

"Yes. So you said last time we met. And, unlike you, I don't drift off in meetings."

She growled and charged into the elevator after him. "I did not drift off."

He pushed the button to the lobby and the doors slid closed. Then he turned that dark, unsettling focus onto her. The air around them seemed to shrink, rendering the already crowded space impossibly tight. "No. I don't believe you did, Elle," he said, his voice as silken as his movements. "You were looking at me with a great deal of intensity. Too much to be on another planet entirely. What was it you were thinking about exactly?"

"Driving a pen through your chest," she said, smiling.

Because she would be damned if she'd say, *Tearing your clothes off and seeing if you're as good in reality as you are in my dreams.*

Even though she felt like that reality was written all over her face, across her skin in the red stain of a blush.

He offered her a wry smile. "You know I can't be killed like that. You have to cut my head off and bury it in a separate location to my body."

"I'll let the hit men know." She turned and smiled at him again, and he offered one in return.

The doors slid open, revealing the rather vacant bottom floor. Matte shared its offices with many other businesses, and with penthouses on the top floor. At this hour of the day not many people were coming and going.

"Where is it you're staying, Apollo?" she asked. "A crypt somewhere in Midtown?"

"The one just next to yours, Elle," he said, his tone light. "After you."

He extended his hand, waiting for her to step out of the elevator. She swept past him, moving through the lobby and going through the revolving doors. She stepped on to the busy Manhattan sidewalk, put her sunglasses on and stood there, tapping her foot.

Apollo emerged a moment later, straightening his suit jacket and standing across from her for a moment.

"Care to continue shouting at me while I walk?" he asked.

"I'm not shouting at you. I'm calmly explaining to you why you're wrong in your methods of handling my company."

He turned away from her, walking down the crowded street, his broad back filling her vision.

"Apollo!" Okay, she was shouting now. "We are not through with our meeting."

"I think we adjourned it."

"The general meeting," she said, upping her pace. "But *we* are not done."

"I'm just here," he said, gesturing to an old boutique hotel only two buildings down from the Matte offices. "Since I'm in town primarily to deal with Matte I thought I should stay close."

"Congratulations. How sensible."

"I have my moments. Judging by the fact that I'm a billionaire who successfully staged a takeover of your father's company, I've had several moments, actually."

"If you were as clever as you think you are you would listen to my plans for Matte. The answer isn't to reduce us down to nothing. You have to let me try and expand it, otherwise we really will die."

"You're assuming I'm trying to save you, dear Elle. Perhaps I just want to pull the plug."

"You... You..." She was sputtering now. She never sputtered. She blamed him.

"Villain. Scoundrel. I answer to any of those really."

"You have always been a competitive son of a bitch, but this is above and beyond."

"You're assuming this is a competition."

"What else could it be? You're ungrateful. For everything my father gave you. And for the fact that he didn't give you everything."

He chuckled, a dark, humorless sound. "Oh, you mean that he didn't give me his corporation, or Matte, in the first place? Why do you think he installed you, Elle? Your competence? No. He gave you the position to keep a foothold once I bought him out."

The words landed hard, hollowing out her midsection. Leaving nothing but a crater behind.

Like you didn't suspect that already.

She had. Of course she had. But the fact he knew it meant it was obvious. Possibly to everyone.

The doorman opened the golden door for them and Apollo paused to tip him before continuing on. Elle opened her purse and produced her own dollar, handing it to the man before going in after Apollo.

She was not allowing him to do her tipping for her.

"I am in the penthouse suite. It's very nice."

"Why am I not surprised that I just got out of a meeting where you were discussing tightening belts for my company, and yet you're staying in the penthouse suite."

He pushed the button for the elevator and the doors slid open. She followed in after, starting to feel slightly out of breath.

"I am not in need of money, *agape*, if that's why you thought I was mentioning cuts."

Agape. She hated that. He'd started using that on her

sometime when she was in high school. Just to make her angry. And some small part of her grabbed hold of it every time, holding it near. *Love.*

Oh, what a ridiculous, stupid…

She really hated her hormones.

"Why else would you mention cuts?" she asked, keeping her tone sweet.

The doors slid shut and she had the uncomfortable feeling of being trapped in a closed-in space again.

"Because *you* need the money. Matte needs the money. In a digital world your print publication is lagging and while you have certainly come up with innovative ways to compete, you haven't leveled out yet."

"But if you have enough—"

He chuckled. "I don't run a charity. I run a business. My corporation turns profits. That's what it does. I make money hand over fist, and I'm comfortable admitting that. I'm proud of it. But that won't continue if I don't refine my assets. Refining is a hot and painful process. It takes fire. And people being fired."

"Ha-ha. You're far too funny for your own good."

He frowned. "Was that funny? It wasn't meant to be."

The elevator stopped and the doors opened on a narrow hallway. Apollo stepped out and walked down a few doors, pausing to open it. "Come in," he said.

She very much had the feeling of being a small, vulnerable creature invited into the lair of a predator.

You are not a wildebeest. You are just as scary as he is. You are a lioness.

She stepped over the threshold and into the room. It was lovely, he was right. Ornate moldings and trim framing the space, the windows looking out over Central Park.

There was a large seating area with a bar, and off to

the left an open door that she could see led to a bedroom with a very large, dramatic bed.

She imagined, as tall as he was, he took up most of the mattress. That thought made her picture him—long, tanned limbs sprawled out on the bed. Would he look more relaxed in sleep? Would he seem less...lethal out of that custom-fit black suit that conformed to every line, every muscle in his body?

He closed the door behind her with a finality that made her jump.

"My team is the best there is," she said. "They have some of the most creative minds in this—or any—industry. You have to admit the fact that the Matte Guidebooks have been hugely successful. And the makeup guide actually helped to increase sales of the cosmetics. It was specific to the brand and that—"

"Again you are telling me things I already know. I didn't get to this position in life without paying attention. I understand that your team is important to you. But if I don't do what must be done, if I don't make the hard cuts, none of you will have a job."

"But I—"

"You seem to be under the impression that this is a democracy, Elle. Be assured, absolutely, that this is a dictatorship. I am not negotiating with you. And it is only by my good graces that your pretty ass remains in the CEO's office."

Heat and fury washed over Elle in a fiery baptism. "And here I thought it was because I'm good at my job."

"You are," he said, taking a step toward her. "But there are a great many people who would be good at your job. People who didn't get handed their position from their daddy."

"Oh, that's hilarious, Apollo. As if you didn't get a leg

up from my father, you Judas." She took a step toward him, rage propelling her now. "My father treated you like one of his own children. He put you through school."

"And I excelled on my own."

"Then you stabbed him in the back."

"I bought him out for much more than thirty pieces of silver, little girl. Perhaps what really hurts is the fact that you were betrayed by your father, not by me. He put you in this position knowing you would fail."

She gritted her teeth, doing her best to shake off his words. To not allow them to take hold. All of this reached down deep. To old wounds. To the way she'd felt she couldn't measure up to Apollo, the son her father had always wanted. To her own fears of being eternally inadequate. And he knew it.

She would not let him win so easily. "He trusted you. When you offered to help he didn't imagine you dismantling everything."

Apollo lifted one broad shoulder. "He made a mistake in trusting me."

"Clearly. You would betray not only the man who set you on the path to success, but your own mother."

"She's fine. Your father is hardly financially ruined. She continues to enjoy her status as his wife. And again, Elle, need I remind you your father sold Matte, and some of his other holdings, to me of his own free will."

"You had him in a position where he couldn't say no."

Apollo took another step toward her. He was so close now that she could see his eyes weren't completely black. She could see a faint ring of gold that faded to copper, then to deep brown. Could see the dark stubble beginning to grow in at his jawline.

Could smell the scent of his aftershave and skin.

"Interesting you put it like that. If dire financial straits take away choice you could argue my mother had little choice in marrying your father in the first place."

"That's ridiculous," Elle said. "She wanted to."

"Did she?"

"Of course."

"A cleaning lady offered the chance to live in luxury after years barely making it in the US? After years of homeless poverty in Greece?"

"That isn't… It has nothing to do with this."

"Maybe," he said. "Or maybe the point is that you can always say no, Elle." He leaned in. "Always."

She could barely breathe, her head swimming, her entire body on high alert. She was almost certain she had no blood in her veins, not anymore. It was molten lava now, heating her from her core.

She remembered so clearly feeling this way every time he brushed past her in the halls of the family estate. Every time she caught sight of him at the pool—his lean, muscular body so fascinating to the girl she'd been.

Only once had they ever come so close to each other. Only one other time had she ever thought he might feel the same forbidden desire that she'd felt from the moment she'd set eyes on him.

Apollo is going to be your new stepbrother.

Everything in her had rebelled at that, immediately. Because she had seen him and wanted him in a way she knew would be wrong once their parents were married. So she had distanced him. She had been…well, sometimes she'd been terrible. But it had been for her own survival.

It was even worse now. He was still her stepbrother. But now, any affection she'd ever felt for him had been twisted by his betrayal. She should have stopped obsessing about him a long time ago.

But she hadn't. She couldn't. She was a slave to this, to him. Always.

She hated it. She hated *him*.

And she had spent nine years resisting him. Embracing the anger, the annoyance and everything else she could possibly use as a barrier between her desire for him and her actions.

Giving in would be a failure. In terms of her self-control. In terms of her relationship with her father. What would he think if he knew she wanted Apollo? What sort of scandal would erupt if the media knew she was helplessly attracted to her stepbrother?

So she had denied it. Pushed it down deep. But she had been aware of it every time she saw him. Every glance. Every accidental brush of his hand against hers. Every time she went to bed at night, hot and aching for something she knew only he could give her.

But he had bought out her father's company. He was gunning for Matte. Her father had installed her as CEO to keep some connection to the company—just as Apollo had said. And she'd failed spectacularly.

She could feel everything slipping out of her grasp. The company. Her control. Everything.

And she'd never tasted him. Never had him. This man who was destroying her whole life. Who commanded her fantasies and called out the deepest, darkest desire from deep inside of her.

For what? For appearances. To triumph.

There would be no triumph here. She was losing. Utterly. Epically.

Why not have this? Why not have him?

It was all going to burn to the ground. She might as well go up in flames with it.

She could see his pulse throbbing at the base of his

throat. If only she had a pen in her hand. It would be so easy from this position to stab him clean through with it. But she didn't.

So instead, she reached up and grabbed hold of the knot in his tie, and wrenched it free.

CHAPTER TWO

APOLLO SAVAS DIDN'T entertain daydreams. He was a man of practicality and action. When he wanted something, he didn't sit around fantasizing about it, he took it.

That was the only reason he knew that it was no hallucination that Elle St. James, his stepsister and mortal enemy, was currently stripping his clothes off, her eyes bright, glittering with rage and desire.

He had resisted her, this, for years. Resisted her. Out of deference to the man he considered a father. Out of respect for all he'd been given.

But all of it had proven to be false, had proven to be a lie. And still he had roped Elle off. Had kept her separate—in many ways—from his plans for revenge.

And David St. James had known he would. Because whether she knew it or not, he had always protected Elle. She had always mattered.

But things had changed. And now she was tugging at his tie. And he was tired of restraint.

He reached out and wrapped his fingers around her wrist, holding her hands still. "What the hell are you doing?" he asked, his voice a growl.

She looked up at him, her green eyes round, those soft, sassy pink lips shaped into a perfect O. "I…" Color flooded her face.

"If you were thinking you were going to take my shirt off, either stop now and walk out that door, or keep going and understand that I will have you flat on your back and screaming my name in a very *different* way before you can protest."

Her color deepened, her eyes growing even wider. He thought she would run. Because Elle was a *good* girl, by the standards of her father. Though, she was stone-cold, aloof and fancied herself far above him.

It had made him want to destroy that facade from the first. He hadn't. Because he knew that she was innocent. Knew that she was nothing more than a cosseted rich girl who would be completely out of her depth with a man like him. A man who had grown up on the streets in Athens, who had learned the hard truths about life early on. About loss. About the true nature of people.

He had known that if he ever touched her it would violate the trust he had built with her father.

But if she was going to touch him now, if she was going to remove that barrier that had always loomed between them, then he wasn't going to put a stop to it.

Apollo Savas was a man who took what he wanted.

With one exception.

Elle.

He had wanted her from the moment she'd transformed from a girl to a woman. A haughty, rude woman who walked by him with her nose in the air half the time. Perversely, it had always made him want to have her even more.

She thought his hands were dirty. Thought he was beneath her. It made him want to put his filthy hands all over her. Made him want to pull her right down with him.

His biggest betrayal had never been buying St. James

Corp's most valuable assets and breaking them off piece by piece.

No, his biggest betrayal had started long before he'd discovered David St. James's true nature. It had begun long before he'd discovered the dark secrets surrounding just why he and his mother had been brought into the St. James home.

His first betrayal had been in the way he'd looked at Elle.

But everything was shot to hell now anyway. Every allegiance broken with his "family." Why not this, too? Why not slaughter the last sacred cow?

He had destroyed everything else. He might as well destroy this, too. And he would relish it.

Her hand was still frozen, holding on to his tie. Then, her eyes took on a determined glitter, her lips curling into a snarl as she yanked hard on the silken fabric, pulling it free from its knot.

He growled, grabbing ahold of that sleek high ponytail that had been taunting him from the moment he had walked into the boardroom today. He wrapped his fingers around her coppery hair and pulled hard, tilting her head backward. Her nostrils flared slightly, her lips parting.

They held their positions for a moment, staring at each other, clearly waiting to see what the next move was.

He had waited too long. He was not waiting another moment.

He would have her now. Strip away every prim and proper layer. Punish her with his kiss as he should have done that day she'd dared him at the pool. The only time the anger between them had given way and revealed the layer beneath.

Of course, she had acted as though nothing had happened after. And so had he.

But he would make sure this time she would not be able to act unscathed after he was through with her.

He wrapped his arm around her slender waist, drawing her up against his body as he backed them both toward the wall. It stopped their progress ruthlessly, her shoulder blades pressed firmly against the hard surface. He bent his head, kissing her neck, his teeth scraping her skin.

The sound that escaped her lips was raw and desperate, her hands clutching his shoulders, her fingernails digging into his skin through the fabric of his suit jacket. Then she slid her palms down flat, grabbing hold of the front of his shirt and tugging hard, sending buttons flying as she wrenched it open. She pushed his jacket from his shoulders, grabbing hold of his shirt and shoving it down, too. He unbuttoned the cuffs, helping her and her progress, and untucking it from his pants and throwing it down onto the floor.

She looked completely shocked, and wholly satisfied by her actions as she regarded his body. Then she pressed her palms to his chest and slid her fingers down to his stomach, her fingernails scraping him lightly as she did. She grabbed hold of his belt, making quick work of that, as well.

"Greedy," he said, taking hold of her wrists and drawing her arms up over her head, holding her there with one hand as he set to work on the buttons of her silk blouse with the other.

She fought against him, the color in her cheeks deepening, her breasts rising and falling with the shallow gasps of her breath. He chuckled when her shirt fell open, revealing an insubstantial red lace bra and he imagined she thought it made her seem daring.

She arched her back, thrusting her breasts into greater prominence. He tightened his hold on her, pressing her hands more firmly against the wall. "You don't get to set the terms," he said. "Not in the boardroom, not in the bedroom. I am in charge in *all* things."

"Always a competition with you, isn't it?" she asked.

"Oh, *agape*, it has never been a competition. How can it be when I always win?"

For the first time, he saw a slight flicker of doubt in her eyes. But it was quickly replaced by a challenge. "So insecure that you have to exert your dominance in such a cliché fashion? You are exactly the same here as you are in the office."

He leaned in, his lips a whisper away from hers. "You're going to pay for that."

"I hope this isn't an empty threat, Apollo," she said, the words throaty, enticing. "You seem to be full of those."

He closed the distance between them, closing his teeth around her bottom lip and biting her. She gasped and he pulled away. The flush in her cheeks had spread to her neck, had down to the full swell of her breasts. She might be angry, but she was aroused, too.

"One thing you need to learn, *agape*, is that my threats are never empty. It's simply that the consequences might be delayed in coming."

She looked down, then back up. "I do hope the coming isn't terribly delayed today."

Those words, coming from Elle's lips, seemed shocking. From any other woman it might have been commonplace dirty talk. Not even all that dirty when it came down to it. But from Elle? It had the desired effect.

He was so hard he thought he was going to burst through the zipper on his pants. His heart was raging, his hand shaking as he undid the last button on her blouse and pulled it from her shoulders.

He couldn't remember the last time a woman had affected him in such a way. If one ever had. But then, he had never been in a situation quite like this. His partner had never looked at him with lust and rage burning from her eyes all at the same time. She'd never looked quite like she wanted to strangle him and have her way with him in the same moment.

And, he had never been with Elle.

"I didn't realize you were a dirty talker, Elle." He scraped the edge of her ear with his teeth. "If you had been negotiating this way all along you might have been a lot more successful."

"You're a bastard," she bit out, turning her head and tracing the line of his jaw with the edge of her tongue. "A complete and utter—"

"And you want me," he said, releasing his hold on her and drawing his face back, pressing the tip of his nose against hers and meeting her fierce gaze. "So what does that say about you?"

"Oh, I know that all of this is the final nail in the coffin of my decency." She grabbed the end of his belt buckle and yanked it through the loops, then set about working on the closure of his slacks.

"Go out with style, I say." He slid his hands down her slender waist, to the full curve of her hip, and down farther, gripping the hem of her skirt and shoving it up roughly over her hips. No surprise, her panties were the same red lace as the bra.

Not that he was complaining.

"I took you for a white cotton kind of girl," he said. "Who knew that you had so many secrets?"

"You're never going to know my secrets, Apollo," she said.

"So venomous," he said, his lips touching hers now as he spoke the words. "And yet, you're dying to have me."

She put her hand between them, pressing her palm against his hardened arousal. "Same goes."

"I'm tired of talking."

And then, he crushed his mouth to hers, claiming the kiss he should have taken years ago.

Elle had no idea what she was thinking. She wasn't thinking. She was feeling. Feeling everything. Rage, need, arousal like she had never known existed.

She would like to be confused about this. About how this could happen. About how she could be doing this with a man she hated so very much. But lust and anger had always been twisted up together where Apollo was concerned. Well, maybe not always. But in the past few years. And that was when her desire for him had turned from a girlish crush into a woman's need.

She wasn't sixteen anymore. She knew what men and women did in the dark. She didn't need her own hands-on experience to be aware.

But somewhere, during all of that, Apollo had gone from being someone she trusted and admired—a member of the St. James family—to their bitterest enemy. And somewhere, as that change had taken place, her desire for him had changed, as well.

And now it was this strange, twisted thing that she couldn't begin to untangle. And there was no other man who made her feel anything near what he made her feel.

It didn't matter that it was sick. It didn't matter that it was wrong. What Apollo made her feel was pure adrenaline. Pure excitement. Even if it wasn't all good.

He made every other man she had ever gone out with seem like a bland, beige substitute.

That was why this was happening. Really, it was why it *needed* to happen. When this was over, she would finally be cleansed.

Her need for him would go down in one fiery ball of pleasure and rage. And when she looked at him she would feel…nothing.

Oh, she wanted that more than anything.

She kissed him back with all of that. All of the anger, all of the lust. His tongue swept against hers, his hold on her hips firm, blunt fingertips digging into her skin. Then he shifted his position, putting his hands between her thighs, stroking his fingers over the thin lace that concealed her desire for him.

She gasped, everything inside of her shaking. She had never been this intimate with a man before, and yet she wasn't afraid. She wasn't experiencing any virginal nerves. She was more than ready for this. It was the combination of years of fantasies. An explosion of… Well, of everything.

His fingers slipped beneath the fabric, gliding through her slick flesh. If he'd had any doubt about how much she wanted him, he couldn't doubt it now.

"Yes," he said, the word a growl.

The way he said that, the absolute, incontrovertible evidence of how much he wanted her in return radiated through her. Spurred her on. She grabbed hold of the waistband of his pants and underwear, tugging them down his lean hips. There was no place for tenderness here, no place for hesitation.

She reached between their bodies, wrapping her hand around his hardened length. It was her turn to shudder, her turn to growl. She had never touched a man like this. She had no idea he would be so very big. She was nearly weak with wanting him. This was why she felt hollow. This was what she needed to be filled.

He slipped one finger inside of her and her breath hissed through her teeth, the unfamiliar invasion shocking and immensely pleasurable.

She took hold of his arms, clinging onto his rock hard biceps as he continued to tease her with a preview of what she really wanted.

She looked up at him, her heart hammering in her chest. He was beautiful. There was no question. And she wanted him. She wanted him more than she'd ever wanted anything in her entire life. It was important that she know it was him. As if it could be anyone else. As if anyone else could ever make her feel this way. This exhilarating mixture of destructive anger and impossible need.

She kissed the corner of his mouth, tracing his lower lip with the tip of her tongue. He moved his hand from between her thighs, lifting it, grabbed hold of her bra and pulled it down, revealing her breasts to his gaze. He lowered his head, drawing one tightened nipple deep into his mouth.

Sensation shot through her like an arrow, hitting her low and deep. A low, harsh sound escaped her lips and she let her head fall back as she laced her fingers through his hair, tugging hard as he continued to pleasure her.

"Please," she whimpered, "please."

He moved away from her, then bent down grabbing ahold of his pants, pulling his wallet out of the pocket before producing a condom.

Her breath gathered up in her chest like a ball and held there, a heavy weight she couldn't move. She could only watch him. Look her fill at his beautiful, masculine form. He was even more beautiful than she had imagined.

He returned to her, his bare chest pressing against

hers as he flattened her against the wall. She looked at his face, his gorgeous, thoroughly despised, utterly beloved face.

She grabbed hold of him, bracketing his face with her hands and tugging him forward, kissing him hard and deep. He put his hand back between her thighs, this time pushing two fingers into her, stretching her gently. She was so ready for him. Beyond ready.

"Do it," she said against his lips.

He moved his hand, gripping hold of her hips, sliding one hand down her thigh and lifting her leg, opening her to him. He tested her slick entrance with the blunt head of his arousal. Then he thrust deep inside.

The pain was sharp, swift. Tears stung her eyes, and she shut them quickly because she didn't want him to see. She didn't want him to know. She had felt powerful a few moments ago, but this made her feel a lot more vulnerable. Vulnerable was not what she wanted. She wanted pleasure, she wanted her desire satisfied. She wanted to rid herself of this toxic, intense feeling she had for him once and for all.

But, she hadn't anticipated this. Not just the pain, but the feeling that she was breaking apart. The feeling that they were connected, closer than she had ever been with anyone.

Somehow, she had imagined the fact that she hated him might buffer against any other emotions.

But it didn't.

So she kept her eyes closed.

If Apollo noticed, he didn't comment. Instead, he fused his mouth to hers and flexed his hips, a flash of pleasure slowly overtaking the pain.

Slowly, all the discomfort began to recede. And she just wanted him. There was nothing else. There was no

ugly history between them, there was no anger, no hatred. Nothing but an intense, burning need to be satisfied. She clung to him, to his shoulders, her lips pressed
to his as he established a steady rhythm, pushing them
both toward the brink.

He thrust hard and she let out a hoarse cry, raking her
nails down his back. He growled, his rhythm faltering.
And then, there was no more steadiness. There was nothing but a frantic race to the finish, his movements rough,
intense. And she took it all. Every last bit.

He gripped her chin, tilting her face up, forcing her to
meet his gaze. And she did. She didn't look away, unwill-
ing to flinch in the face of his challenge. She shivered,
tension growing more and more intense in the pit of her
stomach, her internal muscles gripping him tight as her
orgasm began to build.

He slowed his movement suddenly, withdrawing
slowly before pushing back in hard. White light broke
out behind her eyes, release exploding inside her like a
bomb, a wild burst of aftershocks radiating through her,
leaving her shaken, weak. And then he followed, his entire body going stiff as he shuddered out his own release.

He lowered his head, his teeth digging into her collar-
bone. She let her head fall back against the wall, a sigh
escaping her lips.

They stood like that, for just a moment. And then
slowly, reality started to creep in.

She had done it. She had given her virginity to Apollo
Savas.

And suddenly, horrifically, all she wanted to do was
curl into a ball and cry.

She pushed at his shoulders, and he withdrew. She
began to look around at the ground, realizing that only
her shirt had been entirely discarded. Everything else was

simply askew. That was—frankly—slightly more embarrassing than the alternative. She hadn't even waited for him to undress her completely.

He would think she was completely desperate. He would think that she had been yearning after him for years.

It was the truth. Which was what made it particularly horrifying.

She straightened her clothes, tucking her skirt back into place, fixing her bra as she pulled her blouse back on. He said nothing. He simply watched her with those dark, unreadable eyes.

She smoothed her hand over her hair.

"Too little too late, *agape*," he said.

She froze, her hand still poised over her undoubtedly wrecked ponytail. "Excellent," she said, her voice so brittle she thought it might break.

"I am leaving in the morning."

"All right," she said, the words hollow, echoing in her head.

"I will not see you. I will not make any decisions about staffing changes until the next time we meet."

"I'm relieved to hear that."

"I'll be back in town on the twentieth. Make sure you keep your calendar clear."

With that, she could see she was dismissed. With no more fanfare than if they had simply finished a meeting.

And he was still naked. It was absurd. But she wasn't going to highlight the absurdity. Not when she simply wanted to get out of there as quickly as possible so she could have a complete and total meltdown.

"Then I'll see you on the twentieth."

She collected her purse, drawing the strap over her

shoulder and clinging tightly to it. To keep herself from…
Slapping him? Kissing him again? She wasn't certain.

"Excellent. Should I call you a cab?"

"No," she said, checking her watch. "It's… It's only
three o'clock. I have to go back to work."

She had to go back to work like this. With the impression of his hands still on her skin, her cheeks burning
from the brush of his whiskers against them.

"So it is."

"Goodbye," she said.

He tilted his head. "Goodbye, Elle."

CHAPTER THREE

ANTICIPATING THE TWENTIETH had become something of a reverse Christmas countdown. In that she hoped it would never come. It might have been nice to have an Apollo Advent calendar though. So that every time she thought about him arriving she could eat a piece of chocolate to try to deal with her stress.

When she arrived at the office that morning it was with an industrial-strength coffee, a bottle of ibuprofen and a very fake smile plastered to her lips.

Because Apollo was due to arrive—who knew when— to start handing down edicts from his high horse. And she was going to have to face him for the first time since they had... Since that day in his hotel room.

The very thought of that made humiliating color wash through her face. That day had been an aberration. Something that would never be repeated. She had, after all, gone the first twenty-six years of her life without sex. She should be able to happily get through another few weeks. Then, maybe when everything settled down, when Apollo stopped coming in and poking at her employees, reshuffling her business and in general upending her life, she would contend with the fact that she needed to find a relationship.

That was the problem. She had simply waited too long.

She had allowed Apollo and her desire for him to become so large in her mind that nothing else could compare.

Well, now she'd had sex. With Apollo, as it happened. So, question answered, tension diffused.

She was a modern woman. She wasn't going to allow him to make her feel ashamed about her actions. Even though, considering he was a relic of a man, he would attempt to make her feel ashamed. If for no other reason than he would be actively attempting to assert his dominance over her.

Well, no thank you. She was…indomitable.

She gritted her teeth, opening the door to her office and nearly dropping the coffee in her hand when she saw who was already sitting at *her* desk. "That's my seat," she said, the words coming out crisp and harsh.

"It's lovely to see you too, *agape*."

"Now, Apollo," she said, deciding that she was going to be the one to address the elephant in the room before he got a chance. It was there, she might as well be the one to name it. "Don't try to sweet-talk me just because we had sex."

"I wouldn't dream of it," he said, his lips tipping up into a smile.

"No, I suppose you wouldn't. That would require you to know how to sweet-talk."

"You rocked my world. I saw God. You have ruined me for all other women."

She gritted her teeth against the strange, ridiculous warmth that flooded her when he spoke. He was being a jerk, and she knew it. So his words shouldn't make her… anything. She took a fortifying breath.

"What you said," she said, waving her hand. "Substitute 'men' for 'women', 'slightly disorganized' for 'rocked', and 'God' for… I don't know, maybe 'a really good cheesecake'? Not exactly divine, but adequate."

"You are in *typical* form today."

"I try for consistency, Apollo. It's part of my charm."

"I have rarely seen evidence of your charm. Your *charms* perhaps, but I'm not really speaking of your personality."

"Right, well, for some reason things have been especially difficult between us lately, haven't they? Though, I imagine not as difficult as things have been between you and my father. Have you spoken to him since you rammed that knife into his back?"

"Oh, yes. Of course we have."

"You're sick. How could you do that to your own—"

"He is not my own anything. I am not your blood, *agape*. And a good thing to or what happened between us would be off-limits. Both in the past and in the future."

She gritted her teeth, trying not to blush. She was definitely playing at being slightly more blasé and experienced than she was. But he hadn't called her on it yet. So she was going to carry on. "I would rather run my new Jimmy Choos through the shredder, thanks."

"Is that what the kids are calling it these days? I admit, that doesn't sound very sexy."

"It wasn't meant to be."

"Right. Tell me, Elle, how is my mother?" he asked.

Elle arched a brow. "How long has it been since you've spoken to Mariam?"

He shrugged. "Months? She doesn't approve of my betrayal any more than you or your father do."

"And yet you don't feel any guilt over it?"

"I have my reasons," he said, his tone so cold and hard it could cut glass.

"I'm sure you do, but none of them are compelling

enough for me or my family. I don't care what your reasons are. And your mother is well," she said. "I just talked to her last night."

It had been difficult to talk to her stepmother when memories of what had passed between her and Apollo had lingered so persistently. She had felt…guilty and completely transparent. Thankfully, Mariam had her own topics to discuss and hadn't seemed to notice Elle's general silence.

"Well," she said, clearing her throat, "as charming as this little detour has been, let's get down to business."

He reached up, touching the knot on his tie. "Oh, you meant *actual* business."

"You're a pig."

"I'm wounded. Now, I've been going over projections for the quarter. You have to either increase profits soon or you need to start cutting expenses. I can guarantee one, but I can't guarantee the other." He stood, placing his hands on the desk. *Her* desk.

She tried to cling to her anger. Anger that would hopefully be much more powerful than the attraction that was still surging through her. What was her problem? She was supposed to be cured. She was supposed to have inoculated herself to all future Apollo encounters. Cure yourself from a snakebite with snake venom, and all that. But she didn't feel cured. She did not feel at all inoculated. In fact, she felt a little bit dizzy.

"Of course you can't," she said, the words coming out harsh. "No one can guarantee a profit increase. But trust me, if we keep on going in this new direction—"

"This isn't about trust. It's about the bottom line. I have a great deal more experience in business than you do, Elle."

Those words rankled. In part because they were true.

In part because they dug beneath the suit of armor she had worked so hard to put into place today. It hit the wound beneath it that twinged every day. That she was her father's second choice through and through. When she failed at this, she would prove that she never should have been here in the first place. That if her father had had his way he would have put someone else in her position. That if Apollo weren't too important for it, if Apollo hadn't turned against them, it would likely have been him.

You decided failure be damned, remember?

Yes. She had. But it was difficult to feel committed to that now.

"But I care about this company."

"As do I. It's a part of my bottom line, and there is nothing I care about more than my bottom line."

"Well, Matte is only part of your bottom line because you set out to acquire it when you saw that it was floundering. You knew what you were getting."

"And without my influence this company would probably already be six feet under. Like the rest of the holdings I bought from your father."

"You fired the final shot into them."

"A mercy killing," he said, his tone hard. "Don't oppose me, Elle. I am not doing this for my own amusement. If I succeed, you will succeed along with me. I am not the enemy that you set me up to be."

She didn't know what to say to that. Except, it was a disagreement they were not going to settle. Not without blood anyway. "Yes, but you said you were standing there ready to pull the plug, so let's be honest. You aren't a savior, either."

"I never claimed to be."

"Well, don't stand there and pretend that you aren't the villain."

"Oh, did you think that's what I was doing? You're wrong there. I know full well that I'm the villain here, *agape*. If I had a mustache I would twirl it. Alas. You will have to settle for the assurance that I know full well where I stand in this little play. However, we do not have to oppose each other. I know that my presence is sinister. However, there is nothing you can do to fight it. But understand I will save Matte if it's at all possible."

"You're here to announce cuts today, aren't you?"

"Surprisingly, no. But I did come to discuss something with you."

"What?" she asked, feeling suspicious.

"I would like for you to come to my European headquarters. To get a little bit of an idea for how things run, to attend to some meetings there, and to attend a certain number of charity events."

"What?"

"What I would like to do is help revitalize the image of Matte. I would like to bring you into the public eye. Have you as the public face, so to speak. With a little bit of help you could provide a facelift all on your own. And then, maybe we would be able to avoid cuts."

She hadn't expected this. She was, in fact, struck dumb by the fact that he was extending a hand out. That he was offering her a chance to not only save the company, but to do it in such a public way.

She had been prepared to be the one left standing in the ashes. A phoenix who was not poised to rise. She had been prepared to go down in flames, with her hands on Apollo's naked body.

And now...now he was changing things. Again.

"You just expect me to pick up and go to Europe with you?"

"Yes. And I don't exactly expect you to have a major issue with being asked to spend some time in Greece with me."

"Your headquarters are in Greece still? Are you the last remaining corporation in the country?"

"I am successful. Worldwide. It would be a poor thanks to my homeland to remove the jobs and revenue I provide simply because there's been some unrest."

"Please, don't tell me you have a heart. Only a moment ago you were telling me that your decisions were based on the bottom line."

"I *don't* have a heart. I simply have a strong liking for dolmas and ouzo."

"That I can believe."

He smiled, and for a moment, she felt like she was looking back at the boy he had been. The boy she had known all those years ago. The one who had captivated her from the first moment she had laid eyes on him.

The boy she had proceeded to snipe at and torture with flippant remarks every chance she got. Reminding him that he wasn't really a St. James. Because she'd been nothing more than a little girl with a crush and she'd handled it like they were on the playground.

But though things had never been easy between Apollo and her, he'd been very close with her father. But as close as Apollo and her father had once been, they were just as distant now.

And she had been thrown into the middle of that divide. Tossed into a storm she could never hope to weather. Between two alpha males locking horns. One defending his turf, the other intent on destroying it.

So take control. Do this.

"Well, I'm not going to complain about a free vacation," she said, trying to keep her tone light. She wasn't going to show her hand. Not to him. Wasn't going to let him see that this mattered to her. That she was going to use this—whatever it was to him—to gain a handle on things again.

To redeem herself.

"Oh, this isn't going to be a vacation," he said, rounding the desk and making his way toward the door. "We will go to Greece and work. Additionally, there is a charity event in Athens that we will attend together."

"As business associates," she said, "I assume."

She couldn't even imagine her father's reaction. If he had any idea that she and Apollo— He would be furious. Disgusted.

The idea of disappointing him like that…of losing him altogether, was something she couldn't fathom.

Her mother had left when she'd been a child. She could barely remember her. But she remembered the hole left behind, because it was still there.

She couldn't go through that again.

Apollo gave her a dismissive glance. "What else would we be? The entire idea is to strengthen the brand. Should there be any suspicion that the two of us had—"

"There's no need to keep bringing it up."

"You're the one who seems to persist in bringing it up."

Elle crossed her arms, shaking her head, her ponytail swinging back and forth. His eyes followed the motion.

"You should wear your hair down," he said.

She abruptly stopped shaking her head. "I didn't ask you for fashion advice."

"And yet, I'm giving it. Because you desperately need it." He looked at her, his expression critical. "Yes, you need a slightly younger look. One that isn't quite so… ironed."

"Well, my clothes are ironed. Would you have them look rumpled?"

"I would have you look slightly less like a matron."

She frowned. "I do not look matronly. I have a very classic sense of style. It's chic."

"You certainly know how to flatter your figure." He didn't bother to hide that he was looking. "But you need more than that to be the kind of brand that people remember."

"I'm not a…brand," she sputtered, "I'm a woman. Where are you going?" He had walked past her, heading for the door.

"I thought I might go and speak to some of the staff."

"No," she said, hurrying after him. "I do not wish to unleash you on them. I don't want you talking about how their jobs may be in jeopardy when you make final decisions."

"Their jobs may well not be in jeopardy if you don't fight me every step of the way. People like a public face. You can provide that. You can be strongly associated with the brand, and in effect, become a brand yourself. A young, professional woman. Brilliant, fashionable. You can be that woman."

She rolled her eyes. "That does not sound like—"

"It isn't a negotiation. Either you comply with my plan, or you are subject to Plan B, which is making sweeping cuts and doing my best to lift profit margins that way."

She made an exasperated sound, following him down the hall. "I wish you wouldn't keep walking away from me."

"I have places to be. I want to take a look at the different departments. Get a body count. So to speak."

"We are *talking*." She scampered after him. "Of course I will agree to go."

He pushed the button for the elevator. "I'm glad to hear that. I get the feeling sometimes you're just opposing me for the sake of it."

"And I get the feeling that you're an ass to me just because you enjoy it."

He chuckled and she stepped in just as the doors began to close. "Well, you are possibly correct in that assessment. Anyway, you spent a great many years being an ass to me simply because *you* enjoyed it."

She let out a harsh breath and watched the numbers on the elevator as it moved. Suddenly, she was very aware of the fact that she and Apollo were alone again. She looked at him, just a quick glance out of the corner of her eye. She tried to ignore the restless feeling between her thighs. Tried to ignore the restless feeling in her body.

After what seemed like an eternity, the doors opened again, and they were on the floor that housed the marketing department. He stepped out of the elevator and began to sweep his way through the space like a destructive wind. As he whipped by, heads turned, expressions went from relaxed to terrified.

"See that? Your mere presence lowers morale. I hope you're happy."

"I don't care about morale." He paused by one of the desks. "Hello," he said, clearly attempting to be charming. "My name is Apollo Savas. I'm the owner of this company. What is it you do?"

The girl, a blonde who could barely be twenty-five, blinked rather owlishly. She seemed to be struck dumb by his presence. Either by the fact that he was the owner of the company, or by the fact that he was just so damn good-looking. Truly, it was a problem. Elle felt a moment of sympathy for her.

"I'm on the marketing team for the makeup line," she said, looking a little bit thunderstruck.

"Have you been satisfied with the performance of those products?"

"Well," she said, shuffling the papers on her desk around, "we have seen an increase in revenue this past quarter. And our relationships with vendors—"

"How do you plan to continue the increase? What do you think attracts consumers to this product? Why should they buy this instead of say…any other brand of lipstick? I am a man, I know, but I'm not certain why one sort of cosmetic might be more attractive than another."

"I… I…"

"Enough," Elle said. "You do not need to prod at my staff."

He turned toward her, an amused expression on his face, and suddenly she felt like they were the only two people in the room. That little blonde might as well have evaporated into thin air.

There was no question, she was not remotely as immune to Apollo and she would like to be.

Apollo would question the purity of his motives if his motives were—in fact—ever pure. They weren't, so he was certain there was something self-serving and wretched behind them now. Even if he didn't know precisely what.

He had wanted to impress upon Elle the importance of her complying with his plan. When he had left her after… After the appalling lack of control that had occurred in his hotel room, he had formulated a plan to try to improve things for her company. A foolish thing, perhaps. He didn't know why he should care about the fate of her magazine. Beyond the fact that it was a potential profit machine for him.

Perhaps it was the fact that she had become collateral damage in a war he'd never intended to bring her into. But David had placed her in direct line of the firing squad.

Apollo wasn't a kind man. At least, no one ever accused him of being so. And he had never made it a goal to be seen that way. He had cared about very few people growing up, and it had turned out those he had cared about most had betrayed him long ago.

And so he had stolen his stepfather's empire, started dismantling it. But he had left Elle at Matte. God knew why. He'd known in the end he would destroy it, destroy her.

Perhaps it was because he knew what it was to be caught in the consequences of the sins of the father. Hers and his. Perhaps because he knew that—whether or not Elle had been kind to him when they were younger—she was innocent here.

But now...now it was as though a veil had been stripped away from his eyes. He would have to use her. There was no other choice. There was no preserving her. That much had been made clear when he'd taken her against the wall.

It had been symbolic in many ways of that protection being destroyed. That desire to keep her safe from himself being completely and utterly ripped away.

He could no longer ignore Elle. Could no longer dance around the fact that he would have to destroy her along with her father.

He would use her. And he would discard her.

It had nothing to do with his desire to strip her naked again. To watch her pale skin flush with pleasure once more. It had nothing at all to do with that, because he was not going to allow himself the indulgence.

Indulgence was unacceptable. But revenge? That was sweet.

"Perhaps you would like to give me a tour of the rest of the department, Elle?" he asked, ruthlessly cutting off his train of thought.

"Of course."

They moved away from where they had been standing, and she continued on down the role of desks. "Just don't *talk* to anyone," she said, her voice hushed.

"Why is it that you think you can tell me what to do when I am in my own company?"

"Because I am the boss," she said, her tone sounding slightly petulant. "That has to count for something *somewhere*."

"Sadly for you, I am your boss. Being boss of a lot of other people doesn't give you extra clout. I am the final word. So let it be written, et cetera."

She swept through the little space quickly. "There you have it. And now, I expect you want to be going."

"No," he said, crossing his arms across his chest. "I'll head back up to your office floor and set up for a few hours, get a few things done. I do like to familiarize myself with my acquisitions."

Elle looked livid. Her jaw set, her lips in a flat line. "Can't you do that in your hotel room?"

The mention of his hotel room brought back illicit memories. "I could. But I want to get a greater sense for how things are running here. It is in your best interest to keep me around. I might grow attached. I might yet see the importance of this team you keep talking about."

She said nothing, but her expression took on a rather long-suffering edge. They walked back through the office space and toward the elevators again. She pushed the button, then pushed it again when the elevator didn't immediately appear.

"If I didn't know better I would say you were in a hurry to escape my presence."

"I *am*," she said, flashing a smile. One he very much wanted to kiss right off her pretty face. But he was still calculating. When. Where. What. He wouldn't touch her until he made those decisions.

If he touched her at all.

"I do admire your honesty," he said, instead of kissing her.

"What is taking so long?" She scowled, hitting the button again. Then suddenly, the doors slid open.

"Tenth time's the charm," he said, stepping inside.

She gave him a withering glance before moving inside after him.

The doors slid shut and he had the impression that all the air had been sucked out of the space.

The tension between them was unlike anything he had ever known before. Likely because she was the only woman he had ever bothered to resist. He could remember well the first time he had noticed her as a woman, rather than a girl. Sometime after her seventeenth birthday, when all of her snubs and cutting comments had begun to arouse even as they enraged.

When they'd given way to fantasies of him showing her how base and beneath her he truly was.

His attraction, swift, sudden and abhorrent to him, had hit him low and fast in the gut, so quickly he had not had the chance to guard against it. He had not expected to have to guard against an attraction to his chilly younger stepsister.

He had nearly acted on it back then.

He could well remember the time he'd come home from university to see her getting out of the pool. Sleek curves barely concealed by a hot pink bikini that should have clashed terribly with her red hair, but rather was all the more enticing for how incongruous it was.

And he'd gone over to her, and she'd said something snotty, as she usually did. Then he'd grabbed hold of her arm, and pulled her to him. Her green eyes had gone wide, those pink lips parting gently. Begging to be kissed.

But he hadn't. He'd watched the water drops roll over her bare skin, over her breasts, had imagined lowering his head and slicking up the slow-rolling water. But he hadn't done that, either.

He'd waited. Waited until her eyes had darkened with desire. Until he'd seen her breath speed up, the pulse in her neck beating at a rapid rate. He had held her arm until he'd been sure he'd turned her on. Until he'd been sure the little ice princess was hot all over.

Then he'd let her go, and turned away, hard as iron and fantasizing about what he might have had.

And now… Well, now he'd had her, hadn't he? He had answered the question he'd never meant to ask.

He looked at her now, at the sleek ponytail that begged for him to grab hold of it, to wrap it around his hand. Her long, elegant neck. The soft curve of her pale lips. His stomach tightened. Clearly, his lust for her was not so easily dealt with via one quick screw up against the wall.

"I wish you wouldn't do that," she said, pressing the button that would take them to the floor that housed her office.

"Do what?"

"I wish you wouldn't stare at me."

"I'm trying to unlock the mysteries of your mind," he said. "Or rather, I'm attempting to remember what you look like underneath your clothes." He knew that taunting her was the wrong decision. Knew that it would only push them back to the place he was so desperate to stay away from.

You don't want to stay away. You want her naked and panting in your arms again.

"Stop it," she said.

"You're so desperate to forget what happened between us."

"Nobody likes to remember rock bottom, Apollo. I consider having sex with you my own personal walk through the valley of the shadow of death."

"I'm honored, I'm sure."

"Honored isn't what you're supposed to be." She arched one finely groomed brow, her lips twisted into a sneer. She was so self-righteous when she was just as guilty as he was. So sure she was above this attraction that burned between them when she was just as enslaved.

He wanted her. The angrier he got with her, the more he wanted her. Whatever this thing was, the sick, twisted desire that was exploding between them, he couldn't measure it or assign a number to account for it. He couldn't parse it the way he could a business acquisition. It wasn't the simple desire he felt for the sort of woman he usually picked up to spend a few hours of fun with. It was much, much darker.

It was forbidden. Something he had told himself he couldn't have.

Perhaps that was why it was coming to bite him in the ass now. He didn't typically practice restraint. Maybe by creating forbidden fruit, by placing it in the middle of his personal garden and telling himself he could not eat it, neither could he touch it, he had created temptation.

That made the most sense. Since Elle looked like original sin. A brilliant, shining apple he wanted to bite into.

And why shouldn't he? His reasoning for resisting her didn't matter now. He didn't want to honor her father. And he still wanted to kiss that puckered expression off her face. So why the hell not?

"You don't like me," he said, that darkness compelling him now. "And yet, you do want me."

"Come now, Apollo, don't tell me you like every single one of your bed partners. We both know that sex isn't love," she said, tilting her chin upward, a faint blush spreading across her cheekbones, adding a kind of dissonance to her bold words.

Elle was certainly playing the part of experienced woman. She had gone up in flames in his arms, an equal participant in the conflagration. And yet, it didn't all ring true. Didn't quite piece together in a way that made sense.

He wasn't sure he cared to analyze it. It wouldn't change his actions either way.

"Perhaps. But sex and hate don't typically go together," he said. "And you claim to hate me."

"I do," she said, green eyes flashing. "I hate you for what you've done to my father. To me."

"Not enough to leave the company."

"That would be abandoning it altogether. What he built. What he's trying to keep hold of, in spite of you. I won't do that."

"I do admire your dedication. Your loyalty."

"Why do you admire my loyalty? You don't possess any of your own."

"We admire the things in others we struggle with ourselves, do we not?" he asked.

"I wouldn't know. I certainly don't admire anything in you."

He chuckled, turning to face her, closing some of the distance between them. Her eyes widened and she backed against the wall. It reminded him a little bit too much of what had happened the last time they had been alone in an enclosed space together.

"I think there are a few things you admire about me," he said, moving in a little bit closer. Her eyes widened, her pupils expanding, the green in her eyes reduced to a thin ring. Her mouth dropped open, soft and round, and begging to be kissed. To be explored. "You most certainly admire what I can do to your body. I think we both know that."

"I *do* possess some restraint," she said, her voice trembling.

"Do you?" he asked, his voice sounding rough, ragged even to his own ears. "Perhaps we should test it."

He reached out and hit the stop button on the elevator, his stomach tightening, feeling as though a fist had closed around it.

He reached out and took hold of her arm, mimicking that day out by the pool.

"You want me," he said. "Admit it."

"I will not," she said, reaching out, shoving him. But then her hand lingered on his chest, her breasts rising and falling with her rapid breathing. She looked up at him, her eyes wide, terrified.

"You want me even now," he said.

And it felt imperative he make her admit it.

She tapped against his chest with her fingertips before slowly curling her fingers around the material of his shirt.

Then she pulled him to her, kissing his lips hard, deep.

He tasted anger, and a hint of shame on her tongue. And he knew just how the two mixed together, because he felt it, too.

She groaned, pushing away from him suddenly, but he wrapped his arm around the back of her head, holding her steady, working his fingers through her thick, red hair. "You want me," he growled, "don't deny it."

"Wanting isn't the same as having."

With his other hand, he opened the top button on her blouse. "It's the same for us."

"It doesn't have to be," she said, sounding desperate.

"I think it does," he said, his voice rough. He didn't know himself. Not at all.

She reached between them, pressing her palm over his hard length, stroking gently through the fabric of his dress pants.

"I dreamed about you," she said, her voice hushed, her words rushed. "About this."

"So did I," he said, placing his hand over hers and increasing the pressure of her touch. "Every night."

"Have you had another woman since you had me?" she asked, her tone fierce.

"No." He suddenly thought of her touching some other man like this. "Have you had another man?"

She shook her head, curling her fingers around his arousal. "No."

He growled, pulling her into his arms and kissing her, rage and relief burning through him. The very idea of another man putting his hands on Elle made him angry. He wanted her. It had been too long. Nine years. Nine long years lusting after Elle St. James, even as he hated her family. Even when he was overtaken by the desire to see their destruction, he wanted her. It was unacceptable.

He would burn it out. He would burn it out and then it would be over. Afterward, he could discard her if he wished, but this would finally end.

He stripped her clothes from her body as quickly as

possible, nearly tearing the delicate fabric of her blouse in his haste. Definitely tearing her panties.

She didn't protest. Instead, she made a sweet little sound of pleasure as he wrenched the lace fabric away from her skin, as he stroked his fingers over her wet flesh, so slick, so perfect. She wanted him. There was no denying it, no faking it.

He could feel the evidence for himself.

He stripped all of her clothes from her body this time, leaving her completely bare to his gaze. He had spent so many years fantasizing about what she might look like. The size of her breasts, the color of her nipples. That beautiful thatch of curls at the apex of her thighs.

Yes, he had woken up from a deep sleep many times thanks to a dream about Elle's naked body. He had been—for so long—consumed with the curiosity of what lay beneath her prim clothes.

Now, he didn't have to wonder. Now he knew. But he had a feeling she would still haunt his dreams.

No. Because you will have her until you are finished with her.

Yes, he would. Even if burning it out meant reducing them both to ash.

He stripped his suit jacked off and cast it onto the floor, spreading it as wide as he could. Then he swept her into his arms, and lay her down on the fabric.

He didn't have time to worry about anything. He was too needy. Too desperate. Two more things to add to her list of sins, because ever since he had made his fortune, ever since he had pulled himself up from poverty he had ensured he was never needy or desperate.

He pressed a kiss to her inner thigh and she shuddered. Then he kissed her again, gratified to feel her tremble beneath his lips as he moved closer and closer to the heart of her desire.

"I am desperate to taste you," he said.

She bit her lip, closing her eyes and turning away as he flicked his tongue where she most wanted it. "Apollo," she said, "you don't have to…"

He planted his palms firmly on the soft globes of her ass, pulling her more firmly up against his mouth, tasting her deeply in response to her protest. She wiggled beneath him, and he wasn't certain if she was trying to get away, or if she was trying to move herself closer.

Either way, he didn't care. Either way, he was going to get what he wanted.

He brought his hands into play, stroking her with his fingers, thrusting one deep inside of her, reveling in how slick, how ready she was for him.

She was sweet, like dessert. A flavor he had never realized he craved until he had her on his tongue. And now, he knew that this was the thing he had been missing. This was what he had craved all this time.

He stroked her deeply, adding a second finger to the first. And she shattered beneath him, her internal muscles tight around him as she shuddered out her release.

"Oh, Apollo," she said, leaving no doubt that she knew exactly who she was with. Leaving no doubt that she wanted him. No one else but him.

"Are you ready for me, *agape*?"

She didn't speak, she only nodded.

He freed himself quickly from his slacks, not bothering to undo the buttons on his shirt, not bothering to move his hands any lower than his hips. And he thrust inside of her, the breath hissing through his teeth as she closed around him.

Yes, restraint was for other men. For better men.

He was going to conquer. Conquer his desire, his rage.

He would seize what he wanted. The only question was why he hadn't done it sooner.

He brought his hips against hers, his pelvis coming into contact with her clitoris every time he thrust deep inside of her warm, willing body. And he was lost, lost in this, in her. In Elle. And he didn't give a damn that they were in an elevator, he didn't care that he was using her. Nothing mattered but this.

He gave himself over to it completely, lost himself in the rhythm of her body, the slow, slick glide of their flesh, the soft, sweet sounds she made. The words that poured from her lips, hoarse whispers begging him to continue. To take her harder, faster, just please, *please.*

Inside, he was begging himself to hold off on finding his pleasure. He didn't want to go over the edge without taking her with him.

He wanted to do more than that. He wanted her screaming. He wanted her just as lost, just as obsessed as he was. Just as desperate to burn out the flame before it consumed his entire being. Utterly. Irrevocably.

He refused to be alone in this, in this destructive obsession. He would destroy her along with him.

That thought crystallized, clear and sudden in his mind as his release washed over him in an uncontrollable, endless wave. And then beneath him, she arched her back, crying out her own pleasure, her fingernails digging into his back, even through the fabric of his shirt. And he relished the slight bite of pain that came with the unending onslaught of pleasure. It was the only thing rooting him to the earth. The only thing keeping even part of himself under control.

And as she shuddered out her release beneath him, as

he skinned his hands over her bare skin, he realized exactly what he would do.

He would have her until he was through with her. Would build her up as the public face of the company. And when the time was right, he would drop the blade on the guillotine.

He would remove her from her position as CEO, and with that final move, remove the St. James family from his life. Close the chapter forever.

He would not simply burn out their desire, he would destroy her along with it.

He leaned forward, brushing his lips against hers. "Now there, *agape*, I'm not so bad, am I?"

CHAPTER FOUR

ELLE HAD OPTED to keep her mouth shut from the time she had slowly collected her clothing off the floor of the elevator. She stayed silent as Apollo's driver took them to her apartment and all while she packed her bags, with Apollo looming in the corner of her apartment, until they made their trek to the airport and boarded his private jet.

She attempted to keep the awestruck expression off her face as she gazed around the aircraft. She knew that he was rich. She just hadn't quite realized that he was *private jet* rich. She had been raised in very fortunate circumstances but, even so, her father didn't own his own plane.

Well, he certainly wouldn't *now* even if he had before. Because of Apollo. And it would do well for her to remember that.

The problem was she did remember. While they had made love or…whatever it was you called what the two of them had done, she was aware of who he was. How much he had done to destroy her family's legacy.

Still she wanted him.

She felt… She felt completely and totally frazzled. Somehow, she had ended up kissing Apollo again. And the moment they touched, it didn't stop there. It never stopped there. It *couldn't.*

Apparently.

"Do you approve?" he asked, sinking into the plush leather chair next to one of the windows that looked out on the tarmac. "Or am I to take that expression to mean you are terrified of your surroundings? It's very difficult to say."

"I like the plane. I'm a little bit afraid of being alone at thirty thousand feet with you."

"Afraid you'll join the mile high club?"

Dammit, *yes*. "I think we can both agree that whatever has been going on between us is not a good idea."

"It's a terrible idea. Take your seat so that we can ready for takeoff."

She looked around, elected to sit in the chair farthest from his. "For the record, I still hate you."

"Oh, I'm well aware," he said. "I think that was what you screamed in my ear only a few hours ago. Oh, no, I think what you actually screamed was 'more' and 'harder.'"

"It isn't like you weren't complicit."

"Complicit. *Explicit*."

"What exactly is your goal here, Apollo?" she asked. She didn't trust him. Not one bit. She was not in a position to refuse his command that she fly with him to Greece. Neither did she entirely trust his explanation.

"That depends," he said, leaning back in his chair, his body all leashed power and tension. "Are you speaking of business—" his gaze raked over her body "—or pleasure?"

"I thought we both agreed that the pleasure angle is a poor one for the two of us to take."

"It is. It's a terrible idea, *agape*. We hate each other. As you have stated many times. Or, more to the point, *you* hate *me*. I have no such strong feelings about you."

"No," she said, her tone biting, "you don't feel anything for me or my father. You simply destroyed us for your own pleasure."

"Your father's company was hemorrhaging money long before I came by to deal with it."

"So why didn't you help him?"

"That's a complicated issue, Elle," he said, his words hard.

"I don't have any trouble understanding complexities. Go right ahead and explain."

"There is more between your father and I than you know."

"Enlighten me," she said, the words escaping through clenched teeth.

"Not now. But understand what I'm doing is for a bigger purpose."

"Your ego? Honestly, you're unbelievable. He gave you everything. He loved you best from the beginning," she said, voicing the words that she never had before. Words she had long believed. "And now you've betrayed him for money."

"Love," he spat. "What is love, Elle? Tell me that. Is it what your father feels for you? As he moves you around like a pawn, desperate to put you between me and his queen? Did he love me, or did he see me as another tool he could use? I don't put any stock in love. It has never done anything for me, so I will hardly defer to it now."

Her heart was pounding hard, her throat tight. And she knew what she wanted. She hated herself then, more than she had ever hated him. "What do you want from me?"

"In the short term? I intend to burn this thing out between us. A fire can't keep on forever, can it?"

"Are you suggesting we sleep together while we are away from New York?"

"I'm doing something much stronger than suggesting."

Rage turned to excitement, flickering at the center of her being and radiating outward. The idea of being with him again, of touching him again, made her hands shake. "I didn't realize you got off on coercing women into your bed."

"We both know I didn't have to coerce you into it at all. Also," he said, his tone pointed, "we have never made it to a bed."

The thought of being in bed with him seemed…luxurious. The chance to explore his body at her leisure, rather than finding herself at the mercy of the explosion that occurred between them every time they touched. The force of it propelled her, made it impossible for her to think, impossible for her to resist. What would it be like to make the *decision* to have him? To give herself all night to indulge in that long-held desire for him.

She had always wanted him. And she had hated him for it. She'd been so angry that he was so…untouched. So utterly uninterested. So she'd pushed at him, tried to make him angry if she couldn't make him want her. She'd taunted him. And finally, she'd decided to taunt him sexually.

She could remember very clearly choosing the smallest, brightest bikini she could possibly find—one that absolutely clashed with her red hair, but one she felt would get her the attention she desired—to try to catch Apollo's eye when he came home to the family estate over break.

He had approached her as she'd gotten out of the pool and she'd felt… Naked. Alive. Afraid. So she'd defaulted to her usual position.

She could remember turning to him, her lips curled. *They'll let anyone into the estate, won't they? How my family's standards have fallen over the years.*

His eyes had blazed then. With anger. And he'd grabbed hold of her arm. She hadn't been afraid, though. She'd been…electrified.

He had held her there, looked at her hard, and for one moment, one desperate moment, she had imagined that she had seen lust in his eyes. That she had seen interest. But then, he had released her and turned away, leaving her there as though nothing at all had happened.

But now, somehow, for some reason, he wanted her, too. *This is your chance. To put it behind you once and for all so that you can move on.*

"All right," she said, ignoring the thrill of excitement that shot through her. "I agree. We have to get back on proper footing so that we can deal with each other as business partners."

"You are not my partner."

"Whatever. Terminology aside I am agreeing to the idea of an affair. But it has to stay a secret. Can you imagine the scandal? Me. Dating my wicked stepbrother who stole my family legacy after he wormed his way into my father's good graces."

"Of course. I have no interest in parading my intimate association with you in front of the world. As I already said."

His words, his *tone*, rankled. "I find it funny that you speak of it as though you find it distasteful. Of course *I* do. Everyone who moves in business circles fears you. I can see why I would want to disassociate from you. But not why you would wish to disassociate from me."

He arched a brow. "I have a type, Elle. It is not buttoned-up redheads. As you know, gentlemen prefer blondes. Or, in my case, scoundrels prefer blondes, brunettes or redheads so long as they're willing to part their thighs. I like women who know how to smile. Who know how to have fun. I do not like little harpies who claw at me even as they tear my clothes off."

"You like it when I claw at you."

Heat flared in his dark eyes and she took that as a win. "I consider this a unique circumstance."

She wanted to ask him why he thought heat was exploding between them the way it was. She wanted to ask him if it was ever like this for him and the other women he had sex with. But that would betray her inexperience. And that was something she wasn't willing to do. She wanted to protect her vulnerable places. Wanted to shield everything she didn't know from him.

That was an old defense, and one that she employed daily. She hated asking for help. Hated appearing ignorant.

Her father was a hard man, and she had always had the impression that he was standing by waiting for her to disappoint him. So she never let him see when she was floundering. Never let him detect one bit of uncertainty in her. She had wrapped herself so tightly in her ironed-on exterior, so careful to never show a wrinkle. She had difficulty letting go of it under any circumstances.

And if she was determined to never let her father see her sweat that went even more for Apollo.

That meant she couldn't ask the questions that were gnawing a hole inside of her. They would just have to go unanswered. It didn't matter anyway. Nothing was going to come from her association with Apollo. Nothing except freedom from the bizarre hold he had over her—and her life.

She had spent far too long being preoccupied with him. She would just be glad to have it handled.

And if she was a little bit…giddy over the thought of some time to deal with the attraction…well, that was normal. People acted ridiculous when it came to sex. History was filled with examples. Wars were started over sexual desire. She could hardly expect herself to be above the kind of insanity that captured almost all of humanity.

She spent the rest of the plane ride musing about restraint and dozing on and off while Apollo continued to work. Every time she opened her eyes and looked at where he was sitting, he was maintaining the same position, his focus never broken from his laptop, or the spreadsheets in front of him.

It was strange, watching him from across the darkened cabin. He had changed so much in the past few years. The lines on his face becoming more pronounced, as though each year had left a mark behind, evidence of the living he'd done.

And as a teenager, he had never worn a suit. He had always kept his hair slightly longer back then, too. Now it was cropped ruthlessly short, as though he was trying to look like he had sprung out of the ground a very conservative billionaire.

She wanted to find that boy again. Strip off the layers and layers he'd put over the person he'd been. The one she had… Well, the one she had felt so many things for.

She let her eyes flutter closed again, and when she opened them, they had landed in Greece. Customs and passports and the like were handled in an efficient manner involving people coming to them and apologizing for any delays. After that, they were ushered into a limousine, all their bags packed quickly into the trunk as they departed straight from the plane to the highway.

Athens was an incredible sprawl she hadn't accurately pictured in her mind. The rolling hills were capped with white, not from snow, but from the stone houses packed tightly together, flowing along with the landscape.

The downtown wasn't anything like the glass-and-steel jungle of Manhattan. Ancient structures mixed with more modern buildings, the history and heritage of the nation evident in the intricate stonework, the massive pillars and marketplaces scattered throughout.

"Where are we going?"

"I have a villa just outside the city."

"Of course you do," she said. "But I thought we were going to your offices?"

"We will. At some point. But some adjustments have been made to accommodate some of our new goals."

"Meaning what?" she asked, tearing her eyes away from the scenery to look at him.

"I don't think it's that difficult to guess."

They drove out of the city, winding up the steep, packed hillsides. They escaped the sprawl, moving to an area where trees were more plentiful. Where houses were a little bit less common. Until they reached the top of a completely vacant hill that overlooked the sea. There, behind a secure set of wrought-iron gates was a white stone house that was even more imposing than the St. James family estate in upstate New York.

"Is this your primary residence now?"

He lifted his shoulder. "As much as any place, I suppose. It is my home, after all."

"I *do* know that. You were born here. You left here when you were eight."

His focus sharpened. "Have you been reading unauthorized biographies?"

"No," she said. "I just paid attention when you used to speak around the dinner table. I used to know you, Apollo, as difficult as it is to remember back that far."

An emotion she couldn't put a name to flashed through

his eyes. "I did not realize such memories were worth saving."

"Know your enemy, and all of that."

"I suppose so."

The limousine pulled closer to the house, and the driver put the car into Park. Elle opened up her own door, stepping out and looking up at the house. To her, it looked like a lot of cubes of varying sizes stacked on top of each other, large windows on all sides looking out at the hills behind them, and the ocean before them.

"It doesn't seem like you're afforded very much privacy," she said.

"Are you concerned that the village will see you naked? Because make no mistake, most of the time spent in this house will be spent without clothes."

The dark, sensual promise should have frightened her, offended her. Instead, it excited her.

"The thought crossed my mind," she said. No point in playing the prude now. Not when he knew full well she wasn't.

"Never fear. I can tint the windows at the flick of a switch, and we won't even have to sacrifice the view. But good to know you are on the same page as I am."

"I have great concern for my modesty." And her sanity.

"Well, I hope you don't concern yourself much with it in my presence." He walked ahead of her, moving to the front of the house. "Our things will be brought in momentarily. Come, let me show you around."

She followed him inside, her heart hammering, her mouth suddenly dry. She didn't know what might happen next. If he was going to strip her of her clothing immediately and press her up against a wall again. And if he did, what would she do? She would capitulate. She knew that from experience.

But he didn't make a move to touch her. Instead, he paused in the expansive entryway. "I think this is self-explanatory," he said, indicating the living area with the low-profile couch that was up against the wall, curving around to another. "Beyond that is the pool." He walked ahead, up the open staircase that led to the second floor. She followed him. "My office," he said. "The library, kitchen and dining area. I felt the second floor made for a slightly better view." He continued straight up the stairs, to the third floor and she quickened her pace to keep up. "That way is my room," he said, pointing down to the left. "And then here you will find yours." The opposite direction from his. He began to walk to her room, and she followed, feeling a little bit like a lost puppy afraid of losing sight of her master.

He pushed the door open and revealed a light and airy space. Everything was white. The bedspread, the gauzy curtains that hung around the bed frame. There were no curtains on the windows, just as with the rest of the house. The square, unobstructed glass pane afforded a brilliant view of the jewel-bright sea, and let in the pale, sun-washed light.

"There are several settings for the windows. One is a blackout setting. That way the sun won't disturb your sleep," he explained.

She nodded. "I'm not sure I understand," she said, looking around the room. "I thought we would be sharing a room."

He chuckled. "I don't sleep with my lovers, *agape*. I have sex with them. We don't need to share a bedroom for that."

Dammit. He managed to make her feel completely gauche and out of her depth even though she was doing her best to appear like all of this was commonplace for her. She'd been feeling like she was succeeding. Until this moment. She gritted her teeth. "Of course. How could I be so silly?"

"I imagine you typically date nice boys who like to spend the evening making love before they pull you close and cuddle you."

His mocking tone burned her down deep. She was starting to feel at a disadvantage again. She would not allow it. "Do I seem like the type of woman who enjoys cuddling?" she asked, arching a brow. "You cannot possibly guess at the sort of man I typically associate with. You don't even know me. Not even a little bit. You know what I've bothered to show you, and that's all."

"My mistake. If you will excuse me, I'm going to get ready for this evening. And I have a bit of work to catch up on."

"You worked the entire time we were on the plane."

"Impatient for me?"

She swallowed hard. She swallowed her honest answer, which was most definitely yes. "Just concerned you're going to fall over at the age of twenty-nine from high blood pressure or something."

"Your concern is touching. I will see you this evening for the charity gala."

He turned and walked out of the room, closing the door behind him.

She turned and looked out the window, gazing at the view. For some reason, this time, she had the feeling of being inside of a terrarium, but it didn't feel quite so open. Once that thought entered her mind she felt as if she were some kind of creature he was keeping in a cage until he was ready to take her out and play with her.

Somehow, back in New York this had all felt equal, like they were in the same space, wanting the same things. But not now. Silly, because he owned her company. She should not have felt equal with him in the workplace. Should not have felt like they were on the same footing at all. And yet, for some reason—her pride, her intense dedication to her business persona—she had felt like they were.

But not here. In his house, in this show of his incredible wealth, she felt vulnerable. Powerless. She was in his home country, a place where she didn't even speak the language, trapped in his house on the hill.

She wondered, for a moment, if this was what he had felt. Walking into her family home as a teenager, his mother engaged to a powerful man so far above her station. And he had been greeted by a stepsister so consumed with her own feelings, her own issues, that she'd been nothing but horrible. Had done nothing but try to make him feel completely unequal to the place.

She blinked, pushing back an unwanted wave of sympathy. That was in the past. What she'd done had been out of girlish fear of the strength of her feelings.

Apollo was not acting as a boy, reacting to fear. He wasn't reacting at all. He was a man on the warpath, and God help her if she got in his way.

CHAPTER FIVE

WHEN ELLE APPEARED at the top of the stairs that evening wearing the silk gown that he'd had sent up to the room earlier, Apollo wasn't sure he had the strength to attend the gala. No, most of him wanted to grab hold of her and drag her straight into her bedroom and strip it off her.

The emerald green silk gown seemed almost demure in the front. It had a high neckline, the delicate, shiny fabric skimming her curves. It rippled when she walked down the stairs, flowing over her body like water.

But it was the back he couldn't wait to see. He had selected the dress for that very reason. True to his word, he was intent on raising her profile in the company. All the better to make her family's humiliation more apparent. If no one knew who the St. James family were, if they were only aware of the companies, while the family itself remained faceless, his disgrace of them would not carry the impact he required.

In a few weeks he would cut ties completely. He would let her drown along with her father and the rest of the St. James family.

It was cruel. But what David St. James had done to Apollo's father, the way he had manipulated Apollo's mother...

He forced himself to smile at her. To practice some

form of charm. He did possess it, after all. Though he didn't often exercise it when dealing with Elle. He could have any woman he wanted, and had, even before he had become the man he was now.

The girls he had associated with from nearby all-girls institutes back when he had been a teenager had found him fascinating. None of them had ever intended on taking him home to meet their parents. But a great many of them had taken him to nearby gazebos, backseats of cars and vacant dorm rooms. He might not be the kind of man they could proudly claim, but they had certainly found him attractive enough for certain uses.

Of course, Elle had already proven she had no issues using him for her physical satisfaction while she despised him on a personal level. So, he supposed that there was no point in attempting to be charming now.

All thoughts of charm or anything else were completely emptied from his mind when he saw the side of the gown as she reached the bottom of the stairs. He could think of nothing more than the possibility of stripping it from her body now.

"Turn around," he said, his voice hard.

"Why?" she asked, turning to face him, her hands clasped in front of her, demure, as though she had no idea what she was doing to him.

"Turn around," he said, deciding that he would forgo charm completely.

A flash of color spread up her neck, into her cheeks. Clearly, even if it made her angry, she quite enjoyed it when he gave orders. She turned slowly, teasing him by taking her time. And when she revealed her back fully, his stomach tightened, his blood pooling in his groin.

The back of the dress was a deep V ending just above the curve of her rear, exposing her entire back, the edges glittering with delicate beadwork. The seams over the silken material served to enhance the round shape of her backside, creating an even more dramatic shape to her curves.

He wanted to take her back upstairs, not just so he could have his way with her, but so he could keep any other man from laying eyes on what he thought of as his.

"It does not matter how many men have come before me," he said, not realizing he was speaking the words out loud until they had already escaped his mouth. "You are mine now. You have always been mine, Elle." The words were more raw, more real than he'd intended.

But then, this feeling was more raw, more real than anything that had ever come before it.

He saw attachments for what they were. Saw clearly how easily feelings could be manipulated. But what he felt for Elle was beyond him. It could never be distilled into one neat emotion. Could hardly ever be defined.

He needed it gone. Needed to burn it out. So that in the end he could walk away from the St. James family and never look back.

Walk away from her.

She turned to face him, her signature red ponytail swinging along with the movement. "That's quite possessive," she said.

"I'm kind of a bastard. You have agreed to be my mistress until such time as we have burned out the attraction between us. That means you are mine. And mine alone."

"I hardly make a habit of overlapping lovers."

He took a step toward her, closing the distance between them. He wrapped his arm around her waist, planting his hand firmly at the center of her back and drawing her close to him. "I would not permit it."

"You might own my company, Apollo," she said, her voice low, sultry, "but you do not own me."

"That's where you're wrong, I think," he said, sliding his hand up the center of her back, cupping the back of her head. "Because for now those two things are the same. I own both the company and you."

"You're a caveman."

He wrapped his fingers around her ponytail, tugging hard. "Shall I drag you back to my lair?"

She gasped, the sound one of arousal, not fear.

"You can pretend to hate this thing between us all you want. You can pretend to hate my commands. But we both know that no matter how shocked and appalled you pretend to be, you want this. You want me."

She leaned in slightly, and he kept his hold tight on her hair. Then she pressed her lips gently against his before biting him hard. "I might want you," she said, "but it is not the way a woman *should* want a man."

"Take your hair down."

"I refuse to give in to your every command."

He shifted his hold on her, grabbing the bobby pin that was buried in the ponytail that wrapped one coppery strand around the rubber band that secured her hair, concealing it from view. Then he grabbed the rubber band itself, pulling it free.

Her red hair fell past her shoulders in soft waves, extra full because of the way it had been restrained.

She frowned, her brows locked together. "I can't go like this. My hair is a mess."

"It is perfect."

"I do not have to wear my hair to please you."

"Your hair pleases me however it is fixed," he said. "But this way, this way, all I can think about is burying my fingers in it. Pulling you toward me. Kissing

you deeply. With it like this, I want nothing more than
to take you straight back upstairs and make you scream
my name. And so, I leave the final decision on how you
wear it up to you."

She tilted her chin upward. "Well, it's already down."

He chuckled, the soundboard of satisfaction. "I thought
you might come to that conclusion."

She narrowed her eyes. "I prefer you without a tie."

"It is a formal event."

"Without the black tie, with the first button on your
shirt undone, so that I can just see your chest hair, all I
can think of is you tearing the shirt open the rest of the
way so that I can put my hands on your hard muscles. So
that I can feel your heartbeat raging against my palms. I
can think of nothing but leaning in, running my tongue
over your skin. And so," she said, arching her brow before turning away from him. "It is up to you."

Apollo smiled and began to loosen his tie.

No matter that they were pretending to be merely business associates at the gala, Elle could not help but think
the two of them looked like they had been engaged in
sexual intimacy in the car on the way. Her hair was down,
looking very much like he had already run his fingers
through it. His shirt was undone, his tie long discarded.

And yet, they had not had the benefit of engaging in
any kind of intimate activity.

When they had gotten in the limousine she had
scooted as far away from him as possible, telling him
she needed space, time to collect her thoughts. She did.
She was exhausted, jet-lagged, and the nap she'd had
earlier had only helped a little bit. Beyond that, she was
still raw from their last encounter. And if they were supposed to appear in public together in a platonic fashion,

she did not want the feeling of his touch lingering quite so strongly in the forefront of her mind.

Now though, she was regretting it. Now she sort of wished she had climbed onto his lap in the car and satisfied her desire for him. Anything to take the edge off the extreme arousal that was pounding through her even now.

The gala itself was beautifully appointed, held in one of the oldest and most sophisticated hotels in Athens. When she arrived, she was surprised to see that Apollo's name was on everything.

"You didn't tell me that it was *your* charity gala we were attending."

He shrugged his shoulder, taking a glass of Champagne off the tray of a passing waiter. "It did not seem important."

"I think it is rather important. I wasn't aware that you had founded the charity."

"It's very boring. Press junket stuff. The kind of thing that one says to improve their reputation with the media. It's a game I scarcely have the patience to play at the best of times. I did not see the point in trying to convince you that I was somehow a paragon of virtue simply because I donate money to impoverished families."

"You do?" In spite of everything she knew about him, in spite of her feelings about him, she could feel herself softening.

"Yes. Do not look at me like that. I am a businessman. Believe me when I tell you this benefits me in financial ways."

"Why are you so resistant to being seen as good in any fashion?"

"I do not like to raise people's expectations."

She blinked. "Why?"

"Because they will find themselves disappointed."

She looked around, taking in the beautifully appointed marble interior of the hotel, the impressive pillars, the glittering chandeliers. Couples dressed in the finest couture were already making their way out to the dance floor. She wished she could dance with Apollo. That he would take her into his strong arms and pull her up against his chest, hold her...just to hold her. So that she could relish his strength, his heat, if only for a moment.

She shook her head. That was extreme foolishness. She wanted nothing more from Apollo than for him to leave her alone and allow her to run their business as she saw fit. Well, that and sex for the sake of sex, until they had burned out the attraction between them.

She did not want him to hold her. She did not want to press her head up against his chest and listen to the sound of his heart. Did not want to spend an hour kissing him, just kissing him. *No*, she didn't want any of those things.

"I shall introduce you to some of my associates," Apollo said. "And to some of the members of the press who are in attendance."

"Oh, you're too kind," she said, keeping her tone light.

He pressed his hand lightly on her back, guiding her toward a group of people who were standing there conversing. He made introductions, and dropped his hand quickly back to his side, bringing a great deal of distance between the two of them as he shifted his position within the group.

One of the men was a businessman from Italy, another a Greek, who had his business in the United States. They started to make conversation about staying relevant in the age of the internet and online superstores, and she was so lost in the discussion that it took her a while to notice that

Apollo was no longer standing next to her. She frowned, searching the crowd quickly. And then she spotted him, out on the dance floor with a blonde woman wearing a dress with a hem that fell just beneath her butt cheeks. Rather nice butt cheeks too, Elle was loath to admit.

She fought to keep the scowl off her face. She knew that they were supposed to be playing the part of business associates but she felt this was taking it a bit far.

"I see Mr. Savas has abandoned you," the Greek man, Nikos Vardalos, said.

"Not at all," she said, taking a deep breath. "We are not here together. Mr. Savas is able to dance with whoever he chooses."

"Then I suppose you are free to dance with whoever you choose?"

She could always tell him she had a boyfriend. She often did that when confronted with men she wasn't attracted to in these kinds of situations. But Nikos was handsome enough, and Apollo was dancing with someone else. Really, it seemed rather silly for her to stay hidden away in a corner.

"Absolutely," she said. "I am always free to do whatever I want."

He laughed, treating her to a smile that she had no doubt often made women go weak in the knees. Sadly, not her. Not now.

But she pretended. She offered a smile in return.

"I like a woman who knows her mind. And does your mind tell you that you might want to dance with me?"

"I would be delighted."

He extended his hand, and she accepted it, wrapping her fingers around his. His touch was warm, but it did not light her on fire, not the way that Apollo's did. It was sort of comforting, to have a man touch her like this, and for her to feel so very little.

Every interaction with Apollo, every brush of his skin against hers, was so layered. Was so hot, so intense, she couldn't ignore it, or pretend it hadn't burned. It was never simple. It was always hate spread over lust, spread over a strange attachment that stemmed from all of the years they had known each other. And betrayal. The betrayal that was unique to what she felt for him because of how well they had known each other. Because of how she had felt about him for so long.

Because of the way she had trusted him.

And you betray your father by sleeping with this man. By wanting him.

Still, she couldn't help herself. Still, she could feel nothing as Nikos pulled her into his arms and swept her onto the dance floor. Still, she felt more when she looked across the crowded room and locked eyes with Apollo, who was glaring at her and her dance partner with dark rage.

Fine. He was welcome to be murderous. She didn't particularly care. They were here separately. He was dancing with another woman, and she would be damned if she would play the part of wallflower.

She shifted her hands lightly on her partner's shoulder, tightening her grip on his hand.

"I think Savas wants to kill me," Nikos said, his tone tinged with amusement.

"Oh, I don't suppose he wants to kill you," she said, her tone dry. "Anyway, he and I are associates, as I said before. And neither of us believes in mixing business with pleasure."

"Excellent. Then I shall never do business with you."

She laughed. "Well, that would be a shame. Since

you are in retail, I would very much like to do business with you."

"Perhaps it is crass of me to discuss this during a dance," he said, "but tell me more."

They spent the next two songs largely ignoring the music and discussing the various ways in which they could marry their two brands. She decided that she liked Nikos quite a bit even if he did not make her heart beat faster.

She only wished that he could.

He was Greek, he was wealthy, he had a hint of a gorgeous accent. Truly, if she had a type, this was it. If any other man was going to start a fire in her loins quite the way that Apollo did, this man would. But there was nothing. Absolutely nothing. It was an extreme disappointment.

Still, though she had not found a way to encourage desire toward another man, she had come away with a very promising business contact. They parted at the end of the song, and he did not try to make any sort of romantic overture. He must've sensed the lack of chemistry as profoundly as she did.

She was making her way toward a waiter to get herself a drink when she was all but accosted by Apollo. "Having fun?"

"It's a charming party," she said.

"Yes. I told you already that you would be with me and me alone while we work out the attraction between us, did I not?"

"I'm sorry, I was not aware that a waltz was on par with intercourse."

"You are playing with fire," he said.

"Then you are, too. Don't think I didn't notice your lovely blonde partner."

"It is expected of me."

"And you want my face in the paper. Therefore, I had better do something newsworthy. You put me in this dress that leaves me essentially naked, and now you're going to act as though my getting attention is not somehow essential to your *plan*?"

"All you have to do is simply walk into a room to gain attention, *agape*. Trust me on this."

"I find your assessment flattering, if slightly ambitious."

"I don't care whether or not you find it ambitious. It is the truth." He looked around them. "Even if you have not noticed, I have. Every male eye—and many of the female eyes—have been on you from the moment you walked in. You are absolutely the one to watch here."

"Is that so?"

"Yes. And when you make a large charitable donation in the name of the company, you will become even more of a conversation piece."

Her mouth opened, then snapped shut. "I did not know you were going to make use of my money."

"Of course I am. Anyway, it is a good cause, on that you can trust me. As I said, I provide housing and other necessities for families who have fallen below the poverty line. Surely you can find no fault with that."

"I suppose not."

"You sound so distressed. It must be terrible when I don't rise to the part of blackguard when it suits you."

"Sincerely awful. I can see why you prefer to pretend you're terrible. For consistency."

"I am nothing if not consistent."

She laughed. "If only that were true."

"What is that supposed to mean?"

"Exactly what it sounds like. You are not consistent,

I don't care how you frame it, I don't care what you say. You were a friend of my family, and then you betrayed us. There is nothing consistent about that."

His expression turned dark, fierce. He leaned in and her breath caught in her throat. She thought, for a moment, that he might kiss her. She hoped that he would. He did not. "From the moment I understood there was better than the circumstances I existed in I was determined to find better. When I went to a private school, knowing full well that I didn't belong there, I was determined to rise to the top of the class so that no one could question whether or not I had the ability to succeed in the realms of society into which I had been thrust. I have done nothing but hold myself up from the bottom with my brute strength from the moment I understood it could be done. If that's not consistency, I don't know what is."

"Yes, I know you pulled yourself up quite a bit. But it's quite convenient to forget that my father's money provided a ladder to help you out." She turned away from him and he grabbed hold of her arm, holding on tightly to her and pulling her back to him.

"I was willing to advance myself using any means necessary. Again, I claim consistency." He released his hold on her, straightening the cuffs on his shirt. "Go off and have fun. We will meet again at the end of the night. Do not forget to make your donation."

"Of course not."

"I imagine Luka would like to dance, as well."

"Are you off to find him?" she asked.

"No, but I suggest you should."

"Now you're encouraging me to dance with other men? There's that legendary consistency."

"No, I believe you're right. You should do what you

can to get your photograph in the news. And I shall do
what I have to to get attention of my own. I will see you
at the end of the evening."

CHAPTER SIX

By THE TIME the car pulled back up to Apollo's house later that evening he was in a violent temper. Elle had done exactly as he had demanded and had danced with every businessman within fifteen years of her age. And she had charmed every single one of them. She had no doubt delighted the media.

She had done exactly as he'd asked, and he was incensed. Spending the evening *not* touching her had been akin to torture. But he was ready to move ahead with their agreement. He was ready to claim her. To remind her exactly why she was here, and who she was with.

They had not spoken in the car on the way back to his villa. She was vibrating with indignation next to him, but he didn't care.

When they got out of the car and walked into the house he turned to her. "I want you to go to your room and open up the top drawer of the bureau there. You will find some other items that my staff has procured for you. Make yourself ready for me."

He stormed off to his office then, pouring himself a glass of scotch and downing it in one desperate gulp, relishing the burn as it slid down his throat.

He paced the length of the room, trying to figure out exactly what happened to make him so agitated.

Jealousy.

He could not remember the last time he had ever felt jealous. If he ever had.

He closed his eyes, allowing an old memory to wash over him. Hell, the bikini. Yes, he had been jealous then in a strange way. Of the fact that she was young, with her entire life ahead of her. Of the fact that men had not yet discovered her, and he would not be a part of that discovery. He would have given everything to have been the first man to touch her. To have been the one to awaken her sensuality. Her every sigh, her every moan.

To have been the one who gave her that first climax.

Yes, he would have given anything to be that man at one time. He had been jealous then. Of a man who had not existed. And somehow tonight every man who had danced with her had become one of those nameless, face-less men who had come before him.

He hated them, even without knowing who they were.

He tossed his suit jacket onto the floor, stalking out of his office and going up the stairs toward her bedroom. She had better damn well be ready for him. Because he was not waiting another moment.

He threw open the bedroom door without knocking, and she turned to face him, still wearing the dress she had been wearing to the gala.

"I thought I gave you instructions to change," he said.

Her green eyes glittered with anger. "Yes," she said. "You did. But I have no desire to dress up like some strange interpretation of a fantasy that you have, brought about by your magnanimous staff."

"Expensive underthings offend you?"

"The idea that I might not want to choose my own? The idea that I might be interchangeable with any of the other women you consort with? That offends me."

"What do any of my other lovers have to do with this?"

"Everything. You are treating me exactly as you would any of them."

He clenched his hands into fists, his heart beating so fast it burned. "And you want to be special? Is that it?"

Her cheeks flamed. "I don't want to be the same. I don't want to be just one warm body of any of the ones you could have."

"Still you doubt my desire for you?" He undid another button on his shirt, then another, stripping it off as he walked toward her, feeling every inch a predatory animal. "What must I do to show you that I am your servant, *agape*? What must I do to show you that you own my body?"

The color heightened in her cheeks. "I own your body?"

"Do you think I want this? Do you think I want to be a slave to the desire I have for a St. James? If you think you hate me then just imagine how much I hate you. Your family. Your family name. Everything you stand for."

His words were coming out hard and fast. He was saying more than he had intended. He had never intended to bring this up with her at all. Had not intended to speak any of this to her until he was giving her her marching orders and ordering her to pack her things and vacate her office. He had not intended to reveal any of this until he'd unleashed his ultimate betrayal on to her.

But he couldn't stop it now. He could not stop himself. "If any woman at the party tonight had made me feel even a fraction of what I feel for you I would have taken her into the nearest hallway and pushed her skirt up. Sadly, I only respond to you. You have me on a leash, Elle. I hope you are happy with this revelation."

Her eyes were round, her lips parted slightly. "I don't

understand. You were part of our family. How can you possibly feel that way?"

"Easily. You don't understand what manner of man your father is, you don't understand what manner of man I am. When you were seventeen years old, parading around the family estate in your bikini, I would have liked nothing more than to put you flat on your back. I was a man of twenty, and I would have had you, sweet little virgin that you were. And even knowing how wrong that is, I hate every man who came before me. I regret not taking you then. Such wasted years, Elle. I could have rid myself of my hunger for you then. But I didn't. For what reason? To preserve some semblance of a conscience we both know I don't have? Pointless. But then, I still harbored illusions that I might be good."

"I… You wanted me then?"

"Did you not know? Of course not. You were blind. A little virgin."

"Stop saying that. I wasn't ignorant. It's just that you seemed angry…not…"

"As it always is with us."

"Either way, I'm not ignorant."

"Did I have the wrong end of it then? Please don't tell me you weren't already experienced or I truly will hang myself for being so foolish that I didn't have you."

"Why are you acting like this?"

He didn't know. He damn well had no clue. All he knew was that he was enraged. Over tonight. The other men who'd touched her. The orders she was refusing to obey. Over his behavior nine years ago. Over his behavior now. "Why are you refusing to wear the lingerie I provided for you?"

"Because I will not be one of your whores," she said. "Because I *was* a virgin when you had me at your hotel room. Your jealousy is misplaced while mine is certainly not."

Her words hit him like a punch to the gut. "A virgin?"

"Apparently it matters to you. Apparently you are quite proprietary and possessive, though you have not earned the right to be."

He growled, pulling her into his arms, grabbing hold of the sides of the delicate fabric of the dress and wrenching it down over her shoulders, tugging the bodice down low, revealing her breasts to his hungry gaze. "I am the only man to ever have you?"

"Yes," she said, her voice breathless.

"This pleases me much more than it should," he said, gripping her chin between his thumb and forefinger and tilting her face up to him. "All during the ride back to the villa I was contemplating the different ways I could kill each and every man who danced with you. In my mind, they had become your previous lovers. And I discovered that I felt rather violent about them. About the missed opportunity I'd had. You see, I wanted to be the one to teach you about pleasure."

She bit her lip, as though she were holding back a litany of words. Either curses, or the confirmation that he had indeed been the one to teach her about pleasure. He had a feeling she neither wanted to yell at him at this moment nor give him anything pleasant to latch onto.

"I did teach you about pleasure, didn't I? Against the wall in a hotel room. Dammit, Elle, you didn't tell me."

"Would it have made a difference?"

No. It made no difference at all. Not to anything. Not to what had gone before, and not to what he must do now. The fact that Elle had been a virgin changed nothing. She had been innocent of the wrongdoings of her father before he knew that, and she was innocent of them now. The fact he was her only lover might fill him with a sense of masculine pride, a sense of conquest, but it didn't change the fact that he would betray her in the end. That he would make an example of her and use her to wound her father.

The way her father had wounded his father. The way he had devastated his mother. The way he had devastated Apollo himself.

Whatever sins his father had committed, the rest of them had been nothing more than collateral damage. And so would Elle be. It was not fair. But none of this was fair.

It wasn't about fairness. It was about justice in the way that only he could obtain it.

"Yes," he lied. "It would have made a difference. I would have been much gentler with you." Except he knew he would not have. He would not take that fiery encounter in the hotel room back for anything. When Elle had unleashed all her rage on him. All of her desire. It had been the most singular experience of his life. He would trade it for nothing. It was a moment that belonged to him, one that could not be stolen no matter how low he sunk.

He was a villain, and now, he was embracing it fully.

He leaned in, kissing her, keeping it soft, keeping it light. She grabbed hold of his face, deepening the kiss.

He picked her up, carrying her to the bed and laying her down on the soft mattress, tugging the gown from her body. There would be no more talking tonight.

If he had his way, there would be no more talking until he was through with her. And if that meant spending the next two weeks in bed, then they would spend the next two weeks in bed.

CHAPTER SEVEN

THE PAST TWO weeks at Apollo's villa had gone surprisingly smoothly. It was strange to coexist with him and not fight. It actually reminded Elle of a different time. A simpler time. Back when they had actually liked each other. When she had looked up to him. When he had—apparently—had some sort of attraction to her that he had buried.

Of course, maybe they had coexisted so peacefully because their lives had been essentially separate. Unless they were making love. Which had not been confined to evenings, or to bed. She was certain that at this point, Apollo had taken her on every surface in the entire villa.

She was not complaining. It had been... Well, it had been the culmination of her most heated fantasies. It was strange. Like she was living a life borrowed, one that she could not possibly have in the long term, but one that was in many ways preferable to the one she had been living. She was still seeing to her responsibilities. Sometimes working in his office, sometimes from the office in his home while he was out.

She couldn't complain about the vacation. Of course, it was also difficult to justify the fact that she was sleeping with the enemy. Though, not literally, since they didn't sleep together. They had sex, and then he left.

"It's how I do things, *agape*," she said, amusing herself with her poor imitation of Apollo's voice as she paced the length of her bedroom.

A knock on her bedroom door startled her. She wondered if she had summoned him just by thinking about him. But he had just gone out to work a couple of hours ago, so she doubted he was back already.

She opened the door, to see one of his servants, Maria, standing there holding a package. "This is for you, miss," she said.

"Oh," she said, her whole body getting warm when she realized what it was. "Thank you."

After Maria left, she closed the door and opened the package hurriedly. Inside was a hot pink bikini. She had been planning this for the past few days. Maybe it was juvenile. But she wanted a chance to recapture the moment that both of them had missed. One that seemed to linger in both their minds.

She didn't waste any time getting into it, examining herself in the full-length mirror, watching as her cheeks flooded with color. She didn't make a habit out of wearing things that were so revealing. Though, honestly, after spending so much time naked with Apollo, she shouldn't feel self-conscious.

Still, she did.

That was different. That all happened during the heat of the moment. This was...premeditated. She had never staged anything quite like a seduction with him. And that's what this was. But she was aching for something, searching for something more. She couldn't deny that what she felt for him wasn't hatred at this point. It would be so much easier if it was.

She felt... Well, she felt a lot.

She took a deep breath, opening her bedroom door

and heading down the hall, down the stairs and outside to the pool. She was intent on being there when he got back. Intent on giving him the chance to make a different decision this time when he saw her in the bathing suit.

She slipped beneath the warm water, paddling over to the edge of the infinity pool, looking out over the view of the ocean. It was beautiful here. She hadn't thought it was possible to feel so at peace in Apollo's lair. Certainly not when she had first arrived.

She couldn't say they were growing closer, not exactly. But…it was more than it had been. For one thing, they could be in each other's presence for a full five minutes without screaming at each other. Sometimes they could go that long without tearing each other's clothes off, too. But only sometimes.

The thought made her smile, she lifted her face up to the sky, bathing herself in the warmth of the sun.

"What are you doing out here?"

"I finished work early," she said, turning, her heart slamming hard against her breastbone when she saw Apollo standing there, still dressed in the suit that he'd worn to work.

"Come here," he said, his jaw set, his dark eyes intent on her.

Elle draped her arms over the back of the infinity pool, arching her back slightly, thrusting her breasts up out of the water. "I'm enjoying the water."

"Elle," he said, his tone warning. "Do not make me come in there and get you."

"I think I would like for you to come in and get me. It's what you should have done nine years ago."

He smiled, a genuine smile. It wasn't one that was tinged with cynicism, neither was it mocking or laden with barely contained rage. It made her heart turn over in her chest, made it expand.

He began to remove his suit, starting with his jacket, then his tie, then slowly undoing the buttons on his shirt. There had been ample time over the past couple of weeks for her to become familiar with that gorgeous male physique, but familiarity hadn't made him seem commonplace. Not in the least.

He arched a brow, slowly placing his hands on his belt buckle, working the leather through the loop. Her mouth went dry and she fought to keep herself from moving closer to him. She was going to hang back. She was going to force him to come to her.

He undid the closure on his slacks, pulled the zipper down slowly, his eyes never leaving hers. He pushed his pants down his narrow hips, exposing himself to her. He was everything. Absolute perfection. Everything she had wanted a man to be and then some. No, there was no chance of him ever becoming commonplace in her eyes.

Slowly, he made his way to the pool, climbing down, the water rising up and concealing his body from her.

"You took my show," she said, just as he leaned forward, his sleek, athletic body slicing through the water effortlessly.

"I thought I would bring it to you," he said, approaching her, wrapping his arm around her waist and drawing her up against him.

"Oh," she said, "I guess I can appreciate that."

"I think you can more than appreciate that," he said, looking pointedly down at her breasts, at her tightened nipples, pushing up against the thin fabric of the bathing suit.

"I make it too easy for you," she said, not sounding even remotely regretful.

"I'm not complaining," he said, sliding his hand down her waist, resting his hand on her butt.

"Of course you're not. You're so certain of yourself, and all I have done is make you even more certain."

"I was named after a god. I came into the world with a rather inflated view of myself."

"Of course you did. How could I forget?" She lifted her hand, resting her palm on his chest. "I ordered this bathing suit for you."

Heat illuminated the darkness in his eyes. "I thought you might have."

"We have a chance to make a different decision." She traced the water droplets that were trailing down his chest, rolling into the grooves of his muscles. "I wish that I had done something differently then. Been a little bit bolder."

"You were young. You shouldn't have done anything. I shouldn't have done anything."

"I was young, but I knew what I wanted. And it hasn't changed." She looked up at him. "I still want you. I wanted you all this time, even when I was angry at you."

He wrapped his fingers around her wrist, lifting her hand to his lips, pressing a kiss to her palm. "Yes, I know you did. Believe me when I say the feeling is mutual."

Those words, those husky, delicious words, sent a little shock of pleasure through her. It wasn't strictly physical. It went deeper than that.

Unfortunately, all of this went much deeper than the physical. Much deeper than she wanted it to go.

"I do."

A smile curved his wicked mouth. "Listen to us. We have managed to converse for several minutes without fighting."

"A miracle."

"Perhaps. Though, I imagine we are skirting the edge of sacrilege assigning anything divine to the nature of things between us."

"Perhaps."

He had a point. What they shared was carnal, lustful.

No, not only that. Beautiful. Altering.

Impossible.

He was her stepbrother, he was her enemy. Truly, it was the enemy part that made it most impossible. The stepbrother issue would hardly mean anything. They hadn't been raised together. They shared no blood.

There's no affection, either. Not from him.

She squeezed her eyes shut, unable to look at him while she had thoughts like that. He closed the distance between them, pressing his lips against hers. And she just let it wash over her, warmer than the sun, more refreshing than the water they were standing in.

Desire assaulted her, her stomach tightening, a pulse beating low and hard at the apex of her thighs.

It had been just over a month since their first encounter in his hotel room in New York. Just over a month since she'd been with a man for the first time. It hadn't taken long for her to grow accustomed to it. For her to know exactly what she wanted. For her to learn his body, and to learn what hers desired of him.

He slipped his hand beneath her bikini bottoms, taking hold of her with his large palm. She loved his hands. Loved the feel of them on every inch of her. Loved looking at them. Spent a great deal of time fantasizing about them.

But then, it was like that with every single inch of him.

So many things did not live up to the promise. Did not live up to the hype. Apollo was not one of them. He took her every fantasy and superseded by leaps and bounds.

In comparison with the reality her fantasies of what sex with him would be like seemed childish. Simple.

She had known it would feel good, she had known she would find him attractive. She hadn't realized it would be so raw, so exposing. Hadn't realized it would strip her bare of everything, not just her clothes. She had thought it would just be physical.

That was such a simplistic thought. His body was the missing piece of hers. He was everything she ached for in the dead of night, the reason that she felt hollow sometimes. It was because she was desperate to have him inside of her. Only him.

She parted her lips for him, expecting him to conquer, expecting him to invade. Instead, he was gentle, his tongue sliding slowly against hers, the slick glide sending a sharp pang of need through her. So acute it was almost painful.

She forked her fingers through his hair, deepening the kiss, pressing her body as firmly against his as she could. She knew that if any of his staff members walked out now they would get a bit of a show. But honestly, her brain was too foggy with desire to really get a handle on that reality. She couldn't care. Not for her modesty, not for anyone's sensibilities. There was only this. Only him.

She lost all sense of propriety, all sense of loyalty, all sense of…everything when she was with him.

She became a new person. A different version of Elle.

She had to wonder what might have happened if she had taken the steps to close the distance between them nine years ago. If they would have forgotten about decency back then.

It didn't matter. They were doing this now. She tried to shove aside the thoughts of everything else that had happened in the ensuing years. The wedge that had been driven into the family.

Her father, his mother and her, all on one side of the gulf, with him on the other.

She didn't want to think about them. Not now. Didn't want to think about the father she could never be good enough for. The father who had preferred her stepbrother to her.

Probably still did, in truth. Even though Apollo had taken a chunk out of David St. James's empire, he probably privately celebrated his stepson's ruthlessness.

Apollo might have betrayed them. But Apollo never acted like he wished she were someone else. Apollo never made her feel like she wasn't good enough. He gloried in her body, in the attraction between them. It was more than she had ever had from...anyone.

The thought filled her with a sudden, intense swell of emotion. Whatever they had, whatever this was, it fed her soul in a way nothing else did. Because it was about her. It wasn't about the business. It wasn't about performing to his satisfaction. He cared about performing to hers. They were in this together. They wanted each other.

For once she wasn't striving for approval. Wasn't trying to live up to an expectation she simply never could.

Her father had seen Apollo as his hope. The son he never had. The heir she could never be.

Then he had trusted Apollo to bail him out, never speaking to her about anything. Never consulting her. He had always trusted Apollo above her.

And Apollo had betrayed him.

But that didn't stand in the way of her and Apollo. He didn't look at her and see the unfulfilled promises of someone else. He wanted her. In spite of everything.

It was balm for her soul.

He swept her into his arms, lifting her as though his arms were created to cradle her close. As though she was the perfect weight and size for him. As though this moment had been fated from the beginning.

He carried her up from the pool, striding right into the house, clearly just as unconcerned as she was about being seen. She had a feeling his staff was paid to look the other way when he was conducting affairs in his home. She shoved that thought to the side. She wasn't going to think about other times, other women.

Right now, she was the only one. That would have to be enough.

He started up the stairs, and she put her hand on his cheek, tracing the fine lines on his face. Additions to his features, new and fascinating. She remembered his face so clearly as a teenage boy. Smooth, pretty. Full perfect lips, amusement in his dark eyes, a kind of irreverent quirk to his brow.

He was no longer smooth. Dark stubble covered his jaw, his chin. Deep grooves bracketed his mouth, marred his forehead. The face that had once been pretty was now more rugged, more distinguished. The laughter in his eyes was gone, replaced with a kind of intensity that burned her from the inside out.

The irreverence was still there, though. It was one of her favorite parts of him. That dry, sardonic humor that would make her laugh in the strangest moments. That would take her from anger to entertainment in only a few moments. That would see her kissing him instead of screaming at him thanks to one well-timed comment.

He was one of the few men who had ever stood up to her. Who had gone toe to toe with her and made her feel like she just might lose.

Not for the first time she wondered at the ground

they had covered since then. Wondered about what had happened.

But she didn't have time to turn it over anymore, because they had reached the top of the stairs, and only a second later, her bedroom.

He set her down, water dripping down her body, pooling down around her feet. "I'm going to get the carpet wet."

"I can't say I am very concerned about that."

"Well, it's your carpet."

"Yes, it is," he said, one side of his mouth curving upward.

He regarded her for a moment before taking a step toward her, tracing the line down the edge of her bikini top, the tip of his finger only barely delving beneath. "This is the stuff of my darkest fantasies."

"A fluorescent bikini?"

He chuckled. "You. In this bikini. So much of that beautiful, pale skin on display. Your hair… It should look ridiculous with this color. Instead, you're simply everything bright. I wanted you then. I consider this my reward for good behavior." His smile turned wicked. "You know, I only wish I had known you were a virgin."

"Is that so?"

"Yes. Had I known you were a virgin I would have relished my prize all the more. I was obsessed with having you first. With teaching you about pleasure."

"You did," she said. She had held the words back from him two weeks ago. Because she had not been ready to share that with him. Had not been ready to confess just how much he had meant to her. What it had meant that he was her first lover.

Or why he was.

But there was no use in protecting herself now. She didn't want to.

"It was always you that I wanted," she said. "That was why even though I said I hated you, even though I was so angry at you the first time I kissed you, it went as far as it did. Because it was always you for me, Apollo. No matter how many years have passed, no matter what ugly words were spoken between us, it was always you."

Apollo knew he did not deserve the words that Elle had just spoken. He was using her. For these past two weeks he had been using her. To satisfy his need for her. Biding his time until he could get his revenge, filling the hours with the pleasures of her body knowing that in the end he would betray her.

There was nothing else to do. This thing between them could not last. And he could not deviate from his course of revenge against his stepfamily. Not now.

He had made up his mind. There would be wreckage.

Collateral damage.

But he wouldn't think of it now. Instead, he would take that unearned compliment. Savor it. Hold it close. He would consider this the satisfaction of a desire born years ago. The revenge would be a satisfaction of a different desire, but it was a separate issue. In his mind, she wasn't a St. James. Not now. Now, she was his lover. As he had long fantasized.

When he was finished he would end his association with her and continue on, viewing her again as the daughter of his enemy, rather than his mistress.

He could barely tear his gaze away from her, away from her pale, delectable curves, so effortlessly displayed by the flimsy material of the bikini.

That she had done this for him… It was strange. It

created a shifting sensation at the center of his chest, made him feel as though the earth had tilted slightly. This shared memory that they had of this time when they had wanted the same things… It was strange to have it here in the present.

Just take it. It is a gift.

He would. Whether he deserved it or not. Because, as he had already told her, he was the villain here. Nothing would change that.

Slowly, ever so slowly, he untied the top of the bikini, peeling it away from her luscious breasts, baring them to his gaze. She was pale everywhere except for here. Here, she was pink. Pink and perfect and everything he desired. He leaned in, tracing the edge of her puckered nipple with his tongue before sucking her deep into his mouth.

"So sweet," he said, his voice rough and unrecognizable to his own ears. "Better than honey."

She shivered beneath him and he recognized his pleasure coursing through her body. He was learning to read her. Learning to understand what made her moan, what brought her close to the edge. Had learned how to tease her. How to hold her on the brink of climax without giving it to her completely.

He had never kept a lover for this length of time before. Always, he was finished with them after a couple of nights. A couple of weeks was unheard of. There was something…intoxicating about it. Something singular. To know one particular woman's body in such an intimate fashion. Of course, he was well-versed with the female body, but that was different. This was…

Well, this was Elle.

He imagined it would never be the same with another woman, no matter how long he was with her. Elle was a fiery, living fantasy come to life, everything he had ever imagined she might be and more.

It was a damn shame. He wished she was a disappointment. Wished that she was something he could despise. Wished that she could have done something, anything to confirm that he was right to carry out this revenge plot, and use her as he'd planned.

He wished he had left her as the brittle, buttoned-up woman she had seemed in his mind only a couple of weeks ago.

But now he knew her. Knew her body. Knew her soul. *That's ridiculous. You cannot know someone's soul. You haven't one of your own.*

He pulled her close, taking hold of the tie on her swimsuit bottoms and tugging the thread roughly, then the other side, letting it fall to the ground. Trying to break the spell that she had cast over him with this bright, insubstantial piece of fabric. It was insane. And yet it was so…

He had advanced no further with her than where he had been nine years ago. He was still a slave to his desires. And now he was old enough to know that going out and getting any redhead at any bar would not suffice.

Now that he had had Elle, he knew that there was no substitute. Ever. There had never been another woman like her, and there never would be again.

He dropped to his knees in front of her, suddenly overwhelmed with his desire. He buried his face between her thighs, tasting her, deep and long, relishing the flavor of her desire as it spread over his tongue. He was insatiable for her. Desperate for her. He pushed one finger deep inside her slick channel, then another, loving the way that she bucked against his hand, the needy cries for pleasure that escaped her lips.

She was desperate. Like he was. She was in this with

him. He needed it proven. Needed to know for sure. He felt like he was losing his mind. He did not know himself now. Never in all his life had a woman made him shake. Never in all his life had a woman owned him in such a way. Never had a woman successfully erased visions of any other.

But she had.

He gripped her hips, holding her tightly against his mouth as he continued to pleasure her, until she shook just as violently as he did. Until she was on the verge. Until she was whimpering, crying out for release. Begging for it.

He loosened his hold on her, sliding the flat of his tongue over her as he rose upward, tracing a line to her belly button, up farther, until he was standing. Until he could capture her mouth with his. He pulled her up against him, let her feel the hard, insistent thrust of his arousal against her stomach. Kissed until he was dizzy. Until she was pleading with him to take her.

He rocked his hips against her, relishing the raw sounds she made, the feeling of her fingernails digging into his skin. It was always like this with her. Desire tinged with violence.

And he loved it.

He backed her up against the bed, and they fell onto it. He positioned himself between her thighs, pressing the head of himself to her slick entrance. He pushed into her easily, her arousal easing the way. She was so hot, so tight. She was made just for him.

As he seated himself fully inside her he had the strongest sensation that he was home. That he was complete for the first time in years.

A deep, strong emotion tugged at his chest, a sense of déjà vu that he didn't want to place. This was new and familiar all at the same time. And he rejected it. Didn't want it. But as his arousal built, as she flexed her hips beneath him, meeting his every thrust, he found he could not hold on to his control and keep the emotions at bay.

She wrapped her legs around his hips, and as she gave herself up to her own release, as his own climax crashed over him like a wave, those feelings crashed through him, as well.

And as he was tossed violently in the surf, he could think of one thing. Elle. That she was the port in the storm. That she was the constant. The North Star by which he had been guided for years. A star he had turned away from.

The realization left him feeling like his chest was full of broken glass. As though he had been wounded, invaded by sharp, shattered splinters he could never hope to remove.

He looked down at Elle, at her lips, flushed with desire, swollen from his kisses, her eyes, slumberous, satisfied. Looking at him as though he held answers.

He had no answers. At this moment, he had nothing but questions.

"Stay with me. Tonight," she said, "could you stay with me?"

And as terror tore at him like a rabid dog, he could do nothing but nod and pull her into his arms. But it did nothing to stop the hemorrhaging in his chest. Did nothing to stem the flow of pure, unmitigated fear pounding through him.

But Elle had asked him to stay. And so he did.

CHAPTER EIGHT

WHEN APOLLO WOKE, it was starting to turn gray outside. And Elle was curled up around him like a cat. He had no doubt, even for a moment, who he was lying in bed with. Who he had fallen asleep with.

He had never been close enough with a woman to even contemplate letting his guard down enough to fall asleep with her. In the past, the moment he finished making love with a woman, he left. There was no reason to linger. Sex, in his experience, could be perfectly impersonal. Sleeping with someone had seemed an intimacy he did not wish to contend with.

But he had fallen asleep with Elle, after she had asked him to stay. He had not imagined he would sleep. But it seemed natural. To hold her in his arms while they both drifted off. Bathing in the afterglow of the pleasure they had shared.

Suddenly, panic overtook him. He had a plan. A plan to make the St. James family pay for the sins they had committed against his family. To avenge the death of his father. The loss of his family fortune. The strange relationship Apollo's mother had been forced into by David St. James.

And every indignity he had suffered. Every moment he had been made to feel like he had not earned his position at the prestigious boarding school he went to. Every time he had to defend his placement in the boardroom because he had come from such humble beginnings.

She was weakening that plan. She was weakening his determination. And he could not let that stand.

He extricated himself from her hold, rolling out of bed. He forked his fingers through his hair, looking around, before remembering he had no clothes in her room. He wrenched open the door, walking down the hall completely naked. All of the staff would have gone home. Anyway, they knew better than to stare too long if they saw something shocking in his home.

Instead of going to his bedroom, he went into his office, taking a bottle of whiskey from the shelf to the left of his desk. He poured a healthy amount, and took a fortifying drink. Elle drove him to drink. This was the second time he'd turned to alcohol to deal with the effects she had on him.

Most women didn't affect him at all.

He had been determined to keep her with him until the attraction between them burned out, but he could see that something else was heating up between them, something he had no hope of burning out half so quickly.

Rage took him over. He didn't want to send her away. He could imagine it, telling her to leave. Never touching her again. Never spending another night with her. Anger overtook him, completely, dictating his next action. He took the half-full glass of whiskey and hurled it at the wall, watching the glass shatter, feeling no remorse at all.

The fact that the very thought of her leaving made him feel so helpless, so enraged was only more evidence that he had to send her away.

If he was going to take his revenge, he would have to take it now.

* * *

They had forgotten to tint the windows. That was Elle's first thought when she woke up the next morning. Her second thought was that she was alone. True to his word, Apollo had not spent the night with her. She shouldn't be surprised, but after she had confessed to him that he was her only lover, she supposed she had expected… something.

She supposed that she was foolish.

For wishing that things could be different. For wishing that something had changed between them. She didn't know what.

She sat up, clutching the blankets to her chest. And suddenly, Apollo came bursting through the door. "Good morning," he said, his mouth set into a grim line.

"Good morning," she said.

During all of the time she'd spent here, he had never come into her room unannounced. He had never come in unless it was to make love. He did not look like he had… that on his mind. Not in the least. He looked… He looked like he had come in with demons on his heels.

"I trust you slept well," he said.

"Yes," she said, a strange, uneasy feeling settling in the center of her chest. She didn't know why. She only knew that something wasn't right.

"I think it is time you left," he said, his words cold.

"But we… I don't understand," she said. "Yesterday we…"

"That was yesterday. And this is today."

She thought back to last night, to what had transpired between them. Had she done something wrong? Had he not liked her wearing the bikini and reminding him of that day? No. Yesterday he had enjoyed it. She knew he had.

"I'm not ready to leave," she said. "We agreed we needed to burn this out and I don't think it's burned out."

"A difference of opinion," he said, his tone hard. "For me, it is over."

"Apollo…"

"Also, effective immediately you have been terminated from your position as CEO of Matte."

"I… What?" She couldn't make sense of his words. She was naked, in bed, after having just spent the night making love with him, and he was firing her.

Two weeks. Two weeks she had spent with this man. In his arms. Kissing him, sharing her body with him… sharing everything.

"You heard me," he continued. His tone was flat. His eyes were flat. He was like a stranger. Only yesterday she had felt that she'd known him more intimately, more deeply than any other person on earth. And now she doubted it. She truly did. "I grow tired of the charade, Elle. Truth be told, I was planning on drawing this out longer. I was anticipating feeling a great sense of pleasure when I let you know that I was simply using you to hurt your father. I planned to set you up as the face of the company, to bring you into greater prominence so that when I made it very clear that I had taken all of your father's assets and left him ruined, the world would know exactly who he was, exactly what that meant. But frankly, I find it's just too tiring. So, I will have to be content in my revenge all on my own."

Her head was spinning. Revenge? She had been under no illusions that there was any affection between Apollo and her, but if anyone should want revenge, it was her. "You… You used me."

"Did you really think that I wanted you?"

She felt like he had driven a spike through her chest.

The cold, black words matching his cold, black eyes, making it impossible to pretend she had misheard. "Of course I did. As far as I know men can't fake…" She gestured toward the front of his pants. "They have to at least be attracted to a woman."

"It isn't just women who can lie back and think of England. What I really wanted, Elle, was to let your father know that I've taken everything from him. What would he think if he knew—?"

"Don't you dare, you bastard."

"Then I would have his company, and his daughter."

"You don't have me," she said, her throat tightening. "Two weeks, Apollo. Two weeks I gave you… I did…" She swallowed hard, panic taking over, tears threatening to fall. "I held nothing back from you! I trusted you with my body."

"A bad decision. I am untrustworthy. I have been from the beginning. You were convenient, darling, but let's be honest. Hardly more than a diversion, and one I cannot afford anymore."

"How can you say that?"

"It's true. Elle, be realistic. What could I possibly want with a near-virgin who's so cold she practically leaves icicles on my lips after a kiss?"

His words struck her like a physical blow. None of this made sense. She couldn't process it. But somewhere, in the middle of all the pain, all the anguish flooding through her like an unchecked tide, she found rage. The same rage that had propelled her into his arms in the first place.

And she clung it to it with everything she had. "How dare you?" she hissed, low and hard. "My father did everything for you. He paid for your education. He loved you—"

"No," he said. "He never loved me. He wanted to possess my mother, at any cost. And he did so. His very own Biblical fantasy where she was his Bathsheba and he sent her husband out to die."

"What?"

"Yes. My family was not always impoverished. Your father and mine were business partners, Elle. But they both fell for the same woman. My mother. She preferred my father. Your father bided his time, waited until he saw the opportunity, and then he used his sway with the board to vote my father out of the company. My father was ruined. Ultimately, he killed himself. My mother held out against your father's pleas for him to join her in the US. As his mistress. He was of course married to your mother then."

"I…"

"My mother agreed when I was eight, and we were starving. He established us in a home near his, and he came to visit often. From what I discovered later, he paid your mother off, then waited an appropriate amount of time before bringing my mother to the estate to be his wife."

"No… My father wouldn't… He didn't…"

"He did. He's a manipulative bastard who sees us all as nothing more than pawns. His actions caused his father to kill himself, it ruined my family. But I started to look into the history of my family. And when I found out why my father killed himself…why he was ruined…it all became clear." He paused. "It was your mother who contacted me."

Elle's mother who had long since abandoned the family. Whom Elle hadn't seen in fifteen years. "My mother?"

"Yes. She had seen me rising in business circles and

she…she found me one night at a bar. I didn't know who she was. Just another blonde who was after a night, I thought. But unlike most women, she didn't want sex. She wanted to talk. She wanted to tell me just what your father was."

"She came and found you? After all these years, not speaking to me for any of them, she came and found *you*? Are you that much more compelling to both of my parents?"

"In her case, I think she was compelled by revenge."

"Did she even ask about me?" Elle asked, despising the small sound of her own voice.

He said nothing, and it was his silence that spoke loudest. Of course she hadn't. She hadn't contacted her in years, why would she be concerned now? "I can't… I don't know what to think. I don't know how to process this."

His top lip curled. "Well, you will have plenty of time to process it while you stand in line filing paperwork to collect unemployment."

"Apollo… You can't do this."

His expression was granite. "I am doing this. It was my plan all along, and I am keeping to it. I am simply shortening the timeline."

Her stomach tightened, her entire body seizing up. She thought she was breaking apart from the inside out.

She had believed in him. Believed that he was the first person to see her for who she was. To want her for herself.

That was the worst betrayal of all. The fact that he'd used her. Not even because he hated her, not even because he wanted revenge on her, but because he wanted it on her *father*. Yet again, she was nothing. Nothing more than the most convenient chess piece on the board.

"Get out," she said, shaking now, trembling inside and out.

"It is my house."

"And it is my room. Leave me with what little dignity I have left." He turned away from her, heading toward the door. "I can't believe you. All the things you let me say. All the things you let me do. The bikini. As if I was... As if I mattered. But I never did. You're not any better than my father. Even if what you say is true, every word of it, you haven't risen above anything."

He turned back to her, his expression bleak. "I never wanted to rise above. I only ever wanted to drag you all into hell with me."

And with that, he walked out of the room, leaving her there, desolate and broken and certain she would never be whole again.

CHAPTER NINE

"IF YOU DON'T mind me saying, Mr. Savas, you've been impossible the past few weeks."

"I know *you* don't mind saying it, Alethea," he said, his tone hard as he looked at his computer screen, ignoring his assistant.

"It's true," she said, turning on her heel and walking out of the office. Apollo didn't look up until the door had been shut firmly behind her.

Damned woman. She was always speaking the truth. He should fire her and hire someone stupid, beautiful and biddable.

When he thought the word *beautiful*, only one face came to mind. Of course, that woman was neither stupid, nor biddable. And she was persistently in his head.

Particularly in his dreams. He had woken up hard and reaching for her and she wasn't there. Because he'd sent her away.

It had seemed necessary at the time. Like he needed to put distance between them. But the longer he spent without her, the more he questioned that decision.

After all, his issue had been his loss of control, but sending her away wasn't any more controlled.

He had removed temptation from his path, but he had

not successfully destroyed his lust for her. Because of that, he was suffering now.

There was no reason to do so, of course. She had nothing to do, nowhere to go. No job. He could have her back. Make her his.

The memory of her—the warm weight of her, her sweet scent, the way she sighed and said his name—haunted him. His days, his nights.

He was like an addict in desperate need of a fix. His hands shaking, sweat breaking out over his skin at the thought of tasting her lips. Feeling her softness beneath his palms.

She was his own personal designer drug. One taste had only sent him headlong into an addiction he couldn't shake.

So maybe that was the problem. Cutting himself off completely would never work. It would only leave him wondering what it would be like to have her one last time. To lose himself inside her. To feel her delicate fingertips skimming over his back.

Just the thought sent a rush of need through him, so hot, so swift it nearly sent him down to his knees.

He had never felt like this before. Had never felt the need to keep and possess quite so fiercely.

As her father felt for your mother?

No. This was different. But one thing he knew: he had spent too many years denying this desire. He would not continue on.

He had been forced into denial, into poverty as a boy because of her father.

He would not subject himself to denial of his needs again.

He would not go one more night without her in his bed.

* * *

Elle was certain she was dying. It had been four weeks since she had left Greece. Four weeks since she had left Apollo, jobless, broken and humiliated. At least none of it had made it out into the public.

All anyone knew was that she had been replaced in her position at Matte. No one knew about her relationship with Apollo, and that was about the only thing saving her from melting into a puddle and sliding down the nearest drain, disappearing forever.

As upset as her father was about the entire situation, at least he didn't blame her. Or, maybe she didn't care. She had no idea how she felt. In only a month her entire life had been completely upended. She was avoiding her father. Avoiding dealing with that situation entirely.

Everything Apollo had said, all of the things he had told her that her father was guilty of, had settled down deep inside of her, and created just enough doubt about… everything that she wasn't sure she could deal with right now.

And then, purely selfishly, there was the issue of her firing.

She stood up, the floor pitching beneath her as she rose from the couch for the first time in hours. Being unemployed was bad for her wardrobe choices. She had been wearing sweats for three days, because there was no one there to see her anyway. Yesterday she'd worn flannels with small foxes on them. Today, her pants had owls.

"Very sexy," she said, crossing the length of the apartment and heading toward her fridge. She opened it up, immediately swamped by the smell coming from the inside. She wrinkled her nose. Something did not smell right. But it wasn't like she kept that much food in the fridge.

She dry heaved, and slammed the door shut. She'd forced herself to eat when she'd first woken up, but nothing tasted like…anything. A broken heart did that to you, apparently. But any semblance of an appetite she might have was gone now.

She felt like she had licked the inside of the tennis shoe. Okay, that thought made her stomach feel even worse.

She heard a knock on her door, and she nearly jumped out of her skin. People didn't just gain admittance to the building, so it had to be someone who already lived here. Though, her neighbors didn't speak to her, so she had no idea who it was or what it could be about.

Taking a deep breath, she crossed the apartment and undid the dead bolt and the chain, jerking it open just as she realized she should have looked through the peephole first.

But it was too late. The door was open, and standing there was her worst nightmare.

Suddenly, the vague sense of nausea intensified and she ran from the room, losing her breakfast violently in the bathroom.

"Elle?" Apollo's voice was coming from behind her.

"Stay away," she said, shakily getting to her feet. "I'm…horrifying."

"You're sick," he said, his tone vaguely accusatory.

"I…wasn't." Except she had been—though not this sick—but off her game for the past few days.

"What are you doing here, anyway?" She wandered over to the sink and splashed cold water on her face. "Who buzzed you in?"

"Some young woman who lives down the hall. Nose ring. Pink hair. She thought I looked trustworthy."

Elle laughed. Bitter, hollow. "She thought you looked like you belonged in her bed. I would give her advanced warning, but I imagine she wouldn't really care either way."

"Sadly for her. I'm not on the market."

"Okay. If you aren't here to hook up with my down-the-hall neighbor, why are you here?"

"Would you believe that I came to check on you?"

"No."

"I want you back."

"No," she said, her tone incredulous. "You can't have me back. You were awful to me. You fired me."

"And now you don't have a job. I thought you might be interested in pursuing some sort of arrangement."

She laughed, flinging her arms wide. "And here I am, vomiting as you ask me to come be your mistress. Really, there are probably more romantic settings than the bathroom."

"You need money. You certainly need a way to occupy your time."

"You're despicable."

She swept past him, trying to hold her head high. Difficult to do when the man who had made love to you then humiliated you had just seen you puke.

"Maybe," he said, lingering in the door frame, bracing his hands against it. "But it doesn't change the facts."

"Oh," she said, the world tilting slightly. "I need to lie down."

He frowned. "How long have you been feeling sick?"

"I told you, I only just… That, in the bathroom."

"You've been otherwise feeling well?"

"Not really. But then, you humiliated me and fired

me. So I don't know how well you could possibly expect me to feel."

"I'm not talking about your emotions, I'm talking about physically."

"No. I have not been feeling very well. But your emotions inform things like that."

"Have you gotten your period?"

Her mouth dropped open. "What kind of question is that?"

"The only question that matters to me right now."

Ice shivered down her spine. "I haven't," she said. "But that doesn't... It doesn't mean anything."

"You're here vomiting and looking pale, you haven't had your period in the past month and you don't think that means anything."

"We..."

"Were not very careful."

No, they hadn't been. They hadn't used a condom in the elevator, and again during that last time at his home. So really... She hadn't had a period since the elevator. "No, I guess we weren't."

"And it didn't occur to you until just now that you might be pregnant?"

"No," she said, her hand flying to her mouth, her eyes wide. "No. I'm not... I'm not."

"You have no way of knowing that."

No. She didn't. Because she hadn't taken a test. And, while she had never been particularly regular, that hadn't exactly been a problem because she had been a virgin. Now...it was a bit suspicious.

"I mean, I would prefer to wait a few days..."

He had already pulled out a cell phone. "Yes, Alethea? Find a discreet women's doctor in Manhattan who can see a patient immediately. Text me the information once you have it. When I say immediately, I mean I'm about to get in the car and start driving. They had better be ready to see us."

He hung up, and she could only stare at him. "What are you doing?"

"We are going to answer this question once and for all, *agape*. And make no mistake, if you are carrying my child there is no question that you are coming back to Greece with me. Immediately."

He could do nothing but pace outside the office at the posh, private medical facility he had taken Elle to.

He had found himself back in Manhattan for business reasons, and then he had displayed a characteristic weakness and found himself at Elle's building.

He did not know what manner of witchcraft Elle possessed that she made it impossible for him to forget her. Forget how she made him feel. Whether it was four weeks in the past, or nine years—before he had ever even touched her. She was a woman who lingered in his mind in a way that none before her—or since—ever had.

He wondered now if she had been some sort of bad omen. If the fact that he had never been able to get her out of his mind had been a warning of some kind. If she were truly pregnant with his child, he could not discount that. He had never intended to have children. But the moment the idea that she might be pregnant had entered his mind he had known that he would take possession of his child.

After his own childhood, after the way he had lost his father, he knew he would never subject his own child to such a thing. To a life without the man who was meant to protect him.

He gritted his teeth. His own father's feelings had hardly been his fault. He had been pushed into ruin by

David St. James. The fault would always lie with St. James. Apollo however was standing on his own two feet. No one was pushing him anywhere.

The door opened, and Elle emerged, clutching a few pieces of paper, her face pale. He didn't need her to speak to know what the answer was.

He had never imagined being in this situation. He supposed that any man who was sexually active could potentially face it, but he had always been very careful. So it was never anything he had considered seriously. But he had not been careful with Elle. The theme in their relationship, and the consequences of that, were now coming home to roost.

There was no panic. There was not even any rage, though he had expected it. No, there was nothing but cold, clean determination. He knew exactly what he was going to do. What he would demand.

"I…"

"Yes, I think I can guess."

"I don't know what we're going to do."

"I know exactly what we are going to do."

Her eyes widened. "You do?"

"Yes. You will be coming back to Athens with me. And then, *agape*, you and I are going to marry."

Elle was dimly aware of the fact that she was sitting in Apollo's limo, essentially in a catatonic state. But she had just found out she was pregnant with the baby of a man who despised her and her family, a man who had left her jobless and broken when he had ended their affair.

She had never really thought about being a mother. Her own mother had abandoned her early on and not bothered to keep in touch at all. Her stepmother was a lovely woman, but often silent next to her husband.

And Elle's father was so…imposing. He didn't bend. He didn't show affection. It was like loving a rock.

She had never imagined trying to re-create that parent-child relationship with herself in the parenting hot seat. It seemed…completely unappealing. It also meant she was linked to Apollo. Forever.

As if you weren't before.

She gritted her teeth. She had no idea what to say. No idea what to do next. And as far as she knew she was being shanghaied and sent to Athens again.

That thought sent her into action. "I'm not going to marry you."

He chuckled, a dark, humorless sound. "Then prepare yourself for a custody battle that will drain you of your every resource."

She blinked. "Who said I would fight you for custody?"

The moment she said it, she realized that she would. Not because her parents had been wonderful, not because they had made her long for a parent-child relationship in her own life. But because they had demonstrated in a million small ways how unimportant she was. She would be damned if her own child would walk through life feeling like their mother couldn't be bothered with them.

Just the thought made her stomach clench in agony. Her own little one, believing that she didn't want them. She wanted to apologize to the little life inside her. As though it had somehow sensed her hesitance.

"If you don't feel strongly enough about our child to stand and fight for them, then I would gladly have you step aside."

"I won't," she said, her tone infused with conviction.

The numbness was starting to wear off. And even though she couldn't quite imagine what it would be like to have a child, even though she wasn't sure if she was devastated or happy, she knew that she wouldn't stand aside.

"You just said—"

"Yes, well, I am trying to figure out exactly where I stand. It might surprise you to know this but I didn't exactly fantasize about a life with a picket fence, a husband and children."

"It doesn't surprise me. A woman with as much white in her apartment as you have doesn't seem to be planning ahead for sticky fingers."

"I wasn't. You can be sure of that. But I'm also not one to walk away from my responsibilities. And I don't want any child of mine going through life imagining they aren't wanted."

"Then, marriage it will be."

Her mind was ticking over at a million miles a minute. "I would have a few conditions," she said.

She could not believe she had just said that. She knew that you weren't supposed to negotiate with terrorists or superalpha Greek billionaires who had far too high of an opinion of themselves. So, she didn't know why she was attempting it.

"Conditions, *agape*?" He sounded…angry. But interested.

"Yes. Conditions." Now she had to quickly think of her conditions. "New York is my home. I'm not leaving New York."

"I have a villa in Greece."

"I daresay you have homes all over the world. I know you don't have a permanent residence in New York, but I do."

"Your apartment is the size of a postage stamp."

"It's big enough."

"For you. There is no room for a child. No room for a husband."

She gritted her teeth. "I did not agree to taking a husband. Not yet. I have conditions, but I won't make my final decision until I'm certain that the situation is to my liking."

"I'm not certain you want to challenge my authority. I am a well-respected billionaire, after all, and you are unemployed. The daughter of a businessman on the verge of being washed-up. If your mother hasn't spent all of his payoff money by now, she's certainly close to it. What could you possibly give a child that I can't?"

"Love. Warmth. Human emotion?"

"I'm sure the court will be more impressed with my net worth."

"I don't think so. Everyone agrees that a child needs love above anything else."

"And you feel you are more qualified to give a child parental love that I am?"

She shifted in her seat. "Yes. I do."

"On what grounds? Prior to being unemployed you were a workaholic."

"I was not."

"Did you have a single friend who was not also a co-worker?"

She didn't even have to think about that. She knew the answer to the question. But whether or not they were from work Suki and Christine were real friends. Suki had brought cupcakes after Elle had been fired. *Friendship.*

Though the thought of cupcakes made her stomach turn right now.

"You're a workaholic, too," she said.

"I'm also a man and a billionaire. No one will judge

me for the amount of time I spend working. It is irrelevant. Not so for you."

"The point is, I am the child's mother and I don't think I'm going to have an issue retaining custody."

"I disagree."

"You will have to wait, Apollo," she said, her voice infused with iron, with a strength she wasn't sure she truly felt right now. "I'm not afraid of fighting you in court. To hear you tell it your mother was manipulated into a relationship with my father and now you want to do the same to me? How are you any better?"

"I'm not," he said, his expression bleak, cold. But only for a moment. Then his walls went back up.

"Name your conditions clearly."

"I want to stay in New York. I wish to have the child here. I wish to raise him here."

"The child will be Greek. He should be exposed to his homeland."

"Exposure is fine. But I want him raised here. I want to stay here. Because that leads me to my next requirement. I want my job back."

"The new CEO has only been there for a month. If I let him go I will seem capricious."

"There is a cost to everything. And that is the cost to having me without muss or fuss. Do you accept, or not?"

She wasn't certain if she wanted him to say yes, or if she wanted him to refuse. She wasn't sure what she wanted at all.

"I accept."

A strange mixture of relief and terror washed through her. "Excellent."

He pulled out his phone again. "Alethea," he said. "I require some real estate. A penthouse, Manhattan. Something large, but secure. No rooftop balconies or anything like that. Or, if there are balconies, they need to be secure. Childproof." He hung up.

"Is your assistant finding you a house?"

"No, *agape*," he said, smiling a smile that was not friendly at all. "My assistant is going to find us a home. Now do you agree to marry me?"

Elle took a deep breath and met that coal-black gaze. "If I find the conditions are met to my satisfaction. And if I feel you won't spend my whole life making me miserable. You said I was your revenge, Apollo. Until you see me as a woman—a whole woman, not your stepsister who you harbor rage against, not an instrument of vengeance to use against my father—you will not have me. Not in your life, not as your wife. That's a promise."

CHAPTER TEN

ALETHEA WAS NOTHING if not efficient, and by that afternoon he and Elle were standing in an empty penthouse at the top of the building in Midtown. It was spacious, though hardly the sun-drenched villa he chose to call home in Greece. But it would do.

"Do you find this satisfactory?"

"I have a… I have a house," she said.

"Oh, I have already taken care of listing it for you. Unless you wish to keep it as some sort of workspace, I figured it would be best to sell it."

"You're selling my house?"

"My men have been over there packing your things."

She whirled around, her hands clenched into fists. "Apollo! I can't believe you would do something like that."

He turned to her, arching a dark brow. "Really. You can't believe I would do something like that? And here I thought it was in keeping with my character."

She pressed her fists up against her eyes, as though she was trying to use them to hold back her rage. "Everything is changing too quickly."

"Things have been changing quickly for the past two months. First, we had sex. Then you went to Greece. Then we had more sex. You lost your job. Now you're having a baby and we're working at integrating our lives. It's a fast-moving train, life is."

In truth, his life had been stagnant for quite a few years. Yes, he had more money than he could possibly spend in a lifetime. His business had continued to grow. He had fixated on his revenge plan against the St. James family. But beyond that, nothing had moved significantly in years. His life was an endless array of beautiful women, meaningless events that required him to put on a suit and smile politely at those in attendance. This was...

This was the first time in a long time he had something new.

It wasn't the revenge he had planned when he'd come back to New York, but it was...interesting. He imagined Elle would take exception to him calling her accidental pregnancy interesting.

"Fine. It's very you. But you can't just come into my life and completely reorder it."

"Why not? You have done it to me."

She looked stunned for a moment. "Have I?"

"You are going to make me a father. If that is not up-ending my life, I don't know what is."

"I suppose it depends on how involved you intend to be."

He knew nothing about how to be a good father. He could scarcely remember his own. When the other man had been alive he had all but lived at the corporate headquarters for the business he shared with David St. James. And then, after that, after the disgrace, he had sunk into drugs and alcohol. Affairs. Only a few years later he was dead.

As far as David went...the man had been an attentive stepfather. He had been... Well, none of it mattered now. Because of what he had revealed himself to be.

"I am a busy man. A wealthy man. I plan to keep my involvement somewhat limited," he said.

"Then, I suppose your personal life doesn't have to change much. Oh," she said, her green gaze turning sharp. "Except you are required to remain faithful to me."

Her words hit him low and hard in the stomach. Punched the wound he had just been examining. He could not imagine wanting a woman other than Elle. He had not taken anyone else to his bed in the month since they had parted. Unusual for him.

In fact, from the moment he had taken over her father's company, from the moment he had first taken over the magazine and brought her back into his life on a semi-regular basis, he had not been with another woman. Because the moment Elle St. James had come back into his life his body had reignited its obsession for her. Still, he did not wish for her to know that. He did not want her issuing more edicts.

He had agreed to New York, because that was simple. He had agreed to giving her the position at Matte back because it was also simple. And quite apart from that, the fact that he was providing David St. James with his first grandchild was a whole new, delicious sort of revenge.

He no longer needed to throw her out of the company. No longer required to destroy St. James in that way. He had the man's daughter. She was having his baby. She would be his wife, Apollo was confident in that.

Yes, there was a great deal he could do with that. He was certain.

"I have no experience with fidelity," he said. "I will make no promises on that score."

"Then you will enjoy the single life. If you touch another woman, you certainly won't be touching me."

"I highly doubt that."

He and Elle could scarcely be in the same room together without tearing each other's clothes off. Today
was an exception, brought about by the shock of her discovering she was pregnant and by the need to see to the
logistics created by that circumstance. But he knew that
very soon he would have her on her back begging for
his possession.

Or she will have you on your back begging for hers.

He refused to consider that. Refused to think of things
that way. She was a slave to the pleasure that ignited between them every time they touched, just as he was. He
was not at a disadvantage. He was not alone in it.

"The perk of staying single is that I will be free to pursue other lovers," she said, shaking her head, her coppery
mane shimmering in the sunlight filtering through the
large windows that overlooked Central Park.

"I don't believe that," he said, rage a hot, living thing
in his stomach. The thought of another man touching
Elle was anathema. But she was bluffing, and he would
call her on that.

"Why is that? I may have been a virgin before you
and I met, Apollo, but now that you have shown me just
how enjoyable sex can be I don't think you can possibly
ask me to forgo the pleasure."

"I damn well can."

She laughed. "Careful. Your desperation is showing. You wouldn't want me to understand where my real
power is in all of this."

She hit too close to the bone there, cut him far too
deeply.

And suddenly, he did not care that today had been
an emotional one for her. He did not care that she was
in a fragile state. Only than only a couple of hours ago
she had been sick in front of him, while wearing sweat-

pants. He always wanted Elle. Always. There was never a time when he didn't crave her touch. And this was no exception.

He crossed the vacant expanse of the living area, wrapping his arm around her waist and tugging her up against him, cupping her chin with his thumb and forefinger. "Do not push me, Elle. You will not like the result."

"Do not push *me*, Apollo."

"We push each other, *agape*, that's the honest truth. And look at where it has gotten us."

"Yes. I daresay it is not the most pleasant situation."

"I could make it much more pleasant if you weren't so stubborn."

She glared at him. "The same goes for you."

"You start again at Matte tomorrow. I will give your replacement a generous severance."

He released his hold on her.

"Excellent," she said, smoothing her clothing, her voice making it sound like she thought all of this was anything but excellent.

"I have arranged for all of our things to be moved into the penthouse by tonight."

She laughed. "That isn't possible."

He lifted his shoulder. "It is possible when you pay with cash."

She shook her head. "That's the problem with you, Apollo, you have never been denied anything that you wanted."

"I don't know, Elle, I felt fairly denied of my father after he put a bullet in his brain. And why did he do that? Oh, yes. Because his dear friend and business partner betrayed him. Yes, I know a little bit about deprivation. I refuse to apologize for enjoying luxury now."

She blinked. "I'm sorry. I didn't mean…"

He waved a hand. "I am not so sensitive. Anyway, this is par for the course between us, yes? We must tear strips off each other's hides. Because if we do not, we will tear each other's clothes off instead."

She sniffed. "Maybe once. But not anymore."

"You may cling to that illusion all you want. Either way, your things will be here by this evening. How you choose to spend your time between now and then is up to you."

The next day, when Elle walked into the fully furnished penthouse she felt dazed. Her life was changing so quickly. They were going to be sharing a space while he was in New York. Living together. And he wanted to marry her.

It made her stomach tight. Made her feel dizzy.

The terrifying thing was there was some small, delusional piece of her that felt…excited. As though this were some kind of fairy tale. As though the two of them were embarking on a real relationship. Possibly, a real marriage. As though he wanted her, because she was Elle, because of the heat and fire between them, not because she was carrying his baby.

He came back. He came back before he knew you were pregnant.

She held that close. Turned it over and examined it as though it was some kind of rare treasure that she wanted to keep shielded from the world. That she never wanted to look away from. He had returned to her before he found out about the baby. She didn't know what that meant. Yes, he had said he wanted her to return as his mistress. But she knew full well that a man like Apollo was more than capable of getting any woman he desired. He didn't need her. But he had still come for her.

And the moment he had found out about the baby he had taken charge, taken everything into hand and done everything he could to make their arrangement permanent.

It was perhaps foolish to assign any meaning to that, but she couldn't help it.

At the bottom of it all, at the end of everything, she just wanted someone who wanted to be with her. Maybe that was a sad admission. But she had been lonely for so long. For all of her life. And the way that Apollo looked at her, the way that he commanded her body, so fierce and intense, at the exclusion of all else, made her hopeful that there was more to his attentions than he was willing to admit.

Of course, he would not promise to be faithful to her.

She blinked, swallowing hard, continuing to examine the modern layout of the penthouse. "Which room will be mine?"

"Any one that you choose," he said. "Though the master bedroom already has your things in it."

"Not yours?"

He lifted his shoulder. "I have several other residences. I may not always be here as frequently as you are. My headquarters will remain in Greece. That means I will only spend a small amount of time here."

The idea of him being with other women flooded her mind again. Of course. He wasn't actually planning on living with her. Not really. Not all the time. He was taking possession of her, but he was holding her at arm's length. It shouldn't surprise her. But it did hurt.

And it did nothing to remove the traitorous beacon of hope that still burned down in the pit of her stomach. She should harbor no hope where he was concerned, and still that small part of her whispered: *But he came back before he knew about the baby.*

She wasn't going to let him see her hope.

"That's fine. It will be good for the child, I think, to have us in the same house sometimes. At least there is space. I think I might go lie down," she said, heading toward the stairs that led to the upper level of the penthouse and the bedrooms.

"You're welcome to. But we have a dinner reservation in four hours. I expect you to be ready by then."

She gritted her teeth. "Is this going to be nothing more than a series of edicts?"

"You keep challenging them, I keep trying."

"Well, thankfully a meal is not a marriage."

She continued on up the stairs. Then she walked down the hall and pushed open the door to her new bedroom. In her new house. Suddenly, her knees felt like they were going to buckle. Everything was so overwhelming. The decisions she suddenly had to make. She moved quickly to the bed and threw herself down on the soft surface. And then she did the thing she allowed so very rarely. She buried her face in the pillow and wept.

Elle was always beautiful. That was part of the problem with her. No matter that she was forbidden, either because she was his stepsister or the daughter of his enemy, she was too beautiful. But tonight, in a short cream lace dress, her skin looking as waxen as a doll's, her red hair falling softly around her shoulders, she was like a particularly terrified angel. Otherworldly. Ethereal.

And all he could think of was that he wanted to drag her into the pit with him. Make her fall, as he had done.

He had not lied when he had told her that all he had ever wanted was to bring her down to his level. To somehow make it acceptable for a man like him to touch a woman like her.

What does it matter what is acceptable?

He didn't even know what was acceptable anymore. So the question, he supposed, was moot.

He had not told her what the aim of the dinner was. She would be angry at him, but he could not see her resisting once she saw the ring.

He had gone to a jewelry store today and chosen the ring for her himself. A large square-cut champagne diamond that seemed to capture her particular brand of unique elegance better than a standard sort of engagement ring.

He had also chosen one of the most up-and-coming restaurants in Manhattan to perform the deed. Because there was guaranteed to be paparazzi lurking, even if they were hiding in the hedgerows, so to speak. And, beyond that, there would be people there with cameras ready to take pictures and post what they had seen to the internet. Getting the word out had never been so easy, and since discretion was the furthest thing from his mind, it suited him.

He took her hand, running his thumb over the smooth, silken skin. Some unknown, possessive, caveman part of him relished what was about to happen. The fact that soon he would put his ring on her finger, and the world would know that she belonged to him. He gloried in that. The fact that there would be a sign of his ownership of her.

That made him think of the baby. Of the fact that she would soon grow round with it, yet more evidence of the fact that he had bound her to him, irrevocably, intensely.

He did not know who he was just now. But then, with Elle, he never did.

She looked down at his hand as though it was a potentially dangerous snake. "I don't think you brought me here simply to treat me to a nice meal. Though, it was nice."

"And we have not yet gotten to dessert."

She drew her hand back slowly. "No, we haven't. And you have been perfectly pleasant bordering on solicitous through the entire meal. And so, I need to know what's happening."

"I had planned to wait until you were finished with your cake, *agape*, but if you are feeling impatient then I am more than happy to reveal the reason why I have brought you out tonight."

He reached into the interior pocket of his suit jacket and produced a small velvet box. Though he had not imagined it possible, more color drained from Elle's face. "Is that…"

He shifted from his position in the chair, moving forward, dropping down to one knee in front of where Elle sat. This was yet another thing he had not imagined doing in all of his life. Lowering himself like this. Getting on his knees before a woman. But if the charade was going to work then he had to commit to it. There could be no doing this halfway.

"Elle St. James, I would be very honored if you would accept the offer to become my wife."

He could feel the eyes of all the diners in the restaurant on them, could sense that everyone was watching. And then he heard the sound of shutters. And he knew that it was being documented, just as he had planned. Knew that it would be a headline in the business pages by tomorrow.

"I—I told you I couldn't answer this now," she said, her tone hushed.

If Elle hesitated, she would potentially cause trouble

for him. Perhaps, in his arrogance, he had overplayed his hand.

"I wish for you to become my wife," he said. "You are the only woman I have ever imagined spending my life with. Please, do me the honor of saying yes."

It was the truth, even if it was a misleading truth. In all honesty, he had never imagined taking another woman as his wife. But then, he had not begun thinking about taking Elle for a wife until this morning. So, he supposed there was room for interpretation with those words. But they were not a lie.

Yet her expression remained set.

"Would you like to see the ring?" he asked. If he was not enough enticement then perhaps the jewelry would be.

He opened the lid on the jewelry box, revealing his carefully chosen selection.

She looked at it, her face frozen. Unreadable. She lifted her hand, as though she was going to reach out and touch it, before drawing her hand back quickly, as if the ring was a snake that might bite her.

"No," she said.

"No?" he asked. He was on his knees, on the damn floor in the damn restaurant, and she had refused him.

He felt…at a loss, and that was completely foreign to him. And along with that hollow feeling came…pain. Deep. Stabbing.

She stood suddenly, stumbling around him. "I don't think I want dessert," she said, her voice strangled.

"Are you certain?"

"Yes. I told you I wasn't sure what I wanted and you—" she looked around the room "—you did your best to make this public so that I couldn't say no. You don't get to behave this way, Apollo. I'm not your pawn. I'm not anyone's pawn."

"We will speak more in the car," he said. "There is no point in discussing it here."

"Of course not," she said, "we would not wish for me to make a scene."

He did not have to worry about the check, as the restaurant already had his details, so he took hold of Elle's hand, and the two of them made their way from the restaurant, still with the watchful eyes of the other patrons on them. A quick push of a button on his phone, and his car was brought around to the front. He opened the door for her, then slid inside, and the two of them remained silent until his driver pulled away from the curb. After issuing instructions to take them home he raised the partition between the front seat and the back, shrouding them in privacy.

"Is everything a game to you?" she asked, once they were alone, her expression fierce.

"It is not a game," he said, his voice hard. "It is a strategy. I have spent the past several years planning my revenge against your family. I was finished with it. But now, here you are, and you are pregnant with my baby. I want what I want, Elle, and I intend on getting it."

"So what? You thought you could shock me into saying yes?"

"I thought the ring might do it." It had never occurred to him it might not. Had never truly occurred to him she might refuse.

"If I wanted a ring, I would buy my own. One that did not come with a husband attached."

"Marriage makes sense," he insisted.

"I don't care about sense!" she shouted, her voice filling up the space in the car. "None of this, not ever, not from the first time we touched, was ever about sense."

"Then why pretend it matters now? Why resist me when we both know you're going to give in?"

"Because you would say things like that. Because you think me giving in to you is an inevitability. Because you do not listen, damn you!"

"You're still behaving like you have a choice here," he said, hardening his voice.

"I'm a fool. I keep expecting to discover you feel *something* for me. Anything."

Her words were raw, honest, not the shotgun shells filled with anger her statements typically were. There was a vulnerability here. An honesty he had not anticipated. They scraped at him, tore strips from his hide.

"Of course I feel something for you," he said. "I want you." The words were much more raw, much more shattered than he wanted them to be. But he was rapidly losing control. Of this moment. Of himself.

It was always so with Elle. Always.

She shook her head. "That is not the same thing."

"And yet, it is all I have."

"Because you hate my family so much?"

"Touching you was a betrayal of my father. Of my mother. I had thought to take the thing between us and twist it into something I can use."

"You're that angry?"

"Everything that I built my life around was a lie," he said, his words escaping with a force that shocked him. "I thought your father simply cared about me. Instead, it was all a part of his twisted obsession with my mother. He allowed me to care for him, acted as though he cared for me, while the whole time he knew…he knew he was the reason my father killed himself. So you tell me, Elle, in my position would you not also crave revenge?"

"It solves nothing," she said. "You had your revenge in

hand. You had it for four weeks, you thought it was finished. You had ousted me from my position as CEO. You were done with me. Done with my family, and yet still you were back at my door. So tell me, Apollo, what has revenge solved for you? What has it fixed? Your father is still gone. And you still want me. You are in fact begging me to be your wife. Where is your power in revenge?"

He could not deny it, though he wished to. Though he wished he could tell her that he had been using her all along. He had shown his hand when he had returned to her apartment. When he had asked for her to be his mistress.

And it was not only to her he had shown his hand, but to himself.

"I want you," he said. "Quite apart from any plans for revenge."

"You think that would make a marriage work?"

"It would work because we would make it work. We are attracted to each other, is that not enough?"

"I don't know. I never gave serious thought to marriage. I don't know what I want out of one." She blinked. "Except I would like more than screaming at my husband. I would like more than wondering if he is away having an affair. I would like to be chosen. Just once. Not because of someone else. You know, I'm only the CEO of Matte because it was my father's last attempt to keep hold of his empire. And you… What you really want is to make me your wife so you can lord it over my father."

"I know you don't put stock in my desire for you, because it isn't emotional. I am not capable of the kind of emotion you are talking about. But I will tell you that had I been able to want any other woman, had I had dominion over my desire for you—I never would have given in."

"I'm supposed to rejoice because you didn't *want* to want me?"

"Yes," he said, simply.

"You truly are arrogant. And you don't understand women very well."

He chuckled. "I understand parts of a woman."

"I can't deny that. But I can also tell you that it leaves you cold after, no matter how hot you burn in the moment."

CHAPTER ELEVEN

ELLE FELT DEFLATED by the time they arrived back at the penthouse. She said nothing to him as they went inside, as she walked back to her bedroom and stripped off her jewelry. How had she ever thought she could handle this man? This man who was so twisted by his desire to injure her family that he was willing to consider anyone who stood in his way as collateral damage.

If he acted like a human man, with feelings and emotions and normal connections, then it would be a simple thing to make him understand. But he didn't. She had no idea how to appeal to this enigma. This immovable rock who looked like a man but didn't behave like one.

She remembered thinking only a few weeks ago that he was heartless. She hated that she was more and more convinced it was true.

She had known him for so many years, and yet didn't know him at all. She knew his body. Knew what made him shake, knew just how to taste him, how to touch him. And she had heard that dark edge that crept into his voice when he spoke about his past, that hinted at the pain he had been through. At how he felt about it all. About what it had done to him. But she could not for the life of her imagine him as a husband. As a father. She knew fragments of him. The boy he had been, the man he was now.

The ruthless and cruel businessman, and the solicitous lover. But those things did not mesh in her mind. She couldn't marry the details together.

She sat in her room for a moment longer, not bothering to change out of her dress, checking her emails and wasting time on the internet until an hour had passed since they'd come home. Then she stood, crossing the room before she had time to fully process what she was doing. Making her way through the penthouse toward his bedroom. She paused at the door, placing her palm on her chest, feeling the raging of her heartbeat beneath her palm. Then she pushed the door open. He was in bed, naked, his blankets pushed down low on his hips, his arm flung up above his head. He was not asleep. He opened his eyes when she opened the door, arching one dark brow. "Yes?"

She crossed the room, climbing onto the bed, staying on top of the covers, lying down next to him.

He shifted, leaning over as though he was going to kiss her. She held up her hand. "No," she said, "I want to talk."

"Well, *agape*, I do not talk in bed."

"You also don't get women pregnant, and you don't ask them to marry you. Given that I already had a couple of exceptions made for me, I would ask that you make one more."

"As you wish," he said, moving back into the position he'd been in when she had come in.

"I want to know you," she said.

He paused. "There is little to know."

"I only knew bits and pieces of your childhood. Whatever you told me. But I'm curious now about all of it. With what I know now, with what you know now, I am curious about everything."

Apollo sighed. "Okay. When I was born, I lived in a

beautiful home. But that did not last. My father worked all the time, and I rarely saw him. Then when I was very young, he lost his position in the company he owned with your father. What was done to him was ruthless, as you know. From there, we lost our home. We lost everything. We lived in…modest housing, to put it mildly."

She wanted to touch him. She had just decided touching was easier than talking, that kissing was easier than honesty. Their bodies were so much easier than anything else. But putting healthy distance between them, she didn't interrupt.

"My father did not take our descent into poverty well. He dealt with his issues by taking drugs, by drinking. Eventually, what little money we had was swallowed up by his addictions. We ended up on the streets. Shortly after that, when he saw what had become of us, when he saw what had become of the family, he killed himself. I will never know why. If he felt ashamed, if he thought we would be better off without him somehow. If he simply didn't want to try anymore. I can never know the answer. And in the end it doesn't matter. The decision was made. The years passed. But one thing I do know is that he would want recompense for what happened to him. For what happened to us."

"That he should have taken himself," she said, the words coming slowly, but with conviction. "If he cared that much he would've stuck around to get revenge himself."

"He couldn't. For whatever reason," he said. "Regardless, my mother and I found ourselves on the streets, then eventually in a horrible group home sort of place. That was when we were sent for. My mother gave very few details, but she said we were going to a new home. Starting over in America. There was a house. Small, I suppose, by some standards. But clean. We wanted for nothing. Suddenly my mother was able to be home with me, instead of desperately searching for work. I had a bed every night."

"I… I can't imagine what that would mean to you in those circumstances."

"I can barely remember. Though it's something I try to hold on to. So that I never forget what it means to be hungry. When you lose the memory of your hunger…you forget why you need success."

She nodded in the darkness. "I know what you mean." She was hungry, too. Not for food or shelter. But for approval she'd never gotten before.

"Your father had come to visit us many times. Sometimes a nanny would be sent to care for me and my mother would go away for a weekend. To be with him, though, I had a boy's understanding. Your father was always good to us. To me. And when he wished to marry my mother, when he spirited us both away to your estate, I thought… I thought we had everything. Suddenly, I gained the world that I had only ever seen glimpses of before."

"I remember you arriving. I was awful to you. Because you scared me. You were…the most beautiful thing I'd ever seen and I knew I shouldn't think that about my stepbrother…like that."

"I suppose not," he said. "You were smart to hold me at a distance, Elle."

"I don't know if *smart* is the word I would use. But it was definitely a defense that worked for a while."

He chuckled. "Yes, it did work for a bit." He paused. "I never asked you… I never asked what it was like to lose your mother like you did. I suppose…your father is as responsible for that as he is for the loss of my father."

The thought made her stomach sink. "I know my father isn't perfect but I have a hard time believing he was so manipulative. But then, I guess maybe I don't... He's a man who likes control, and a man who thinks nothing of pitting his children against each other. So why wouldn't he have always done this, with every person he could? He does it to his own flesh and blood." She moved closer to him, only a bit. "My mother mostly cared about parties and handbags. Lunches with her friends. She was a trophy wife. Her identity was in who my father was, and I suppose that's why I wanted so badly to find something else. To succeed at Matte. To make my own achievements. Except...they were my father's too, really. I was living out my father's plans in my need to please him, in my need to rebel against my mother. I did miss her," she continued. "I really did. Even though I was mostly cared for by nannies. She was my mother, and she smelled of Chanel and vanilla shampoo. And I loved her."

"Of course you did," he said. "My father was distant, a workaholic and an addict, and still I loved him."

"I was happy to have your mother. Mariam has always been good to me."

"But she is not your mother."

Elle's throat tightened. "No. She isn't."

"Nothing can replace what we've lost."

"I guess in a way both of our parents chose to leave us," she said. "Though...my mother could have chosen to come back."

"Or perhaps not. Perhaps she doesn't feel like she can. Not now."

"Maybe. When it became clear the takeover of the company was...hostile... When it became clear you weren't helping...my father put me in control of Matte. And I knew why. I knew it was to use me as a shield. But still, I accepted the position. He's...all I have, really, and I wanted to please him," she said. "I wanted so badly to be accepted. I just wanted him to be proud of me. And then you came in and bought everything out. I thought maybe if I could hold on to my position he would see that I have deserved it all along. But you fired me."

"Had I known your position as CEO was such a contentious one, I might have left you alone."

"I don't know that you would have, Apollo. It isn't in your nature."

"I don't suppose it is."

"I wonder what I would have done," she said, "if he had not selected for me. If I had not been so determined to prove to him that I could be everything that...that you weren't for him."

"You can try and find out, you know. You don't have to go back to work as you. You feel trapped there... There is no reason for you to be there."

"I feel like my team is counting on me. I poured endless hours into it. So much time and energy."

"But you do not have to be there. You are the mother of my child and whatever happens, I will support you financially. You can simply stay home with our child if you prefer. You can go back to school."

She laughed. "I feel like it's too late, really."

"I hope it's never too late to change what you are," he said. "In part because I have been many things in my life. A child of privilege, a gutter snipe, a charity case, wealthy again... We can always change what we are, as long as we stay on earth to breathe one more time."

His words settled heavily on her chest. His father had stopped breathing. And so he had ended his story. "I understand that," she said.

"So if you could do anything, what would you do?"

"I would like to advocate for people who can't do it for themselves. To use the fact that I enjoy challenging people to accomplish something good. A lawyer. But for children, maybe. For women who have been abused."

"That's a very worthy goal," he said.

She shrugged. "It's a fantasy. Anyway, I feel like I was making so much progress with the brand. Really bringing it into the modern era. I know profits aren't off the charts, but the books and cosmetics and the other tie-in products have really taken us to a new level. I want the chance to fight for my staff, for my team."

"Then that is what you will continue to do," he said.

"Why are you doing all this? Saying all this?"

"The baby," he said.

"Of course."

Her eyelids felt heavy now. It was on the tip of her tongue to say that it wasn't really what had brought them together, because he had come back for her before he knew about the child. So she had to wonder what exactly really had. But she was too tired, her brain sluggish, her body even worse.

They had never had a whole conversation without it ending in them yelling at each other or sex. She was almost entirely certain she had never felt comforted by his presence. But she did now. Just being near him. This man who had walked for so long, to gain everything he had.

Everything in her possession had been thrust onto her by her father, whether she wanted it or not. And yes, that came with its own burden. But he had been forced to make the choice to succeed. Yes, her father had paid for his schooling, but if he hadn't taken it seriously, nothing would have come from it.

Had she truly understood the sort of man Apollo was she would have been more terrified of him the first mo-

ment he had walked into her company. He was a man
who set his sights on things with terrifying single-mind-
edness. With a kind of intensity unmatched by anyone
else she had ever known. If she had realized when he
had reappeared in her life that he wanted revenge and
he wouldn't hesitate to use her, she would have been
much more afraid. Would have behaved much differently with him.

Would you?

Or perhaps, they would be in the same place. In the
same moment, in the same bed. Because as much as she
wanted to believe she had a bit more common sense, the
fact remained that when she fell for him it had nothing
to do with common sense.

No, nothing at all. It was so much deeper.

She reached out, resting her palm on his chest, felt his
heartbeat beneath her fingertips.

She had dreamed of this. Of simply holding him. Of
listening to him breathe. Of sharing the sweet and simple intimacy that came from being near each other. Of
touching just to touch.

It felt so good. To simply be with him. Not fighting.
Not having sex. Just being.

For the first time in weeks, she felt some peace. She
didn't want to sleep. She wanted to prolong this, for as
long as possible. If she could choose one moment to stay
in, it would be this one.

But sadly, time moved forward. And as it did, she
drifted off to sleep.

When they woke in the morning Apollo was still there.
Elle had half expected him to have gone off again, to
awaken to him standing angrily at the foot of the bed and
demanding that she leave. But that didn't happen. Instead,

he was wrapped around her, his legs laced through hers. He wasn't wearing any clothes. She was still wearing the dress from last night.

He was awake, and he was looking at her, a strange expression on his face. "Good morning," she said, her voice coming out a little bit like a croak.

"Good morning."

"This is a strange morning after," she said, looking around the room.

"We didn't have sex."

"Yes, that's exactly what I mean."

"How are you feeling?"

"Oh, you mean after...all of that."

He let out a long, heavy breath. "Yes, after I behaved so poorly."

"Wait a second. Are you, Apollo Savas, actually acknowledging the fact that you behaved poorly?"

"Please, don't press the issue, or I will retreat back behind my rock wall of a heart."

"Sometimes I think maybe your secret is that you are not as heartless as you appear." After being convinced of the opposite last night, this was a refreshing feeling.

"We must all maintain our mysteries, must we not?"

"Maybe. I don't think I'm all that mysterious. I think that I reveal myself to you very easily."

"If only that were the case. I should like very much for you to be easier for me to read. And yet, I can't seem to decode you."

"Then you aren't paying attention. The fact that you thought I would crumble at the sight of an engagement ring says that you don't know me very well."

"You never let me."

She let his words take root inside her. They were not untrue. She knew that.

"I know. But after last night you know why. I was afraid. If I had let you touch me at seventeen then we would have been in this position back them. And as poorly as we're handling it now can you imagine how we would have handled it if we were still that young?"

"A nightmare," he said, laughing bitterly. "Yes, it would have been a nightmare."

"I was very afraid of you. Of what you made me feel. I've always been afraid of you." He had the power to devastate her. To tear her apart from the inside out. Apollo possessed so much more dominion over her than she wanted him to know about. Than she would like to admit, even to herself. But the fact of the matter was it had always been so.

"You must not be feeling particularly wonderful, considering you slept in your dress."

She scrubbed at her face. "I suppose I do feel a bit day-old."

"Stay right here." He released his hold on her and got out of bed, crossing the large expanse of the room and heading into the bathroom. She could hear the water start running. Her heart began to beat faster. He was doing something for her. Something thoughtful. Something kind. She wasn't sure how to handle it. So she just lay there, her heart putting a dull, unsteady rhythm in her chest. He returned a moment later, standing in the doorway, naked, and thoroughly unashamed. Of course, he had nothing to be ashamed about. His body was the stuff you could write poetry about.

But she had never been very good with poetry. She would rather lick his body instead. All over. From head to glorious toe, and every muscular inch in between.

Last night, and the no touching, had been… There had been something altering in it. The fact that they had been able to lie together and neither scream at each other nor tear each other's clothes off had been something of a revelation. But that didn't mean she was ready to give up touching him entirely.

Bad idea. You don't even know what kind of relationship the two of you have.

No, she didn't. But if she wanted to move it toward a real relationship, it might be best if she maintained a physical connection with him. At least, that was a handy justification for getting what she wanted. Which was to be back in his strong arms once again. To be brought to the peak of pleasure by his talented hands and mouth.

She shivered.

"If you are cold, *agape*, I have a warm bath for you in here."

For some reason, his tender words made tears prick the back of her eyes. "Okay," she said, standing up on wobbly legs and walking toward him. She paused in front of him and he gripped the hem of her dress, pulling it up over her head. He took over after that, dispensing with her underwear quickly. Then he lifted her up into his arms and set her gently in the deep tub. The water was perfection, as though he had somehow been able to reach down inside of her and figure out exactly what her perfect bath might be like. And then—further proof that he might be reading her mind—he got down into the tub with her, positioning himself behind her, having her press her back up against his broad chest.

"We have not gotten off to the best start. And when I say that, I mean going back more than a decade, we did not have the best start."

She nodded, not saying a word. He ran his hands over her damp skin and she shivered, her nipples tightening and hardened to points in spite of the warmth of the water.

It had nothing to do with temperature, and everything to do with arousal.

"But I think things can be better between us. I'm not… I am not angry at you, Elle. I was, I admit that. I was angry at you for making me want you. For creating a desire within me that I could not satisfy. That was… That was wrong of me."

"Are you apologizing to me?"

"Yes," he said. "I am apologizing to you, because you deserve my apology. I was cruel to you in ways that you did not deserve."

"But my father deserved it," she said, her voice hollow.

"Your father has nothing to do with this. Right now, he has nothing to do with you and me. We can forget that our parents are married. That I feel a sense of betrayal where your father is concerned. We can forget about all of it. Here, right now, we have to do that. Because if we are ever going to bond with one another, if we are ever going to come together and raise this child then there is history we must erase."

"What does that mean? What does it mean for my relationship with my father?"

He reached out and picked up a bottle of shampoo from the edge of the tub, squirting a little bit into his hands. "I don't know." He began to work the lather through her hair, and her heart contracted tightly in on itself. This was what she had wanted, what she had craved all along. This attention. This wonderful, luxurious attention.

He was focused on her now, wholly and completely. In a way that no one else ever had been. It made her want to cry. She would, if she wasn't so afraid of showing that weakness in front of him. Strange how even now, while he was being kind to her, she felt like she had to have her guard up. Like something was still missing.

That made her chest ache. Because she knew it didn't have to be that way. But she didn't know what else they could possibly have, either. They had spent so many years being unkind to each other. Those were the seeds they had planted for their connection, for their relationship. He was right. Maybe all that was left to do was start over. Maybe they had to forget their family. Maybe they had to forget their prior connection. Maybe there was nothing else but this. Maybe that was all there could be. Maybe it was the only way.

She suddenly felt desperate. For him. For his touch, for everything. Suddenly felt like the world would end completely if her mouth wasn't joined to his.

She turned slightly in the water, pressing her hand to his cheek and angling her head, kissing him, slowly, deeply. Trying to make it different from the other times they had kissed. She wanted this to be different. She wanted this to be the new beginning. To be the new start to something that wasn't toxic. To something that wasn't so deadly. Wasn't so dangerous. Maybe it would even be less all-consuming. Maybe it could be something easier. Something freer.

Maybe it would never be a normal relationship, but if he didn't want to use her, and she could trust him…then maybe it could be something.

He was motionless for a moment, as though he was deciding how to react. Then, he gripped her chin with his thumb and forefinger, holding her steady as he deepened the kiss. He kept it slow, too. Tasting her deeply, his pace leisurely as he swept his tongue over hers. As though he really did have all the time in the world. As though they might in fact have forever.

She turned completely, getting on her knees between his size, leaning in, tracing a line on his chest with her tongue, all the way up to his neck where she pressed an openmouthed kiss to his skin. She looked up at him, at the feral light in his eyes, signaling his very tenuous grasp on his control. She affected him. She really did. This had nothing to do with anger, nothing to do with revenge. It was Elle and Apollo, and nothing else in between.

Oh, how she craved that. That connection that was about the two of them and nothing else at all. She moved closer, straddling his lap, bringing the heart of her up against the uncompromising ridge of his arousal. She flexed her hips, rubbing against him, sending a sharp shock of pleasure through her body. He lowered his head, sucking one nipple deeply into his mouth, those two points of pleasure on her body joining up to create a sensation that threatened to overwhelm her completely. She grabbed hold of his face, held him steady, locked her eyes with his as she rose up slightly onto her knees, then lowered herself onto his arousal, taking him deep inside, sighing heavily as he filled her, satisfied her. Completed her.

Apollo Savas had been sex to her from the moment she first met him. From the moment she understood what transpired between a man and a woman in the dark. She had always acknowledged that. Had always known it to be true. But she had missed something. She had missed the most important part of the equation. He wasn't only sex. He was something more. Something deeper. Had it only ever been about sex she would never have been so afraid. But she had known that beneath that desire, beneath that base arousal, was something much darker, much deadlier, much more dangerous.

It had never simply been desire. It had never simply been anger. It was love. It was love then, it was love now.

She loved him. The thought sent a crack of lightning

through her, threatened to split her in two with the pleasure that was building deep inside her. It created a tidal wave of emotion. Completion, satisfaction, despair. She'd never wanted to love him. She had always known that he could never love her back.

No one did. Why would he? Why should Apollo love her for who she was when her own father couldn't do that? When her own mother couldn't seem to manage it? Why should this man ever love her?

And only then could she acknowledge the fact that she had never hated him. Not really. She had loved him.

From the time she was a girl she had loved Apollo Savas. And when he had betrayed her family it had twisted into something new. Because she couldn't understand how the man she cared for so much could do that to her family. When she had thrown herself at him in the hotel room it had been the last gasp of that love, desperate to be heard, desperate to be expressed. And when she had said she hated him it was only because hate was the other side of that coin. So close to love. So perilously close, she understood now. Because it was love twisted, turned into something ugly.

She realized then, as Apollo looked down at her with his dark eyes glittering, that he had loved her father. That he had loved her family, and that was why it had been twisted into this. That was why, in the beginning, he had gone so far to seek his revenge. To use her. To harm her.

Because of how love could get twisted up.

He gripped her hips hard, taking control of their movements, thrusting up inside her, chasing his release. And she was grateful, because she had gone weak. She could no longer take control of this, no longer claim control over this interaction. No, she was now at the mercy of it. At the mercy of him, at her desire for him.

He slid his hand around to cup her bottom, gripping her tightly, his fingertips brushing up against where they joined. That added bit of contact was enough to send her over the edge. Her mind went blank for one glorious moment, pleasure stealing over her, rocking her like a crack of thunder.

And when it was over, when it all settled, when she was still straddling him, their eyes on only each other, pleasure coursing through her like an endless wave, there was only one bright, brilliant thought in her mind.

She loved Apollo Savas. She always had, she had a suspicion she always would. And she knew, with just as much certainty, that he would never love her in return.

CHAPTER TWELVE

ELLE HAD BEEN quiet ever since they had woken up that morning. Or, more specifically, ever since he had given her a bath. He could feel her slipping out of his grasp. Even as they had reached the peak together, he had felt her pull away, and he didn't know what to do about that. He didn't even know what he thought about it. If it mattered. Except that for Elle, he had a feeling emotion mattered. That it was key.

He could take or leave it. He wanted nothing more than a connection based on honesty, on a contract. It was why he wanted marriage. He wanted to have a guarantee.

He didn't trust emotions. Not in the least. Not when his mother had led such a tangled existence based on the men who had professed to love her. Not when the man who had behaved most like a father to him had revealed himself to be the worst sort of liar. How could he even fathom putting stock in emotion under those conditions?

But Elle was most certainly a more emotional creature. If only he could figure out how to read her. If only he could figure out how to connect with her. He had tried talking, he had tried kindness. And then, she had initiated sex. Neither was the magic key. He wasn't sure there was a damn magic key. He found that disconcerting.

He walked around the expensive penthouse, learning the layout of his new home. Regardless of what he had said to her earlier about how much time he would spend with her and the child, he was anticipating trying to accomplish most of his work in the States, from now on. His own father had abandoned him through suicide. His stepfather had proven to be an imposter. He would not have his child living life with that sort of cloud over them. Money only solved certain things. He knew that for a fact. Coming out of poverty and into financial gain had shown him that there were still things that money couldn't buy.

If only Elle's undying affection was one of the things money could buy. It would make things much simpler. Instead, he was left trying to untie one of the great mysteries of the modern age, or any age. Feminine emotion.

As he was brooding on this, his phone buzzed in his pocket. He picked up quickly without bothering to look and see who it was. "Savas."

"What the hell are you doing with my daughter?"

It was the voice of his least favorite devil on the end of the line. "That depends on what you've heard."

"I have seen the headline in this morning's society pages. You proposed to her last night at a restaurant. By all accounts she refused you and stormed out."

"Then I fail to see why you're calling me. Obviously Elle is up to the challenge of handling herself."

"I am calling because I feel that I have the right to know exactly what led you to a place where you thought proposing to my daughter might end in a *yes*. Do not tell me you set yourself up for public humiliation on purpose, Apollo. I would not believe it."

"It's almost as though you know me," he said, his tone easy. "I had thought she might say yes."

"After all I have done for you—"

"Yes, after causing the suicide of my father, after blackmailing my mother into a relationship, how dare I not be more grateful?"

"I hardly orchestrated your father's death, Apollo, as you are well aware. Your father made his own choices. I was certainly ruthless in my desire to push him out of the company, but what happened after that was his choice, not mine."

"In my mind, you pulled the trigger. There is nothing on earth that will convince me otherwise."

"And so you're using Elle to get revenge?"

It was on the tip of his tongue to tell him that's exactly what he was doing. To let the older man know that Apollo had corrupted his only daughter. That he had gotten her with child. That he now held all the power. It all belonged to him. But then, she walked into the room, wearing soft, baggy pants, and a loose-fitting top. Looking soft and vulnerable, not the least bit hard and glamorous. And he realized that he could not say those things. He could not use her that way. She had asked him to see her as a woman, and he did. He had been the one to suggest they put it all behind them, to start new. And so, he would choose to do so. Now, he would choose to do it for her. For them.

"Whether you believe it or not, my association with your daughter has nothing to do with you."

Elle's head snapped in his direction, her eyes rounded.

"I don't believe it," David said.

"That is inconsequential. It is the truth. I intend to win her over, one way or another. I will obtain her hand in marriage."

"Why is it so important to you?"

"Because I want her."

"And you love her?"

The question hit its mark like an arrow striking a target. Nearly made him fall to his knees. He thought about love, what it meant to him. Certainly, his mother loved him, in her way. She was a fragile woman, not unsurprising considering all she had been through. And at times he wondered if she simply had no choice but to detach in order to protect herself from further pain. After the loss of her husband, after being blackmailed into marrying a man she had not chosen.

His father, his biological father, had been so consumed with the acquisition of material things, with his status, that he had preferred death over staying and protecting his wife and child. In that sense, Apollo could not deny David's words. Suicide had been his father's choice. And not anyone else's. Though he knew that there were many complicated factors that played into that. Depression, mental torments that he could not possibly understand.

It did not stop him from retaining a boy's perspective on it in many ways. He felt abandoned. He felt angry. Whether or not his father deserved more sympathy than that was irrelevant. Apollo could only feel what he felt.

And then there was David St. James. He had truly taken him in. Truly accepted him as part of the family.

He had been a father to him. More of a father than his own had ever been. He had raised him, taught him the value of hard work, paid for his education, taught him to take nothing for granted. Though he was a hard man, though he was distant at times, he was a solid, steady figure in Apollo's life. The man he had sought to pattern himself after. Discovering the depths he had sunk to in order to obtain Apollo's mother—as though she were an item to be acquired and not a human being, as though Apollo himself and his father were incidentals—that had shown him just how deep a lie could run.

The fact that his feelings for the older man had not been eradicated overnight—if ever—showed him just what a fickle and dishonest emotion love could be.

Worse still, all of that, every bit of it, was proof that his love twisted things. Changed them in permanent and ugly ways. He was like a lit match brought up against the edge of something fragile. Making the edges curl and darken, altered beyond recognition.

He couldn't do that to her. He wouldn't.

"No," he said. "No, I don't."

"Then you don't deserve her."

And with that, the line went dead. Those words echoed in his head as he turned to look at Elle, who was regarding him with a confused expression. "My father?"

"Yes. He is unamused with me."

"Did he see it in the paper? Was it in the paper?"

"Yes," he said. "Apparently your rejection of me has made headlines."

"Well, I would apologize but it really is your own doing."

"This is true."

"What did he ask you?"

"He asked if you were my revenge," Apollo said. "I told him you're not."

"Yes, I gathered as much. But what was the last question he asked you?"

His stomach tightened, dropped low in his midsection. "He asked me if I loved you."

She closed her eyes, her face going pale. "You said no."

Elle felt as though the ground was dropping out from beneath her feet. She had been shocked, thrilled, when Apollo had not taken the chance to eviscerate her father. When he had not used her as a weapon. Had not trotted out the baby, their affair, in a crass and unnecessary way. That when he had been asked directly if he was using her, he had said no. Even if it was a lie, even in part, he had stopped using her then. He had honored her request.

But then he had been asked if he loved her. And his answer had been no.

She realized then that it was nonnegotiable for her. She needed love. She needed for him to love her. There was nothing more important. Nothing at all.

She had dressed it up in all kinds of fancy descriptions. Had tried to convince herself that all she needed was respect. That they needed to find common ground. That she simply needed someone to want her as she was, and not as a weapon in some kind of scheme. But after their encounter in the bath, after that pleasure radiated through her, after she had felt the intensity of her own feelings for him, she knew that that wasn't the case. She needed more. She needed everything. And anything else would be doing herself a terrible disservice.

She wanted more for herself. More than simply heading up a company because she wanted to prove to her father that she could. More than marriage to a man for his convenience. In truth, as much as she wanted to give her child a home with both parents she knew that if they were living together under sufferance, if she made him miserable because he eventually bored of her, and he made her miserable because her love went unreturned, their child would know. He or she would sense the unhappiness, and for them to even suspect that their presence was the cause of that kind of relationship was something she could not place upon her child.

"I can't marry you," she said.

"What are you talking about? You showed me this morning just how irresistible you find me."

"That's sex, Apollo. We have had that through every-thing. When I was terrible to you, you still wanted me. When you took over my business, betrayed our family, I still wanted you. Even while I was thinking about stab-bing you through the chest with a pen, I wanted you. But that isn't enough for marriage. And right now? It isn't enough for me. I realized something this morning."

"That you are a contrary little thing who makes ab-solutely no sense?"

"That I love you. I love you with everything I have. It has always been that way. But I cannot, and will not, continue to accept this strange, leftover existence that I have cobbled together with the discarded pieces of yours and my father's manipulative plans. I'm the CEO at Matte because he wanted to play me against you, not because he thought I was suited to the position. I'm pregnant with your baby because you wanted to hurt him, and while I appreciate the fact that you didn't rub it in his face just now…that's our foundation. It's what we are."

"No," he said, his voice rough. "That is not our founda-tion. There was no calculation when I took you up against the wall in my hotel room, no ulterior motive when I had you in the elevator."

"How can I believe that?"

"Because it is the truth. I decided after I had you the second time that I would use what was between us to get revenge. Only because I was desperate to find some jus-tification for what you did to me. For wanting to indulge in this thing between us."

"And why'd you come back?"

"Because I wasn't finished with you!"

"But that's the thing," she said. "I am not a thing that you can pick up and put down at your convenience. Not a weapon that you can use at your discretion. I am a human being. I have feelings. I love you and I deserve to be loved in return." She shook her head. "If you cannot give me that then I will have to go out and find someone who can."

All of the anger drained from his face, his expression turning to stone. "You are correct. If that is what you want, then that is what you must find."

Her chest felt hollowed out, her heart thundering hard in the empty space. "That's it?"

"We are at an impasse, Elle. I cannot love, and you require it. I do not wish to hold you prisoner. I see no satisfaction in making you miserable. There was a time when I might have, but things have changed."

"Maybe that means you have feelings for me?"

"No," he said, his tone hard, definitive. "I cannot."

She felt like she'd been stabbed clean through, like she would bleed out on the floor, her pain, her love, everything for him to see. She wouldn't be able to hide anymore, as she had done for so many years.

She waited for something to come, for a cutting remark to rescue her, but it wasn't there. There was nothing to hide behind. Nothing but pain and love in equal measure.

And she wanted him to see it. Wanted him to know. She was done hiding. She'd done enough damage pushing him away so that she wouldn't be hurt.

She had hidden everything for years. Her pain, her desire, her love. And she was done. Pride be damned, she wouldn't hide herself anymore.

"Why?" she asked. "Why are you doing this? There is nothing stopping us, nothing stopping this except you, and I can't understand why."

"Everything I love turns to dust, Elle. I would not have you so diminished."

"I've been diminished already!" she shouted. "All of my life. To keep the peace, to try and do what my father wanted, to try and avoid…well, exactly this, with you." She swallowed hard, shaking, all of her repressed emotion, decades of it, pouring out now. "I'm done with that. I'm making demands now."

He stared at her for a moment, his dark eyes hollow. "I can't meet them."

"You won't."

"It amounts to the same thing."

And then he turned away from her, and walked out of the penthouse, closing the door softly behind him. She had a feeling that he would not be back.

She didn't want half a life, half a love. She didn't want a future with a man who wouldn't give her what she'd just realized she so desperately wanted.

So, she let him go. And she did her very best not to cry.

Elle approached her father's office with great trepidation. She was going to let him know that she was officially resigning from Matte. She was also going to tell him about the baby, and the fact that she would not be marrying Apollo. She took a deep breath, trying to ease the knot in her chest. Then, she raised her hand and knocked on the door.

"Come in."

She turned the knob and opened the door, stepping inside quickly. "Hello, Father," she said.

"Elle," he said, gesturing at the chair across from his desk, as though she were a business appointment he was keeping. "Have a seat."

She did. "I imagine you're wondering why I wanted to speak with you."

"Not particularly. I assume it has something to do with Apollo."

"Well," she said, "you aren't wrong."

"Have you decided to marry him?"

"On the contrary, I have decided that I cannot continue my association with him."

"I fail to understand why there was an association with him in the first place. He turned against me."

"Yes," she said.

"He fired you. Then, you got your job back, did you not?"

Her face got hot. "I know what you're implying, but it didn't happen that way. Anyway, I'm stepping down at Matte. I'm going to go back to school. I'm going to figure out what *I* want to do. Quite apart from your expectations, or his. I have been caught in the cross fire for too long. I just can't do it anymore. I have to find out what I am beyond this…desperate people pleaser. I have to find out if I can be more than your shield to block you from Apollo's wrath."

"Is that what you think?"

"Why would I think anything else?" she asked.

"And yet, you have never said anything."

"Yes, well, I wanted to keep the peace. I wanted to do the right thing, be the daughter you needed. But I'm over that now. I need to be the person I'm happy with, not the person you're happy with."

"Did I force you into the position at Matte?" he asked, his tone hard.

"You can't deny that you used me to try and stand between Apollo and the destruction of the company. It had nothing to do with me. You never intended to give any of it to me. You always wanted a son, and until he went rogue, Apollo was that son for you. I was never supposed to be the one in that position. You used me."

He lifted his shoulder, the lines on his face looking suddenly more pronounced. "Yes, I did use you. But how else could I defend my legacy? I knew you could do it, Elle. I had no concerns about that. I knew Apollo had… feelings for you. Feelings of some kind, and I thought that perhaps he would modify his actions if you were in the line of fire."

"And so you used me as a target."

"I knew you were strong enough. You might think it's because I don't respect or value you, but it is to the contrary. You're strong. I would not have shielded a son from such a thing, and I did not shield you."

"Am I supposed to be grateful?"

"I could see no other way," he said, his tone uncompromising.

"Is that why you ousted Apollo's father from your company all those years ago? Because you could think of no other way to be with Mariam?"

"Yes," he said, simply. Calmly. "It was the only way I could think of to win Mariam. And so I did what I could. But she stood by him. Had his child. And for all my sins, I never held that against Apollo. That he was the product of a union I despised."

"You don't get a medal for that, Dad," she said. "Not when you were so…horrible."

"I was horrible," he said, his tone hard, his eyes ice blue. "And I would do the same thing again. Make the same choices. I didn't intend for his father to kill himself, Elle. I am not a mind reader. I could not predict the outcome. I did, however, think that it was likely Mariam would leave him when he had nothing and I had everything. I was wrong."

"She loved him."

Her father nodded slowly. "Yes, she did. But she has learned to love me, I think."

"You think?"

"Yes. I do."

"Have you ever asked her?"

Her father's face went blank. "No. I haven't. But then, I'm not certain it matters. Not now."

Elle's heart crumpled. "I think it always matters. It doesn't matter when love comes, as long as you know it's there. Does she know you love her?"

"I destroyed her world to move her into mine. I cleared my world to make room for her. If that is not love then I do not know what is."

He didn't. Elle could see that. He truly and honestly knew nothing of love being two-sided. Of giving rather than taking.

He was an unbending man. Unyielding. All arrogance and a stiff neck. Unable to truly turn and look at anyone else.

"I think perhaps love isn't destroying worlds. Or moving people around like chess pieces," she said, her voice shaking. "I think maybe it's giving more than you take. Showing it, even when someone may never show it back. Being kind even when the other person is cruel. I think love isn't always balance, but if both are willing to give more than they take…it might be a beautiful, rare sort of treasure."

"I don't know about any of that, Elle," he said. "I do know that I have you, and I still have Mariam. In that I find some success, I think."

"Do you love *me*?" She might as well ask. She had already been rejected by Apollo, so there was really no reason to protect herself at this point. She had been flayed already. She might as well allow some salt to be rubbed into the wounds.

Her father only looked at her for a moment, his gaze unreadable. "Did you not know?" he asked.

"How would I?" she answered.

"I am your father, Elle."

"That doesn't make any guarantees."

"I am a man who has built my life on a foundation made of ruthless decisions. I did not become rich by following the rules. I did not obtain my wife by playing fair. I hurt Hector. I hurt your mother. I have never known quite how to handle the people in my life. But for all of that, I do love you."

It was still indirect. Still impersonal. But she felt it was very likely the best he could do.

She also saw, for a moment, herself in the old man's gaze. Waiting to be given what she wanted, all of her conditions met. No, she wasn't being unreasonable wanting love from Apollo. But she had to consider where he had come from. What he knew.

Apollo had been broken. Battered by life. People he had trusted had abandoned him. Betrayed him. He needed someone to show him something different. Needed someone to stand by him, no matter what. To take what he could give now, and trust there would be more in the future.

She would do that for him. For her. Just because he couldn't meet her here now didn't mean he never would.

She loved him. She would love him enough for them both.

"I love you," she said, because she thought she might as well practice saying it again, to another man who had difficulty hearing it, saying it. To continually practice this new start, where she didn't hide. Where she didn't try to make herself palatable. "In spite of everything."

"I haven't changed," he said. "I am the man you have always known. You just know a bit more of the story."

"Yes, well, the whole story is important. It doesn't mean I think you made good choices."

"I never asked anyone to sign off on my choices. I made my bed, and it has the woman I love in it. How can I have regrets?"

"Well," Elle said, "I'm going to go after the man I love now. Because he's pigheaded and stubborn and scared. And I'm okay with that. As long as I can be with him. Oh. I'm having his baby, also. That might be relevant, too."

That seemed to successfully shock her father. His gray eyebrows shot upward, his mouth dropping slightly open. "You didn't see fit to mention that sooner?"

"We got philosophical. I imagine this will be the only time. But… Apollo is the father of my child. You're married to his mother, you're both the grandparents of the baby." She frowned. "It's very complicated. And you're going to have to make some kind of peace with him."

"It may not be possible. As you said, the whole story changes things. And for him, I think it transformed me into a villain. One I cannot deny I have been in years past. I tried to make it up to him by giving him all I could. But as you have pointed out to me, my demonstrations are not always clear."

"You've both caused a lot of damage. Fighting, seeking vengeance, going after what you want with no care for others…it just has to stop. If it can't be anything more than a cease-fire then let it be that. But it has to stop. I can't be in the middle. I won't allow my child to be in the middle."

"And if you have to choose between me or him?"

"It would be him," she said, not even hesitating. "Assuming he felt the same way."

Her father nodded slowly, his lips curving into a smile. "Maybe you even understand my more ruthless decisions."

"Where Apollo is concerned I have no doubt I could be ruthless. Where my child is concerned… I would shed blood."

"I fear I was too selfish to make that choice," her father said. "And that I did not have the pride that you do."

"What do you mean?"

"I did not care if Mariam felt as strongly as I did. I only cared that I had her."

"Well, I lived too much of my life that way and I won't do it now."

Her father regarded her with…pride. For the first time she could honestly say she felt it. A strange moment because she didn't feel particularly triumphant. She only felt…broken. Sad. Pride was a poor salve for a broken heart.

"I need to be loved," she repeated, for herself as much as anyone. "And I need to be assured that my son or daughter will not be used as a pawn. Not for Apollo to hurt you, not for him to hurt me. I think you will find my love for my child the most ruthless of all."

"Then go," her father said. "Tell him. Go and be ruthless for love."

CHAPTER THIRTEEN

APOLLO WAS NO stranger to despair. While he had not been terribly conscious of the loss of wealth as a boy, the loss of his comfortable bedroom, his bed, had certainly been things he'd felt deeply. After that, the loss of his father. Then, the loss of the man he had come to think of as a father.

But he had never once experienced loss like this. A loss that was, in many ways, his own doing. There had been no control in his hands when they had lost their livelihood and their money, there had been no control when he had discovered the true nature of David St. James. But here… With Elle, he'd held the power. The power to tell her what she wanted to hear, to find a way to be the man she needed. And he had turned away.

"Coward," he said aloud to the empty space in his office. He paced in front of the window, looking out over the city below. He had gone back to Greece, because he had not known what else to do. Had not known where else to go. He felt helpless, and it had been a long time since he had felt helpless. He despised the feeling. More than anything. It was one of the many reasons he had turned so sharply, so hard, on David St. James.

Because when the revelation had struck him it'd been with the force of a killing blow. It had chopped his legs out from beneath him, left him gasping, shocked. He was not a man who took kindly to such a thing.

Wounded pride, Apollo? That is a very small reason to seek revenge. A very small reason to hold on to anger.

But what his father had been through… What his mother had been through…

He knew he should speak to his mother. But the simple fact was he was afraid to hear what she had to say. He had been from the moment three years ago when the revelations about David had become clear. He didn't want to hear what she had to say. For fear that she loved him. For fear that she was happy. For fear that she supported the decisions her new husband had made because it had resulted in the two of them being together.

But he knew now that he needed to ask her. He knew that he needed to find out why she had stayed.

He picked up the phone, dialing her number, dimly aware that it was very early in the morning in New York. "Hello?"

His mother's faintly accented voice came over the line. "Hello, Mother," he said.

They had barely spoken over the course of the past three years, and when they had, it had been very carefully. Because she had known that he was actively pursuing vengeance against her husband, and while she had kept her feelings to herself, he could always sense the fact that she didn't approve. Certainly, she didn't necessarily support him, as she had not demanded he take her with him, back to Greece. He was more than capable of supporting his mother now. She did not have to stay with David St. James. And yet, she did.

"Why?" he asked, with no preamble at all. He had not meant to launch straight into it like this, but he had been unable to help himself.

"Why what, Apollo?"

"Why do you stay with him? I don't understand. The truth about David St. James was hidden from me for all of my life. But it was not hidden from you. You knew exactly what manner of man he was. And yet, you remain with him. You could leave. I could take care of you until the end of time, and you would never want for anything."

There was silence on the other end. "Yes," she said softly. "I do know what manner of man he is. I have known David St. James since long before you were born. I knew him from the beginning. I met him when I met your father. I don't know why, but I have a tendency to love hard men. Though perhaps that is a good thing for you, I think."

Apollo chuckled. "I suppose it is."

"I did love your father. And I stayed with him even when we lost everything. Even when David ousted him from the company."

"Which David did to hurt him."

Mariam continued as if he hadn't spoken. "I do believe that at the time, your father already had a bit of an issue with drugs. Though they had not yet consumed him as they did later. He was working long hours, and he needed something to help him keep up. It was competitive. He didn't want to sleep. I rarely saw him. And I would be… I would be lying if I said we were perfectly happy. But I was never unfaithful to him. I knew that David had feelings for me. But I had chosen Hector. And so I remained with him. I remained with him until the end, when everything became so twisted, and so hard. By the time he died he was not the man I had first known."

"Because of David St. James."

"Yes, and no. Business is harsh and uncompromising.

It has always been so. Many men lose all their earthly possessions and come out the other side."

Apollo was having trouble processing what she was saying. "You're saying you harbor no anger against him over what he put us through?"

"I am sorry to tell you that I put much more of the blame at your father's door than I do at David's. Yes, he ousted him from the company, but had your father taken better care of our assets we would not have been destitute. Had he not completely given up, we could have come back from it. I had no skills. I was nothing more than a village girl who knew how to do little more than sew. And while that could support us in a very modest fashion it was never going to pull us out of poverty. When David contacted me… I am not proud of what happened after that, because for all of my sins, for all of my divided loyalty, the one thing that I truly regret was any part I might have played in the destruction of his marriage."

Apollo swallowed hard. It was difficult to hear such things. To take on the knowledge of his own mother's part in all of this. "Yes, well, you had a child to take care of."

"He did not force me into an affair," she said, her voice soft. "That was my choice. When he discovered how we were living he asked us to come, he offered to buy me a house, and to care for you. A relationship was not part of that. But I… I was lonely. And I recognized what I might have had. I regretted not choosing him, I think. Because he seemed stronger. That was my mistake, Apollo. His as well, but do not blame it all on him."

"Well, his ex-wife didn't care enough about her own child to stick around after she was deposed."

His mother sighed. "No, she did not. Again, it does not excuse my actions. But I do love Elle, almost as if she were my own."

"She knows that."

"I hope so. There was a time when I thought you knew that David loved you as a son, as well."

"I did believe that," Apollo said. "But when I found out the level he had stooped to to bring you to him, to get revenge because of his love being spurned, I could not simply stay in his home, stay as his son."

"It is done," she said. "It may have been wrong, but it is done."

"I loved him," Apollo said. "What kind of a son does that make me? I cannot love without it becoming something horribly twisted. You had to care for me, and that forced your hand. I loved my father, but it wasn't enough to make him stay... David..."

"None of this, none of the tangled web, is your fault. You should not place more consequences onto yourself. We were badly behaved adults, who got our children caught in the cross fire of terrible games. Neither of you deserved it. I wish very much your father had not killed himself. But he was not simply a victim, either. Your love didn't bring out the worst in us, Apollo. Your love was the best of us."

He swallowed hard, his throat suddenly tight. "None of it is simple," he said. "None of it. So I do not understand how I am supposed to sort through it all."

"I can't answer that question for you. I do know that it doesn't benefit anyone to hold on to anger. To hold on to the past. It twists you. That's what it did to Hector. It broke him completely. All of the anger that he felt toward David... I would hate for you to suffer the same fate."

"And so...you would simply forgive?"

"I cannot make the decision for you, Apollo. I should like, for the sake of our family, for you to find it in you to forgive. But it is your journey. Perhaps I was wrong to forgive. I do not know. I only know that I had choices before me and I took the one that made me happiest."

"We can never be a family as we were," he said, "in part because while you may love Elle as a daughter, I do not love her as a sister."

That declaration was met with silence. "I know," she said finally. "I have always known."

Those words nearly broke him. Shattered him entirely. She had always known, because his feelings had always been there. Every action, every cruelty, all the anger that had passed between them over the years had been there simply to disguise that fact.

From himself.

He had never managed to hide it from his mother.

"I do not know how I can be with her."

"We can only carry so much, Apollo. I have lived an imperfect life, and if I have learned anything it's that, at some point, we must put some of our burdens down so we can pick up things we would more gladly carry. These are decisions we make. We cannot wait for the pain to go away. We cannot simply expect the anger to fade, or the grief to stop biting. We must make choices. They are the hardest choices to make. But if you want to move on, then you must begin on your own."

"That simple?"

"No," she said. "That difficult."

"I know what I want," he said. "I just don't know if I can have it."

"You're angry at David, and that is understandable. You want revenge, and that I understand, as well. But I think you can see the way that revenge twists your own life. If you deny your love for Elle simply because you want to punish David St. James, then it isn't truly him you're hurting. Then the only person whose life you've destroyed is your own."

"You stayed because you love him?"

"God help me, but I do," she said. "Though I should not. Though he perhaps doesn't deserve it. There are many days when I don't deserve it, either. Though, in his way, I believe he loves me."

He could not say he envied his mother her relationship, her marriage. And yet, he could see that they had love for each other, even if it wasn't the sort he recognized. And what sort did he recognize? That, he supposed, was the question. Did he recognize it at all?

He had. With Elle, he had recognized it for the first time. And he had run, because it had been too much. Because, as his mother said, he was carrying too much anger to accept the love that she was asking for, that she was offering.

"I suppose I have a decision to make," he said.

But it was already made. There was no question. He loved Elle. And that meant whatever the risk, whether he was able to trust himself or not, whether he truly believed he knew how to love and how to accept love, he wanted to give her what he could. What he had. He wanted to give her everything. "I will have to get her back," he said finally.

"I hope that you do," his mother said. "I hope it isn't too late."

He hung up the phone and turned back to the sprawling city before him. He would need to get the first plane out. Or perhaps he should call her. But he didn't know if apologies such as this one should be done over the phone. He had hurt her, had said terrible things. Hurtful things. He did not deserve to ask forgiveness. But dammit, if David St. James could earn the love of the woman he wanted after all he had done, why couldn't Apollo?

He turned back to the door of his office just as it opened. In strode Elle, looking red-faced, pursued by his assistant Alethea.

"I'm sorry, Mr. Savas," Alethea said. "She insisted that she had to see you."

"I do," Elle said, looking stubborn. He adored that expression. That uncompromising, demanding expression. Elle was not an easy woman. She never would be. But he didn't want easy. He wanted her. Always. Forever.

"It's okay, Alethea. I would like to see her."

Alethea shook her head. "Best you work out your problems, Mr. Savas. You have been mercurial of late, and I find it irritating," she said, turning on her heel and storming out of his office.

"That is not the sort of assistant I expected you to have," Elle said.

"Yes, well. At this point she knows where all the bodies are buried and I can't get rid of her. Sadly, she knows that."

"I had to see you," she said.

"Why is that, *agape*?"

"Because I have something to tell you."

Suddenly, his stomach plummeted. "It isn't about the baby, is it?"

"The baby is fine," she said.

"I'm relieved to hear it."

"It isn't about that. I mean, it is. But nothing is wrong."

"Well, before you launch into your speech, I must tell you, I was on my way back to see you."

"You were?"

"Yes," he said, "I was. There is something I need to tell you to. I spoke to my mother this morning."

"That's funny. I spoke to my father about… Well, I guess it must be fifteen hours ago or so. Since I am here now."

"I see. I needed to understand why she stayed with him. I needed to understand how she had managed to let go of everything that had gone on in the past. She helped clarify some things. For one, your father did not force her into a relationship. That is important for me to know. She admits they handled things poorly. But he did not force her."

Elle looked visibly relieved by the revelation. "I'm glad to hear that. That isn't something my father would willingly admit. He's such a stubborn old man. I think talking about his feelings is the thing he dislikes most in the world. But he did admit to me… He does love your mother. For all of his sins, he does."

"She loves him," Apollo said. "Somehow, she was able to let go of everything that had happened all those years ago. Somehow she fell in love with him."

"We don't have half of that baggage standing between us, and here we are unable to sort out our differences."

"There's a simple enough reason for that," he said. "I was a coward."

"You're not a coward, Apollo."

"Yes, I am. I was unable to admit my feelings for you nine years ago, and I found myself unable to admit them last week. Even to myself. But I love you, Elle. I always have."

Elle could only stand there, shocked, staring into Apollo's intense, dark gaze. He said that he loved her. He said that he always had, that he had simply been unable to admit it. That was not what she'd been expecting. She had flown to Athens, stormed into his office expecting a fight. Expecting to engage him in a knock-down, drag-out battle as she told him there would be no revenge. That they would be putting everything aside for love. Not theirs, but the love of their child. And yet, here he was…saying he loved her.

"I had a speech prepared," she said, her voice sounding hollow.

"Did you?" he asked, his eyebrows arched.

"Yes," she said. "I was… I was going to make sure you knew that our child was everything. That I would never use a child to get revenge on you, nor would I allow you to use our child to hurt me. And that under no circumstances would I allow our son or daughter to be caught in the crosshairs of your issues with my father."

"There is no danger of that."

"I… I see that. Because you… But I…" She suddenly felt a sharp pain in her chest. "I'm sorry."

"For?"

"You do love me. I knew you did. I really did. But I didn't trust it."

"Why should you take less than you deserve, Elle? Why should you take less than you deserve simply waiting around for me?"

"Because love isn't about what you deserve."

"Thankfully for me," he said.

"For all of us. We're about to have a child, and we're evidence of the fact that…parents make mistakes with their children. Even children they love."

"That is true."

"Love is…bigger than keeping score. It costs more than we could ever hope to earn. At least, it's supposed to. I need you to know, here and now, that I love you without reservations. That I believe you *do* love me. I understand what you've been through. I understand that you were used badly." She took a deep breath. "Your mother may have been able to easily forgive my father, or at least forgave him eventually, but she knew everything from the beginning. Your trust was betrayed in a way that hers wasn't."

Apollo shook his head. "The guilt that I felt over considering David a father figure to me was what truly enraged me."

"I recognized that. That what you felt was badly-used love. I did. Because I had experienced it with you. But even recognizing that, I was unbending."

"I want you to be unbending, my sweet, beautiful Elle," he said.

Her chest swelled, her heart feeling large and tender. "You do?"

"Yes. Because I want everything you are. Everything you will be. Because I want the woman you are, not simply the woman that makes my life easiest. I do not want you simply because you are the mother of my child. I do not want you because you are biddable, because you fit easily into the life I have created. I will rearrange it all for you," he said. "Somehow, I think I knew I would have to do that. And it frightened me. Again, you must understand that I am a coward."

She shook her head. "No," she said, the word coming out broken. "You are the bravest man I have ever known. Because you would open yourself up to love again even when your love had been so abused before."

"I hardly deserve a medal for accepting a gift so beautiful as your love," he said.

"Yours is beautiful too, you know."

His chest pitched sharply, his dark eyes glittering. "I was so convinced my love killed things. That it was toxic. How could I trust something that always turned into something so painful? So I denied it. What I felt for you. It was always there. I wrapped it up in anger, I wrapped it up in hate, because I wasn't ready to reach out and take it."

"I did the same," she said, her throat tight. "I told myself that I hated you, that I couldn't stand the sight of you, because in truth you were the most glorious, wonderful sight I had ever beheld. And I called my feelings something else, anything else, rather than accepting the fact that I might never have you. I pretended I didn't care rather than opening myself up and risking being humiliated. Rather than risking admitting what I might lose and how badly it might hurt. I hid my feelings, even from myself. See, I am more like my father than it seems on the surface."

"But you're here. You're here telling me now."

"If we can't learn from the mistakes of the people who came before us, then I fail to see the point of any of it."

"Yes." He shook his head. "You are very right about that. When I look at the mistakes my mother made, your father made, that my father made, in their pursuit of love, of money and success, I see nothing but a sad, tangled web. And in the end, I suppose what our parents have found is love, as best as they can have it."

"Yes," Elle said. "I think that's true."

"But I want more than that. I want deeper. None of the anger, none of the pride, none of those wasted years."

Elle laughed softly. "I suppose we already have a few wasted years."

"But no more. It is you for me, Elle. Only you. I want to make a life with you. With you and our child. I will get down on my knees and beg if I must, because my pride is nothing more than dirt if it keeps me from you."

"As enjoyable as I might find that, I don't need you to

beg. I love you already. I don't need you to do anything to gain that acceptance."

He crossed the space between them and her heart lurched, a thrill racing through her as he took her into his arms. This would never fade. It would never get old. Things had never been hotter, more intense between them because of the anger. The anger had simply covered the true intensity. It was only bigger now. Brighter, deeper. Now that she knew the racing of her heart, the intense surge of adrenaline that raced through her every time she saw him was not hate, but love after all.

"I love you," he said. "And I will lay down all of my anger, my need for revenge, my distrust and anything else that might hinder my ability to give you all that you deserve. Because if I am to be full, then I would have myself be full of nothing but my love for you."

"I was so hurt, Apollo, because I was afraid that you wanted me only for revenge. To hurt other people. And I never felt like my father loved me for *me*. I never felt like anyone in my life loved me simply because of who I am. But here you are, asking me to be difficult, asking me to be stubborn, asking for me to be myself. And I... I can hardly believe it."

"Then I will spend my every day, from this moment until the end, showing you just how much I love you, for all of the good, all of the bad and everything in between. I will do my very best to ensure that you never doubt that you are the one I love. You are the one I want. Whether you're a CEO, a lawyer, a cupcake maker, a police officer."

"I have never given any indication that I want to be a baker or a police officer."

"But you could be. You could be anything you wanted

to be, and you would still be Elle. And I would still love you."

"There is a remarkable amount of freedom in that," she said, her chest swelling with emotion. "I don't think you can possibly know what that means to me."

He pulled her closer, kissing her lips. "Then show me, Elle. Show me."

EPILOGUE

SHE DID. AND she spent every day after that showing him, demonstrating her love for him. And he did the same for her.

It was one of Apollo's proudest moments when Elle graduated at the top of her law class. One of his happiest moments, sitting there, cheering her on as she walked onstage while he held their daughter in his lap, with their new baby in the crook of his other arm. He was so proud of what she had achieved, of what she had decided to go after. Of how she had decided to use her uncompromising nature and sharp tongue.

She was, in his opinion, the best lawyer in New York City, eternally advocating for women in difficult circumstances, and for children who had had injustice done against them.

If someone would have told him when he had first married Elle that he would only grow to love her more over the next decade, he would have told them they were insane. After all, how could anyone love more than he had on the day of his wedding? But he discovered just how deep, just how wide, love could grow. Each year, each child, each achievement and each failure added a texture and a richness to what he felt for her that stretched far beyond what he could have ever imagined.

On the night of their tenth anniversary, Elle came home from work, exhausted, frowning, possibly because the case she was working on was so intense.

He took her into his arms, not saying a word. And she wrapped her arms around him, leaning on his strength.

"I'm glad you made it," he said.

"Of course. This is the only place I want to be tonight." She looked up at him and smiled. "Are the kids taken care of?"

"I believe Alethea is reading them a bedtime story. But she is not a nanny, Elle. She made sure to tell me that as she went to perform the task. This was after hovering around them at dinner trying to get them to eat their vegetables."

Elle laughed. "Of course."

"And tomorrow David and my mother will be by to take the children for the weekend. They wish to contribute to our alone time."

"Very nice of them."

"Indeed." He brushed his thumb over her cheek. "Are you ready to go out tonight?" He examined the faint shadows under her eyes. "Or would you rather stay in?"

"I would love to go out. Because I want to go show off my wonderful husband."

"You cannot possibly wish to do that more than I want to show off my wonderful wife."

"We'll have to argue about it later." She let out a sigh, a long, contented sound. "We've been together for more than ten years. It's amazing how different this last decade has been from the one before it."

"The one where we both wanted each other, but wouldn't allow ourselves to have each other?"

"Yes. I have no clue what we were so afraid of. What we were waiting for."

"The more I think about it, the more I believe we were waiting for the right time. Where we could be brave enough, give enough, love each other in the right way. Had I kissed you for the first time when I was twenty years old, I would have only messed it up later. I would not have been a man who could have given you the support you needed through all of this."

She nodded slowly. "I don't think I would have been a woman who could have gone for her dreams."

"Do you want to know a secret, Elle?"

She nodded. "Of course."

"I like everything that we have. I treasure it. I enjoy my job. I am proud of yours. But you're my dream."

Elle smiled, all of her exhaustion fading, tears filling her eyes. "Oh, Apollo. You're my dream, too."

She drew up on her toes and kissed him, and it was like the first time. Every time with her was like the first time.

"Perhaps we won't make it out after all," he said.

She smiled, her expression a little bit wicked. "Yes, perhaps it would be best if we stayed in."

* * * * *

*If you enjoyed this story, check out these other
great reads from Maisey Yates
THE QUEEN'S NEW YEAR SECRET
A CHRISTMAS VOW OF SEDUCTION
BOUND TO THE WARRIOR KING
MARRIED FOR AMARI'S HEIR
Available now!*

*Don't miss Lynne Graham's 100th book!
BOUGHT FOR THE GREEK'S REVENGE
Also available this month*

"A marriage like this is nothing but a game."

Brittany made herself pout at Cairo when he only continued to stare down at her, as if he really was trying to see inside of her.

"Why not take it into bed as well?"

"You told me there was to be no sex in this marriage."

His gaze was on her mouth. Her heart pounded hard, like a sledgehammer.

"You told me that wasn't your style," she countered.

She didn't know when she'd noticed that he'd angled his torso toward her. That he was holding her there against the wall so easily. Brittany knew she should have hated it. She should have felt caught. Captured. Compromised.

She didn't.

His eyes glowed the dark amber that made her chest feel tight, and she couldn't seem to pull in a full breath to save her life. His palm was surprisingly hard and warm against her cheek. She could feel it in her toes. His chest pressed against hers and made her breasts ache. And that beautiful mouth of his was set in a stern, resolute line that made something giddy and wild race through her, then coil tight, low in her belly.

"I already told you I want you, Brittany," he told her.

It had the ring of a vow. Of something stitched together. Need and command as one. And a red-hot punch straight to that place that already melted for him.

"That hasn't changed."

Wedlocked!

Conveniently wedded, passionately bedded!

Whether there's a debt to be paid,
a will to be obeyed or a business to be saved…

She's got no choice but to say, 'I do!'

But these billionaire bridegrooms have got another
think coming if they think marriage will be easy…

Soon their convenient brides become the object
of an *inconvenient* desire!

Find out what happens after the vows in

The Billionaire's Defiant Acquisition
by Sharon Kendrick

One Night to Wedding Vows
by Kim Lawrence

Wedded, Bedded, Betrayed
by Michelle Smart

Look out for more *Wedlocked!* stories
coming soon!

EXPECTING A
ROYAL SCANDAL

BY
CAITLIN CREWS

First Published in Great Britain 2016
By Mills & Boon, an imprint of HarperCollins*Publishers*
1 London Bridge Street, London, SE1 9GF

© 2016 Caitlin Crews

ISBN: 978-0-263-92116-8

Printed and bound in Spain
by CPI, Barcelona

USA TODAY bestseller and RITA® Award–nominated author **Caitlin Crews** loves writing romance. She teaches her favourite romance novels in creative writing classes at places like UCLA Extension's prestigious Writers' Programme, where she finally gets to utilise the MA and PhD in English Literature she received from the University of York in England. She currently lives in California, with her very own hero and too many pets. Visit her at caitlincrews.com.

Books by Caitlin Crews

Mills & Boon Modern Romance

Castelli's Virgin Widow
At the Count's Bidding
Undone by the Sultan's Touch
Not Just the Boss's Plaything
A Devil in Disguise
In Defiance of Duty
The Replacement Wife
Princess From the Past

The Chatsfield

Greek's Last Redemption

Scandalous Sheikh Brides

Protecting the Desert Heir
Traded to the Desert Sheikh

Vows of Convenience

His for a Price
His for Revenge

Royal and Ruthless

A Royal Without Rules

Scandal in the Spotlight

Heiress Behind the Headlines
No More Sweet Surrender

Self-Made Millionaires

Katrakis's Last Mistress

Bride on Approval

Pure Princess, Bartered Bride

Visit the Author Profile page
at millsandboon.co.uk for more titles.

To Maisey, who fixed the book once
when it had all turned a bit grim,
listened to a lot of ranting on street corners
with very broad hand gestures, and then
loved it when it was done.

CHAPTER ONE

THERE WERE SOME invitations a wise woman did not refuse.

The invitation in question tonight had been handwritten by one of the most famous men on earth on luxuriously heavy card stock and then hand-delivered to her door by a servant. The message itself had been intriguingly mysterious, asking her only to... *Meet me in Monte Carlo.*

And Brittany Hollis was many things by the ripe old age of twenty-three—including widely reviled on at least two continents thanks to her collection of strategic marriages, a reality show appearance in which she'd played the widely loathed villain and her trademark refusal to confirm or deny any and all scandalous rumors she heard about herself—but she'd always considered herself wise enough.

Too wise for her own good, in fact, or so she'd always thought. That was how an untouched virgin let herself be known across the planet as one of the most shameless women alive. Yet all the while, she stayed in control and above the snide remarks—because she, and maybe only she, knew the truth.

And no matter what names others called her, like *mercenary* when they were being polite, her ability to keep her eyes on the prize as if none of that bothered her was the best way she knew to propel her toward the tropical island paradise of her dreams.

She'd get there one day. She knew she would. She'd

spend the rest of her life in a flowing caftan sipping pitchers of mai tais with cheerful flowers in her hair, and she'd never spare a single thought for these harsh days of hustling or the cruel tabloid stories in which she was always cast as the evil villain.

Not one stray thought. Not ever again.

Brittany could hardly wait. She'd spent years sending half the money she earned back home to the family members who proclaimed her lost to the devil in public, cashed her sinner's checks in private and then shamelessly asked her for more. Again and again. Her beloved grandmother would have expected Brittany to do her part after Hurricane Katrina had wiped out what little Brittany's single mother had possessed over ten years ago, leaving them all wretched and destitute and close enough to homeless in Gulfport, Mississippi.

Brittany had done her best. Year after year, the only way she knew how, with the only weapons she possessed—her looks and her body and the wits she'd inherited straight from Grandmama, though most people assumed she was entirely witless. Her youngest half sibling was ten this year. Brittany figured that meant she had eight years left before she could suggest her family members support themselves for a change.

Though maybe she'd use stronger words.

Meanwhile, the other half of the money she made she hoarded, because one of these days she was headed for a remote Pacific Island to take up residence beneath a palm tree and the deep blue sky on a deserted white sand beach. She'd seen pictures of the archipelago of Vanuatu while still in high school, and she'd decided then and there that she needed to live in that kind of paradise. Once she made it to those perfect islands west of Fiji, she wasn't coming back to the mess of the world or her place in it.

Ever.

First, however, there was all the elegant splendor of Monaco and the man who had summoned her here to meet with him in the spectacularly iconic Monte Carlo casino where blue-blooded men like him whiled away casual evenings at gaming tables that had been specifically designed to part Europe's wealthiest from their vast, multigenerational fortunes. *To discuss a proposition that would benefit us both*, the message he'd had delivered by hand had said, though Brittany hadn't been able to think of a single thing that could possibly do that. Or anything they had in common, come to that, except a certain international notoriety—and his, unlike hers, was based on documented fact.

Documented and streamed live on the internet more than once.

Still, Brittany entered the casino that evening right on time. She'd dressed her part. Monte Carlo's achingly civilized sins were draped in the veneer of a certain old-world elegance and therefore so was Brittany. A girl liked to match. Her gown shimmered a discreet, burnished gold, sweeping from a knot on one shoulder all the way down to flirt with the gleam of her sleek heels. She was aware the dress made her look edible and expensive at once, as befitted a woman whose own mother called her a whore to her face. But it also suggested a bone-deep sophistication with every step she took, which helped a white-trash girl from Mississippi blend in with the gold-leaf and marble glory surrounding her in all directions.

Brittany was very, very good at blending.

She felt the impact of the man she'd come to Monaco to meet long before she saw him, tucked away at one of the more high risk tables in the usual throng of lackeys and admirers who cavorted about in his shadow. Even without his selection of courtiers circling him like well-heeled satellites, she would have found him without any trouble.

The whispers, the humming excitement whipping through the crowd, the not precisely subtle craning of necks to get a better view of him—it all marked him with a bright red *X*. He might as well have sent up a flare.

Then the crowd parted, and there he was, sitting at a table in a desultory manner, though his attention was on the crowd—broadcasting the fact that the man formally known as His Serene Grace the Archduke Felipe Skander Cairo of Santa Domini was so supremely wealthy and jaded he need not pay attention to his own gambling endeavors even while he was undertaking them.

Cairo Santa Domini. The exiled hereditary king of the tiny alpine country that bore his surname and the only surviving member of an august and revered family line stretching back some five hundred years. The scourge of Europe's morally compromised women, the papers liked to call him—though it was also said that a woman of impeccable reputation *became* compromised merely by standing too close to him at an otherwise staid and boring function. The living, breathing, epic scandal-causing justification for the military coup that had overturned his father's monarchy and was widely held to have assassinated the rest of his family years later, leaving only Cairo the sybaritic degenerate in their wake, like a profligate grave marker.

Largely because there was no point in targeting him, the pundits had agreed for years. He redefined *disgrace*. He did an excellent job of reminding the world why the excesses of ancient monarchies should never be tolerated, simply by continuing to draw his pampered and ill-behaved breath and cavorting about the scandal sheets like a one-man bacchanal.

Cairo Santa Domini, right there before her in the sleek, superbly fit, astonishingly handsome flesh.

His had been the name on the invitation she'd received,

of course. She'd expected she'd see him here. Yet she was somehow unprepared for him all the same.

Brittany realized she'd stopped walking and had, in fact, stopped dead in the middle of the casino. She knew better than that. Hers was a game of mirrors and sighs, of soft suggestion and affected disinterest. She did not stand about staring in shock like the yokel she hadn't been in years. That wasn't the impression she liked to give off. Yet she couldn't quite make herself move.

And then Cairo glanced over and met her gaze, bold and lazy at once, and she wasn't certain she'd ever move of her own volition again. She felt bolted to the floor—and painfully, at that.

She'd seen a thousand pictures of this man. Everyone had, and of significantly more of him than necessary. She already knew he was beautiful. Many celebrated things were from a distance, she'd found, only to prove a bit more grimy and weathered and unfortunate up close. Hollywood, for example, and many of its best-known denizens.

But not Cairo.

He had one of those full, captivating, startlingly European mouths that made her feel edgy and hollow down deep inside. That mouth of his made her imagine hot, desperate kisses in cold, unfamiliar cities bristling with baroque architecture and laden with strange pastries, when she hadn't thought about *kissing* anyone in years. He had a full head of shaggy dark hair that was obviously left mussed and careless on purpose, yet still managed to make him appear as if it had *happened* to him on the way to Monte Carlo.

And his eyes! They looked pretty enough in photographs. More than pretty. This close, a mere stone's throw across the casino floor, they were nothing short of marvelous. There was no other word to describe them. They were the color of exultantly wicked caramel and made her feel like spun sugar all the way to her toes. Her mouth watered despite herself, and she felt the heat of him in a bright blaze down deep in her belly.

This had never happened to her before. Not ever.

Brittany had been more or less immune to men since her mother's early, appalling boyfriends had raged drunkenly through their miserable trailer during Brittany's formative years. The fact she'd married three men of her own volition and for her own very practical reasons hadn't altered her opinion on the drawbacks of the male sex one bit—and not one of her husbands had affected her blood pressure like this.

Or at all, if she was honest.

It didn't make sense. She jerked her gaze from Cairo Santa Domini's too aware, slightly arrested one to take in the rest of him, not surprised to find he wore the usual uniform of all the very wealthy European men she'd ever seen out at night in this city or that, clogging up the nightclubs and restaurants and boulevard cafés. Though his version was…better.

Much better.

His dark, exquisitely tailored shirt clung to that expected glorious male torso of his that no doubt looked equally delicious framed by various Italian coasts or the yacht-choked harbors lining the French Riviera outside. His gorgeously cut dark jacket somehow made his masculine chin, with just a bit more than five o'clock shadow, seem that much more decadent and attractive. His legs, athletic and muscled and longer than most, were packed into the sort of bespoke black trousers that cost more than some people's mortgages. His shoes whispered with the quiet confidence of Milan as he stretched out his legs, continuing to lounge there, awash in his followers, as if the famed Monte Carlo tables were but a prop for a man like him.

As was she, she understood, when one of his dark brows arched high in some mixture of weary boredom and very royal command. A prop for a game she didn't yet understand—but she would. That was why she'd come.

That and she'd never before met a man who would have been an actual king, barring all that unfortunate civil unrest when he'd been a child.

Cairo crooked an imperious finger, beckoning her near, and Brittany really, truly didn't want to go to him. Every instinct inside her screamed at her to turn on her heel and run in the opposite direction. To walk all the way back up north to her efficient little flat in Paris if that was what it took.

Anything to get the hell away from him before he destroyed her.

That thought shivered over her like some kind of prophecy, bone and blood. *He will destroy you.*

She tried to shake off the feeling. She told herself she was being fanciful. Silly. Two things she'd never been in her entire life, but maybe the sight of a would-be king in a place like Monte Carlo was too much for all the broken shards of the Cinderella fantasies she knew she had rattling around inside her somewhere, scraping at her with their jagged edges when she least expected it. Making it hard to breathe in strange little moments like this one.

She started toward Cairo, affecting a faintly quizzical expression as if she hadn't recognized him. As if she'd stopped in the middle of the casino floor because she'd been uncertain where to go, not because she'd seen him and been struck by the sight. As if their gazes hadn't clashed like that, in a tangle of caramel breathlessness that was still scraping through her and making her feel almost…raw.

Brittany ignored all those inconvenient feelings, whatever the hell they were. She sauntered toward her doom, and no amount of shouting at herself to stop being so fanciful convinced her that the dissolute aristocrat who watched her approach was anything but that: her sure destruction packed into a recklessly masculine form.

"Are you Cairo Santa Domini?" she asked brightly as she drew near, letting a little more Mississippi flavor her words than usual. For dramatic effect—because people drew all sorts of conclusions about folks with drawls like the one she'd grown up using. Mostly that they were as dumb as a pile of rocks, which she'd always enjoyed using to her advantage.

As expected, her feigned inability to identify one of the most recognizable men alive was met with gasps, outraged sniffs and muttered condemnations from his entourage. Cairo's mouth, a study in carved sensuality that seemed to be wired directly into an echoing heat deep her belly, curved in appreciation.

"I regret that I am." His voice was like melted dark chocolate. Rich. Deep. Faintly, intriguingly accented, as if his use of English was an afterthought or perhaps a gift. He didn't move from his languid position, though she had the strangest notion that his decadent caramel gaze had sharpened as she approached. "But only because no one else has stepped up to take the position, no matter how I try to give it away."

"A pity." She stopped when she was *just* inside the span of his carelessly outthrust legs. She felt certain he'd appreciate the symbolism. Sure enough, that arrested, *aware* gleam in his gaze intensified. It told her she was right. And that he wasn't as bored as he was pretending to be. "Then again, no one else in all the world can boast of your indefatigable penis and its many salacious conquests, can they? What's a lost kingdom next to that?"

Brittany was aware of the ripple that deliberate slap caused all around them, ruffling the feathers of his courtiers and his more distant admirers alike. She'd meant it to do just that. And yet she couldn't seem to jerk her gaze away from the man who stood there before her—smiling, though she noticed it went nowhere near his deceptively warm eyes or the cool, calculating gleam there.

"Ms. Hollis, I presume?" he asked.

Brittany was certain he'd known her at a glance. But this was the game. So she merely nodded, all gracious condescension, as if it had been a true inquiry.

"I've been in exile most of my life," he said after a moment, his mild tone at odds with the way he was studying her. "Only the revolutionaries call me any kind of king these days. Best not to invoke their brand of fealty. It comes with toppled governments and ruined cities, generally speaking." He inclined his head, reminding her with that single, simple gesture that whatever he was now, however far he'd fallen, he'd been raised to rule. "I do hope you found your way here tonight without incident. Monte Carlo is not quite the burlesque halls of the Paris sewers—that is what we call such places in polite company, is it not? I trust you do not find yourself too far out of your accustomed, ah, *depths*."

Brittany had misjudged him. She hadn't expected a playboy royal, draped in well-dressed tarts and trailing scandal behind him wherever he roamed like some kind of acrid scent, to be anything like *sharp*. It hadn't crossed her mind that he could possibly insult her with any dexterity.

Or at all, honestly.

Some part of her shifted, deep inside, in what she told herself was grudging admiration. Nothing more.

"Water seeks its own level, I'm told," she said, and smiled all the brighter as she switched up her tactics on the fly. "And so here I am."

His impossibly carnal mouth curved again, deeper this time, and she felt it tug at her, low in her belly, where there was nothing but fire and an edgy need she didn't really understand. It seemed to intensify by the second. With every breath.

"You should, of course, feel elevated by my notice in the first place. To say nothing of my invitation." He shifted against the table at his back, propping himself up on an elbow. It only drew attention to the fact that he had to look down at her, though she stood in three-inch heels that made her nearly six feet tall. "You do not appear to be glorying in your good fortune tonight, *cara.*"

"I feel very fortunate, of course," she said in an insultingly overpolite tone, as if attempting to pacify a dimwitted child. "Truly. *So* lucky."

Brittany was used to reading rooms, the better to contribute to her own tarnished legend by playing it up whenever possible. A wink here, a smile there and another rumor spread like wildfire and ended up a tabloid headline. But this was different. It wasn't only that there were no cameras allowed in this place, which made playing to them difficult. She should have been cataloguing bystander reactions to this meeting and gathering information the way she usually did—but instead, the whole of the casino seemed cast in shadow with Cairo the unlikely sun at its center, a streak of glaring brightness she found unaccountably mesmerizing.

As if he was powerful beyond measure when she knew—when everybody knew—he was at best a modern-day wastrel. He shouldn't exude anything but the latest party-boy cologne. She told herself he was a snake charmer, nothing more. Why she couldn't seem to hold on to that thought was a question she'd have to investigate in depth when she was somewhere far, far away from all this insane magnetism of his, which was far too riveting for comfort.

Cairo watched her in his oddly intent way, though every

other inch of him shouted out his pure indolence. It gave her the distinct sensation of whiplash.

"I saw your act," he said after a long, tensely glimmering moment dragged by, and Brittany found she was holding her breath. Again.

He'd been there? In the audience in that grimy little club that Europe's most pampered imagined was a walk on the wild side of their indulged little lives? Brittany couldn't believe she hadn't *felt* this intensity of his, somehow.

She hated that she felt it now. She caught herself in the act of scowling at him and softened her expression—but she was sure he'd seen it anyway.

She was certain, somehow, that Cairo Santa Domini saw a great deal more than he should.

"You have a very interesting approach to the art of the burlesque, Ms. Hollis. All that stalking about the stage, baring your teeth in such a terrifying manner at the punters. Effectively daring them to deny you their pallid offerings of a few measly bills for a glance at your frilly underthings. You'd be better off cracking a whip and dispensing with the fiction that you are at all interested in appealing to the usual fantasies, I think."

Brittany tucked her bright gold clutch beneath her arm, as languid as he was, though something in her shook at his horrifyingly accurate picture of the side gig she'd taken to make a few more scandalized headlines, and let her smile flirt with a bit of an edge.

"Are you reviewing my performance?"

"Consider it the studied reaction of a rather ardent fan of the art form."

"I don't know what's more astounding. That you sullied your aristocratic self in a burlesque club in 'the sewers of Paris,' as you call them, or that you would admit to such shocking behavior in the glare of all this fussy Monte Carlo elegance. Your desperate acolytes can hear you, you know." She leaned closer and dropped her voice to a stage whisper she was fairly certain carried all the way across the Italian border less than ten miles to the east. "You'd better be careful, Your Exiled Highness. The chandeliers themselves might shatter at the notion that a man of your known proclivities attended something so prosaic and tedious as a *nightclub*."

"I was under the impression my behavior no longer shocked a soul, or so the wearisome British papers would have me believe. In any case, do you really feel as if a return to the dance halls of your storied past are a good investment in your future? I'd thought your latest marriage was a step in a different direction. A pity about the will." That half smile of his was—she understood as it sliced through her and reminded her of the very public way her most recent husband's heirs had announced that Brittany had been excluded from the bulk his estate—an understated weapon. "I ask as a friend."

"I would be quite surprised if you truly had any friends at all." She eyed him and amped up her own smile. Polite and charming fangs. Her specialty. "But I digress. In some circles a glance at my frilly underthings is considered something of a generous gift. You're welcome."

"Ah, Ms. Hollis, let us not play these games." Something not quite a smile any longer played with that stunning mouth of his, marking him significantly more formidable than a mere *playboy*. "You did not strip, as widely advertised. You hardly performed at all, and meanwhile the chance to get a glimpse of Jean Pierre Archambault's disgraced widow in the nude was the primary attraction of the entire exercise. The whole thing was a regrettable tease."

She shrugged delicately, fully aware it made the gold fabric of her gown gleam and shimmer as if she herself was lit from within. "That must have been a novel experience for a man of your well-documented depravities."

His head tilted slightly to one side and his gaze was not particularly friendly. Somehow, this made him more beautiful. "You were a high school dropout."

Brittany knew better than to show any sort of reaction to the shift in topic. Or to what was likely meant to be a hard slap to shove her back into her place. Trouble was, she'd never much cared for her place, or she'd still be in Gulfport scraping out a miserable existence with the rest of her relatives. No, thank you.

"Did they call it something different when you failed to finish one private boarding school after the next?" she asked sweetly. His Royal Jackass wasn't the only one with access to the internet. "There were how many in a row? Six? I know the obscenely rich make their own rules, but I was under the impression your numerous expulsions meant you and I are both somehow making it through the big, bad world without a high school diploma. Maybe we'll be best friends after all."

Cairo ignored her, though she thought there was a certain appreciative gleam in those deceptively sweet-looking eyes of his. "A runaway at sixteen, in the company of your first husband. And what a prime choice he was. He was what we might call..."

He paused, as if in deference to her feelings. Or as if he'd suddenly recalled his manners. Brittany laughed.

"We called Darryl a way to get out of Gulfport, Mississippi," she replied. She let a little more twang into her voice, as emphasis. "Believe me, you make that choice when it comes along, no matter the drug-addled loser that may or may not come with it. Not the sort of choice you had to make, I imagine, while growing up coddled and adored on one of your family's numerous foreign properties."

The word *exile* called to mind something a bit more perilous than the Santa Domini royal family's collection of luxury estates; here a ranch, there an island, everywhere a sprawling penthouse in the best neighborhood of any given city. It was hard to muster up any sympathy, Brittany found, especially when her own choices had been to live wherever she could make it work or end up back in her mother's trailer.

"Your second husband was far more in the style to which you would soon become accustomed. You and he became rather well known on that dreadful television program of yours, did you not?"

"*Hollywood Hustle* ran for two seasons and is considered one of the less appalling reality shows out there," Brittany said, as if in agreement. "If we're tallying them all up."

"That's a rather low bar."

"Said the pot to the kettle." She eyed him. "Most viewers were obsessed with the heartwarming love story of Chaz and Mariella, not Carlos and me."

"The tattoo artist." Cairo didn't actually crook his fingers around the word *artist*, but it was very strongly implied. And, as Brittany recalled, deserved. "And the sad church secretary who wanted him to follow his heart and become a derivative landscape painter, or some such drivel."

"Pulse-pounding, riveting stuff," Brittany agreed dryly. "As you clearly already know, if you feel you're in a good place to judge the behavior of others despite every cautionary tale ever told about glass houses."

It had all been entirely faked, of course. Carlos had been told the gay character he'd auditioned for had already been cast, but there was an opening for a bad-girl villain and her hapless husband—as long as they were legally married. Brittany was the only woman Carlos had known who'd wanted to get out of Texas as much as he did, so the whole thing was a no-brainer. The truth was that after Darryl, Brittany didn't think too highly of the institution of marriage anyway. She and Carlos had been together long enough to get reality-show famous—which wasn't really famous at all, despite what so many people in her family seemed to think—and then, when the show's ratings started to fade and their name recognition went with them, Brittany had dramatically "left" Carlos for Jean Pierre, so Carlos could complain about it in the tabloids and land himself a new gig.

But to the greater public, of course, she was that low-class slut who had ruined a poor, sweet, good man. A tale as old as time, blah blah blah.

She raised her brows at Cairo Santa Domini now. "I wouldn't have pegged you for a fan of the show. Or any reality show, for that matter. I thought inhabitants of your social strata wafted about pretending to read Proust."

"I spend a lot of my time on airplanes, not in glass houses and very rarely with Proust," Cairo replied, a glint in the caramel depths of his gaze as he waved a careless hand. "Your show was such a gripping drama, was it not? You, the heartless stripper who wouldn't give up your tawdry dancing for the good of your marriage. Carlos, the loving husband who tried so desperately to stay true to you despite the way you betrayed him on those poles every night. The path of true love, et cetera."

Brittany felt the flash of her own smile as she aimed it at him, and concentrated on making it brighter. Bolder. It was amazing what people failed to see in the glare of a great smile.

"I'm a terrible person," she agreed merrily. "If a television show says so, it must be true. Speaking of which, didn't I see you featured on one of those tabloid programs just last week? Something about a hapless heiress, a weekend in the Maldives and the corrosive nature of your company?"

"Remind me," Cairo murmured, sounding somewhat less amused—she was almost certain. "Were you still married to Carlos when you met Jean Pierre?"

Brittany laughed. A sparkling, effortless, absolutely false laugh. "You appear to be confusing my résumé with yours."

"And speaking of Jean Pierre, may he rest in peace, what was it that drew you together? He, the elderly man confined to a wheelchair with a scant few months to live. You…"

Cairo let his gaze travel over her form, as hot and buttery as a touch. He didn't finish that sentence.

"We had a shared interest in applied sciences, of course," Brittany replied, deadpan and dry. "What else?"

"An interest that his children did not share, given they wasted no time in ejecting you from the old man's chateau the moment he died and then crowing about it to the press. A shame."

"Your invitation didn't mention that we'd be playing biography games," Brittany said brightly, as if it didn't bother her in the least to be so publically eviscerated. "I feel so woefully underprepared. Let's see." She held her bag beneath her elbow and ticked things off on her fingers. "Royal blood. No throne. Always naked. Eight thousand women. So many sex tapes. So scandalous the word no longer really applies because it's really more, 'there's Cairo Santa Domini somewhere he shouldn't be with someone he shouldn't have touched and blurred out bits in a national newspaper. La la la, must be Tuesday.'"

"Ms. Hollis," Cairo said in that drawling way only extremely upper-crust people could manage to make sound so condescending. When it was only her name. He reached over as if nothing had ever been more inevitable and then he traced a very lazy, very delicate path from the gold knot at her shoulder to the very top of that shadow between her breasts. Sensation detonated inside of her. She flashed white hot. She saw red. She *felt* him, everywhere, and that voice of his, too, all dark chocolate and stupendously bad decisions melted into something that shivered through her, dessert and desire and destruction all at once. "You flatter me."

Brittany didn't like the way her heart catapulted itself against the wall of her chest. She didn't like the way her skin prickled, hot and cold, as if she was sunburned from so small and meaningless a touch. Since when had she reacted at all to a man? No matter what he did?

She didn't like the fact that she'd completely lost sight of the fact that they were in public, even if the public in question was mostly his circle of pseudosubjects she knew trotted around with him everywhere he went—or that all she'd really seen since she walked in here was Cairo. As if she'd come here to compete for his attention, like one of his usual horde of panting women.

She liked that part least of all, and she didn't care to ask herself why that was. It didn't matter. None of what had happened here mattered. This spectacularly messy and inappropriate man wasn't in any way a part of her grand plan, and would do nothing but delay her dreams of a getaway to her solitary tropical island paradise in Vanuatu. He had that kind of total disaster written all over him, and too much exposure to him made her worry it was written on her, too. She'd accepted his invitation because she was curious and he was Cairo Santa Domini, and now she knew.

He was her ruin made flesh. Nothing less than that. At least she knew it now, she told herself. That meant she had the chance to avoid it. To avoid *him*.

"Your Almost Highness," she breathed, in exaggerated shock.

She wanted to snatch his lazy finger away from her

overheated skin, which was why she leaned into it instead. His finger slipped into the valley between her breasts, *just there* beneath the edge of her angled bodice, but neither one of them looked down to see what both of them could feel. Their gazes were locked together, tangled up hot and a little bit wild, and Brittany was slightly mollified to see she wasn't the only one affected by…whatever the hell this was. She raised her voice so they could hear her everywhere in Monaco, the trashy American that she was, every inch of her offensive to each and every highbrow European eye that tried its best not to see her.

But Brittany wasn't any good at being invisible. "Are you *flirting* with me?"

CHAPTER TWO

A SHORT WHILE LATER, Cairo stood with his back to the disconcerting American, his brooding gaze fixed on the seductive glitter of Monaco's harbor out there in the sweet summer dark. The night pressed in on the glass windows of his penthouse suite the way that woman seemed to hammer against his composure, even when all she was doing was sitting quietly on his sofa. He could see her reflection in the glass and it irritated him that she looked so calm while he had to fight to collect himself.

That he had to do any such thing was nothing short of extraordinary for a man who was alive today precisely because he could so expertly manage himself in all situations.

But then, nothing tonight was going according to plan.

Brittany Hollis wasn't at all what he'd expected. When he'd watched that cringe-worthy television program of hers she'd been all plumped-up breasts and an endless Southern drawl, punctuated with supple flips and melting slides on the nearest stripper pole. All the advance research he'd done on her before selecting her for the dubious honor of his proposal had suggested she might possess the particular cunning native to the sort of women whose life revolved around strategic relationships with much wealthier men, but he hadn't expected any great intellect.

Cairo had been delighted at the prospect that she'd be exactly as gauche as her tawdry history suggested she was.

Someone capable of injecting the embarrassing spectacle of her risqué burlesque appearances into everyday life and making certain the whole world found her deeply embarrassing and epically shameless at all times.

The perfect woman for him, in other words. A man so famously without honor or country deserved a shameful match, he'd told himself bitterly the night he'd seen her dance. Brittany Hollis seemed crafted to order.

Instead, the woman who had walked up to him tonight was a vision, from the pale copper fire of her hair to the hint of hot steel in her dark hazel eyes, and there wasn't a single thing the least bit dumb or plastic about her. He didn't understand it. Meeting her gaze had been like being thrown from the saddle of a very large horse and having to lie there on the hard ground for a few excruciating moments, wondering with no little panic if he'd ever draw breath to fill his lungs again.

He still didn't know the answer to that.

His long-term head of security, Ricardo, who'd suggested this tabloid sensation of a woman in the first place, had a lot to answer for. But here, now, Cairo had to navigate what he'd expected to be a very straightforward business conversation despite the fact he felt so…unsettled.

"Have you lured me back to your hotel suite to show me your etchings, Your Usually Far More Naked Grace?" Brittany's voice was so dry it swept over him like a brush fire, igniting a longing in him he'd never imagined he'd feel for anyone or anything aside from his lost kingdom and its people. He didn't understand what this was—what was happening to him, when he'd felt absolutely nothing since the day he'd lost his family and had understood what waited for him if he wasn't careful. What General Estes, the self-appointed Grand Regent of Santa Domini, had made clear was Cairo's destiny if he ever so much as glanced longingly at the throne that should have been his.

"What a dream come true. I've always wanted to join such a vast and well-populated parade of royal paramours."

That the girl was perfect for his purposes wasn't in doubt, dry tone or not.

Cairo had known it the moment Ricardo had handed him her picture. Even before Ricardo had told him anything about the pretty redhead who wore so little and stared into the camera with so much distance and mystery in her dark eyes. He'd felt something scratch at him, and he'd told himself that was reason enough to conceal himself and sneak into one of her scandalous performances in Paris. He'd been far more intrigued than he should have been as he'd watched her command the stage, challenging the audience with every sinuous move of her famously lithe and supple figure.

He'd sent one of his aides with his invitation and he'd continued interviewing the other candidates for his very special position, but his heart wasn't in it once he'd seen Brittany. And that was before he'd read all the unsavory details of her life story, which, of course, rendered her an utterly appalling if not outright ruinous choice for a man some people still dreamed would be king one day. General Estes might have routed Cairo's father from the throne of Santa Domini when Cairo was still a small child, but the passing of time only ever seemed to make the loyalists more shrill and focused. And that made no one safe—neither Cairo nor the Santa Dominian people, who didn't deserve another bloody coup in a thirty-year span, much less the empty-headed playboy prince Cairo played for the papers as its figurehead.

Besides, Cairo knew what the loyalists refused to see—there was nothing good in him. He'd seen to that. There was only shame and darkness and more of the same. Play a role long enough and it ate a man alive. The desperate American stripper who'd made an international game out of her shameless gold digging was an inspired choice to make certain that even if no one listened to Cairo about who he'd become, no coup could ever happen and his people would be spared a broken, damaged king.

And then she'd walked up to him in a dress of spun gold and pretended not to know him, and he'd forgotten he'd ever so much as considered another woman for this role at all.

"Was it a lure?" he asked now. He turned to see her rolling her glass of wine between her palms, an action he shouldn't have found even remotely erotic. And yet… "I asked you to accompany me to my hotel suite and you agreed. A lure is rather less straightforward."

"If you say so, Your Semantic Highness."

Cairo had expected to find her attractive. He'd expected a hint of the usual fire deep within him and the lick of it in his sex, because he was a man, after all. Despite what he needed to do here. He'd been less prepared for the sheer wallop of her. Of how the sight of her made his breath a complication in his chest.

And he certainly hadn't imagined she'd be…entertaining.

The pictures and even the stage hadn't done her any justice at all, and the tidy little marriage of convenience he'd imagined shifted and re-formed in his head the longer he looked at her. Cairo knew he should call it off. The last thing he needed in his life was one more situation he couldn't control, and the blazing thing raging inside of him now was the very definition of uncontrollable.

And *she* was something more than a gorgeous redhead who'd looked edible in a down-market burlesque ensemble, or even a former American television star in a shiny dress that made her look far more sophisticated than she should have been. Brittany Hollis should have been little more than a jumped-up tart. Laughable in the midst of so much old-world splendor here in Monaco.

But instead, she was fascinating.

Cairo was finding it exceedingly difficult to keep his cool, which had never happened to him before in all the years since he'd lost his family. He hardly knew whether to give in to the sensation, unleashing God knew what manner of hell upon himself, or view it as an assault. Both, perhaps.

"Is this the part where we stare at each other for ages?" Brittany asked from her position on the crisp white sofa where she perched with all the boneless elegance of a pampered cat. "I had no idea royal intrigue was so tedious."

It was time to handle this. To handle himself, for God's sake. This wasn't about *him*, after all, or whatever odd need he felt licking at him, tempting him to forget the dark truths about himself in earnest for the first time in some twenty years.

"Of course it's tedious," he said, drawing himself up to his full height. He brushed a nonexistent speck of lint from one sleeve. "That's why kings are forced to start wars or institute terror regimes and inquisitions, you understand. To relieve the boredom."

"And your family was drummed out of your country. I can't think why."

Cairo had long since ceased to allow himself to feel anything at all when it came to his lost kingdom and the often vicious comments people made about it to his face. He'd made an art out of seeming not to care about his birthright, his blood, his people. He'd locked it all up and shoved it deep inside, where none of it could slip out and torture him any longer, much less trip him up in the glare of the public eye.

No stray memories of graceful white walls cluttered with priceless art, the dizzy blue sky outside his window in that particular bright shade he'd never seen replicated anywhere else, the murmur of the mountain winds against the fortified walls of his childhood bedroom in the castle heights. No recollections of the night they'd all been spirited away in the dark before General Estes could get his butcher's hands on them, hidden in the back of a loyalist's truck across the sharp spine of the snowcapped mountains that ringed the capital city, never to return.

He didn't let himself think of his father's roar of laughter or his mother's soft hands, lost forever. He never permitted himself any stray thoughts about his younger sister, Magdalena, a bright and gleaming little girl snatched away so easily and so unfairly.

He didn't have the slightest idea why the usual barbed comments from yet another stranger should lodge in him tonight like a mortal blow, as if the fact this woman had surprised him meant she could slip beneath his defenses, too. No one could do that. Not if he didn't let them.

And he was well aware that even if he'd wanted someone close to him, to that tarnished thing inside of him he called his soul, he couldn't allow it to happen. He couldn't let anyone close to him or they'd be rendered so much more collateral damage. One more weapon the general would find a way to use against Cairo and then destroy.

Why was Brittany Hollis making him consider such things?

He studied her. Her coppery hair was caught up in a complicated twist, catching the light as she moved. Her neck was long and elegant, and made him long for a taste of her. More than a taste. Her skin looked as if it was dusted a fainter gold than the dress she wore, which on any other woman might have been a trick of cosmetics, but on this one, he thought, was actually *her*. She was far prettier than her photographs and infinitely more captivating than her coarse appearances on that stupid show. She was all impossibly long legs, those lovely curves shimmering beneath the expert cling of the gown and that enticing intelligence simmering there in her dark eyes.

That same thing scratched at him, the way it had in Paris when Ricardo had given him her picture, and he knew better than to let it. This was already a mess. A problem, and he had enough of those already. He needed a clear path and a solution, or what was the point of this game? He might as well hand himself over to the general for the execution that had already been meted out to the rest of his bloodline and call it a day.

Some part of him—a part that grew larger all the time—wished he'd done just that, years ago. Some part of him wished he'd been in that car with the rest of his family when it had been run off the road. Some part of him wished he'd never lived long enough to make these choices.

But that was nothing but craven self-pity. The least of his sins, but a sin nonetheless.

"You are very pretty," he told her now. Sternly.

"I would thank you, but somehow I doubt it was a compliment."

"It is surprising. I expected you to be attractive, of course, in the way all women of your particular profession are." He waved a hand.

She smiled, managing to convey an icy disdain that would do a royal proud. "My profession?"

Cairo shrugged. "Dancer. Television personality. Expensive trophy wife, ever open to the appropriate upgrades. Whatever you call yourself."

Her smile took on that edge that fascinated him, but she didn't look away.

"I do like an upgrade." She fingered the rim of her glass and he remembered the feel of her skin under his hand, hot and soft at once. Touching her had been a serious miscalculation, he was aware. One that pounded in him still, kicking up dark yearnings and desperate long-ings he knew he needed to ignore. "Are you going to tell me why I'm here?"

"No insulting version of my title this time? I'm wounded."

"I find my creativity wanes along with my interest." She leaned forward and set her glass down on the table before her with a decisive *click*. "Monte Carlo is wasted on me, I'm afraid, as I'm not much of a gambler." Her smile didn't reach her eyes. "I prefer the comfort of a sure thing. And I loathe being bored."

"Is this what boredom looks like on you? My mistake. I rather thought you looked a bit...flushed."

"I find myself ever so slightly nauseated." He knew she was lying. The glitter in her bright eyes told him so, if he'd had the slightest doubt. "I can't think why."

He thrust his hands into the pockets of his trousers. "Perhaps you dislike penthouses with extraordinary views." He smiled. "The coast or me. Take your pick. Both views, and I say this with no false modesty at all, are stunning."

"Maybe I dislike spoiled rich men who waste my time and think far too highly of their overexposed charms." The edge to her smile and that glittering thing in her gaze grew harder. Hotter. "I've seen it all in the pages of every tabloid magazine every week for the last twenty years. It's about as thrilling as oatmeal."

"I must have misheard you. I thought you compared me to a revoltingly warm and cloying breakfast cereal."

"The similarities are striking."

"A man with less confidence than I have—and no ac-cess to a mirror—might find that hurtful, Ms. Hollis."

"I feel certain you find whatever you need in all the reflective surfaces available to you." She eyed him. "I suppose that almost qualifies as a skill. But while that confirms my opinion of your conceit, it doesn't tell me what I'm doing here."

Cairo hadn't decided precisely how he would do this. Somewhere in his murky, battered soul he'd imagined this might prove a rare opportunity to be honest. Or as near enough to honest as he was capable of being, anyway. He'd imagined that might make purchasing a wife to ward off a revolution a little less seedy and sad, no matter his reasons. A little self-deprecating humor and a few hard truths, he'd imagined, and the whole thing would be easily sorted.

But he hadn't expected to want her this badly.

"I have a proposition for you," he forced himself to say, before he made the unfortunate decision to simply seduce her instead and see what happened. He already knew what would happen—didn't he?—and the pleasures of the moment couldn't outweigh the realities of the future bearing down on him. He knew that.

He couldn't believe he was even considering it.

"I'd say I'm flattered," Brittany was saying coolly, "but I'm not. I'm not interested in being any man's mistress. And not to put too fine a point on it, but your charms are a bit…" She raised her brows. "Overused."

He blinked, and took his time with it. "I beg your pardon. Did you just call me a whore?"

"I'd never use that word," Brittany demurred, and though her voice was smooth he was sure there was something edgy and sharp lurking just beneath it. "But the phrase *rode hard and put away wet* comes to mind." She waved a hand at him. "It's all a bit boring, if I'm honest."

"Do not kid yourself, Ms. Hollis," Cairo advised her quietly. "I've had a lot of sex with a great many partners, it's true."

"That's a bit like the ocean confessing it's slightly damp."

He smiled. "The media coverage of my sex life might indeed be boring. I wouldn't know as I make a point never to follow it. But the act itself? Never."

"You'd be the last to know, of course. Even a man as conceited as you are must realize that."

"I suppose the first hundred or so could simply be interested in my dramatic personal history," Cairo said, as if considering her point, though he kept his gaze trained on the increasing color high up on her cheeks. *Interesting.* "And the second two hundred could be in it for my personal wealth. But *all* of them? The law of averages suggests not *all* of them would come apart like that, screaming and wailing and crying beneath me. The same reasoning applies if you suggest they were faking it. Some, I imagine, because there are always some. But all?"

"I'm sure you saw whatever it is you wanted to see." He could have sworn there was a huskiness in her voice and a deeper shade to the red of her cheeks, and he didn't care what she said. He knew passion when he saw it. She was as affected as he was. "Ninety times a day, or whatever the horrifying number is. The mind boggles."

Cairo was no saint, by design or inclination. But he was also not quite the epic sinner he'd played all his life. And in all the years he'd performed his role in the circus that was his life, he'd never felt the slightest urge to tell a woman that. What the hell was happening to him tonight?

"I'm only good at one thing," he told her, the way he'd have told anyone else. He pretended he couldn't hear the intensity in his own voice. He pretended he had no idea how little in control of himself he was just then. "And as it happens, I'm very, very good at it."

She swallowed, which he shouldn't have found even remotely fascinating, no matter how elegant her neck. "Is that your proposition? My answer is an emphatic no, as I said. But also, your pitch needs some work."

"That I'm an excellent lover is a fact, not a pitch," Cairo said with a small shrug. He found he was enjoying himself, which was almost as unusual as the claws of need that still raked through him. "The proposition is far less exciting, I'm afraid. I'm not in the market for a mistress, Ms. Hollis. Why would I bother with such a confining arrangement? I rarely meet a woman who wouldn't do anything I ask for free, no need to provide room, board or baubles on demand."

"I'm overcome by the romance of it all."

"Then this will delight you." Cairo eyed her, a column of gold tipped in all that sweet copper he wanted to bury his hands in, and he found his blood was pumping much too hard through his body then, as if he was out on a long, hard run in a harsh winter. He ignored it. "I find myself in need of a wife. I've been considering a number of candidates for the position, but you are far and away my first choice."

He expected her to say something scathing. Perhaps let out a scandalized laugh. He even braced himself for the lash of it, and damned if he didn't enjoy the anticipation of that, too. But she only considered him for a moment, her dark hazel gaze unreadable, and he found he had no idea what she might say.

That, like everything else with this woman, was a new experience. He told himself he hated it. Because he should have. He needed an employee of sorts, at minimum. A partner if at all possible. What he did not need was any more trouble, and Brittany Hollis had that stamped deep on every inch of her lovely skin.

God knew he had enough trouble. It lived inside him. It was his world.

"Who's your second choice?" she asked when the silence had drawn out almost too long.

"My second choice?"

Brittany didn't *quite* roll her eyes. "I can hardly determine whether to be insulted or complimented if I don't know the field, can I?"

Cairo named a famously orphaned Italian socialite, primarily well-known for her bouts of sulky nudity on board the superyachts of her questionable Russian oligarch boyfriends.

Brittany sighed. "Insulted it is."

"She's a far second, if that helps. Far too much work for too little return."

This surprising American, who he'd expected would fall at his feet in an instant and who cared if that was as much about his credit line and his title as the charms she'd called *overused* to his face, only gazed at him a moment, her dark eyes narrow. He thought he could *see* her thinking and he didn't understand why or how he could find that the sexiest thing he'd seen in years. It was that glint in her hazel gaze. It was moving through him like something alcoholic.

"You don't actually want to get married, then. You want to inflict your wife on someone—the world, perhaps? As any girl would be, I'm of course delighted to be considered an infliction. It's all my dearest fairy-tale fantasies made real, thank you."

He couldn't help but smile at her dry tone, though the curve of his own mouth felt as hard as granite. "I'm sorry, did you expect protestations of love? I could do that, if you like. You can even believe them, if it helps. But the offer is for a job. A position. Not a romantic interlude."

Those too-dark eyes held his for a moment that stretched on a little too long for comfort. Then even longer. And Cairo had never wanted to read another person's mind as much as he did then.

"I feel certain there's a middle ground." She stood, running an unnecessary hand over the sleek fall of her gown as she did, and Cairo found he wanted her with a raw fervor that shook through him, making him a total stranger to himself. Making him a traitor to his cause. Making her nothing less than a calamity—which only made the wanting worse. "I'd suggest you find it before you approach the socialite. I've heard she bites."

And then Brittany Hollis—so far beneath him that she should have been prostrate with gratitude at his attention to her and appreciative of the faintest bare crumb of his interest—actually turned on her heel, showed him her back as if he really did bore her silly and walked out.

Halfway through her burlesque performance a few nights later, Brittany felt an electric ripple go through the crowd. And seconds later, through her.

She told herself she was imagining things as she strode across the stage to the pulsing beat, but she knew better. She knew that feeling, like being lit on fire and forced to stand still in the crackling flames. That was exactly how she'd felt in Monte Carlo, burnt to a crisp where she stood on the casino floor.

Brittany concentrated on the pounding music and on the lazy choreography she could perform by rote. Something she was even happier about than usual, because she could hardly pay attention to this kick or that shimmy when she could *feel* Cairo's presence like some kind of tsunami, washing through the club. She didn't have to squint to see him past the swirling lights the club owner went a little overboard with during her number. She didn't have to try to make out his features as he moved through the dark.

She could track him by the murmur and shift in the crowd as they swiveled around in their chairs to watch him pass. She could feel the way that deceptively lush gaze of his settled on her and stayed there. It was a little too much like the dreams she kept having, the ones that spun out different, far more erotic endings to that night in his hotel suite in Monaco—when she'd never wanted a man's touch in her life. She felt that same great rush of complicated, messy feelings, the way she did each time she woke up with her heart pounding and her breath tangled in her throat, her body too warm and somehow no longer her own.

And suddenly the crimson corset she wore seemed a good deal tighter across her breasts and the black lace choker at her neck lived up to its name with a vengeance. She was aware of the creamy expanse of her upper thighs that peeked out above her garters, and the way the sleek sleeves that hooked over her pointer fingers, but covered her forearms to her elbows, left her upper arms bare. The frilly, puffy shrug she wore that made her look one step away from steampunk seemed insubstantial, suddenly, and she understood what Cairo had called "the art of the burlesque" in a different way than she ever had before.

Brittany didn't want to investigate that—much less the great swirl of *feelings* that nearly knocked her sideways on the main stage. She simply danced toward it.

Toward him.

Toward Cairo as he moved to the reserved table that had been kept empty right there in the front all night, so there was no pretending she didn't see him when—at last—he stopped showing off for the goggle-eyed audience and settled himself in the chair closest to the stage as if he owned this place and everything in it. The dancers before him, most of all.

It was Brittany's turn then, and she took it.

He'd been right about her previous performances. She'd been phoning it in, having promised the club owner eight weeks of shows and not caring too much about it after the first rash of appalled tabloid headlines. Tonight, however, seven weeks into her run, it turned out she had something to prove.

To him, a little voice clarified.

She didn't ask herself what she was doing, just as she didn't question why the things he'd said to her and the proposition he'd made—far less offensive than most of the things she'd been called and a huge percentage of the offers she'd fielded in her time—had needled her ever since. Brittany simply danced.

For him, something inside her whispered.

Up there on the stage, dressed in bright red, frilly almost underthings, she didn't care if he knew it. She danced as if there was no one else in the room. She danced as if they had long been lovers, a cheap, trashy girl like her and a man who could have had a throne. She danced as if this whole cavernous club was a king's harem, and she had no goal in all the world but to please him.

Because he wasn't the only one who was good at what he did.

The truth was, the only thing in her life Brittany had ever really loved besides her grandmother was dancing. It had gotten lost there, in the brutal reality of her first marriage and the Hollywood fakery of her second. She'd turned it into pole tricks and barely there G-strings and all manner of mugging for the camera to pay her bills. She'd used it to inform the way she moved and breathed and insinuated herself in the path of tabloid reporters and future husbands alike. But deep down inside of her was the sheer love of movement and music and the fusion of the two that, once upon a time, had been her only way out of the grim realities of her life in Mississippi.

Brittany drew on all of that now.

She danced to him, for him. She wound herself around the poles and she strutted across the stage, until she felt as if she was flying. She'd gone completely electric by the

time she skidded to her dramatic finish—sliding across
the stage on her knees with her hands stretched out in front
of her, ending up face-to-face with Cairo as the music
ended.

And it was as if she'd tipped off the side of the world,
straight into that hot caramel gaze of his. Spun sugar and
hot sex.

The crowd made noise all around them. She could hear
the DJ on the microphone as if from a great distance. She
was aware of the stage beneath her knees and the hands
she'd stretched out toward Cairo in some or other form
of supplication—

All feigned, she reminded herself sternly. All part of
her performance, no matter how oddly right and real it
felt to be stretched out before Cairo Santa Domini as if he
was the only man in the whole club. Or perhaps the world.

As if nothing could possibly matter but him.

That should have set off all kinds of alarms inside of
her, especially when she knew exactly what he wanted
from her and, more than that, what he must think of her
in the first place to offer it. That it was what she'd gone to
excessive lengths to make sure everyone already thought
of her didn't seem to matter.

The world didn't hurt her feelings any longer. Yet somehow, Cairo had.

Did you expect protestations of love? he'd asked, his
voice scathingly amused. It had cut her. Deep.

She told herself she didn't know why.

Yet here, now, at the end of a silly dance in a stupid costume that had never affected her one bit before, all Brittany could see was Cairo. Caramel eyes burning bright
and hot and that intoxicating mouth set to something far
too edgy for her peace of mind. She could feel it move
in her, from the breasts that wanted to break free of her

constricting corset, to that low, odd ache in her belly that she tried her hardest to ignore.

"That was perfectly adequate," Cairo said, his voice pitched to slice through the clamor pressing in around them, his mouth set in a little crook.

It went straight through her all over again, little as she wanted to admit it.

Brittany shifted, rolling back so she kneeled upright on the stage above him, no longer at eye level. That felt safer, no matter that her heart clapped wildly against her ribs. She forced herself to gaze down at him coolly. Challenging and wholly unbothered, as he'd accused her of being in Monte Carlo. How she wished it was true, the way it always had been before, with every man she'd ever met in all her life. Except this one.

"Are you slumming, Your Most Graceless?" She raised her brows as she swung her legs around in front of her and then slid from the stage to stand before the chair where, once again, he lounged as if he'd presented himself for a study in aristocratic laziness. "Maybe you don't know the rules this far from the golden embrace of the Champs-Élysées. If you want a private chat, you need to pay for the privilege."

He didn't quite smile. And his eyes seemed to darken the more his mouth curved.

"Let me hasten to assure you I know my way around establishments of ill repute." He tilted his head to one side and that gaze of his went very nearly lethal. She felt it like his hand wrapped tight around her throat, rendering her choker superfluous. Or maybe that was her heart, pounding so hard she thought it might tip her over. He indicated his lap with a jerk of his chin, never shifting his gaze from hers. "Come, Brittany. Show me what you've got. I promise, I can pay."

CHAPTER THREE

HER NAME IN Cairo's decadent mouth, instead of that drawled *Ms. Hollis*, was like a lick against the hottest, sweetest part of her. It jolted through her, lightning need and the same dancing fire, making her melt. Everywhere.

Brittany couldn't seem to jerk her gaze away from his, and even knowing how dangerous that was didn't make it any easier. Her heart was a hammer against every pulse point, slamming into her again and again, but she made herself smile as she shifted position into something more pinup worthy, as was expected of a woman wearing as little as she was.

She told herself it was the game. What the costume demanded.

And so what if she'd never given an audience member the time of day after a performance before? *This is different*, she told herself, with starch. *This is our own little war, him and me, and I'll win it.*

"Was I unclear in Monaco?" she asked him. She was aware that they were attracting all kinds of stares as the music cued up the next act, but she couldn't bring herself to pay attention to that the way she knew she should. She couldn't break away from the tractor beam of his arrogant gaze long enough to read the room and react accordingly, and she didn't want to think about the implications of the situation. "I thought my walking off without a backward glance was a fairly straightforward message."

"I assumed that was a ploy," he replied in that same deceptively mild way of his that really shouldn't tear through her the way it did, making her feel hollow and needy and too many other raw things to name. "I thought I'd come here and speak to you in the language you understand."

"Rather than in Pompous Ass, the language of rich men? Don't worry, I'm fluent."

He didn't answer that directly. Still holding her gaze with his, he reached into the inside pocket of the sleek coat he wore and pulled out a leather billfold fat with euros. Very, very fat. He didn't so much as glance at it, he simply peeled a purple note from inside and slapped it on the table. Then another. And another.

"You appear to be suggesting I'm motivated by five-hundred euro notes," Brittany said. Through her teeth. "Surely not."

Cairo didn't say a word. He merely added another note to the pile. Then another. One after the next.

"I'm sure I'm mistaken," she bit out, as the pile continued to grow. "You can't possibly be calling me a prostitute, can you?"

He didn't quite laugh. Not quite.

"Of course not," he replied, in a scrupulously innocent voice that made the lie of it feel like a slap. "Your prices are much higher and you require legal vows, if your matrimonial history is any guide. Hardly a rendezvous in a back alley, is it?"

"True," Brittany replied, her voice a different sort of slap that her palms itched to replicate against that dark-shadowed jaw of his. "But I have no intention or interest in making vows of any kind with you."

That sharp smile of his edged over into something feral.

"So you say." He threw another few bills onto the table-top, carelessly and insultingly. Deliberately so, she imagined. "Then a lap dance it is."

Brittany jerked her attention away from him for a moment to see the club owner over by the bar, furiously gesturing for her to sit down. To stop blocking access to the stage, she realized, now that the next act had started. And it was simple, of course. She should merely walk away from Cairo again the way she'd done once already. She should pretend she'd never met him. She wanted nothing more than to do exactly that.

So she had no idea why instead, she settled herself on the arm of his chair and gazed down into his face as if she really was the hardened stripper she'd played on TV instead of the innocent sometimes even she forgot she really was.

"I don't give lap dances," she told him loftily, pretending she hadn't surrendered something critical in sitting down like this. As if that blaze in his caramel gaze didn't show sheer male victory and something edgier besides. As if she didn't recognize she'd lost what little ground she'd gained by denying him in Monaco. "Though I'm happy to take your money, of course. You appear to have far too much of it."

Cairo shrugged as if it was nothing to him, the thousands of euros in a purple pile on the table. What were mere thousands to a man who had untold billions in property alone?

"All I want is a dance," he told her, and he was so much closer now than he had been in Monaco. Too close.

The arms of the seats were made deliberately wide and comfortable, all the better for the girls to perch upon, so she wasn't touching him—because Brittany didn't do *touching*. Especially not with men. And she told herself she didn't recognize that craving in her for what it was, elemental and obvious, so close to that magnificent body of his as he lounged there that she could feel the heat he generated in the space between them.

Then he made everything that much more mad and wild when he reached over and started to trace a lazy little pattern against the skin of the thigh nearest him, right at the top of her stocking and below the ruffled red-and-black underwear she wore.

Back and forth. Back and forth.

She wanted to leap up. She wanted to slap his hand away. She wanted to slap *him* like the offended virgin she actually was, but she didn't dare give herself away like that. And the more she sat there and let Cairo touch her, the more she seemed to forget why allowing this to happen was such a terrible idea.

They both watched his idle finger for a while. Maybe entire years—decades—while inside, everything Brittany had ever been and everything she knew about herself crumbled into dust and shivered away until there was nothing left of her but that pulsing heat between her legs.

Her worst fear come true.

But she still didn't move.

"Or perhaps you prefer a private room after all," Cairo said, the low rumble of his insinuating voice adding to the spell he cast with that impossibly elegant finger against her thigh rather than breaking it. "Is this how you upsell the punters, Ms. Hollis?"

Brittany jerked her attention away from that mesmerizing, addictive pattern he kept drawing against her flesh, and told herself it was the insult of what he'd said—not that he'd reverted back to *Ms. Hollis*. But his gaze was worse than his touch. Too bright, too hot.

And the last thing in the world she wanted was to be locked away in some private room with this man. She knew she couldn't trust him, of course. He'd made the fact he couldn't be trusted something that practically required a celebration. But she was suddenly so much more afraid she couldn't trust herself.

"I think not," she managed to say, but she didn't sound like herself. She sounded as thrown as she felt.

Something flashed over his famous, beautiful face. She felt it echo inside of her like a roll of thunder and then, suddenly, he wasn't lounging there idly any longer. She hardly saw him move. All she knew was that one moment she sat there on the arm of his chair, barely clinging to the pretense of some civility and everything she'd ever known about herself, and the next she was sprawled across his lap.

She wanted to scream. To fight. She wanted that more than anything—so she had no idea why she simply melted against him, as if she'd lost all control of the body that had done her bidding the whole of her life.

She had never been tempted, by anyone. She had never *melted*, ever.

Cairo was hard beneath her, hot and perfect, his legs so strong they marked his studied laziness as yet another lie. His arms closed around her, holding her against his sculpted chest and she couldn't seem to *breathe*. She couldn't breathe and she couldn't speak and she had no idea why she was letting any of this happen.

Especially when he bent and brought his face so close to hers.

So. Damned. Close.

"You'd better brace yourself," she managed to tell him, though she sounded far more thrown by this than she would have liked. And still it was nowhere near as thrown as she *felt*. "The security guards take a dim view of unauthorized touching in the main room."

"When will you learn that the rules do not apply to me?" Cairo's mouth was a breath away from hers, and the thick, glossy fall of his shaggy hair brushed her cheek as he bent over her, his dark eyes gleaming. "And that sooner or later, all mere mortals do exactly as I ask?"

"I'm not giving you a lap dance," she told him, though

her heart was drumming at her again, so hard she was glad she wore that lace choker so there was no chance he could see it there in the hollow of her throat. "And I'm not marrying you, either. I don't even like you."

"What the hell does that have to do with anything?" Cairo muttered, sounding less like a king and more like a man than she'd heard him yet. "This has nothing to do with *like*."

And then he yanked her mouth to his.

He never should have tasted her.

It was a terrible mistake in a night brimming with too many of them already. He should not have come to this crass place in a temper. He should not have indulged in that temper in the first place, for that matter. He should have laughed at the absurdity of a woman of so little breeding declining his offer to better herself so spectacularly and then moved on. Hell, he should have forgotten she existed at all the moment the door of his suite in Monaco had shut behind her.

Instead, he'd brooded over it. Over her.

"The world is full of inappropriate women, Sire," Ricardo had pointed out earlier this evening. "It's one of its few charms."

"It seems I require a particular blend of inappropriate and interesting," Cairo had replied, having spent the days since Monaco convincing himself of precisely that. It wasn't that only Brittany Hollis would do. It wasn't that he was unused to rejection. Both of those things were true. But what mattered more, he'd assured himself, was that his very *requirements* had changed. "If there are more who fit the bill, by all means, present them to me."

But Ricardo had wisely said nothing, and here Cairo was.

And this inarguably terrible mistake he was making

felt like sweet, hot glory and all manner of dark and lovely sins besides. He wanted nothing more than to commit every last one of those sins, with impunity, and with her. Cairo was only a man, after all, and he knew better than most what a terrible one he was, straight through to his core. And Brittany was sprawled across his lap, dressed in a sleek red corset and very little else, tasting of mint and longing.

He shifted, opening his mouth against hers, and he lost himself in the fire of it. The sheer, exultant perfection of the scrape of her tongue against his, the press of her breasts against his chest, the way she clung to his shirt as if she wanted him even a small fraction as much as he wanted her.

Cairo could work with a fraction.

He poured everything he had into the kiss, taking her mouth again and again. Lust and need. All the dark longings that had haunted him since she'd walked away from him in Monaco. All the sweet, hot desire that had flashed through him as he'd watched her performance here tonight.

All the fire in his twisted, haunted soul.

He wasn't surprised when she tore her mouth from his, and his arms tightened around her as if he expected her to twist out of his hold. She didn't—and it was a measure of how out of control he'd become that he counted that as a victory.

"I don't want anything to do with you," she hissed at him.

Cairo couldn't blame her. Neither did he. But that was beside the point.

"Of course not," he agreed, their lips practically touching, his hands full of her sweetness. "I can tell by the way you kiss me."

And then he set his mouth to hers once more.

Because kissing Brittany, he discovered quickly, was fast becoming his favorite vice in a life fairly overflowing with them.

This time when she pulled away, he discovered his hands had found their way to her thick hair in its tempting copper twist, and he'd pulled the fragrant curtain of it down around them. Her lips were sweet and full, her breath came as fast as his did, and her eyes had gone wide and dark.

Cairo thought he might never get enough of her, and it was a measure of how obsessed he was already that the notion failed to alarm him.

"You can't do this," she told him, and he had the strange thought that this was the real Brittany, after all her edge and flair. She sounded a little bit shaken. She looked a little bit fragile. He should have felt a surge of triumph at that, but instead, the thing that turned over inside him felt a good deal more like regret. He knew all about *regret*. "You know you can't."

"I don't think you've been paying attention, *cara*," he told her, and he shifted one hand from her thick, gorgeous hair to drag his thumb over the plump seduction that was her lower lip. He ached to taste her again. He didn't know how he refrained. "I am the last of the Santa Dominis. Some still call me a king. I can do as I wish."

"Not with me, you can't." She jerked her mouth back from his touch and shoved her way to a more vertical sitting position on his lap, and the sweet agony of it all threatened to unman him where he sat. "I want nothing to do with your little game of lost thrones, thank you. My life is complicated enough."

"Marrying me would uncomplicate it."

"Right. Because that's exactly what you are. *Uncomplicated.*"

He could see the moment it occurred to her that despite

the hard tone she'd used, what she'd said might as well be a compliment. Little did she know. He could teach darkness to the night, and that was on his good days.

"I want to be inside you," he told her then, raw and untutored, as if he was a stranger to himself. He felt her shiver, as if the electric charge of it had seared straight through her. "So deep inside you, *cara*, that neither one of us can tell who is a king and who is a stripper. Until there is nothing in all the world but that sweet, wet heat and what burns us both as we drown in it."

He was close enough that he could see the way her pupils dilated at that, so close he could feel the goose bumps beneath his hand as easily as he could see them rise up all over her exposed skin. So close he could feel all that intense heat as it burned through her, like a wild flame incinerating them both.

"I can tell who is who, though," she said, and Cairo was certain he wasn't mistaking the sheer misery he could hear in her voice, as if this was as hard and mystifying a thing for her as it was for him. That was something. He told himself that had to be something. "Just as the tabloids certainly can. And I doubt that would ever change."

"Why would you wish it to change?" He hardly sounded like himself. Or maybe he'd forgotten what it was like to be so honest, about anything. His whole life was a collection of misdirection and straight-out lies, wrapped tight around the blackened, shriveled heart of a man who should have died years ago. "You've crafted your public persona with exquisite precision. Why not take it to its logical end?"

"I know exactly where my public persona is taking me," she gritted out at him. She shifted in his lap, brushing up against the part of him that yearned for her the most, and they both froze. She swallowed, her eyes dark on his, and he had the most absurd notion that she looked *panicked* for a moment. "And it's not to your bed."

"That is why you melt against me, I am sure. Why you cannot look away."

"I'm trapped in your lap. *You* are trapping me."

"We're in a public place," he continued, and though his palms itched to move over her, to learn her in the best and most tactile way possible and prove his point besides, Cairo didn't do it. He let his voice cast that spell instead. "How many people do you think are watching us instead of the stage?"

"All of them." He didn't imagine the sheen of something harder in her gaze then, or the way she tilted her chin up. "You saw to that."

"And yet, were I to slip my fingers just a little bit higher, what would I find?" He moved the hand on her thigh a scant centimeter higher, letting his fingers toy with the satin edge of her underwear. Her breath came in a rush even as she shivered out the truth again. "How wet are you, Brittany? Right here in a strip club where everyone can see you? Would you even protest if I slid my hand beneath those silly red underthings? Or would you lean in closer so no one could be sure and ride my hand instead?"

"Neither." But her voice was soft then. Too soft. As soft as he imagined she was only a fraction of an inch from the place his hand lingered. "I'm going to stand up and get back to work."

"Work?" Cairo laughed and moved his fingers again, and the flush on her delicate cheekbones told him she felt that precisely where he wanted her to feel it. So did he. "This place is an ill-mannered salute to your late husband's family, not your work. We both know what your true calling is."

Her lips pressed together and that melting heat in her dark hazel eyes faded. "If you mean that I'm a whore, you'll have to come up with a better insult. My mother's used the word so many times I've come to consider it an endearment."

"Then marry me," he heard himself say, quite as if it was a real proposal and he was truly as raw and ruined and *desperate* as he felt inside just then. As if there was any real thing inside him at all, when he knew better. But no matter that he told himself he was playing a role, he couldn't seem to stop this electric collision course he found himself on. Worse, he didn't want to stop it. "And we shall see what words your mother uses to address my queen."

"Evidence has never persuaded my mother away from the things she's decided are true," Brittany said, and what was remarkable, Cairo thought, was how she didn't sound bitter at all just then. Only matter-of-fact. It made that same temper he couldn't afford to indulge flare inside him all over again. "But thank you. I'm sure a season as queen to the King of Wishful Thinking would be a delight. But my dance card is full." She nodded at the stage before them. "Literally."

And this time, Cairo felt a kind of hitch in his chest when she pulled away from him. He let her stand, and watched her as she stood there before him, making no attempt to hide the evidence of his need. Her cheeks burned, her eyes gleamed dark, that marvelous copper hair of hers tumbled all around her in unruly waves, and Cairo understood that role or no, he would never, ever rest until he had her.

In his bed, to start.

But no other queen would do. He ignored the part of him that questioned that—the part that reminded him he was a king without a throne and in need of any unacceptable woman to make sure he stayed without it—and indulged the part of him that had the blood of five hundred years of Santa Dominis pounding in his blood. Five hundred years of autocratic rulers who knew what they wanted and took what they wished, and brooked precious little disagreement as they did it.

He might have lost his kingdom. He might never set foot in the palace his family had built from a primitive fortress into a splendid fairy tale ever again. But he was still who he was, who he'd been bred to be, and no matter the darkness he knew he carried inside of him—or else how could he make himself such a believable disgrace?—none of that mattered in the end. He was still Cairo Santa Domini.

"You can't have me," she told him, as if she could read his mind. As if she could see the truth of him, stamped in his bones, deep in his veins, all the kings and queens who'd gone before him.

"Silly girl," he drawled, and made no attempt to sit up straighter from his lazy position. Or to rein in the desire he was certain she could see stamped all over him, from his face to his sex. "Don't you know that only makes me want you more?"

"You'll have to learn to live with the disappointment somehow," she said dismissively, and Cairo only smiled.

"That," he murmured, like the threat it was, "is one thing you can depend upon me never, ever to do."

Brittany woke late the following morning in her little flat, four narrow flights up in a weathered old building on the outskirts of Montmartre. It was laughably tiny, although if she stood on a chair in her small kitchen there was enough of a view of the Parisian rooftops and the smallest bit of the famous Basilica of Sacré-Cœur that she could forget her worries a while as she craned her head to see a sliver of its pale white dome.

She did not think about what had happened the night before. She did not think about the dreams that had haunted her through the night, waking her again and again until she finally fell into something dreamless and exhausted near dawn.

She didn't think about any of it and yet she could still feel Cairo's touch. She could still taste him on her lips.

Her body was still in that insane tumult over him, from her breasts that felt swollen to twice their size, to the shivery hot knot low in her belly that clenched and clenched and clenched. Her body, which was supposed to be entirely hers. Her body, which she'd kept a pristine little fortress ever since her first wedding night, when she'd hidden from the whiny boyfriend turned drunken lout and had decided, there and then, that she'd rather die untouched and alone than let anyone else touch her against her will.

She'd never imagined that her body and her mind could disagree about what *her will* was.

Brittany took a very long shower to wash the night away. Then she went on her daily run at her gym, moving much faster than usual today through her usual miles, but the dreams and the memories stuck with her no matter how quick her pace.

It was never a good sign when the treadmill felt more like a metaphor than simple exercise.

Brittany was already in a dark, uneasy mood when she made it back to her flat. It did not improve when she picked up the private mobile phone she'd left plugged in on her bedside table to see her mother had called at least three times.

She was scowling at the screen as she scrolled through the logged calls, no messages, when it lit up with a fourth call from her mother.

Something cold snaked down Brittany's spine. The last time her mother had called repeatedly like this, Brittany's former stepchildren—all old enough to be her parents, a fact that perhaps only she and Jean Pierre had found amusing—had taken to the tabloids to sound the trumpets about how shoddily they'd treated her and how they had "expunged that harlot" from the family home at last.

Brittany's mother had not called to commiserate about yet another tour through the slag heaps of the tabloids. She'd called, as ever, to complain that her daughter's disgraceful behavior was humiliating the whole of the Hollis clan back in Gulfport and *had Brittany no shame?*

"Do you want me to have shame, Mom?" Brittany had asked coolly. Someday, she'd vowed for the nine millionth time, she would stop answering her mother's calls altogether. Someday when she'd finally come to terms with the fact that the woman was never, ever going to treat her as anything more than a source of income. Much less love her. *Someday.* "Or do you want me to keep paying your rent?"

Today was not *someday*, regrettably, but Brittany tossed the mobile aside without answering, letting her mother go to voice mail. She powered up her laptop instead.

She didn't even have to Google herself, as she sometimes did. Oh, no. The headlines were right there on her launch page.

His Royal Stripper?
How Low Can Cairo Go?
Black Widow Brittany Trades Up!

Her heart was already causing a commotion in her chest as she clicked on the first article, as if she already knew what she'd see—

But it was worse.

Someone had taken a series of pictures in the club last night. And the pictures made the whole thing look much more sordid than Brittany remembered it. Much hotter.

Much more desperate and *much* more public. If she hadn't known better, Brittany might have assumed that Cairo actually had bought her for the evening. The papers certainly insinuated he had.

He might as well have, she thought now. It came to the same thing, and if she'd let him, she'd have a paycheck to comfort herself this morning. Meanwhile, that scraped-raw, heavy feeling in her chest wasn't going to help a soul. It was better to ignore it. Starting with the little sound she didn't mean to let out as she sat there gaping at those awful pictures that told her far too many hard truths about herself and her own longings. She lifted up a hand to try to rub that harsh, hollow feeling out of her own chest.

It didn't really work.

She felt betrayed. By herself, not by the devastatingly handsome man whose entire life was a monument to wreck and ruin. She should have seen this coming. She should have known there was no way *Cairo Santa Domini* could turn up in her life *without* leaving his dark mark all over her.

This was what he did. Exactly this.

She should have assumed not only that someone would have photographed the whole of their encounter, but also that, of course, they'd sell it to the voracious tabloids. In point of fact, it was likely Cairo had engineered the whole thing and the photographer in question was on his payroll. Why hadn't she thought of that last night? *Of course* he'd play this up to the paparazzi. *This was what he did.*

She should have been prepared for this—why wasn't she?

But she knew why. Brittany hadn't been thinking after that kiss, which looked even more carnal and impossibly sexy in the pictures than she remembered it. And her memories were explicit. She hadn't been thinking when she'd staggered away from him and hid backstage, where none of the other girls talked to her and she could pretend she was utterly at peace as she changed back into her street clothes. She hadn't been thinking when she'd opted to walk home despite the hour and the questionable neighborhood, hoping the exercise and the night air might clear her head.

He'd kissed her. She'd kissed him. It had been the most sensual experience of her life, and she hated herself for that. She hated that she'd responded to him like that.

That kiss had been the only thought in her head.

The truth was, she hadn't been doing a whole lot of actual thinking since she'd walked into that casino in Monaco.

The fact that Cairo was certain to destroy her had loomed so large inside of her from her first glimpse of him that even now, it was making it hard for her to breathe. It was clouding her judgment, confusing her, making her *react* to him rather than act in her own best interests the way she always had before.

The way she'd been doing all her life, or she'd never have made it this far.

"Pull yourself together, Brittany," she ordered herself, her own voice loud in the quiet of her little studio, her own face much too big and exposed on the laptop screen before her, looking vulnerable and needy and entirely too aroused.

It horrified her to see that expression. Or it thrilled her, because she could still *feel* that kiss.

Or maybe she couldn't tell the difference. "This is an opportunity. Since when do you turn down an opportunity?"

Destruction wasn't a good enough excuse to avoid something. If it was, she'd never have left Gulfport at sixteen in the company of Darryl, whom she'd known perfectly well was nothing but trouble.

The kind of destruction Cairo was likely to cause, she understood in the wake of his kiss in a way she hadn't before, was purely internal. He wouldn't take a swing at her the way Darryl had. He might rip out her heart with his royal hands. He might tear it into pieces, mash it into a pulp beneath his feet. She didn't understand why a man she should find laughable in any real sense instead posed such a risk for her neglected little heart, but there it was. She didn't know why. She only knew it was an inescapable truth. She'd known it the moment she'd laid eyes on him.

"But so what?" she asked herself now, digging the heel of one palm into her chest as if that could make the feeling of immensity and inevitability go away.

Because other than the small issue of her inevitable ruin, Cairo Santa Domini was perfect for her purposes. More than perfect. He was *Cairo Santa Domini*—he was a dream come true. Richer than sin, possessed of more blue blood in the tip of one toe than her entire family tree put together and not in the least put off by her sad, tacky and deeply checkered past. Most of the wealthy European men Brittany had met after marrying Jean Pierre, including his own sons, had indicated that they would be happy to sully themselves with her in private of an afternoon, but would never allow anyone to see them in her gauche presence in public, lest their ancient claims to aristocracy collapse into so much deeply inferior dust.

Cairo was quite the opposite.

And if she still felt that strange pang at the fact he wanted her *because* of the image she'd crafted instead of despite it, to say nothing of her low-class upbringing, well…of course he did. Why else would a man like him notice a woman like her? That silly *pang* was between her and the heart he was going to break without even trying very hard, and the truth was, she could as easily live on her far-off island with a shattered heart as without it.

The point was the palm trees and the fruity drinks and the solitude. Who cared what happened to her heart?

So when her other mobile phone rang—the one she kept for paparazzi, tabloids and whoever else wanted to reach her yet didn't know her personally—she answered it.

"Please hold for His Serene Grace the Archduke Felipe Skander Cairo of Santa Domini," the cultured voice on the other end of the line intoned.

Brittany didn't hang up, despite that spike in her pulse. Because her own internal destruction was a small price to pay. Cairo Santa Domini might be as dangerous as he seemed. After last night, she knew he was.

But he was her only escape. He was the light at the end of the tunnel as much as he was also the train.

She had no choice.

"Darling," she purred when he came on the line, that voice of his dark and sinful and good enough to eat. God, she was in so much trouble. But she told herself it would all be worth it. One day, all of this would be worth it. Vanuatu waited for her across the planet, white sand beaches, peace and anonymity at last. "I saw our engagement announcement in all the tabloids. You shouldn't have."

CHAPTER FOUR

CAIRO APPEARED IN so many tabloids with so many women that even when the woman in question was notorious in her own right, like Brittany, it could only cause so much comment. There was the initial carrying on and then it was on to the next set of celebrity shenanigans. Football players were forever embroiling themselves in bitter custody disputes with B-list actresses, politicians were ever hypocritical and blustery in turn and the papers never lacked for seedy stories to tell in their breathless, insinuating headlines.

"We appear to be less interesting than the custody tussles of a striker for Real Madrid," Brittany said brightly when they met after the initial frenzy started to fade that first week, to plot out their next few moves. That sweet smile she could produce on cue did absolutely nothing to soften the edge in her voice—which was a good thing, Cairo thought, since he was a perverse creature who liked the edge better. "The entire world has been overexposed to Cairo Santa Domini scandals. A few pictures in a strip club are too run-of-the-mill to captivate the public interest after a steady diet of far worse. I'm afraid your shenanigans are good for a shudder, nothing more."

"It's usually more than a shudder," Cairo assured her, because he couldn't seem to help himself. "It's really more of a drawn-out scream, with many a religious conversion along the way. Oh, God. Oh, Cairo. *Oh, God.*"

Brittany sighed as if he was a deep and enduring trial to her. A sound Cairo was certain no woman—no *person*—had made in his presence in all his life, except himself.

"I'll keep that in mind," she said, as if placating a child having a tantrum.

"You do that," he murmured, and then they discussed how best to prepare for the second phase of their plan.

Cairo very rarely appeared with any woman more than once. It was difficult to maintain a reputation as an inveterate playboy if he seemed interested in quality rather than quantity, so he'd never tied himself down to anyone for more than a long weekend. Sometimes he'd throw in a repeated date or weekend years later, just to keep people guessing, but that didn't happen very often.

"I become rather boring after three consecutive days," he'd once told a smarmy journalist in Rome when questioned about this pattern of his, flashing a knowing smile as if he could already read the fan letters his secretary would be forced to wade through, each declaring him anything but *boring*. Some complete with enclosed panties, as punctuation. "It is less a pattern and more of a public service, you understand."

The second time the paparazzi "caught" him and Brittany in the sort of restaurant famous people would only patronize if they were trying to avoid being seen, five days after that night in the strip club, it caused a buzz. It suggested that an actual relationship of some kind had survived both what was called *Cairo's Scandalous Lap Dance* and the resultant tabloid screeching over the photos of the two of them kissing.

"Had I known this would cause such a commotion," Brittany told the pack of cameramen who surrounded her when she emerged from an expertly timed trip to Cartier, flashing her megawatt gold digger's smile and a sizeable cocktail ring on her right hand featuring a deep blue sapphire the approximate size of the Mediterranean Sea, "I would have asked for something a whole lot bigger."

Then, days after that dinner, they were seen exiting Cairo's private residence in the unfashionable morning light, suggesting they'd spent the night there. Or perhaps several days *and* nights, now that Brittany had finished her run at the strip club.

"Are you *dating*?" a clearly appalled television tabloid reporter asked Cairo as he made his way through the heaving mass of paparazzi outside a charity event in London a few days later. "You and the Queen of Tacky?"

"You will be the first to know." He smiled, all teeth and noblesse oblige. "You and all of your viewers are foremost in my thoughts as I navigate my romantic life, I assure you."

"Why isn't she with you tonight?" another reporter demanded. A bit too hotly, Cairo thought, as if these people had personal stakes in Cairo's continuing bachelorhood. He supposed they did. And in that darkness in him he paraded around in so many fine clothes, calling it a man and letting them call him the worthless one he'd always known he was. "Did you already break up?"

"I cannot keep track of this relationship according to all your conflicting headlines," he told them. "On, off. Playboy, gold digger. Maybe she and I are simply two people who enjoy each other's company. But of course, that makes no snide headlines for you, so that will never be printed as a possibility."

Cairo Calls Bad-news Britt a Gold Digger, screamed the papers the following day, right on cue.

After that, Cairo squired Brittany to the lavish wedding of an old boarding school friend of his, currently one of the richest men in Spain. The speculation about what they meant to each other surged into what could only be called a dull roar.

Had Cairo ever attended a wedding with a date before, therefore keeping him from finding several dates there? Answer: no. Did a man who was only after a bit of fun take that fun to a very old friend's wedding in the first place? Answer: of course not, as there was nothing fun about a date with high expectations that a man was only going to dash cruelly. The papers were agog. Could Cairo Santa Domini possibly be getting serious about the most unsuitable woman in the world—even after she'd finished her stint in that horrible Parisian club?

Answers on that last varied, especially after "a wedding guest" released a photo of Cairo and Brittany in their wedding finery, clinging to each other on the dance floor in what was called "the would-be king at his most tender and affectionate—friends claim they've never seen playboy Cairo lose his head like this before!"

"I had no idea you could dance so well with your clothes on," he'd murmured to her as they'd swayed to the wedding band.

"How many of the bridesmaids here have experienced what *you* do so well without your clothes?" she'd replied, not missing a step as she smiled up at him, and he was certain only he could see how razor-sharp that smile was.

After that, they took it to a new level and introduced a series of romantic holidays.

First a weekend in Dubai. Then a week in sun-drenched Rio, and an endless series of photographs of the happy couple on the famous beaches in very, very little. "The better," one online gossip magazine asserted dryly beneath a photo of Brittany in a tiny bikini, "to remind you why Brittany Hollis is dating your husband Cairo Santa Domini and you aren't." Then, after a low-key week or so in Paris, they embarked on an elaborate fortnight in Sub-Saharan Africa, from the sweeping deserts of Namibia to the glory of Victoria Falls to an elegant, fully catered safari in Botswana.

All photographed extensively and then carefully curated to look like a sweepingly luxurious trip so epic it redefined romance. A love letter to all the world, from two of the least likely people to fall in love around. A masterpiece.

If Cairo said so himself.

"Oh, please," Brittany replied when he actually did say it, sitting on one of the camp chairs in the spacious tent they shared, piled high with rugs and linens and tables laden with succulent foods, that had been set up for them a stone's throw from the nearby river bristling with hippos and crocodiles. She was reading yet another book on her e-reader while he tracked their headlines on his mobile, and they were the only ones in the entire world who knew that they slept on opposite sides of that tent the same way they'd slept in different parts of all the hotel suites he'd booked. Night after torturous night, not that it was driving him mad. "*Romance* is not the word being used when people discuss us. I think you know that."

He did know it. What he didn't know, out there in the deep Botswanan night so thick with stars, was why he wanted to change the conversation. Or why some part of him hated it every time another tabloid skewered her. When that, of course, had been the whole point from the start.

Has Brittany Stripped Her Way into Cairo's Heart? howled one New York gossip rag.

Will Cairo Be Lucky Number Four for Much-wed Brittany? asked a British paper, pretending to be slightly less salacious.

Another British paper was far less circumspect: *Brittany's Big-game Hunt in Botswana—Will She Nab Herself a Crown?*

And more starkly by far, in the most popular Santa Domini paper over a picture of the two of them gazing adoringly at each other: *Queen Brittany?*

He should have been pleased, Cairo told himself. Everything was going according to plan. He should have been *exultant*.

But he didn't sleep much on that holiday, and he told himself it had nothing to do with the fact she was in that tent with him, yet a world away. He told himself it was for the best, and he should *exult* in the fact this woman seemed so immune to him.

Exult, he told himself as they smiled and laughed and pretended so well the whole world gasped and carried on over every new photograph.

Exult, he ordered himself when they were in private and she held herself so far away, all cool smiles and distance and her face forever in a book.

He shouldn't find her a mystery and he shouldn't want so badly to solve that mystery that he was up half the night. If this was exulting, Cairo thought as the safari wrapped up and they returned to their regularly scheduled lives in Europe, he was going to require a whole lot more caffeine to survive all the nights he spent asking himself if she really was the only woman he'd ever met who saw only the darkness in him.

That and why, if she was, he was masochistic enough to find that attractive.

"I'm getting the sense that the world is not so much rejoicing in our relationship or even avidly watching it unfold so much as they're craning their necks at us, the way people do at a terrible accident," Brittany said as they flew back to Paris from an exceptionally glorious charity ball in Vienna one night.

She set aside the paper she'd been reading and eyed Cairo as he lounged on the sofa across from her in his preferred position: lying flat on the white leather sectional with his feet propped up on the far arm, his dark suit in disheveled disarray all around him because the more rumpled he looked, the more the papers speculated about his sexual prowess and giddily imagined he performed sex acts behind every potted plant in Europe.

Who was he to deny his public?

He waved a negligent hand and let the ice cubes rattle around in the drink he held. The more noise the ice cubes made, he'd discovered long ago, the drunker people assumed he was. And it was astonishing, the things people said and did when they assumed another person was too drunk to remember, respond or protest.

Cairo wondered if he'd ever simply live through a moment, without mounting any kind of performance to survive it. Or if he even knew how to do that, when there was nothing in him but lies atop lies.

Then he wondered why, when it had been this way since he was a young man, he found the realities of his life and all its necessary untruths so terribly constricting now.

"We are a delicious accident, *cara*," he told her, and experimented with a faint, fake slurring of his words. "That's the whole point."

"My mistake," Brittany replied. "I was starting to think the point was you cavorting about the globe so you could better rub your wealth and careless lifestyle in the face of every last person alive."

"That is a mere side benefit. One I greatly enjoy."

Cairo swung around to sit up, raking his hair back from his forehead as he did. He put his drink down on the coffee table in the expansive jet cabin that better resembled a hotel suite, and he told himself there was no reason in the world for this *gnawing* thing inside him.

She'd agreed to everything after that night in the strip club. After that kiss he'd been torturing himself with ever since, as if it had been his first. She'd come to his residence in the car he'd sent for her in the middle of the night that week, to keep the meeting a secret. All the hints he'd seen of some kind of vulnerability in the strip club had been gone by then. Long gone, leaving her as smooth as glass. She'd merely discussed their strategy with him, offered her own thoughts and ideas and then signed all the papers. No theatrics. No hint of any emotion at all, as if everything between them was strictly business.

Brittany had insisted that was how it should remain.

"You must be joking," Cairo had protested after she'd dropped that little bomb. It had been well into the wee hours that night in Paris, and she'd sat there across from him in one of his ecstatically baroque salons as if she'd been carved from stone.

"I rarely joke at all," she'd replied, deadpan. "And never about sex."

"But sex is one of the great joys of life. Surely you must know this."

"No wonder you are widely held to be such a bright beacon of happiness. Oh, wait. Laziness is more your style, isn't it, Your Indolent Majesty?"

He hadn't known quite what to make of such a strange, stilted conversation about sex with a woman whose taste was still tearing him apart. A woman who, even then, had that same high color on her cheeks that told him she wanted him as badly as he wanted her, no matter what cold, repressive things she said to deny it.

"I know you want me," Cairo had said, baldly. As if he'd never finessed a situation in his life. As if he didn't know how. As if he couldn't help himself or keep himself from being more alarmingly honest with this woman than he was with anyone else alive. "Do you imagine you're hiding it?"

"I don't care who you sleep with, of course," Brittany

had continued as if he hadn't said a word. She'd waved a negligent hand in the air, but he'd seen the way her eyes glittered. He'd been certain that meant something. Or he'd wanted, desperately, for that to mean something. "I only ask that you keep it discreet, so as not to distract from what we're trying to accomplish, and that you make certain to keep it far away from me. That's only courteous."

"No threesomes, then?" he'd asked. Drawled, really. Entirely to watch her reaction—but she'd given him nothing but that glass exterior of hers, smooth and clear.

"You can have all the threesomes you like." Her brows had arched and he'd felt skewered on that hard gaze of hers. "Unless, of course, a man of your appetites finds that number restrictive. Believe me when I tell you I couldn't care less where you put your, ah, royal scepter. As long as it isn't anywhere near me."

"That's hurtful." He cocked his head to one side as he considered her. "My scepter is considered the toast of Europe, if not the entire world."

A faint gleam in her dark eyes then. "I doubt that."

"Naturally, the savage, rutting creature you seem to think I am will only view your denial of what we both feel as a great challenge."

"I don't feel anything." Her voice then had been crisp, her gaze clear, but he still hadn't believed her. Wishful thinking or the truth? How could he still not know? "Am I attracted to you? Of course. You're a remarkably handsome man. I can't imagine any woman alive wouldn't react to you, especially when you decide to turn all of that smoldering on her to get your way."

"Is that what I did? I thought I kissed you and you kissed me back and we very nearly broke a few decency laws right there in that strip club. It wouldn't have bothered me if we had. I have an unofficial diplomatic immunity. You, of course, might not enjoy a stint in a French prison."

"I don't find it necessary to act on every attraction I might feel," Brittany had said, again as if he hadn't spoken. He hadn't been able to think of any other person alive who'd ever treated him as if he was annoying. What was the matter with him that he found that as intriguing as anything else she did? How much must he hate himself? But, of course, he'd already known the answer to that. And she'd still been speaking, still fixing him with that stern glare of hers that he'd doubted she knew made him almost painfully hard. "And I feel certain that as time goes on, the attraction will fade anyway."

"I'm told that never happens. Such is my charm." Cairo had smiled when she'd shaken her head at that. "I'm only reporting what others have said."

"How would they know?" she'd retorted, settling back in her chair as if its stuffy, hard back was comfortable so long after 2:00 a.m. "You never spend more than a weekend with anyone. I'm signing up for far more exposure to your…"

"My scepter?" he supplied.

Her smile in return had been that sharp, edgy thing he found far too fascinating. "Your charm. Such as it is."

"I think you're kidding yourself," he'd said softly then, because he couldn't seem to maintain his game with this woman. "Sex is inevitable."

"I'm sure you believe that," she'd replied, her tone crisp, as if she didn't care either way, and he'd found that needled him far more than if she'd seemed horrified. "And I told you I don't care who you have it with, so I certainly don't need to hear about it." Then she'd shrugged as if she'd never encountered a topic more tedious in all her life. "Have at, with my blessing."

Except the most curious thing had happened since that conversation. Cairo had discovered that he hadn't had the slightest urge to touch any woman but her. He told himself it was because she'd proven herself to be such an excellent partner. A perfect costar in this little bit of theater they were performing for the masses and for their own complementary ends.

He told himself a lot of things. But the only woman he saw was her.

"Why would you do this?" she'd asked him that first night when Ricardo had ushered her into the elegant salon that had stood more or less unchanged for centuries. "What can you possibly hope to gain?"

He'd only shrugged. "I need an infliction, as you said, for any number of shallow reasons. Why are you doing it?"

She'd sniffed. "I want to retire to Vanuatu and live on the beach, where no one can take a single photograph of me, ever."

Cairo didn't think they'd believed each other, but there it was. And here they were now, weeks into this thing. She dressed perfectly, reacted perfectly, gazed at him with the perfect mix of adoration and mystery whenever there was a camera near. She was tailor-made for her role.

That had to be why he'd lost his drive for his favorite vices, women and whiskey, in no particular order. He was too busy taking in the show.

"Why are you staring at me like that?" she asked now. She'd changed from her stunning ball gown the moment they'd boarded the plane, almost as if she couldn't bear to be in all that couture a moment longer. She did it every time. The moment she could be certain no cameras would follow her, she threw off all the trappings of her larger-than-life presence and left nothing behind but a real, live woman.

Cairo was fascinated. He found he liked her in what he considered her backstage uniform. Low-slung, high-end athletic pants that clung to every lithe curve and long-sleeved T-shirts made of the light, remarkably soft cotton she preferred. Usually, like tonight, she also wore an oversized cashmere scarf she would wrap several times around her neck. He liked it. He liked her gleaming copper hair piled high on the top of her head, so he could see her delicate ears and the line of her neck and that sweet, soft nape he had every intention of getting his mouth on, one of these days.

"Forgive me," he said when moments dragged by and he was still staring. "It occurred to me that you're the only woman I've ever seen in casual clothes." He smiled, and had no idea why it seemed to come less easily than usual. "My lifestyle has never really leant itself to such intimacies."

Brittany blinked. Then again. Her expression shifted from that bulletproof cool he despised and admired in turn to something else. Something that made that gnawing thing in him dig deeper and start to actually hurt.

"You work so hard to pretend otherwise," she said after a moment that dragged on far too long and made his chest hurt. "But beneath all the smoke and mirrors, beneath the Cairo Santa Domini spectacle, you're a completely different man. Aren't you?"

Cairo didn't like that at all. He'd worked too hard for too long to make certain no one ever bothered to take him at anything but face value, because he knew exactly how black and cold it was beneath. Why was this woman the only person on earth who never seemed to do that?

"There is no 'beneath the spectacle.'" His voice was too grim. Too gritty. Too damned revealing. "There is only spectacle. The spectacle is how I survive, Brittany. Believe that, if nothing else."

It was possibly the most honest thing he'd ever said to her. Or to anyone.

"Sometimes I think you're a monster," she told him. "I think you want me to think it. And then other times…"

Her voice softened, and everything inside him ran hot and wild, terror and need. "I think you're possibly the loneliest man I've ever met."

His heart kicked at him. Cairo wanted to kick back. At her, and this situation, at his whole wasted, twisted life.

"I don't know an orphan or refugee who is ever anything else," he said quietly. He knew he shouldn't have said it. He should have made a joke, laughed it off. Said something appalling or shallow, as expected. But he couldn't seem to look away from her. He couldn't seem to breathe. He didn't understand what was happening to him or why he couldn't stop it. There was nothing in all the world but her lovely face and that searing gleam of recognition in her dark hazel eyes, and the words coming out of his mouth, filled with a truth he knew he shouldn't tell. "I am both. All I have—all I will ever have—is the spectacle."

He slumped back down after that, pretending to lapse off instantly into sleep like the lazy ass he was so good at playing would.

But he felt the weight of her dark gaze on him for a long time after.

"The general is rumored to be in ill health," Ricardo told him some days later. "It has been widely suggested that this ill-conceived fling of yours at a time the kingdom might actually need you may finally have put you beyond the pale, even in the eyes of your most die-hard supporters."

Cairo did not look up from his laptop, where he was managing his investment portfolio with a shrewdness he knew most would not believe he possessed, but then, he had worked hard to live down to any and all expectations. He sat at the gleaming, polished table in his Parisian residence that had welcomed all manner of European royalty in its time. It, like everything else in this house he'd inherited from his late family and got to rule over like the high king of ghosts, was a monument to nostalgia.

He included himself in that tally.

"I would have thought that I was so many shades lighter than pale that I'd gone entirely translucent before my eighteenth birthday," he said, more to the screen than to Ricardo. "That was certainly the goal." He sat back then and eyed the closest thing he had in the world to a friend, this man who had been at his side since before his family had died and who would support him to the bitter end. "What will it take? A murder conviction?"

"The loyalists would only claim you'd been framed, Sire. And then you'd simply be in prison, a situation that I doubt would suit you."

Cairo did not state the obvious: that he was already in prison. That he had been born into one sort of prison and then, after the revolution that had sent his family into exile, thrust into an entirely different one. And that the way he'd lived since he'd survived his adolescence was yet another jail cell, all things considered, no matter how elegantly appointed.

No one had any sympathy for a man like Cairo Santa Domini. Cairo, least of all. He knew he deserved it.

"You are correct," he said instead. "A life sentence would not suit me at all."

Ricardo smiled slightly, as if he knew exactly what Cairo hadn't said. "The scandal sheets are having a field day and there appear to be more than the usual number of appalled citizens registering their dismay at your antics, but I'm afraid the rumblings from the most deluded of your followers grow ever louder. It's as if they think they must act before you commit an unthinkable crime."

"Not an actual murder, I assume. A marriage." Ricardo nodded and Cairo rubbed a hand over his face. "But the general is unwell?"

His murderous heart, one of the many reasons he would never be a good man, wanted that evil man dead, as painfully as possible. It would be a good start.

"The palace is trying to keep it quiet, but my sources tell me it is serious," Ricardo said quietly. He aimed a swift, dark look from Cairo. "The loyalists think this relationship of yours is a distraction. Merely a game you play as you bide your time and wait for the usurper to die."

Cairo thought of the loyalists, true believers who had opposed the general's coup thirty years ago and had only grown stronger and louder in the years since. The more the general hunted them down and attempted to silence them, the louder they got and the more furiously they agitated for Cairo to return and take his throne.

They didn't seem to realize that his attempting to do so would lead to nothing but slaughter. Had they learned nothing from his family's "accident"? General Estes was as much a butcher today as he had ever been. Perhaps even more so, if his power was slipping away.

"The loyalists believe what they want to believe," he said now.

"The key points they wished me to pass on all concern your current companion," Ricardo told him. "She is inappropriate, they claim. Unacceptable, though stronger language was used. She is a slap, and I quote, 'in the face of centuries of the Santa Domini bloodline.'"

"Heaven forfend the bloodline that ends in me suffer a slap. The monarchy might be lost in shame forever—ah, but then, there is no monarchy and hasn't been for thirty years."

Ricardo had heard all of this before. He inclined his head. "They want to meet."

They did not want to do anything so innocuous as *meet*. They wanted to plan, to scheme. They wanted to talk strategies and possibilities. The practical loyalists wanted their seized lands and confiscated fortunes back. The idealists wanted the country of their forefathers, the fairy-tale perfection of "the kingdom in the clouds," as Santa Domini had been known in previous centuries. Cairo was as much a figurehead to them as he was to their enemies.

And figureheads too often ended up sacrificed to the cause, one way or another. What the loyalists failed to realize was that they'd be served up along with him. Cairo had been trying to avoid that very outcome since the general had assassinated his family.

As long as the general lived, nothing and no one Cairo cared about was safe.

"Impossible," he murmured now. "My social calendar is filled to bursting and I am, quite publically, falling head over heels in love with an American temptress reviled on at least three continents, rendering me stupendously unfit to be anyone's king."

"That is what I told them, more or less. It was not received well."

This was the problem with royal blood. History was littered with the executed and deposed relatives of this or that monarch, all of whom had been pressed into service by exactly the sort of people Cairo knew better than to actually speak to directly. The fact of his existence was enough of an irritant to General Estes. The general had claimed the throne of Santa Domini, but everyone knew he'd taken that throne by force and, because of that, there would always be whispers that he could only hold the throne by the same force. Meanwhile, Cairo hadn't set foot on Santa Dominian soil since he'd been a child and had made himself one part a laughingstock and two parts too scandalous to bear, but there was no doubt that he was his country's legitimate heir.

If he'd hid himself away somewhere and stayed out of the public eye as his parents had advised him to do when he was a child, Cairo wouldn't have survived to adulthood. That he lived, that he drew breath daily, was a constant reminder to the general that he was not legitimate and could never be legitimate no matter whom he bullied. That he had not won his position by popular vote or historic right, but by violence and betrayal.

Cairo had spent a very long time making sure no one could possibly imagine a known fool like him, vapid and excessive and usually scandalously naked besides, as any kind of king. Secret meetings and murky discussions with those who would use him to take back the country would undo all of that work. It would put not just Cairo at risk, but all of those who had ever supported his family. From the sweet nannies who had raised him and his lost sister, to Ricardo, to say nothing of the ancient families that had stood with the kings of Santa Domini for centuries.

He might have risked himself, now that he was no longer a grieving and terrified boy. But he had already lost everyone he'd ever cared about. He could not risk anyone else.

He would not.

"I suppose there is only one course of action, then," he said after a moment, when the air in the old room, so much like a mausoleum, grew tight. "To put the final nail in my coffin."

"Not literally, I hope." Because Ricardo would always do what was asked of him, Cairo knew this as well as he knew his own heart within his chest, but that didn't make the man any less of a loyalist at heart.

He made himself smile, and pretended, as he always did, that he didn't know how deeply the other man longed for Cairo to stand up one day and announce he'd had enough—that he was taking back the kingdom. That day would never come. Cairo had made certain of that, as surely as he'd made sure to become exactly the sort of creature his beloved father would have loathed.

"Indeed, that is what we always hope, Ricardo," he said instead, and for the first time in a long while, he found he actually meant it.

Cairo turned his attention back to his laptop, telling himself that he was perfectly calm, because he should have been. That his heart was not beating too hard, that he was not tense with sheer anticipation—for all the wrong things—because he should have been as composed as he was when he handled his investment portfolio.

That he was not should have concerned him a great deal more than it did.

Because it was finally time to propose to Brittany, his inappropriate consort who functioned as the perfect sucker punch against his splendid ancestry, royal blood and claim to the throne of Santa Domini.

He would make her his wife and ruin the dreams of all those loyal to him, once and for all.

He should have viewed this necessary step with a measure of satisfaction. Possibly with a touch of nostalgia for the country he'd not laid eyes on since he was small boy.

But he found that instead of his kingdom, what he thought about was Brittany. Copper fire and the sweet, hot insanity of her slick mouth against his. Her lean, muscled curves in his lap and her scent all around him like a fist. The torture of these last weeks, of having her so close and yet so far away. Every touch he stole in front of the cameras that he relived for another sleepless hour when alone at night. The agony of her smile, of that mysterious distance in her eyes. It had been unbearable from the start.

But the time had come at last.

He would finally, finally make her his.

Cairo found he couldn't wait.

CHAPTER FIVE

"PAY ATTENTION, PLEASE," Cairo said from across the small table, which was how Brittany realized she'd been lost in her own head somewhere. She snapped her gaze back to his and saw that same brooding, amused impatience in those caramel depths that she was starting to crave a little bit too much.

Maybe more than a little bit.

She shoved that thought aside and cranked up her smile to something melting and adoring, as befit the occasion. She assured herself it was completely feigned. She'd worn a gown of glorious red that clutched at her breasts and then tumbled down to flirt with her knees, and the sort of fancifully high and delicate shoes that impressed even the most glamorous French women. She'd pulled back the front part of her hair and let the rest of the heavy mass of it swirl down from that gleaming little clip to tumble past her bare shoulders, a sleek fall of copper that she knew caught the light.

She would look beautiful in all the engagement pictures. Elegant, even; the better for all the nasty "compare and contrast" photos the papers would run the moment they heard the news. This side a future almost-queen dressed for the part, that side a stripper in a G-string and a bikini top upside down on a pole.

The vicious articles wrote themselves.

Brittany told herself, the way she seemed to do more

and more these days, that she didn't mind at all. That this was what she wanted. That she was as pleased with the public persona she'd created as she ever had been, and welcomed the way she and Cairo were using it to their own ends.

I have never been happier in all my life, she told herself now, surrounded by fine china and Michelin stars. Again and again, hoping it would sink in. *Not ever.*

Cairo looked devastatingly gorgeous. Cairo always looked devastatingly gorgeous. The things the man did to a jacket and a pair of dark trousers defied description. It was as if a light shone upon him from a great height, making him seem something like angelic despite his rather more earthy reputation. He turned heads. He inspired sighs. He couldn't walk across an empty street without someone gasping aloud, and there'd been a chorus of dreamy sighs all the way across the restaurant floor when they'd entered.

He was the most dangerous man Brittany had ever met, and sometimes, when he lost that smirk of his and stopped saying his usual absurd and provocative things, she was sure it was as obvious to the world as it felt sloshing about inside her.

Tonight he'd chosen the best table in Paris's current darling of a restaurant, where the paparazzi could crowd about outside and take telephoto pictures of their meal. He'd picked her up from her flat in a flashy sports car, a muscular Italian bit of fancy in a deep, glossy black, and had swept her into the restaurant in a hail of flashbulbs that hardly seemed to register to him at all. A surreptitious glance at the mobile phone in her evening clutch told her the pictures were online before they'd ordered their first course.

There's no getting out of this, a little voice kept whispering to her from that place, deep inside her, where everything was fluttery and terrified and all because it recognized how susceptible she was to this man. How vulnerable. He made her *feel things* and that was unforgivable. *There's no taking it back.*

"You seem bored," Cairo said after one silent moment bled into the next. He leaned back in his chair in that exultantly male way of his, a negligent finger tracing the stem of his wineglass as he spoke. "Surely not."

From a distance she would look enthralled with him, she knew. Or she hoped. She leaned forward and rested her chin on her hand, to underscore that impression. Too bad it made it far too easy to forget that she was supposed to be acting.

"It's only that I've done this so many times before," she said.

Laughter flashed over his extraordinary face, and that didn't help. Brittany might as well have plugged herself into an electrical outlet and switched on the power to full blast. She *felt* it when he laughed. Everywhere.

She was in so much trouble. That truth shivered through her, making her stomach flip over and then knot tightly, and it took everything she had to pretend it wasn't actually happening.

Cairo watched her, close and hot, as if he knew every last thing she wanted to hide from him. "Did your teenage first husband propose to you in the finest restaurant in…wherever you came from?"

"In fact he did," she said loftily. Brittany forgot herself again and grinned at him, remembering. "It was the parking lot of a McDonald's with a bag of cheeseburgers from the drive-thru."

"Be still my heart."

"That counted as highly romantic to a sixteen-year-old girl with no prospects, I'll have you know. Darryl had even bought the cheeseburgers, which made the whole thing especially fancy."

He smiled at that. Brittany looked away. The sapphire ring she wore on her right hand caught the candlelight and reminded her exactly how far she'd come from a fast-food parking lot in Gulfport, Mississippi.

Cairo wasn't done. "And what about poor Carlos, who you treated so hideously on television like the callous creature the papers tell us daily you truly are?"

"He came into the bar where I was working—"

"Is that a euphemism? Do you mean another strip club?"

"I mean the bar where I was working as a waitress," she said, shaking her head at him. Then she relented. "The strip club was my second job."

Cairo's mouth moved into that smile of his that she'd discovered made her silly straight through. Completely and utterly foolish, and something like shattered besides. The only defense she had against it was to act like an icicle. But somehow, she couldn't seem to do that tonight. Her ability to freeze had disappeared, lost somewhere in the dancing flames of the candles between them. Or in that smile of his that made her feel like just another flickering bit of the light surrounding him.

Maybe it wasn't the worst thing, to be caught up in this man. To flicker and dance around him like the candles on the tables, or his loyal subjects, who followed him from party to party without end, or every woman who'd ever laid eyes on him. Maybe she was trying too hard to resist the inevitable. It was possible that giving in to it would make this latest transactional, cold-blooded marriage... easier.

Sweeter, anyway. She had to believe it would make it so much sweeter.

"Carlos came into the bar and he said he was moving

to Los Angeles and I should go with him." She shrugged away the other parts of the story that had little to do with what he'd asked. She didn't like to think about that time. The usually angry, rough clientele and the places they tried to put their hands. That ever-present sense of danger that, still, had been better than a life dodging Darryl's fists. She might have been a virgin, but her experiences had made sure she never felt anything like innocent. "He was pretty sure he could get us both on a television show if I did."

"Better than a sonnet."

"I asked what the catch was, because who walks around claiming they can get on television shows? He said we had to get married, I said okay. The end."

Cairo didn't actually move to put a hand over his heart, but the gesture was implied in the way he watched her then, his caramel gaze looking darker in the candlelight. More like whiskey than candy, and it made Brittany feel a little tipsy, instantly.

Maybe more than just a little tipsy, she thought.

"Sheer poetry," he said, his mouth in that tempting curve. "And Jean Pierre? Or did he have one of his nurses do the honors as he lay in his sickbed?"

"That one was much more fun." Brittany couldn't seem to stop smiling at him tonight, when she knew better. These past weeks had been sheer torture. Cairo was not the sort of man whose potency wore off the longer she spent time with him, like every other man she'd ever known. Not Cairo. He intensified. He got *worse*. "He came backstage after one of my shows."

"This time we really are talking about a strip club again, yes? For the purposes of clarity?"

"He said some lovely, complimentary things." She raised her brows at him, daring him to comment.

"I'm sure he praised the strip club's choreographer to the moon and back." Cairo nodded, that sharp gleam in his gaze telling her he knew very well Jean Pierre had done no such thing. "Or perhaps the set design?"

"Something like that," Brittany murmured.

Jean Pierre had told her something that bordered on filthy, that he'd somehow made sound charmingly bawdy instead—but Brittany suspected that Cairo, with that sharp gleam still in his gaze as he waited, wouldn't find it nearly as amusing as she had at the time.

She didn't want to dig into how she knew that. Much less what it meant.

"And then he told me he had very little time left to live and a handful of deeply ungrateful children. 'Marry me, *cherie*,' he said." She affected a dramatic French accent and had the enormous, very complicated pleasure of seeing Cairo's dark amber gaze gleam with pleasure. "'And we'll give them hell.'"

"This proved sufficiently compelling for you? I'll make a note."

"Jean Pierre had a certain charm."

"By which, of course, you mean his net worth."

There was no particular reason for that to slice through her, especially not tonight. Brittany didn't know what was the matter with her, especially because it was true. She didn't know why she felt so…fragile. She couldn't scowl at him with so many people watching them, inside the restaurant and out, so she had to settle for a bright sort of smile that made her own mouth hurt.

"I make no apologies for that or any other choice I made, then or now," she told him, and she chose not to concentrate on how difficult it was to keep her voice in the neighborhood of calm. "Only people who never have to worry about money look down on those who do nothing but. Besides—" she let her gaze sweep over him, from that reckless dark hair to his careless smile, and the sheer masculine beauty of that body of his he packaged to perfection "—you're no different from me."

"I must beg to differ, *cara*. I do not sell myself to the highest bidder."

Her smile still hurt. Worse, then. "Keep telling yourself that. Tabloid after tabloid after tabloid."

Cairo's eyes flashed with an emotion she couldn't read. He inclined his head slightly, very slightly. He did not say *touché*. Brittany supposed he didn't have to say it out loud. The fact she'd scored a direct hit seemed to simmer in the air between them.

"Cairo," she said, and she didn't know what she was doing. She was performing, yes, but all she wanted was to…do something about the fact it seemed she'd hurt him, when she'd have said that was impossible. "You're not the man you play in public." She didn't know where that came from, only that the moment she said it, something shifted inside her. She knew it was true. She reached her hand out across the table, but he didn't take it. "It won't kill you to admit that, if only to me."

He let a bitter sort of laugh, and Brittany had the impression he was as surprised by the sound as she was. He leaned forward. He still didn't reach for her hand.

"That is where you are wrong," he told her, and she went still. His dark eyes were so dark and something like tortured, and she realized in the same instant that she'd never seen him look like this. Not remotely indolent. Not the least bit lazy or pampered. No trace of that smirk on his beautiful mouth. "It very well might kill me. Did you imagine this was a game?"

That sat there between them, stark and harsh. Brittany's head spun. Then he pulled his gaze away and ran an unnecessary hand down the perfect line of his lapel.

"What do you mean by that?" she asked, her voice

barely above a whisper, her hand still reaching across the table. She couldn't seem to move a muscle.

"I mean nothing by it." But it took him another long moment to look at her again, and she didn't believe him. "I am a creature of well-documented extremes, that is all. The theater of it all goes to my head sometimes and I imagine I am starring in some great tragedy. I think we both know I am not the tragedy sort."

"Cairo…"

But he changed again, right there before her eyes. He didn't appear to move a muscle, and yet he changed. He looked as useless and lazy as ever, that stark moment gone as if it had never been.

"This proposal will be unmemorable, I'm sure," he told her, his voice amused and his gaze more like his usual caramel again. Light. Easy. Why couldn't she believe it? "Especially for a woman as vastly experienced in this area as you. Are you ready?"

Brittany pulled her hand back from the center of the table and told herself this was none of her business. *He* was none of her business. She should never have acted as if she wanted to know *the real him* anyway. What an exiled king chose to hide behind his public mask was his affair, not hers.

"It can't possibly be as heartwarming as cheeseburgers in a parking lot, or off-color remarks in a strip club," she replied, and it was a fight to make her voice cool again. As if that strange moment that still spiked the air between them hadn't happened. "But you do like a challenge, don't you?"

Cairo's mouth moved into its usual amused curve, though his eyes remained dark on hers. He reached into the pocket of his suit coat and pulled out a small box. An instantly identifiable jeweler's box that could really only contain one thing. And still, Brittany found herself staring at it as if she didn't know what it was. As if she didn't know what was happening. As if they hadn't decided he would do this here, now, tonight.

The frightening part was, she was only partially acting. She felt too hot, then too cold. Her tongue felt glued to the roof of her mouth.

He moved then, shifting from his seat to kneel down beside her chair, and her heart started drumming wildly in her chest. She couldn't tell if the restaurant around them went quiet. She couldn't tell if the earth had stopped spinning. The point of this was the spectacle he'd mentioned, the endless show that was both their lives—but all she could see was this. Him.

The last man in the world who should ever have been kneeling down before her, and yet there he was, doing exactly that.

The whole world narrowed as he took her hand in his.

Then disappeared entirely.

This isn't real, this isn't real, this isn't real, she chanted at herself.

But the truth was, it felt more than real. It felt like a fairy tale, the kind she'd lectured herself against loving or believing in all her life. It felt like magic and hope and something sweet besides.

His Serene Grace the Archduke Felipe Skander Cairo of Santa Domini smiled at her, Brittany Hollis, from the worst trailer park in Gulfport, Mississippi, as if she thrilled him. As if she really, truly did. That treacherous part of her, not buried as deep inside her as it should have been, wished that was possible. Oh, how she wished it.

He cracked open the small box he held and presented it to her with flourish, and Brittany's heart stopped.

She knew that ring. Everybody knew that ring. That glorious, incomparable diamond for which songs had been written and blood had been shed, across the ages. She knew its sparkle, its shape, even the delicate, precious stones that surrounded it like a whimsical halo. It had been painted by any number of great masters over the centuries, was known as one of the finest legacy jewels in all of Europe, and was so beloved by so many that various paste representations were sold all over the world.

"It was my mother's," Cairo said quietly, his eyes on hers. She knew that. He must have known that everybody alive knew that. "And my grandmother's before her, going back hundreds upon hundreds of years. It was commissioned a very long time ago, crafted by my kingdom's finest artisans, and is known as the Heart of Santa Domini. I hope you will wear it proudly."

"Cairo…" Her voice was a whisper. She couldn't wear such a ring. She couldn't bear it. It was a symbol of hope, of love, and this was nothing but a sideshow performance for a baying crowd. But she couldn't seem to open her mouth and tell him so.

She'd forgotten her internal chant entirely. She'd forgotten her own name. She'd forgotten the fact they were in public, the paparazzi right there outside the window, even the fact that all of this was staged.

There was only the look in Cairo's caramel gaze. That hot, dark, gleaming thing that wrapped around her and pulled tight. There was only the way he took that fairy-tale ring from the velvet box and then slid it onto her finger, as if she was the princess in the tale, not the joke he was playing on the world.

"Marry me," he said, and his voice was different, too. Deeper. Richer.

As raw as she felt.

And Brittany understood how foolish this game of theirs was. There was nothing the slightest bit cool about her then. No icicle. Nothing even close. She felt… everything. She didn't know if she wanted to cry or if she wanted to scream. If she wanted to fall into his arms or run away. She only knew that she'd been married three times and not one of them had ever felt like this. Not one of them had ever made her shake, inside and out.

Not one of them had ever been anything but expedient.

She tried to remind herself that Cairo was the same, if on a grander scale. That it was all he was. She tried to tell herself this was no different from the rest, and no matter that she was wearing one of the most romantic diamonds in the history of the world on her hand.

"Must I beg?" he asked then, though he looked as comfortable on one knee as he did lounging in a chair or sprawled out on a sofa. As if he could inhabit whatever posture he found himself in and make it his own, and easily.

"Of course not," she said quickly, and she wasn't faking the way she shook. Or the sting of tears that threatened to spill over from behind her eyes. "Of course you don't have to beg."

"Say it," he ordered her, every inch of him the king he wasn't, even as he kneeled in what ought to have been a supplicant position. It took her breath away. It made her imagine that all of this was something much, much different than it was, and that, she knew on some distant level, was the most dangerous thing of all. "I find I require it."

"Yes," she told him, this exiled king on his knees before her. *Her.* Brittany Hollis, reality-show villain and scourge of Europe, destined for nothing but infamy and then irrelevance. In that order, if she was lucky. "Yes, I'll marry you."

"I hoped you might." He didn't move. His eyes were lit up with that drugging heat she didn't want to recognize, but she did. God help her, but she did. She could feel it echo inside of her, making that sweet, hot knot in her belly bloom into something more like an ache. "Come now, Brittany. We need to sell this scene for our adoring public."

"I said yes. What more do you want? A song and dance?"

"I think you know." He smiled when all she did was stare at him, so outside herself she hardly knew where she was, and shivering inside as if she'd never get warm again. She wasn't sure she wanted to. "Kiss me, please. And make it good."

Brittany felt dizzy then. Hot and wild and pierced straight through.

But it didn't occur to her not to obey him.

You want *to obey him*, that voice inside her accused her.

She sat forward in her seat. She let go of his hand and indulged that part of her she'd been denying all this time, sliding her hands over that marvelous, ever-roughened jaw of his to cup his beautiful face between her hands.

Her breath caught. She saw nothing but fire in his hot, sweet gaze, this stunning man whom she should never have met. Whom she should never have touched. Whose kiss weeks ago still worked in her like a fire she couldn't stamp out and whose gorgeous male body, sculpted to impossible perfection, had been *right there within reach* on all those little holiday jaunts they'd taken, in all those rooms and tents they'd shared without ever sharing a bed.

She hadn't touched him. She hadn't dared. She didn't know what would become of her if she followed that flame. She couldn't imagine what waited for her on the other side—and she hadn't known how to handle the fact she'd *wanted* things she'd never, ever wanted before, from anyone.

But tonight, she'd agreed to marry him. Tonight, they were in public, where it was safe. Where they could both wear the masks they preferred. Where there could be no real surrender to lick and scrape of all that fire in-side of her.

Tonight, she felt as if she could dare anything. Even this. Even him.

Even the terrifying things she felt inside.

So Brittany slid forward and pressed her mouth to his.

It was better than she'd remembered—better than she'd dreamed. She tested the shape of his lips, shuddering at the warmth, the contact. He tilted his head to change the angle and took the kiss deeper, hotter.

His taste exploded through her, fine wine and devil-ishly perfect man.

God help her, but he was perfect.

Brittany kissed him as if fairy tales were real, and as if the two of them were, too. She kissed him as if they were nothing more than a man and a woman, and this kiss was all that mattered.

No kings, no strippers. No tabloid personas. No calcu-lation whatsoever.

She couldn't seem to do anything but pour herself into him, no ice and nothing hidden or left back. No self-preservation at all.

Brittany kissed him as if she was falling in love with him, raw and wild and heedless, and her heart flipped over in her chest at the very thought.

And as if he knew it, Cairo pulled away. He brushed her hair back from her cheek, handling her as if she was infinitely precious to him. Something bloomed within her, warm and bright. Because she wanted that. She wanted to be precious.

To him.

"I promise you," he said, his voice husky with what she might have called a kind of pain, or maybe it was the honesty she'd asked for earlier, "you won't regret this."

"Neither will you," Brittany heard herself say, her voice as swollen as her lips, but a solemn vow even so.

It hung like that between them, shimmering and real.

And that was when the first paparazzo reached their table.

Six frantic and over-photographed weeks later, Brittany stood in a tiny stone chamber high in an ancient castle built into the side of the Italian coast, letting a set of smiling attendants lace her into her wedding gown. She kept her eyes trained on the tapestries that adorned the walls, all showing this or that medieval battle or glorified feast.

She tried to remind herself that this day, like all the conflicts and celebrations on display before her, would fade into blessed obscurity soon enough.

In five years, ten, a hundred, no one would care that Cairo Santa Domini was the first of his bloodline in three hundred years to marry outside the iconic cathedral that had stood for centuries in the Santa Dominian capital city, not far from the grand palace where his family once ruled. No one would care that he was—as a particularly vicious reporter had said to Brittany's face with obvious relish—polluting himself and the Santa Dominian line of ascension by consorting with her at all.

Time would pass. They would be messily and extravagantly divorced, as planned. They would make sure to drag it all out across the tabloids, the better to ensure the entire planet was heartily sick of them both. And then Brittany would fade off into obscurity and be remembered as nothing more than a tiny little footnote in the long, celebrated tale of Cairo's family that would end, ignominiously, with him.

It was too bad this particular footnote was fighting off a panic attack.

"Are you well, my lady?" one of the attendants asked

in heavily accented English as they finished the lacing. "You look pale."

"I'm fine," Brittany said, though her tongue felt strange in her mouth. She made herself smile. "I'm excited, that's all."

The women smiled back, the bustling and fussing continued, and then the church bells were ringing out the hour and it was really about to happen. In sixty short minutes she was going to walk outside to the chapel set high above the Mediterranean Sea and marry Cairo Santa Domini.

She dismissed the women from the room and stood there in the middle of it, fighting to keep her breath even and her eyes dry. Fighting to keep upright instead of sinking to her knees and staying there. Or worse, crawling into the four-poster bed that commanded the whole of one wall, hauling the covers up over her head and pretending she was the child she didn't think she'd ever been. Not really.

"Vanuatu," she muttered to herself. Fiercely. "Palm trees and white sands. Freedom and mai tais and life in sarongs."

Get your head into this, she ordered herself, in a pitiless sort of voice from down deep inside her that sounded a great deal like her harsh, bitter mother. *Right now. You have no other option.*

Brittany only realized her hands were clenched into fists when her fingers started to ache. She straightened them as the door to her chamber opened behind her, and then she smoothed the dress where it billowed out below her waist and—according to the mirror angled on its stand before her—made her look like a confection. She looked past it and out to the Italian hills that sloped toward the deep blue sea, dotted in marvelously colorful houses seemingly piled on top of each other while the staunch cypress trees stood like sentries beside them. She tried to breathe.

She kept trying.

"I'd like a few moments to myself," she managed to say after a moment, and was proud that her voice sounded much, much calmer than she felt.

"It is my role in life to disappoint you, I am afraid."

Cairo.

Of course.

Goose bumps swept over her, and she hoped he couldn't see them through the filmy, gossamer veil she wore pushed back to cascade over her shoulders toward the stone floor. His voice was richer than usual. Deeper and darker, and suddenly there was a lump in her throat that made it hard to swallow.

Then she turned to look at him and it was all much worse.

He was resplendent in white tie, lounging there in the doorway like a decidedly adult version of Prince Charming. The long tails of his morning coat did marvelous things to his lean, powerful frame, as if he'd been born to wear such formal clothes. A bubble of something giddy and inappropriate caught in her chest, and she had to swallow down near-hysterical laughter, because, of course, he had been. Bred for centuries on end to look nothing short of perfectly at his ease in attire most men found confining and strange.

"You are staring at my boutonniere as if you expect it to rise from my lapel and attack you," he said in his lazy, amused way, as he shut the heavy door behind him.

Brittany had never been a coward. She'd never had that option. And she didn't think she was one now, no matter how she felt inside. Still, the hardest thing she'd ever done in her life was to lift her gaze to meet his.

This glorious man. This would-be king. This inscrutable creature who was about to become her fourth husband.

Fourth, a small voice whispered deep inside of her,

with a certain feminine intuition she chose not to acknowledge, *and last*.

She shrugged that away, and the shiver of foreboding that crept down her spine, and let herself drink him in.

He looked exactly the way she'd expected Cairo Santa Domini would look on his wedding day. If, perhaps, more stunning. That careless dark hair of his was actually tamed. He'd even shaved his deliberately scruffy jaw, so he looked a bit less like a renegade than usual. He looked every inch the gleaming, impossibly wealthy and powerful royal he was.

And his eyes were more whiskey than caramel again. They seemed to see straight through her, pinning her to the wall like yet another decorative tapestry.

"What are you doing here?" she asked, and she hated that she sounded so much more stern and *bothered* by him than she'd intended. Or was wise. She cleared her throat. "Aren't you supposed to be waiting for me in the chapel?"

"It is not as if they can start without me." He eyed her, and she had no idea what he saw. No idea what that dark awareness that gleamed in his gaze was, only that it seemed to echo inside of her, growing bigger and wilder by the second. "I wanted to make certain you were not seized with any bright ideas about tossing yourself out the windows. A bridal suicide, while certainly bait for the tabloids, would simply mean I needed to start this process all over again. And I do hate to repeat myself."

"The papers we signed were clear. Death means no money at all. And if I abandon you at the altar I only get a quarter of what I would if I go through with it." She made herself shrug, as careless as he always was despite the fact she felt so soft and shivery. "It wouldn't be in my best interests to climb out the window, even if it wasn't a steep fall off a very long cliff to the sea."

Something occurred to her then, and gripped her so hard it was like a brutal fist around her heart.

"Why?" She didn't want to ask the next question, but she forced herself to do it anyway. "Have you changed your mind?"

Brittany understood far too many things in that airless, endless moment while she waited for his response. Too many things, too late. Too much she didn't want to admit, not even to herself.

This wedding was nothing like her others, two rushed courthouse visits and the small civil ceremony on the grounds of Jean Pierre's chateau that had been all about the gown she'd worn specifically to infuriate the old man's heirs. It had done its job. It had proclaimed her more Vegas showgirl than the solemn bride a man of Jean Pierre's standing should have been marrying, just as he'd wanted. She'd expected the dress for this even more dramatic performance today to be along those same lines. She'd been prepared for it, despite some drawings Cairo had showed her weeks ago that suggested a more classic approach.

But instead, the gown her attendants had dressed her in really was the one Cairo had showed her. Simple, elegant. It made her look like an actual, blue-blooded princess worthy of marrying a royal, not a tabloid sensation. Her breasts were not the main attraction. They weren't even on display. Her legs and thighs were not exposed every time she moved. Her veil, handed down in his family for generations and smuggled out of Santa Domini years ago, was almost as old as Cairo's title.

This wedding—this man—was nothing like the others. And it made her feel things she'd never felt before. *He* did.

"I have not changed my mind," Cairo said.

His gaze was too bright and too assessing at once, and he seemed to fill the whole of the room, stone walls and the four-poster bed and ancient tapestries be damned. Then he stepped closer to her and that was worse. It was as if he took over the entire world while her heart simply hammered at her, telling her things about herself she didn't want to know.

Brittany had to order herself to stand still. To simply hold her ground, tilt her head back to keep her eyes on his face and keep herself from reacting when he reached over and took her hand in his. Idly, lazily, his fingers found the Heart of Santa Domini and moved the famous ring gently this way and that on her hand.

It was such a small, civilized sort of touch. It was so restrained, so conservative—nothing like that kiss in the burlesque club or the one staged for the slavering press in one of the finest restaurants in Paris. They were both wearing so many fine, carefully crafted clothes today, all of them formal and stuffy and exquisite. There was almost no flesh on display at all, in contrast to almost every other time they'd been together.

Not to mention, they were alone.

That word seemed to pound through her. *Alone.*

Maybe that was why his seemingly inconsequential touch *hummed* in her, stark and wildly electric, as if he'd done something far more wicked than take her hand in his. Something in her wished he had. She felt soft and desperate and deep inside her, high between her legs covered in yards and yards of shimmering white, something clenched hard and then pulsed.

She wished she wasn't a virgin. She wished she was as experienced as she pretended. Then she would know how to handle this. Then she would know what to do.

"Have you?" Cairo asked. Quiet and close, his attention trained on the ring.

"No," she said. It was not quite the set down she'd wanted to give. She was lucky she got the words out at all. And was that relief she saw chase across his gorgeous face? But that made no sense. It disappeared and she told herself she'd imagined it. "No, I haven't changed my mind."

There was no reason on earth that she should. Except, of course, that overwhelming sense of doom and ruin and longing and insane hope that was filling her nearly to bursting. She planned to keep right on ignoring the lot of it, straight on into the financial benefits of this arrangement that would have her feet sunk deep in the South Pacific sand within five years, tops.

All she had to do was keep herself from toppling over. Especially while Cairo was watching her...and touching her.

How could he manage to do this to her with so meaningless a touch?

"The guests have assembled," Cairo told her, as if none of this was getting to him. She envied him that. "The overbred scions from all the noble families in Europe or their more embarrassing relatives in their place, depending on how personally offended the sitting monarch is by my assorted shenanigans over the years."

"Of course, your friends and very distant family are here, as expected."

"In the sense that all of Europe's aristocratic families were related at some point or another?" He shrugged at that, though Brittany knew that he was listed in the lines of succession of at least five different kingdoms. "I would not call them my family. It would be rather presumptuous, among other things. But I cannot help noticing that your family are nowhere in evidence."

She wanted to tug her hand from his, but she suspected that would be too telling. Too revealing, when she already felt wide open and much too vulnerable, and this was the man who had showed her his real face in a restaurant in

Paris and then claimed she'd misread him. She needed to remember that. Cairo *wanted* these masks they wore.

She had no idea when she'd stopped wanting it, too.

"Mine weren't invited," she said. Abruptly.

Cairo's brows rose. He opened his mouth to say something that would no doubt cut her to the quick, and Brittany couldn't take it. She felt too exposed already. And suddenly she didn't care if he knew it. She pulled her hand back, but that didn't help. She could still feel that deceptively simple touch everywhere, as if he'd branded her.

"My family didn't sign up for this spectacle." She did nothing to ease that snap in her voice. "And it's not as if our marriage will last long anyway. It would take longer for them to get here than we'll stay together. Why bother?"

Brittany regretted her words almost the instant she said them. Cairo seemed turned to the same stone as the walls around them, and she knew, deep inside, that she'd offended him.

He looked away for a moment, toward the cliff and the sea and the Italian villages clinging to the hills in the distance as if the view could soothe him. When he looked back, there was a speculative expression on his face.

"You cannot be nervous, *cara*, can you?" He adjusted his crisp cuffs, one after the next, though his gaze never left hers. "This should be like falling off a log, as you Americans say, should it not? I am the wedding virgin here, after all, not you."

Later, she would reason that it was *that word*. She hadn't heard that ridiculous, archaic word in a long time, because who would bother to use it in the vicinity of such a well-known slut and, according to the more salacious papers, possible prostitute? It hardly came up in the strip clubs or dive bars where she used to spend all her time. Much less in Hollywood, the most virginless place she could imagine.

But here, now, in an old castle on the Italian coast, it hardly mattered *why* she flinched at the sound of the word. Only that she did, right there where Cairo could see her do it.

And then, much worse, she blushed.

Bright red and unmistakable.

She could feel the heat of it sweep over her, making her sweat and let out a harsh, loud breath. Her dress felt itchy all around her, suddenly. The combs that held her swept back veil felt prickly against her skull.

And worse than all of that was Cairo, who watched her with wholly undisguised fascination.

That and a very hungry sort of focus.

"Brittany," he said softly, so softly. "Do you have something you want to tell me?"

"No."

He laughed at her reply, but the way he watched her with those dark whiskey eyes of his only seemed to deepen. And then expand inside of her. "Can it be? Is it possible?"

The mortification and all that red heat seemed to roll tight inside of her, and she didn't know what to do with it. Only that if she didn't do *something*, she'd explode. She fought for some composure—but then came up hard against the far wall of the small, ancient room.

She hadn't even realized he'd been coming for her, or that she'd backed away from him. All the way across the room.

And now it was too late.

Cairo leaned in close as if he wanted to inhale the fine tremors that moved over her body, one after the next. Then he laid his hands on the cool stone wall, one palm on either side of her head, caging her where she stood.

"Stop lying to me," he ordered her, in that same quiet voice that did nothing to disguise the fact it was another steel-tipped royal command.

"We're about to get married for money so we can lead a tabloid life," she managed to bite out in some semblance of her usual composed, measured tone. "I thought lies were a given."

"Brittany," he said, and again, her name in that mouth of his *did things* to her she wished she could ignore, "are you the best-disguised and least likely virgin in the whole wide world?"

CHAPTER SIX

SOMETHING SHOOK THROUGH BRITTANY, long and deep.

She had to stop this. She had to distract him. She couldn't let him think she was an innocent, not today of all days. She didn't think she'd manage to survive it if he thought she was anything but the hard-shelled, cold-eyed creature she'd spent so many years pretending she was that she sometimes believed it herself.

Because she couldn't allow herself to be vulnerable. Not here. Not with him.

She didn't know how to handle the fact that Cairo was the only person she'd met in years who didn't see exactly what she wanted him to see when he looked at her.

Masks, she snapped at herself. *This relationship is about masks, not what's beneath them.*

"Of course I'm not a virgin," she said crisply, frowning at him. "Do people still use that word? Did it become the seventeenth century while I wasn't looking?"

He didn't look convinced. And Brittany knew, with every last fiber of her being, that she had to convince him he was mistaken and she had to do it *right this very minute* before it was too late—

Some part of her whispered that it already was.

That it had been too late from the moment she'd set foot in Monte Carlo.

And still Cairo looked at her in that deeply unsettling

way of his, as if he could see straight through to her battered old soul.

As if he already knew she was a virgin, whether she bothered to confirm it or not. As if a small fact she'd considered essentially meaningless for years told him everything he needed to know about her.

She couldn't have this. She couldn't let him think this, especially because it was true. It would ruin everything, she knew it.

"Impossible," she said when he didn't respond, but continued to watch her in that same considering way. It was much harder than it should have been to affect her trademark arch, amused voice. "Everyone knows I'm a whore, Cairo, and here's a news flash. They're not wrong."

"Including your own mother, I believe you mentioned."

Brittany would have said the names her mother had called her over time were a collection of very old scars set over wounds that had long since healed, and yet she ached when he said it. Still, she made herself smirk at him as if there were no scars, no ache, and never had been. Not beneath *her* mask.

"Especially my own mother."

That it wasn't strictly a lie gave her voice a little power, she thought. After all, some members of her family believed that listening to certain kinds of music rendered a woman instantly and irrevocably fallen. It was a slippery, easy slope from that to whoring about. Her mother had always been the first to say so, when it suited her.

Cairo shifted then. He left one hand on the wall as the other moved to trace a lazy pattern along the line of her jaw. Down the length of it, from near her ear to her chin. Then back again. And the look in his eyes was more than simply dangerous, then. It was possessive. Triumphant.

And very, very male.

Brittany felt that shaking thing inside of her again,

insistent and terrible. Some part of her wanted nothing more to surrender to it. To tell him the truth he'd already guessed. To stop lying about herself for one little second in all these years of living those lies to the hilt.

Just here. Just to him. Just to the only man whose kiss had made her feel like a woman, not a means to an end.

But that was insanity. That bordered on *intimate* and she knew better than to risk such a thing. Not with *Cairo Santa Domini*, in the name of all that was holy, given his version of intimacy likely involved cutting down to three orgies a week from seven.

What the hell was she thinking?

She blamed the dress. The elegant princess dress that gave a woman *ideas*, even a woman who should know better. The dress that looked as if it had fallen from the pages of a fairy tale and made even a trailer-park Cinderella like Brittany imagine princes were real and charming and right here in front of her at last.

Life had taught her better than that. Over and over again.

So she smiled at Cairo, suggestively and wickedly. She reached up and covered the hand he held to her cheek with hers, and arched herself into him. She pressed her breasts against his chest and she tilted back her head to keep her gaze on his, and she did her best to ignore the way those things made the fire inside her sear through her.

"I can play a virgin if you want me to," she murmured, her voice sultry. "Why am I not surprised that the most famous playboy in Europe likes a little role play?"

That hot blaze in his eyes deepened. The air between them seemed to pull tight, as if something huge clenched around her, then squeezed. Hard.

"Are we playing?" he asked quietly.

"A marriage like this is nothing but a game." Brittany made herself pout at him when he only continued to stare down at her, as if he really was trying to see inside of her. He shifted, dragging his chest against hers so that tendrils of flame curled through her and made it hard not to squirm where she stood. And harder still to remember she was supposed to be acting. "Why not take it into bed as well?"

"You told me there was to be no sex in this marriage." His gaze was on her mouth. Her heart pounded hard, like a sledgehammer.

"You told me that wasn't your style," she countered.

She didn't know when she noticed that he'd angled his torso into her. That he was holding her there against the wall that easily, and Brittany knew she should have hated it. She should have felt caught. Captured. *Compromised.*

She didn't.

His eyes glowed that dark amber that made her chest feel tight, and she couldn't seem to pull in a full breath to save her life. His palm was surprisingly hard and warm against her cheek. She could feel it in her toes. His chest pressed against hers and made her breasts ache, the peaks pinching into hard points. And that beautiful mouth of his was set in a stern, resolute line that made something giddy and wild race through her, then coil tight low in her belly.

"I already told you I want to be inside you, Brittany," he told her, and it had the ring of a vow. Of something stitched together, need and command as one, and a red hot punch straight to that place that already melted for him. "That hasn't changed."

She rotated her hips, pulling him closer to her, and then she slid both of her hands around his neck. Her pulse was a riot, hammering through her veins and striking rapid blows in her temples, her throat, her wrists. And deep between her legs, where she ached and melted and ached some more.

And Brittany forgot that she was playing a role. She forgot everything but the fact she wanted him, as extraordinary as that was. *She wanted him.* And the whole world already thought he'd had her a million times, so who was she saving herself for if not this curious man who got beneath her skin as no one else ever had?

"Then why aren't you?" she asked. Cairo seemed to freeze there before her, save the hand that had gripped her jaw. He dropped it then, but his eyes stayed locked to hers. "Why aren't you inside me, when you are renowned the world over for your inability to keep it in your own trousers? Why have we spent our entire relationship so chastely and demurely?" She laughed at that, because she didn't know the answer herself when the only thing inside her was this edgy, delirious need. "Or is this terrible reputation of yours no more than the fevered imaginings of an overworked publicist somewhere?"

His gaze took on a light she'd never seen before, but she felt it. God help her, but she felt it, deep inside of her, where she was nothing but slippery longing and very bad ideas.

"Why don't we find out?" he murmured, his voice like silk.

Silk and danger and too much heat besides.

He shifted again, then. He reached down between them and began pulling up her heavy white skirt, never moving that demanding gaze of his from hers.

Brittany couldn't have said a word if she'd tried.

She didn't try.

And this time, when he traced patterns over the top of one thigh and then dipped into the valley between her legs, he didn't stop there. He found the silken panties she wore and smoothed his way beneath them, and then it was happening. It was really happening.

He was touching her where no one else had ever touched her.

Him.

Cairo.

He made a low, approving noise that rolled over her like another caress, as if finding her heat made him feel as raw as she did, and she surrendered herself all over again.

She had the distant thought that she always would.

Cairo stroked her tender flesh with his fingers, his eyes glittering darkly as her lips parted. Brittany did nothing—could do nothing—but lean back against the wall. And die from the pleasure of his touch, over and over and over. And let her hips rise to meet him with every slippery, decadent stroke, as if she was learning how to dance for the very first time.

As if he was teaching her the steps to the most perfect dance of all.

"It almost feels as if I know what I'm doing," he murmured, his voice a low, throbbing thing that mixed in with the slick, delicious movement of his hand, there against an old castle wall. "I can almost imagine no publicist has been involved in the creation of my reputation. What do you think?"

But everything else was lost in that fire he built in her and she couldn't respond. She wasn't sure she would have responded if she could. Not when she could disappear into the sweet glory of his touch instead.

And that was when he found the center of her need. He pressed against it once, then again, making her moan out loud. She told herself an experienced woman wouldn't react the way she did—but she couldn't seem to help herself, not when he ground his hand against her.

"Let's consider this an object lesson," Cairo murmured, dropping his head beside hers, his breath against her neck. "You have a habit of saying things no other person alive would dare say to me. Perhaps I have finally found the appropriate way to respond."

He twisted his wrist, plunging a finger deep inside her

molten heat while the rest of his hand rocked hard against the place where she ached the most.

It was an invasion. *It was perfect.*

He did it again, then again, then added a second finger and did it once more.

And Brittany simply…broke apart.

She shook and she shattered, and she fell into a thousand pieces right there in her wedding dress with her fingers dug deep into his arms, and the only thing she knew in all the world was his hard hand and his rough voice at her ear. She might have fallen apart forever, tumbling this way and that into a million little shards of who she'd been. She felt as if she had.

And when she came back to herself she was slumped against the smooth wall and the only thing holding her up was the arm she hadn't realized Cairo had put around her waist, securing her there against him.

He was watching her closely when she finally focused on him again, with an expression she'd never seen on his royal face before. Hard and solemn at once, and lit from within with a kind of hunger that made her clench tight all over again, against the fingers she could still feel inside of her.

Inside of her. Brittany let loose a shudder, low and deep, through a brand-new lick of need and heat.

Cairo smiled at that. He took his time pulling his hand away. He smoothed the silken fabric over her heat and then he drew his hand away entirely, letting the heavy wedding dress fall back into place to cover her weak knees and legs.

As if none of it had happened, when she was still soft and soaked and trembling.

"Brittany," he began, as if that wasn't the same sensual hunger that stormed through her turning his gorgeous face stark.

And something surged in her then, shocking her back

from that syrupy sweet place he'd thrown her into so easily, so expertly. Some kind of heightened awareness, or desperation. She didn't know what it was, she only knew with every inch of her body that she had to act instantly or lose everything.

"Is that it?" she asked, and she'd never sounded more bored. She heaved a sigh and pushed away from him, taking advantage of the look of arrogant astonishment on his face to swish her great skirts around him and start toward the other side of the room. "Clueless teenagers commit more interesting sins while fully clothed in the hallways of their high schools. I expected a little more finesse from a man who calls himself a king."

"Finesse," he repeated, as if he was unfamiliar with the word, and he sounded far closer to her than she'd expected. And far more cutting. Every hair on the back of her neck stood, but she didn't turn around. "The excitement of our wedding day must be playing havoc with my hearing. I just imagined you questioned my *finesse* mere seconds after you climaxed in my hands. Surely not."

She turned around then and her stomach flipped over, because he was *right there.*

He kept coming. Brittany decided to stop moving and stood there at the foot of the four-poster bed, trying to exude bored experience while her knees still felt like jelly.

"It's okay," she murmured, as insincerely as possible. She rolled her eyes. "I'm sure you're great."

His head tilted slightly to one side and the way he smiled then, slow and hard, made her think of a wolf.

"Oh, I am at that." Cairo reached over and ran a finger down the length of her hair, then tugged on the end. Once, then again. Not precisely hard—and yet that small hint of sharpness seemed to rebound through her overheated body, blooming into something much hotter and more intense in the place that still ached for him the most. "But by all means, *cara*, do not take my word for it."

And then he bent down and swept her up off her feet, huge dress and veil and all, and tossed her onto the bed.

Cairo hardly let himself think.

She landed on the bed with a soft exhalation and then he was there with her, levering himself above her and holding himself up on his elbows.

"Cairo—"

"Quiet, *cara*. Allow me to meet the challenge you issued, if you please."

His voice was a lash of command. He hardly recognized it. But that didn't seem to matter. Nothing seemed to matter except this woman dressed in white, with those dark eyes still so hot and wild and all for him. This woman who would shortly be his wife. *My wife*, he repeated, and the words seemed to reverberate inside of him, growing so big and so loud they filled him up—then crowded out everything else.

The world. His sense. *Everything.*

Cairo didn't care. He traced her lips with his fingers and hoped she could taste her own need when he did. She flushed that intoxicating red again, and it made him feel dizzy. It made a beast he hadn't known that lurked so deep inside him roar.

For once in his life, he didn't calculate the outcome of this encounter or worry about his performance. He'd left that somewhere behind them on the stone floor, tangled up in those abandoned little moans she'd made that left him so hard and so wild for her he ached.

He ached.

"Cairo," she said again, and this time her voice was little more than a whisper. But he recognized the heat in it. The impossible fire that burned in him, too.

He forgot how they'd come to be here. He only knew that finally, *finally*, Brittany was beneath him. *Where she belongs*, that beast in him growled.

What else could possibly matter?

He reached between them and pulled her dress up and out of his way. She made a soft, high sound, but when their gazes clashed she pulled her lower lip between her teeth. Then rocked her hips against him as he settled himself between her soft, leanly muscled thighs in wordless welcome.

God help him, but she was perfect.

He leaned in close and took her mouth with his, with all the desperate ruthlessness of a man about to explode. Her taste washed through him, sweet woman and all Brittany. He lost himself in the sheer perfection of it. He tasted her again and again, then angled his head for a hotter, slicker fit and did it all over again.

She lifted herself to meet him, her tongue meeting his and then driving him slowly, inevitably, gloriously insane.

Cairo had been acting a part for a long time. He'd pretended to be lost in a thousand kisses, usually for the benefit of the cameras that always waited nearby. But there were no cameras here and the longer he indulged himself in this woman, the more he forgot he'd ever treated a kiss like a stage.

This time, he really was lost.

He wanted her naked. He wanted her without a stitch of clothing on her perfect, delectable body, spread out before him like the feast she was. He wanted to take his time. He wanted to wallow in sensation, bathe in passion, throw himself completely into this woman and never come up for air—

But the bodice stopped him. It was a piece of understated elegance, embroidered and close-fitting, and it penetrated the fist of need that had him locked in its grip.

Just enough to remember that there were people waiting. That there were other things he needed to do to Brittany today, like marry her.

He could think of only one thing he wanted more, just then.

He deepened the kiss. His mouth mated with hers, taking her and taunting her. Making her flush and buck against him, her hands clutching at him and urging him on.

"Are you ready?" he asked her.

"I've been ready for weeks," she retorted, as he should have expected.

Cairo reached down between them and worked at his trousers, then smoothed his hand back beneath her silken panties, still beautifully damp from before. She was still molten hot and mind-numbingly soft, and she was *his*.

He'd been waiting for this moment since the moment he'd seen her picture, so long ago now. He'd longed for this since the night they'd met in Monte Carlo. He'd imagined this a thousand different ways since she'd walked out on him that night and left him to stew in his own wild need.

Cairo had never wanted another woman more.

He lined himself up with her slick, ready entrance *at last*, then thrust himself home.

It hurt.

He was huge and hard and so deep inside her, and the sensation that burst within her was too much. *Too much*.

Brittany went stiff, unconsciously slamming her hands in fists against his chest, and Cairo froze.

She'd imagined she could play it off. She'd been so sure that all her years of dancing would have loosened her up, made this a nonissue, the way so many of the other girls had claimed it had for them. She'd wanted him so much that she'd been positive she could simply throw herself into this thing without him pausing or even noticing that it was her first time.

But his eyes were dark and faintly accusing as they met hers now. His beautiful face was taut. He held himself very, very still above her, but there was no mistaking the steel length of him still sunk deep inside her, or the utter foreignness of the big, hard, decidedly male body nestled tight between her thighs.

He was stretching her. He was inside her and he was stretching her and she could *feel him* everywhere. With every shuddering breath she took.

But far worse than that, he had definitely noticed.

Brittany felt tears pool in the corners of her eyes, when she hadn't *cried* in longer than she could remember, and she couldn't believe she felt so *undone*.

"Do you care to explain this turn of events?" Cairo asked, conversationally, which only made that particular hot gleam in his eyes seem more dangerous.

She tried to blink back the tears in her eyes and swallow down that lump in her throat, but only made a snuffling sort of sound instead. She *snuffled*. She was flat on her back in the most beautiful wedding dress she'd ever seen, His Serene Grace the Archduke Felipe Skander Cairo of Santa Domini braced above her and deep *inside* her, no longer a virgin no matter what happened next if she understood the mechanics of these things correctly, and she'd *snuffled*.

Like some kind of animal.

"Do not cry," he ordered her. His gaze gentled as it met hers and it was astonishing how comforting Brittany found that. "Don't you dare cry, *tesorina*. You have lived through far worse things than me, I am confident."

A moment ago she'd had a sob inside her chest, so big she'd been afraid it would burst straight out through her ribs like some kind of alien creature and engulf them both, and now she wanted to laugh. She loosened the fists she still had clenched against him, uncurling her fingers and then smoothing them over the elegant morning coat he wore. Almost as if she was comforting *him*.

She opted not to analyze that.

"I haven't yet determined whether or not I'll live through this," she pointed out after a moment, and though her voice was thicker than normal, there were no tears in it.

She could feel him, hard and so astonishingly hot, still wedged deep inside her. The very thought of it made her a little bit breathless, and then there was how it *felt*. Or maybe it was just him, braced above her so that thick hair of his fell down his forehead the way it always did. But there were still no tears. And then his mouth curved, and Brittany couldn't imagine why she'd ever felt like crying.

Cairo lowered himself to his elbows and cradled her face in his hands. It made him move the slightest bit inside of her, the faintest bit of friction where she was nothing but tender and new and scared, and it hurt again. She stiffened in the same instant she recognized that the pain was far less than before.

"You will live," he assured her. He held himself still again. "I promise."

He was heavy and hard, and her dancer's thighs, which she'd thought could handle any amount of stretching, felt… different. They almost ached from this strange position, pressed down and wide open by another person so much larger and more solidly muscular than she was. Still, it wasn't a painful ache. Not quite.

"It is your maidenly virtue that we must mourn here today," Cairo continued, sounding almost as lazy as he normally did, despite that caramel gleam in his dark eyes. "That and your penchant to lie directly to my face are two topics I imagine we will spend some time discussing in the days to come."

"Let's not get carried away." She frowned at him. "I might not have had sex before, but that doesn't make me—"

"A virgin? I think you'll find that is, in fact, the textbook definition."

"Virtuous." Her frown deepened. "I haven't been remotely virtuous since I was a kid and I was never much of a maiden, either. I have three husbands who would agree."

"Three husbands, yes." His gaze held hers, hot and gleaming, and he moved then. A simple little slide. An adjustment, nothing more, and it made her breath catch as she clutched at him. But it didn't hurt. Not at all, this time. "But no one has ever been here but me."

She scowled at him.

"I will take that as the confirmation I do not actually require," he murmured.

He pulled her closer to him, and Brittany was astounded to feel herself begin to melt all around him again. That look in his eyes changed again, and this time, the flush she felt was from something that felt a great deal like shame.

"You should have told me." Cairo's voice was reproving, and there was that edge to it she didn't quite understand. Once again, she had the wild notion she was looking at a Cairo no one else had ever seen, this man who looked at her with something akin to tenderness in his gaze. Deep inside, she trembled. "I did not wish to hurt you. I am not quite that monstrous. Not quite."

"I…" This was so far outside her experience. She didn't know what to do, what to say. She'd never *felt* so many things at once, physical sensation mixed with a flash flood of emotion, and all the while Cairo simply held himself there. Not hurting her. Not rushing her. Not leaving her. As if he could stay like that forever. "I didn't want you to know."

"Because you thought I would mind?" he asked, and though his voice was mild enough she thought she heard an edge in it. He still didn't move. "Or because you thought it would give you better leverage to throw your virginity at the highest title in your vicinity?"

She tipped her chin up as if she wanted to fight him for saying that. Maybe she did. Or maybe that was her only defense when he accused her of something so outside her imagining that she felt lacerated.

"I can't imagine a single person alive who would imagine that Cairo Santa Domini, patron saint of the lascivious, would have the slightest interest in whether or not someone was a virgin. You are whatever the opposite of a virgin is. Times a million."

His dark eyes gleamed. "As it turns out, I find myself deeply interested and also deep inside you. Perhaps they are related states."

She tilted her head back to glare at him more fully. "If I'd known the possibility of a truly white wedding mattered to you, because you are apparently a giant cliché masquerading as a man, I would have made certain to demand more money for going through with it." Her voice was as icy as possible, and yet even she could hear she sounded much too rough. And that it was far too revealing. She soldiered on, "And if I'd known you were a walking caveman, I would have turned you down the way I wanted to do from the start, no matter how many provocative pictures you sold to the tabloids."

"I am a king, Brittany."

That rang out between them, and she thought she saw something like amazement on his face for a moment, though he blinked it away. He seemed to get harder, bigger. Propped over her like that, still lodged inside of her, he became the whole world.

And Brittany found she couldn't seem to say another word.

"Not a cliché, not a caveman, not common in any way," he told her, in that same quietly ringing tone. "And I may not have a kingdom or the subjects I deserve, but I will have a wife before this day is done. I will have you. Like this. As long as we are together, I will have you exactly like this."

Cairo said it as if they stood at the altar already and these were the promises he was making to bind them together. She shook again, deep inside. Then, following an urge she didn't entirely understand, she moved her hips. She rocked them against his. His eyes darkened. And she pulled in a breath.

Because that didn't hurt at all. In fact, it felt…interesting.

"And whatever games we play in public, Brittany, what we do in private is ours. More specifically, mine."

"Cairo," she whispered. "I think I want you to start moving now."

Something flared in his gaze then, a deep, male satisfaction and that same hunger she recognized.

"Your wish is my command, *tesorina*," he told her. "But first you must say it."

"What do you want me to say?" She rocked against him again, against that impossible length of his buried so deep inside her, and shivered when sensation swirled through her. Lighting her up from the tips of her ears to the hard points of her nipples, past the molten place where they were connected, down into the toes that curled in the delicate shoes she still wore.

"Tell me," he urged her, and he pulled back then. Slowly. Slowly and steadily, inch by inch, and it made Brittany flush. Then try to meet him when he reversed himself and sank back into her. Deep and sure. "Tell me that in this, I am your king if no one else's. That here, you are mine."

She would have told him absolutely anything just then. Anything at all.

"Yours," she agreed, her head moving against the bed as he repeated that luxurious slide. Even more intense, delicious sensations coiled in her and flashed like wildfire through her entire body. Again and again. "I'm all yours."

"You have no idea how true that is, *tesorina mia*," Cairo muttered, dark and urgent, and then he really began to move.

And Brittany simply surrendered herself into a mass of pure sensation.

Cairo set a lazy, easy pace, and he encouraged her to meet him. Brittany moved her hips as he directed her, growing bolder with each stroke until she wrapped her legs around his hips.

He built the fire between them high and bright and so intense she didn't see how anyone could live through it. She also didn't care. He thrust harder, deeper, and she gloried in it. In him. As if she'd spent her whole life searching for this. As if this, right here, was exactly where she was meant to be.

As if her body knew things her mind didn't want to examine.

Still, he urged her on. Still, he swept her along with him, until she was hovering on another precarious cliff of his making.

"I can't…" she whispered.

"But you will," he replied, fierce and sure. "For me."

He reached between them and stroked her where she needed him the most. Brittany tipped her head back and gripped him tight as he pounded into her. Again and again—

Until finally, she hurtled off into nothingness, breaking apart into too many scattered little bits to name.

And this time, he called out her name and followed her right over that edge.

She had the vague notion they floated out in that silken, beautiful darkness together for a very long time. It could have been years.

But Cairo was already up and moving when she finally thudded back into her own skin and opened her eyes again.

"Stay where you are," he told her, in that bossy tone of voice she thought she really ought to object to.

But she didn't say a word. Nor did she move. She felt loose and lazy as she lay there on the old four-poster bed. There were all manner of thoughts and problems and issues hovering there, waiting for her to acknowledge them, but she ignored them. She listened to the cries of the seabirds on the other side of the windows instead, wafting in on the sweet summer breeze. She felt the sunlight dance over her face. She imagined she could hear the sea against the rocks, far below.

She felt bright and sunny straight through, as if she could drift away into the blue sky forever.

Cairo came back to her then, and she blinked, because he looked immaculate as he stood there at the foot of the bed. Not a wrinkle, or a hair out of place. As if none of this had happened when she could still feel him between her legs, where she was deliciously tender. She knew that should have bothered her. It should have done *something* other than make her shudder with a little more of that heat. He moved to put a hand on her belly and she shivered at his touch, then again when he used the cloth in his other hand to tend to her.

"You did not bleed much," he told her matter-of-factly, and she flushed at that. As if the words were more intimate than the act they'd shared. He tucked the cloth into her panties, pulled them back into place over her hips and then helped her to her feet, smoothing her dress down around her as she stood. "Leave that there until just before you walk down the aisle."

"What?" She wanted the floor to swallow her whole. She stared at the stones, willing it to do just that. "I don't want to talk about this with you."

"Brittany." She couldn't help but obey him when he used that voice, but he took her chin in his hand to make certain. "You are wearing a very white dress and you will be standing in it before a large congregation and a great many cameras. This is no time for modesty."

She pulled away then and stepped around him, amazed that her legs held her up when she felt as if she'd been swept away. As if she wasn't entirely herself anymore.

As if the mask she'd worn all her life had shattered, leaving her with nowhere to hide.

"This was a mistake," she said, sounding stilted to her own ears. "That shouldn't have happened."

It took everything she had to pull herself together. To lift her chin, run her hands over her veil, manage to smooth out her expression. She moved to the mirror and was as amazed as she was oddly disappointed that she looked exactly the same. The same as she had before he'd come into this room and more, wholly unruffled. As if nothing had happened between them but a little chat, like all the other little chats they'd had over the past weeks. All she needed to do was reapply her lipstick and no one would ever be the wiser.

She decided to take that as a sign. A portent, even.

"That will never happen again," she told him, raising her gaze to meet his in the mirror.

He moved to stand directly behind her, and her body knew him. It ached for him. She felt herself soften, everywhere, and had no idea what to do about it. As if he

knew it simply by looking at her, Cairo smiled. He slid
his hand around to hold her there before him, stretching
his palm against the tight waist of her gown.

She felt the heat of it everywhere, like a promise. She
wanted to lean into it, into him. She would never know
how she kept herself from doing it. How she kept her spine
straight and her knees locked.

"You are going to marry me in approximately five minutes," Cairo told her, and she couldn't help but remember
the way he'd said "I am a king," as if he'd never said such
a thing out loud before. She could hear the echo of it again
now, and more, feel it deep inside her. Like a command
from on high. "You are going to remember what happened
here with every step you take down that aisle. I have no
intention of a carrying on a sexless marriage, Brittany.
Certainly not with a woman who wants me as badly as
you do. Almost as badly as I want you."

"I…"

But she didn't know what she meant to say. What she
could say, when every last cell in her body wanted nothing more than to throw herself back onto that bed again.
To tear off her clothes and all of his and actually explore
him this time. Then lose herself in all that marvelous
shattering all over again. Right here, right now, and who
cared how many noble personages waited for them below?

"I was always planning to seduce you, Brittany," Cairo
told her as he pulled his arm from around her body. He
righted her when she started to slump over because her
knees really weren't working, and she flushed at his touch
all over again. His firm lips moved into that small curve
that set off explosions all through her. "Now I will simply
take comfort in the fact that inevitably, I will ruin you for
all other men. I likely already have. What a great pity."

"That's a lovely sentiment," she managed to say, trying desperately to sound as composed and as dry as she

wished she was. "I'm signing up to be your wife for a little while, not become your…"

She faltered, not knowing what word to use. What this was, what she was.

Or, worse, what she wanted to be. With him. For him. Much less for herself.

Cairo smiled at her then, and this time, it reached his eyes. And it was as lethal to her as the way he'd touched her, as the way he'd moved inside her, as the way he'd made her feel. It was almost too much to bear, too bright and too perfect, like the impossible Italian summer on the other side of the window.

He was her ruin made real and today she'd ensured it. She felt something inside her crack wide open and she was terribly afraid it would suck her in and destroy her right then and there, whatever it was. It felt that brutal and that permanent.

The trouble was, some part of her wanted to see what would happen. Some part of her imagined the wreck of it—of this—would be worth it, no matter what came after.

"Don't worry," Cairo told her, as if he felt it, too, that great, wide, open thing that was already changing everything. As if he knew exactly what it was and what it meant. As if this was as real as it felt—as real as that silly, fairy-tale-headed fool inside of her wanted it to be. "You will be both. My wife, yes. My countryless queen in all your glory. But most of all, Brittany, you will be mine. Do you not understand? You already are."

CHAPTER SEVEN

THE LAST OF the Santa Dominis married his stripper bride in a private chapel that dated back to the Italian Renaissance, the first of his family to marry in a place other than the Grand Cathedral in Santa Domini's capital in centuries.

Three whole centuries, to be exact.

As the old hymns were sung and the old words intoned, Cairo stood at an altar his ancestors had built with a woman for whom he felt entirely too many complicated things to name and found it hard to remember that he was baiting a trap. It was much too difficult to focus on the real purpose of this performance.

Because all he could think of, all he could see, all he could concentrate on was Brittany.

Who had somehow seen beneath every last mask he wore. And was already his.

Princes and counts and the assorted minor arcana of Europe sat in the pews arranged behind him, yet all Cairo could think about was the fact of her innocence and his taking of it. Her sweet heat and her addictive taste. The untutored rawness of the way she'd moved beneath him and the greedy little sounds she'd made as she'd found her release. He had to shift slightly as he stood to mask his body's response to the onslaught of memory, lest he appall the gathered throng of European nobles even more than he already had by making them bear witness to this ceremony in the first place.

Pay attention to the game, you fool, he ordered himself as the priest waved his hands over his bride's elegantly veiled head and intoned sacred words down the length of the chapel.

He was making this woman his in every conceivable way today, and despite the niggling sense that he was forgetting something critical, he exulted in it. If was up to him, he thought, he'd lock her up somewhere far away and out of the public eye, and indulge himself in her forever.

But that, of course, was not the game they played. No matter that she wasn't at all the practiced trollop she'd pretended she was for years. Nobody alive could possibly know that except Cairo—and in any case, it changed nothing.

The fact he felt he could show her the truth in him didn't mean he should, or that it altered the course they'd set out. It only made him hate himself that much more.

"I don't understand," Brittany had said weeks ago. It had been a few days after their engagement dinner. Enterprising paparazzi were attempting to scale the gates of his Parisian residence and the sketches he'd commissioned from his preferred Italian dressmaker had been spread out between them on the coffee table in one of his salons. "This looks like something a proper English princess would wear. I assumed we'd be taking the loud and tacky route."

"Everyone will be expecting that, of course." He'd eyed her, all copper fire and that distance in her gaze. He'd had the fleeting notion she'd been protecting herself—but he'd dismissed it. Why should she need protection? She was the one marrying up. "I have something else in mind."

A different sort of color bloomed high on her lovely cheeks, his mother's ring gleamed on her finger and it was a dangerous game he'd been playing. He'd known that all along, but perhaps never so keenly as in that moment.

"I don't understand." He'd had the impression she'd thought about how to respond. Her words were too precise. "I thought the point was to horrify the entire world with your marriage to a bargain-basement upstart like me."

"I want something slightly more complicated than a circus of a ceremony and a parade of bad taste," he'd said quietly. "That would be an obvious stunt. And not only because that was how you did it the last time you married above your station."

There had been a hint of misery in her dark hazel gaze. Then she'd blinked it away and lifted her chin, and he'd wondered if he'd only wanted that kind of reaction from her. If that was why he kept baiting her.

If he'd *wanted* her to feel all the things he was terribly afraid he felt himself.

"You want them to pity you," Brittany had said softly.

She hadn't met his gaze then. The iconic ring he'd slid onto her finger so recently had seemed to dance in the Parisian morning light between them, hoarding the sunshine and then sending it cartwheeling across the room.

Like joy, he'd thought. Not that he would know.

Brittany had still been talking. "You want them to think you believe that the sheer force of your feelings for me makes me somehow appropriate. You want to present a sow's ear all dressed up like a silk purse and pretend you can't tell the difference. You want them to laugh at you. At me."

She'd met his gaze then and it had taken everything he had to keep from flinching. He, who had never so much as blinked at all the tawdry things he'd done in his lifetime. He, who had always known precisely what his mission was and how best to achieve it, no matter how many reports he received that the general's health continued to decline.

"I do," he'd said, and he'd pretended that he hadn't seen

her pretty eyes go darker at that. Or, more to the point, he'd pretended he didn't care.

He said the same words now.

His voice was strong and sure to carry throughout the chapel and dispel any possible doubt that he was marrying this woman—*his woman*. He kept his fingers clasped tight around hers. And he waited.

But it wasn't until she replied in kind, sending relief arrowing through him, that Cairo realized he hadn't known what she'd say. Some part of him had truly believed that Brittany might change her mind at the last moment and take off running, like some captured bride of old. Another part of him wouldn't have blamed her if she had.

Here in this church, as he slid a new ring onto her finger to proclaim her his without any doubt or wiggle room, Cairo found absolutely nothing amusing about the idea of Brittany anywhere but here. With him.

The whole world thought they knew her, but only he did.

She was his in every possible way.

"You may kiss the bride," the priest intoned.

Cairo wanted to do a great deal more than simply kiss her.

But this was a stage, he reminded himself. This was an act. This was his opportunity to paint himself the besotted fool for the cameras.

He told himself he was a lucky man, indeed, that it was so easy.

Brittany tilted her face up to his, her pretty eyes darker than usual. He wanted that to be evidence. He wanted her to be as swept away in this as he was. He hated that he couldn't quite tell how much of her was real and how much of her was a performance.

It had been different up in that old stone chamber. When he'd been able to feel the truth of her, of them, in the way she shook apart in his hands and then again beneath him. When he'd ridden them both into all that glorious fire and let them burn and burn and burn.

God, how he wanted to do it again.

He pressed his mouth to hers. He felt her tremble against him when he deepened the kiss, holding her against him a beat or two longer than was strictly polite, and he saw the vulnerable cast to her temptation of a mouth when he finally released her.

She was thinking about what had happened between them, too. About him sunk deep inside her and her legs wrapped around him. He knew it as well as he knew his own name.

"Next time," she murmured, right there against his lips, "why don't you brand me with your initials instead? Or perhaps urinate in a circle around me, like a dog?"

"Is that a request?" he asked, in a low voice pitched for her ears alone. "Or a dare?"

And then he pulled back and presented her to the assembled crowd, before she could answer back in her usual tart way. His queen at last, and who cared what those vultures thought of her?

He knew what he thought: that his honeymoon couldn't come fast enough, because one taste of her wasn't nearly enough.

Cairo couldn't remember ever wanting a woman the way he wanted this one. *His wife*, he thought as they made their way down the chapel's long aisle and then stepped out into the exuberant Italian sunshine. It was such a small word, and yet he couldn't seem to process it. *His wife*.

There was only one other thing in all the world he'd ever wanted so badly it had consumed him whole. Thinking of his lost kingdom as they moved, Cairo thought he should be ashamed that he'd lost sight of it for even a moment. No matter how his new queen's smile caught the sun and made the whole world a little brighter all around her as they walked from the chapel. The wedding breakfast that waited for them, arranged in artistically laden long tables in the old castle keep, was not the place to forget who he was or the role he needed to play here.

Because it had never been more crucial to keep up his usual act than it was today.

"I never thought I'd see the day," one of his supposed best and oldest friends said with an entirely feigned congratulatory grin, slinging his arm over Cairo's shoulders in a show of his usual drunkenness as Cairo made his rounds sometime later. Cairo could see right through it, but then, there wasn't much of Harry Marbury—a man constructed of as many impeccably pedigreed English forebears as cast-off morals—that wasn't entirely transparent. "It's not as if you must marry to secure the kingdom, Cairo. It's been lost all your life and no matter those rumors that the old soldier is on his last legs. What *is* this preposterous wedding all about?"

"We all must fall in our time," Cairo replied lazily, as if mention of the general didn't scrape at him. And he hated himself when he continued, as he knew he must. "Better to cushion that landing in a woman who knows her way around a stripper pole, in my opinion."

"One does not marry the trash, friend," Harry said, laughing in his condescending way—and raising his voice just enough that it carried across the gathering and over to where Brittany stood with that fake smile on her face. Cairo saw her stiffen and he hated all of this. These lies, these performances, when what had happened between them had been real. Raw and real and entirely theirs. The most real and unscripted he thought he'd ever been in his life. "One uses it and then one's servants puts it out. In bins, I'm told."

Cairo would never know how he managed to keep himself from murdering the man—his supposed oldest, dearest friend—with his own two hands just then, right where they stood in the medieval courtyard of the old castle keep.

But he didn't, because this was exactly what he'd wanted. What he'd gone to such great lengths to make happen, precisely like this. He had no one to blame but himself if he didn't like how it felt now.

Now that she was his wife. His exiled queen.

His, damn it.

That was the part that mattered. That and the headlines Harry's little comment would likely generate from all the hangers-on that Cairo knew full well spent half their time in his presence texting the tabloids with choice snippets that usually bred headlines. And that was why Cairo laughed indulgently and clapped Harry on the back as if he'd told a rousing great joke instead of exterminating him like the cockroach he was.

You deserve a medal of valor for letting him live, he told himself grimly as he smiled and laughed and encouraged all these parasites to pity him as the reception wore on. Just as he'd planned.

Though it was hard to mind any of that when he had Brittany in his arms again.

She tilted her head back as they danced together for the first time as husband and wife, exiled king and nominal queen, smiling up at him for the benefit of the crowd.

"You look as if you are head over heels for me," he told her, and tried to sound as if he was chiding her when all he could think about was keeping his hands where they belonged. Instead of where he longed to put them. He was sure everyone could see it and with it, his real face. His true self. And yet all he wanted to do was continue to gaze down at her. "The papers will not know whether to call you smitten or materialistic."

"It must be the romance of the day," she said dryly. "It's

going to my head. Next thing you know I'll be reciting poetry and telling all the papers it was love at first sight, right there in that nightclub in the sewers of Paris where they think we met."

Two things happened then, in an instant.

First, a hard kick in the vicinity of Cairo's chest, making him clasp Brittany tighter as he fought it off. He tried to tell himself he didn't know what it was—but he did. Of course he did. Anticipation, desire... As if he wanted this to be real. As if he wanted this to be the mad, epic romance they were pretending it was.

As if it already was.

But that wasn't possible. He knew that as well as he knew his own, cursed name.

Because the second thing that happened was a vicious punch, straight to the gut. Cairo knew what happened when love was involved. He'd lived it. He was still living it. Grief and horror and crushing, interminable loss. A lifetime of pain and guilt when the people he'd loved were taken. He wouldn't go near it again. He *couldn't* go near it again.

But God help him, he wanted things today he'd never imagined he'd ever want. *Ever.* It was the way she'd come apart for him earlier, so soft and hot beneath him. It was the way she'd watched him in the chapel, her eyes solemn on his.

It was the simple, searing fact that no one had ever had her but him. No one had ever touched her and therefore nobody truly knew her, except him. Cairo didn't need to be told that she'd given him a gift far more precious than her maidenhead today.

He'd spent his whole life doing what he had to do, not what he wanted to do. He always made the smart choice no matter how it hurt him, no matter what it cost. He'd learned long ago to think of himself and his own feelings last, if ever, because what the hell did *he* matter when there were so many lives on the line? He'd never questioned any of it. He'd become his own worst nightmare, an utter disgrace to all he held dear. And because of that, he'd survived.

He gazed down at the woman who fit as perfectly in his arms as he had inside her, and he didn't know if he could do it this time. For the first time in as long as he could remember, Cairo wanted to do more than simply survive.

He wanted *more*.

"You're staring at me." She sounded edgy, despite the smile she aimed at him. Because, of course, they were still in public. They were always in public.

"You are my wife." He sounded like the man he'd taken such care, all his life, to keep from becoming in word or deed or public perception. He sounded like his memories of his father, commanding and sure. His father, who had refused to fight the coup because he'd thought that meant fewer of his subjects would die. His father, who had always viewed his exile as a mere interlude. His father, the king of Santa Domini Cairo would never, ever become. "My queen."

Her dark eyes glittered despite the sunlight, and she seemed as far away then as if she was up on the stage in that club again. On display to all, available to none.

But he'd seen beneath that mask. He'd removed his own.

Everything was different now.

He didn't want to watch her distance herself from him or what had already happened between them today.

He wanted anything but distance, even when they were out in public for all to see.

He dipped her then, slow and romantic and not entirely for show, and let himself enjoy the way her gaze spit fire at him despite the smile she kept welded to her lips. He pressed a kiss against that smile when he pulled her back to standing, and let that kick between them.

That lick of fire. That spiked edge of need.

And the murmurs and applause from the crowd he'd half forgotten all around them.

"That felt like a threat," she told him through her teeth, her smile as bright as her clever eyes were dark, making her even more beautiful to him, somehow.

"It was a promise," he retorted.

Searing and hot, that promise.

One he had every intention of keeping.

And keeping and keeping, until he wore them both out.

Soon.

Brittany woke up sprawled across the wide bed in one of the private jet's guest chambers. She was still wearing the pale yellow shift dress that had been set out for her to change into after the wedding breakfast, and in which she'd been photographed by a sea of paparazzi as she and Cairo had boarded his plane in Italy the night of their wedding.

She'd staggered on board, put as much distance as possible between her and the brand-new husband who'd gotten under her skin in more ways than she could possibly count already, and then slept like the dead the moment she'd tossed herself across the soft coverlet.

She was all too aware he'd let her go. Let her retreat from him.

And now you're waking up married, she told herself—perhaps a little more sharply than she should.

After all, it wasn't as if that was anything new.

The fact that she was no longer a virgin, on the other hand, was.

Lying there on her stomach, she pulled her hand out from beneath the pillow and stared at her rings. She'd worn wedding sets before, of course. Her first husband had been as deficient in that department as in everything else, but Carlos had dutifully presented her with not only the expected solitaire engagement ring and a platinum band to match, but also a bill for her half of the investment they were making in their Hollywood future. Jean Pierre had preferred yellow gold and had given her an ornate ruby he'd claimed was a family heirloom when they'd gotten engaged, then two guard bands of rubies and diamonds at their wedding ceremony. His fifty-year-old matron of a daughter had sneered at the rings and told Brittany it looked like her hand had been dipped in blood.

"Success," Jean Pierre had murmured into Brittany's ear, the conniving old fool.

But today she wore the Heart of Santa Domini and next to it, an eternity band of heart-stoppingly perfect diamonds that sparkled with their own, deep fire.

Because this time she was married to a legend. She was Cairo Santa Domini's queen. Whatever happened next, however their fake little marriage worked and then ended, she would always—*always*—be the first woman he'd married. She would appear in all his biographical information, in history books and encyclopedias alike.

Just as he would always be the first—something inside her whispered *only*, but she shoved it aside as so much damaging wishful thinking—lover she'd ever taken.

Brittany rolled over and sat up, looking around the compact room as if she expected to see her new husband lurking somewhere. As if Cairo was the sort who lurked. But she was alone. The little room was dark. She had no idea what time it was, how long she'd slept, or even where they were flying. Cairo had announced that they would honeymoon for a month or two and that had been all the information he'd offered. She hadn't asked where they were headed because it hadn't much mattered. The Maldives, New York City, the moon—who cared?

Their act was their act wherever they took it.

She scraped her hair back into a knot at the nape of her neck, wishing she'd had time to comb it all out and shower after the wedding. Wishing she hadn't slept in all her makeup, come to that. She ran her index fingers below her eyes and sighed when they came away smudged with black mascara. *How regal and queenly*, she chided herself. No wonder Cairo had married her for the sole purpose of parading her embarrassing low-class behavior in front of the whole world. She couldn't even manage to wash her own face.

None of this felt real to her, the fact she'd married the most famous exile alive, and not just because she didn't like thinking about *why* Cairo had married her.

Her other marriages had felt real. Too real, in all the wrong ways. Her first wedding night had been spent locked in the bathroom of the run-down motel Darryl had taken her to before he'd started drinking himself into a rage. She'd been so naive then, thinking *drunk* was the worst thing a man could be. Darryl had quickly taught her otherwise. Her marriage to Carlos had been pure business all the way through, and their life together had been entirely conducted to be filmed, from their choice of apartment in the gritty outskirts of Los Angeles's Echo Park neighborhood, a far cry from the Hollywood tourists loved, to their plotted outings to Southern California hot spots. Even her time with Jean Pierre, which had been all about creating a commotion, had been conducted as a shared vision and business enterprise.

Her new marriage didn't feel particularly authentic in that sense. She certainly didn't feel like any kind of queen, exiled or otherwise. But *she* felt something far more than real. Cairo knew her deepest, darkest, best-kept secret.

She felt raw all the way through.

Brittany moved to the edge of the bed and helped herself to the bottle of spring water that had been left there, gulping down half of it in greedy swallows, but she still felt parched.

You are going to remember this moment with every step you take down that aisle, he'd promised her, and he'd been right. She'd felt soft and shivery all the way through the ceremony. She'd *felt* the vows he'd made as if he was still moving deep and wild between her legs, and she'd hardly managed to get her own out in turn.

There were a thousand things she should have been thinking about now that she was awake. She knew that. That they hadn't used any protection, for one thing. But she couldn't worry about that. Not now. Her mind skidded away from that and she found all she really wanted to know was where her brand-new husband was and why he wasn't in this bed with her, teaching her more of all the many marvelous things he knew.

She wanted to learn each and every one of them, and she didn't care how vulnerable it might make her feel. Or she'd care later, she told herself firmly. After he was gone and she had the rest of her life to live without him.

Not that she wanted to think about that inevitability. It would come soon enough. And in the meantime, she could indulge the sensual side of herself she hadn't known she possessed. Until Cairo.

Brittany heard a muffled buzzing sound then and it took her a long moment to realize it was her mobile phone. She looked around the room, finally spotting her handbag on the floor near the foot of the bed, where she must have dropped it in her earlier exhausted haze. She moved to yank the bag up from the floor, thinking as she did that the fact it was buzzing at all meant they had to be above land somewhere, not an ocean, or there wouldn't have been a signal.

Brittany glanced at the display, saw it was her mother and then answered the call anyway.

A choice she regretted almost instantly.

"Well, well," Wanda Mae Hollis said in her gravelly smoker's voice, thick with its usual resentment. "How nice of your uppity majesty to pick up the phone. I've been calling you for weeks."

"Hi, Mama," Brittany said, and it was harder than it should have been to mask her emotions. It annoyed her that there were any to mask. Phone calls from her mother were always assaults of one sort or another. She should have been used to it by now—and she was. That was why she usually avoided them. "I've been a little bit busy."

She sounded more Mississippi when she spoke to her mother than she did at any other time, ever. Her voice flattened out into the drawl she'd worked so hard to leave behind her when she'd left home, as if she was still that miserable child trying to make herself small in the corner of her mother's trailer while another drunken adult fight raged on.

"You don't need to tell me what you've been up to," Wanda Mae said bitterly. "It's all anyone can talk about today, no matter where we go. I hope you're happy with yourself."

This was why Brittany limited phone conversations. She didn't know why she'd answered this one. Did she want to punish herself? But she suspected she knew what it was that had made her pick up the call: that tiny little shred of hope she kept tucked away, deep inside of her, and only took out from time to time when it whispered things like, "maybe your mother might be happy for you for once."

That little shred was always wrong. Hope, she'd discovered long ago, was a big fat liar.

Brittany snuck an arm around her own waist and held on tight, then dug her bare toes into the carpeted floor beneath her as if she needed to remember that she was solid. That she was real. That she had a whole life that had nothing to do with Wanda Mae Hollis, and nothing her mother said could matter one way or the other unless she let it.

But she still didn't hang up. She didn't know why.

"Thank you," she said instead, and made an effort to sound as if she'd never visited Mississippi, much less grown up there. "I appreciate you calling with your good wishes."

Wanda Mae snorted. "I couldn't walk three feet today without someone else throwing your latest exploits in my face. Do you know what they're saying about you? Do you care?"

"I'll assume they're not praising me and calling me the next Kate Middleton," Brittany said, and was proud of the fact she sounded amused. Or close enough to amused, anyway, that the mother who barely knew her wouldn't be able to tell the difference. "But that's just a guess."

"Trust you to marry a king and screw that up, too," Wanda Mae snapped.

Brittany sighed. "I did it to hurt you, of course. You've discovered the truth."

"You think you're so smart, don't you?"

Her mother didn't wait for an answer. She kept right on talking, the way she always did.

The sick part, Brittany understood then as she listened to the usual litany of complaints and accusations that followed after that rhetorical question, was that she found this comforting on some level. She clenched her free hand into a fist and felt her rings dig into her flesh, but still, this was some kind of cold, bracing comfort. It reminded Brittany who she was and, worse, who she might have become.

Nothing had ever made Wanda Mae treat her eldest

child as anything but an embarrassing burden, no matter how much money Brittany had sent home over the years, which was never, ever enough. Nothing had ever made Wanda Mae act as if she loved Brittany at all, for that matter. Not Grandmama. Not her other kids, most of whom Brittany had basically raised herself while Wanda Mae was out cavorting in bars. Not the fact Brittany was the only one who hadn't gotten in any trouble. She hadn't gotten pregnant and she hadn't gone to jail. She'd just left.

And still, somehow, Brittany found her mother's predictable fury soothing. She knew what to expect, and no matter that it was the same endless font of vitriol every time. It was her mama. It was the way things had always been. *You probably need to take a look at that*, she told herself, not for the first time.

After all, she'd lost her virginity at last. She'd never thought that would happen. Didn't that suggest anything could?

But not today. Not when she felt so…ripped up inside. It was as if those stolen, heated moments in the castle had done a whole lot more than throw her over a cliff she hadn't known existed. They had crumbled her foundations into dust.

Cairo had.

She didn't know what to do about it. She didn't know if anything could be done about it, come to that. And her mother was still shooting off her mouth, the way she liked to do when she got going.

No wonder she'd answered this call. Somewhere deep inside, Brittany had obviously wanted to know that something, somewhere, would remain the same no matter how much she might have changed. No matter how much Cairo had already changed her, from the inside out, leaving her flailing about without a mask when she needed one the most.

"Only you could manage to marry the one person on earth more sinful and shameful than you are," Wanda Mae was saying as if personally affronted by this. "How am I supposed to hold my head up in town, Brittany?"

"I've never known how to answer that question, Mama," she replied, unable to keep the weariness from her voice. "But I'd imagine you should use your neck, like anyone else."

"I'm glad you can still make smart remarks. I'm glad you think this is one more big joke, like everything else in your life. Everyone knows exactly what kind of sick pervert that man is. Everyone knows what he's like. It's probably why you chose him. You *like* degenerate, disgusting—"

Brittany didn't know she meant to move and she had no memory of doing it, but then she was standing there by the side of the bed as if she'd *jumped* up. Her heart pounded at her, suggesting she had.

"Careful, Mama," she said, and her voice was cold. A kind of blade, slicing through her mother's stream of words and shocking them both, if her mother's gasp was any indication. "Be very careful. Keep running your mouth about him and you might find the bank dries right up. Then how will you keep yourself in cigarettes and beer?"

"You would threaten your own mother?"

"I don't want to hear your thoughts on this marriage."

Wanda Mae sniffed. "This is the influence that man has on you. This is the kind of ungrateful, selfish creature you've turned into, in such company. Flaunting yourself all over the world and then taking it out on your poor—"

"This is your last warning," Brittany said, even colder. "I'm not playing with you, Mama. He is off-limits to you."

Her mother fell quiet, and Brittany couldn't seem to feel that shocking little victory the way she should. She felt too unsteady. Her stomach was twisted into a knot and her heart was pounding at her. And she couldn't remember the last time she'd defended her choices to her mother. Had she ever?

But she refused to listen to her mother vent her spleen on Cairo.

She refused.

She didn't really want to ask herself why.

"You listen to me, Brittany," her mother said after a long pause, and her voice had gone quiet. Brittany closed her eyes and braced herself. "You think I don't know anything. You lit out of Gulfport and never looked back and believe you me, your opinion of the folks you left behind couldn't be more clear. You think we're all dumb country trash."

"I think nothing of the kind," Brittany gritted out, and what she hated herself for the most was how guilty she felt when her mother said these things. As if Brittany's snobbery had been the problem instead of Wanda Mae's patented blend of neglect and malice. "I think you'd find just as much about me to criticize if I lived next door."

"But I know a few things about rich men and poor girls," Wanda Mae continued as if Brittany hadn't said a word. "There's nothing new about it."

"Haven't you heard, Mama? I'm not all that poor any longer. If I was, you wouldn't get all those checks."

"This is one of the oldest, saddest, most run-of-the-mill stories around." Her mother's voice was upsettingly even. Not harsh. Not cruel. As if she was relaying a simple fact, nothing more. "Rich men like to play their games. They like to put a pretty girl on their arm and make a show out of it. They like to make sure everyone knows what a sacrifice they're making, taking on a charity project like her, so young and so desperate. And then they make those girls pay for the privilege. They make them pay and pay and pay. You might end up with more money, but you better believe that man will take whatever's left of your soul."

Brittany opened her mouth to say "you don't know him," but stopped herself just in time, horrified.

As if she did? As if anyone did? He'd been *inside her body* and she didn't know him at all.

"Thank you, Mama," she forced herself to say through lips gone stiff. "I'll keep that in mind."

She ended the call as her mother launched into another part of her lecture, then tossed the phone on the bed.

But she couldn't control the way she shook. The way her stomach flipped, end over end. Or the way her mother's words spun around and around in her head. As if Wanda Mae knew exactly how precarious this all was. As if she'd seen what Cairo had done to Brittany in that castle. How he'd touched her and, worse, how he'd made her feel.

What was going on with her that she'd tried to defend Cairo to her own mother when she hadn't defended *herself* in years?

"She's a lonely, bitter woman," Brittany told herself furiously, scowling at the mobile phone on the coverlet as if it was her mother's face, flushed with her usual anger. "You shouldn't listen to a word she says."

But her words disappeared the moment she said them, as if sucked out of the plane's windows and tossed off into the dark.

And her mother's words seemed to echo there instead, like a curse.

Like something worse.

Like prophecy.

CHAPTER EIGHT

THEY LANDED ON the small, private island in the Vanuatu archipelago as the South Pacific dawn eased its deep blue and fresh pink way across the sky.

"Vanuatu," Brittany murmured as they made their way down the jet's stairs to the private runway. She sounded shell-shocked. "You brought me to Vanuatu."

Cairo found he couldn't look away from her as she stopped at the bottom. There was the sea and the white sands and the sprawling house he'd bought on this faraway spot, but all he could see was his wife in a crumpled yellow dress and her hair in a tangled coil at her nape.

His wife, who he'd had to force himself not to pursue when she'd barricaded herself in that cabin for the whole of their twenty-hour flight. He'd reasoned she needed time. Space. Some peace and quiet after the circus that was their wedding. To come to terms with what had happened between them in that castle, perhaps—before they'd exchanged vows. To accept that they were truly married, in the classic sense of the term that involved the kind of consummation she'd never experienced before.

And if he allowed her space, he could pretend he hadn't needed it himself. That he wasn't shaken by what had happened. That it was nothing but sex, that moment she'd given herself to only him. That this marriage was yet one more circus sideshow, nothing more.

But she was his wife even so. The morning breeze from

the sea all around them was cool and soft, and teased the ends of the hair she'd braided to one side and tossed over her shoulder. She swallowed hard as she looked around, and he found himself watching the lovely line of her throat as if there were clues there. Answers to questions he didn't know how to ask.

"It looks exactly as I imagined it would," Brittany said quietly. Perhaps too quietly.

"Did you not wish to come here?" Cairo asked.

His own voice sounded unduly harsh in the quiet morning, with no other sounds but the surf and the breeze. He felt like a parody of himself. Even the clothes he wore seemed to brand him a fraud. A T-shirt that clung to his torso. Casual linen trousers. He felt like a beach bum instead of a king, or even the Euro-trash version of a king he'd been playing to the hilt all these years, and he found that made him...uneasy.

As if she would forget who he was if he gave her the chance. Or he would.

"I've always wanted to come here." She swallowed again, then blinked, as if she was shaking something off. Him? Their wedding? He didn't much care for that notion. "Eventually, I wanted to come here and stay forever."

"The island is yours," he said shortly. Gruffly.

Her gaze moved to his and he didn't like that it was troubled. He didn't like that at all.

"Mine? What do you mean, 'mine'?"

Cairo nodded to the waiting servants to handle their baggage and then took Brittany's arm, threading it through his. She didn't resist, and he found himself turning that over and over in his head like some hapless boy obsessing over his first sweetheart. It appalled him. Deeply. He was frowning as they started up the winding path toward the house that waited at the widest part of the small island, all rolled-up walls and high ceilings to let the tropics inside. An island paradise, if he said so himself.

But all he could concentrate on was the feel of her skin against his. Her arm on his. The smallest, most innocuous touch he could imagine, and yet it pounded through him like fire.

He had never felt so naked in all his life.

"Consider this place a wedding gift." His voice was even rougher then.

Cairo didn't know what was wrong with him. He'd spent twenty hours sitting on a jet plane becoming more and more of a stranger to himself. As if he'd left every careful mask he'd ever worn behind at that castle in Italy. As if here, with this woman, he was a man. Not an exiled king. Not a disgrace.

He didn't have the slightest idea what that meant, only that it spun in him, making him feel something like drunk.

Brittany was frowning now. At him. "You can't hand out islands as presents. That's insane."

Cairo ignored that. He reveled in the simple feel of her arm against his. Her lithe body moving beside him as they walked through the gathering daylight. The silky tropical breeze that danced around them and over them, making him remember those moments he'd been deep inside her—

Remember them. Who was he kidding? He hadn't thought of anything else since it had happened. He hadn't really tried.

"I was beginning to think I'd married Sleeping Beauty." He thought he felt her stiffen slightly beside him, and he thought there must be something deeply wrong with him that he'd view that as a good thing. Or any other reaction she had, for that matter. As long as he got to her. "And here I am, a king without a country instead of the necessary Prince Charming. It would have been quite the PR disaster, don't you think?"

She glanced at him, then back toward the path that stretched ahead of them. "I was tired."

"Are you certain?"

"Am I certain I was tired?" She frowned at him then. "Yes. But if I'd been confused, the fact I've slept for hours and hours would have cleared it up for me."

"It was a twenty-hour flight, give or take."

"Then, yes, Cairo. I'd say I was tired."

He tried to smile. That same casual lazy smile he'd used all his life. It should have come easily to him, the way it always had, but his own mouth betrayed him. "Because I was starting to think you were hiding in that bedroom."

She didn't pull her arm from his and Cairo didn't know why that felt like a gift.

"Do I have a reason to hide from you?" she asked. Carefully.

He thought they were both a little too aware that she hadn't exactly denied it.

"You tell me."

But she didn't. They walked for a moment in silence. The waves surged against the shore and the palm trees clattered overhead. Her bright copper hair, thick and wild, unwound itself from her makeshift braid as it moved and flowed around her, and he knew how she tasted, now. He knew how soft and molten she was for him, and the noises she made when he moved deep inside her. He knew her.

Maybe that was why his heart kicked at him, making his whole chest hurt.

"I appreciate the thought," she said in what he thought was a remarkably stiff voice, here on a tropical island in the middle of a perfect blue sea in all directions. "But I can't accept an entire island. As a…bridal present for a wedding that has the shelf life of organic fruit."

A swift glance her way showed him nothing. Her expression was smooth. Composed. The way it always was, as if he'd never held the heat of her in his hand.

His chest hurt. Worse than before. He was fairly certain it was that temper of his he normally kept locked away. Or worse, the truth of himself he'd been hiding from all these years.

"I am afraid it is already done." He stopped moving when the path ended at the bottom of the sweeping lawn that led up to one of the house's many lanais. "The island is yours, as is everything on it. My attorneys transferred ownership the moment you said 'I do.'"

She managed to pull her arm from his without seeming to do it on purpose. Cairo might have admired the sheer efficiency of the gesture if he hadn't hated that he was no longer touching her.

"No."

Her voice was low. She crossed her arms and frowned out toward the horizon. And Cairo could have pretended he hadn't heard her. That she hadn't spoken.

He didn't know why he didn't.

"I apologize that the gift does not please you," he said stiffly. "Is it the size of the island? The house? Would you prefer something larger or more ornate? Dubai, perhaps?"

"Of course not." She shook her head, but she still didn't meet his gaze. "I grew up in a trailer with my mother, whatever boyfriend she had that week and four other kids. Any house containing a room I don't have to share is like heaven to me. This…" She jutted her chin toward the house and when she finally looked at him again, her eyes were much too dark. "The house is beautiful, Cairo. Everything here is beautiful. It's so much more than I imagined."

"Then I fail to see the problem."

He felt rooted to the ground. Frozen into place. Completely out of his element—and how could that be? How had this woman turned him so upside down? What the hell had she done to him?

But he thought he knew. He hadn't expected her to be a virgin. To be innocent. There was no place in his sad, soiled life for *innocence*. And because he hadn't been prepared, even after she'd given herself away and he'd guessed the truth, he'd simply...reacted. He hadn't planned out what he'd do. He hadn't performed his usual role.

Those moments with her on the bed in that castle were the most genuine he'd been in at least twenty years, and it was addictive. He wanted more. He wanted her. He wanted to be the man he was with her, not the role he played.

He wanted everything.

"This is the problem," Brittany said, and her tone was too even. "This is my dream. I told you that. *Mine*. You have no right to use it as part of this sick little farce we're acting out for the world's amusement."

"By which I am to assume you mean our marriage."

"Marriage, performance art—whatever you want to call it." She shrugged. "It's not real. Coming to Vanuatu is a dream that's sustained me for years. It's what I've held on to through every single horrible thing that's written about me or said to my face. It's what allows me to shrug it all off. How could you possibly imagine I'd want to pollute it with this thing? With—"

She cut herself off.

"Me?" Cairo supplied coolly, because she did not see a man. She saw the game. The roles he played. The creature he'd become.

"I don't know what you dream about," she threw at him, and his particular sickness was that he found that to be progress, that little show of temper. "I couldn't begin to guess."

"I am a king without a kingdom." Cairo laughed at that, though the sound was hollow, and he thought the breeze stole it away anyway. "What exactly do you imagine it is I dream about, Brittany?"

"I dream about something that's mine," she snapped at him, and he saw the way she gripped herself tighter, as if she was holding herself back. Or holding herself together. "All mine. Where no one is watching me and speculating about me and making up stories about me. I dream about a perfect, unspoiled place a million miles away from the rest of the world, where I can disappear. Do you have the slightest notion what that means?"

"I'd imagine it means a well-staffed house accessible only by boat or by air, in the farthest reaches of one of the most remote island nations on earth." He eyed her, standing there with her feet in the sand and the South Pacific around her because he'd imported her straight into her fantasy. "Wherever will we find such a place, do you think?"

"I play a part, Cairo. A role." Her words came fast and hard now, and he found he enjoyed watching her unravel far more than he should. It meant this was getting to her, too. That he was. Cairo couldn't regret that. "I've been playing it since I was a kid. Vanuatu was supposed to happen when I finally left it all behind, not while I'm neck-deep in the middle of yet another performance!"

Something eased inside him then, though that pressure in his chest remained. He thought the way she scowled at him was beautiful. He thought *she* was beautiful—even more so than the island paradise that waited all around them.

He saw the way her lips trembled slightly before she pressed them together. He saw the way she leaned back, as if she'd wanted to put more space between them, but had forced herself to stand still.

This wasn't affecting only him. He wasn't the only one without a mask.

"Come here," he said. It was more of an order.

Cairo had the distinct pleasure of seeing that melting expression move over her face before she balked, visibly, and straightened where she stood. He *felt* it, everywhere. In that pressing thing in his chest. In his sex.

"I'm standing one foot away from you," she said, crossly, and he was insane to find that tone of voice comforting. He was a madman, there was no other explanation.

But he didn't care.

He sighed in the officious manner that had servants at aristocratic balls leaping to tend to his every whim, and then he merely reached across that one foot of space, hooked his hand around her neck and hauled her to him.

She hit his chest an instant later, made one of those soft noises that made the hunger in him burn white-hot and threw her head back to look up at him. She was scowling, of course. She was always scowling. But that meant she wasn't hiding behind her mask of composure, and Cairo loved it. He craved it. He wanted more.

"Cairo—"

"This is not a performance," he told her, holding her where he wanted her, her body flush against his. *Where she belongs*, something in him whispered. "You, me. Here. None of this is for public consumption. It is only ours. It is real."

The truth was the way she flushed at that. The way her eyes darkened with the same need he felt careening around inside of him, changing him. Changing the whole world.

"There's no such thing as *ours*," she whispered. "There's nothing *real* here."

"Tesorina," he murmured, "of course there is. It tastes like this."

And then he bent his head to claim her mouth, and showed her exactly what he meant.

* * *

The weeks that followed were like a dream. The best version of her favorite dream, in fact.

Brittany never, ever wanted to wake up.

It wasn't only that the house and island were even more beautiful than she could have imagined they'd be. It wasn't that they were staffed to the extraordinary level of discreet, nearly psychic level of service that Cairo demanded. That meant that almost the moment they had a thought or a desire, often before it was expressed, the plate of food was laid out or the tray of drinks was presented. That meant fresh towels and a selection of new, tropical clothing to better while away the days every time they exited one of the property's pools, or wandered out of the sauna. That meant the tiki torches were always lit the instant the sky began to turn colors at the end of the day and there was always a hammock waiting between two palm trees should they take a walk along the beach.

All of that was divine. Luxurious pampering far beyond anything Brittany had ever imagined. But far more remarkable than the level of service was the solitude. Their first night there, after Cairo had carried Brittany off to the vast master suite they'd shared ever since and after they'd worked off their jet lag in the most delectable manner possible, they'd agreed to simply…shut out the world.

"No one will miss us for five weeks," Cairo had said when evening had started to creep across the sky, orange and red, outside the open floor-to-ceiling spaces where walls would be in another house. "They will barely notice we are gone, with so many other headlines to keep them occupied."

He'd been sprawled out on his back on the bed, the sheets in complicated tangles at his feet. Brittany had been stretched out over him, the dizzying heat they'd built in each other still there where she pressed against him, even as the lazy ceiling fan moved the cooler air around on her back. Her head had been a cascade of images of all the ways they'd had each other already in that single, perfect, endless day. All the things he could do with his hands, his mouth. All the places on that stunning body of his she'd tested with hers.

Her body had still been humming. She thought perhaps it always would.

"I suppose we have the rest of our lives to be terrible," she'd agreed drowsily, unable to think of much beyond the simple perfection of the way their bodies fit together. The way they seemed perfectly crafted to come together like this and drive each other wild—

There had been something in her that had balked at that, deep down beneath the layers of satisfaction. She might not have had sex with anyone before Cairo, but she wasn't a complete idiot. She knew sex made people crazy. It made them imagine intimacies that didn't exist outside the bed. Hadn't she watched her own mother make that mistake again and again? Brittany had always vowed she'd never be one of those deluded fools, no matter what.

But she could put that aside for a little over a month, too, she'd thought then. She could simply sink into this thing and not worry about what came after or how she'd have to play it when they went back to their carefully scripted, relentlessly public lives. She could decide not to worry about it—about anything that wasn't Cairo, or herself, or how they made each other feel—until this honeymoon was over. And until then, they could lock their phones and laptops in one of the cupboards and let themselves soak in the peace and quiet of this little island so far away from anything.

"I think this is the purpose of a honeymoon," she said.

Cairo smiled, his hand moving lazily down the length of her spine, then back up again. "I thought it was an opportunity to post pictures from exotic locales onto one's social media pages, the better to maintain one's presence and public brand. No? Are you sure?"

"Ask me in a month," Brittany replied, grinning as she buried her face in that tempting hollow between his pectoral muscles.

Their days bled one into another, long and sweet. They walked on the beaches in the sun and in the intermittent rains that kept the plants lush. They sat beneath the impossible confusion of stars at night, out on one of the terraces or huddled together on a blanket on the sand. They talked, ate, swam. They argued politics and classic movies. They read books from the house's eclectically stocked libraries, discussed them, then read more.

And they explored each other, with a ferocity and focus that would have shaken Brittany to her core if she'd stopped to think about it. She didn't. It seemed part and parcel of these stolen blue-sky weeks. It seemed as inevitable as the afternoon rains, the kick of the tropical winds, the smudged blue line of the horizon far away in the distance. She abandoned herself to Cairo's touch the same way she lost herself in a novel or sank beneath the sea to listen for whale songs. No thought, no concern, no self-preservation.

There were no kings on this island, no class divisions, no strippers and no scandal. There was only the glory of the way her body took him in, again and again. There was only the sweetness of the way they came together in the lazy heat, the bold explosions of need and hunger they weathered in the pool, on the beach, standing near the trees, down on the floor of the room they liked to read in.

Brittany had never known another person's body as well as she came to know Cairo's. Every inch of his skin. Every tiny imperfection that made his intense male beauty that much more fascinating to her. She tasted her way across

the acres of his sculpted chest and lost herself in the taut
ridges of his abdomen. She licked him where he was salty
and slept tangled up with him in that great big bed. She
learned how to straddle him and take him into her, how to
ride them both blind, and how to tease him with the slow,
careful rhythm of her hips until he could only groan. She
learned how to love him with her mouth, sucking him
and licking him until he sank his fingers in her hair and
bucked against her, emptying himself between her lips.

And she had never been known so comprehensively
in return.

Oh, the things Cairo taught her about herself. About
her appetites and her capacity for both pleasure and need.
There was no boundary he wouldn't cross, no limit he
wouldn't push, if he thought it would make her scream.

It usually did.

He was insatiable. She lost count of the times he
reached for her at night, or the times their gazes snagged
during the day and led to more of that bone-melting fire
they fanned high in each other again and again.

It couldn't last. She told herself that *of course* it couldn't
last, but perhaps that was what made it so poignant.

Or that was what Brittany told herself as the weeks
rolled by, slow and bright and more beautiful than anything she'd ever dared imagine. Better than she ever could
have dreamed that night she'd rejected his initial proposal
in Monte Carlo. Just…*better*.

Because the other thing they did with all their time together was talk. Rambling conversations that started one
day and ended the next, and that Brittany only realized
later were deeply revealing. Stories comparing their very
different childhoods, painted in broad strokes and told
as if they'd been amusing, when they weren't. Current
events, popular culture in at least three countries, even
the odd conversation about sports—all these things, taken

together, meant not only that she knew the exiled king of Santa Domini better than anyone alive, but that he also knew her the same way.

Inside and out, that little voice inside her reminded her daily. *No masks. No act. Just you.*

She told herself it didn't scare her, such astonishing intimacy. Because she wouldn't let it.

One night, after they'd had their usual dinner of fresh grilled seafood and an array of perfect fruits, they sat out on one of the terraces beneath the night sky. The flames on the tiki torches danced in the faint breeze from the water, and they were tucked up together on one of the loungers. Brittany sat between Cairo's legs, her back to his chest, and absently ran her fingers through his.

It had been a month, and the fact of that had been echoing inside her all day. It reminded her that this wasn't forever. That this relaxed, smiling man who was all caramel and whiskey when he looked at her here would disappear, and soon. They would put on more clothes and walk back onto the stage where they conducted their lives and had already made plans to end their brand-new marriage, and these weeks would be the anomaly.

She would have to wake up, and she didn't want that. More to the point, she would have to deal with the growing worry deep inside of her that the fact she'd missed her period for the first time in her life, two weeks into their stay, was from something more than the stress of such a major life change.

Brittany didn't want to consider that, much less what it might mean if her suspicions were correct. All the things it might mean, when their relationship had a built-in expiration date. A child was forever, no matter their messy divorce.

A child would change everything.

"You seem far away."

Cairo's voice was rich and lazy, but Brittany knew that, here, it was because he was actually relaxed. She couldn't bring herself to ruin that. She felt the words on her tongue and swallowed them back.

They had so little time left before they were back in the world. It could wait.

"We only have a week left here." She blew out a breath and told herself it was kinder to wait until she knew for certain. Better. "It's going to be hard to leave. To get back onstage and into the headlines."

Her hair curled as it pleased in the humidity here, and after the first day or two of fighting it she'd simply let it do what it would. Behind her, Cairo wrapped a long curl he found around his finger, winding it tighter and tighter, then let it loose only to start all over again.

"What would you do?" he asked idly. Or perhaps not idly at all. "If there were no headlines. If there was only a normal life to live."

"A normal good life or a normal bad life?" she asked, tipping her head back to better rest against his shoulder.

His mouth, still the most gorgeous thing imaginable, grazed her forehead in a glancing kiss that still managed to make that glowing heat deep inside her spike.

"I believe that is the trial of normal life, is it not? One cannot tell, day to day. One is without the constant intervention of the press, there to interpret every move and fashion it into a narrative that sells papers. If that is good or bad is up to you."

"I want picket fences," Brittany said, surprising herself. But once she said it, she warmed to the idea. "I want to cook things, feed a family, worry about the school run and the ladies at the PTA. I want the life they live in minivan commercials, with golden retrievers and a good soundtrack."

She felt his laughter, deep in his chest.

"You would not get to dance in that life. The picket fences forbid it, I think."

She smiled at that. "I'd dance for fun, not money. That's the problem with being good at what you love. You turn it into your job and then it can't be about love anymore. It has to be about bills." She laughed. "Not that you'd know much about bills, I think."

"I pay my bills." Cairo's voice was ripe with the same laughter she'd felt in his chest, and that wealth of affection that she knew would fade, out there. Out in all those spotlights and flashbulbs. And it would likely happen very quickly if she really was pregnant. She shoved that aside. "Larger ones, I imagine, than most."

He pulled her closer to him. She could feel the heat of him through the gauzy layer of the flowing dress she wore. The heat and the steel-edged strength that was all Cairo. With his arms around her and his body surrounding her, Brittany felt hollowed-out and whole at once.

"What would you do?" she asked. "If you could choose a normal life, what would it be?"

He was quiet for a long time. Brittany could feel the solid weight of him behind her and feel the soothing beat of his heart against her back. She listened to the waves in the distance as she waited, and tried to tip herself over and out into the stars spread out so thickly above them.

"I do not think I know what normal is," Cairo said, when she'd stopped expecting that he might respond. He sounded quieter than before. "I do not know what it looks like."

"You could be an accountant," she said, crinkling up her nose at the image of his highness, the imperious accountant. "Or, I know, a traveling bard. Can you sing? That would work better if you sang, of course."

"The only thing I know how to be is me," Cairo said, and there was a strange note in his voice then.

Brittany didn't think. She shifted around on the lounger, moving so she could straddle him and loop her arms around his neck. She looked down into his perfect face. Those impossible cheekbones, that purely Santa Domini jaw he deliberately left unshaven, as if that could obscure the truth of him. As if anything could, exile or a thousand mocking headlines or his own penchant for self-destruction.

She felt him stir beneath her, and felt her own body, so attuned to him now, instantly ready itself for his possession. But she made no move to impale herself on him, to throw them both back into that slick, breathless heat. She only searched his royal face in the starlight, and that odd expression in his dark amber eyes.

"Then that's normal," she said. "That's your normal life. Why should you change?"

Cairo's mouth curved. "I like it when you are fierce on my behalf, *tesorina*. The truth is I have never adapted." He shrugged, and she expected him to kiss her. To change the subject with his touch as he usually did. She was shocked when he kept speaking. "I was bred to be the king of Santa Domini. My father might have been exiled, but he always imagined that was a temporary state of affairs. He had every intention of reclaiming his throne." His jaw hardened, and though his hands were at her hips she could see his attention was far in the past. "Even after he died, nothing changed. I was the unofficial king. I was always me. It didn't matter how many ways I made it clear I was unfit to rule. Every person I trusted expected that someday, I would take back the kingdom. All these years later, they still do." His gaze found hers, hard and stirring and filled with a darkness that tugged at her. "What is normal for me, Brittany, is to be the greatest disappointment my people have ever known."

"No." The word was out before she knew she meant

to speak, but she didn't stop. She continued, feeling very nearly furious—but *for* him, not *at* him. "Nothing about you is disappointing."

Something sparked in his gaze then. He lifted a hand to slide it over her cheek, anchoring his fingers in her hair as if he'd hold her there forever. As if he could.

"You cannot be trusted," he told her softly. "You make me imagine I could be not only a decent man, but the man I was intended to become. You are so far under my spell you cannot see straight."

"You're wrong, Your Majesty," she whispered back, still fierce and sure, and finally using the title that he deserved. *His* title. "You're pure magic."

The way he looked at her then, so certain that that was the sex talking and it could never, ever be true, broke her heart.

And that was when she knew. It wasn't a jolt or a shock. It was as inevitable as the next wave against the gleaming white sand. The sun sinking into the sea. It washed through her, changing her completely from one moment to the next, though nothing had changed. She loved him. She wondered if she always had, even back in that first moment when she'd seen him across a casino floor and had been struck dumb. She'd known this would happen from the start.

This was the ruin, the destruction, she'd feared all along. *Love.* As simple and as terrifying as that.

She'd spent a month here with absolutely no mask. She'd given him her virginity. She'd opened herself up to him in a thousand ways she hadn't known were possible, and she thought that no matter what happened next, even if she really was pregnant, she couldn't regret it. She wouldn't.

But she couldn't tell him, either.

Because she knew without having to ask that love was

the one thing that could ruin everything between them. Worse, perhaps, than the possibility of a child.

"No, *tesorina*," Cairo said, that look in his eyes that made her heart feel shattered. Sad and wise and lost, as if they were already back in Europe. As if she'd already had to give him up, the way they'd planned. As if he'd known all along that this dream of theirs could never last. She'd known that, too. And it hadn't done a single thing to stop this. Any of this. "You are the magic."

And then he pulled her mouth to his.

She kissed him back, a sharp desperation snaking through her. Because every kiss was measured now. Every touch was closer to their last.

She wriggled against him, lifting herself up so she could find him in his linen trousers and free the satin length of him between them. The fire that always raged in them both was a madness tonight, the flames wild and almost harsh, and Brittany shook as she waited for him to handle their protection, as he'd done every single time save their first. She let out a soft sound of distress when he pulled his mouth from hers, and he didn't laugh at her the way he usually did.

Neither one of them was in a playful mood.

She felt the blunt head of his sex against her softness, and she rolled her hips to take him inside of her. She worked herself down, rocking gently until she was seated fully against him.

Cairo let out a long, hard breath. Brittany wrapped her arms around his shoulders and then, giving in to an urge she didn't want to name, tipped her forehead to his. For an eternity, they sat there like that, drinking each other in. Her husband. Her king. Possibly the father of her child. For as long as she had him.

He was huge and hard within her, she was soft and trembling. Their mouths were so close she could breathe with him if she liked, and it was as if they'd both realized how close they were to losing this. How very short, indeed, the week they had remaining to them was.

She started to move then, and this time, it was a dance. It was joy.

It was love.

Brittany couldn't say it, she didn't dare say such a thing to the man she'd married purely for the headlines, so she showed him. Every roll of her hips, every lift and every slide. He peeled the straps of her dress down and took one of her hard nipples into his mouth, driving her wild as she loved him with every last part of her being. He pulled hard and she let her head drop back, and then it really was as if she'd fallen off into all those stars.

It was hard to tell who did what. There was only sensation and fire, bliss and longing.

Love, she thought, with each delirious thrust, but then she stopped thinking altogether.

And there was only Cairo.

He reached down between them and pressed hard where she needed him most, and Brittany exploded—but he didn't stop. He surged into her, pounding her straight through one exultant climax and high again toward another.

He flipped them over on the lounger, coming over her in the soft, silken night as he thrust himself home.

Deeper. Harder. Better than perfect.

Again and again and again.

Until they flew over that edge together.

And stayed there beneath the quiet glory of the southern stars until the first hint of a brand-new morning, when everything changed.

CHAPTER NINE

RICARDO ARRIVED ON the island via very noisy helicopter from Port Vila, Vanuatu's capital city, not long after the break of dawn.

He was not welcome, Cairo thought uncharitably as he watched his most loyal subject walk toward him over the otherwise deserted beach, the crisp suit he wore that was so appropriate in Paris looking nothing but out of place here.

It was a stark reminder of how far away Cairo had been from the world this last month—and how much he'd like to remain here forever.

"Was I expecting you?" Cairo asked. He led Ricardo onto the lanai where breakfast was usually served, and nodded toward the carafe of strong, hot coffee he knew the man preferred. "I feel certain I was not."

It was more of an effort than it should have been to keep his tone light. Lazy and careless, as expected. He'd grown unused to speaking to anyone but Brittany—and he'd thought he'd be able to keep it that way a while longer.

The truth was, he didn't *want* to speak to anyone but Brittany. He hadn't wanted to leave her when the sound of the helicopter had woken them both where they'd drowsed off together beneath the light blanket he'd pulled over them sometime in the middle of the night. He'd had to let her go, and he didn't like that edgy, pointed sort of feeling that had moved into his chest lately, to go along with that pressure that never really eased.

He didn't like any of this.

"You have been out of reach for a month, Sire," Ricardo replied, pressing a mug of coffee to his lips. He took a pull, relaxed his shoulders, then focused on Cairo again. "Completely out of reach. There were rumors that you were dead."

Cairo waved a hand. "There are always rumors."

"These were more convincing, given the absence of the usual photographic evidence to the contrary."

"I would never die in so obscure a fashion," Cairo murmured, and some part of him was dismayed at how easy it was to pick up his role again. To slip back into that second skin of his and treat it like it was the only one he knew. "Especially not so tragically young. I would make certain to die theatrically in a major city, the better to leverage good media coverage of my pageant of a funeral."

"Sire." Ricardo's expression was…not grim, exactly. *Solemn*, Cairo thought. And something rather more like *expectant*. "General Estes suffered a massive heart attack a few days ago. He collapsed in the palace and was rushed to the hospital, where, after many attempts to revive him, he died." He watched Cairo's face as if he expected a reaction. When Cairo only stared, he cleared his throat. "His ministers have stepped in and are trying to maintain the peace, but they have never been anything but puppets. You know this. And, Sire. The people…" Ricardo made no attempt to hide the gleam in his gaze when he trained it on Cairo. The fervor, the belief. "Sire, the people are ready."

Time seemed to spread out. To flatten.

Cairo remembered his father's hand, heavy on his shoulder as they'd walked together through a foggy British morning on a remote estate, years ago now.

"What if we never go home?" Cairo had asked. He

could not have been more than eight years old. His father, then the exiled king to Cairo's crown prince, had seemed so old to him then. So wise and aged, when in truth he'd been an athletic man midway through his forties.

"It is your duty to carry Santa Domini within you wherever you go, whether we return home or not," his father had said. "You must serve the kingdom in all you do and say. All you are. Every step and every action, Cairo. That is your calling. Your destiny."

He'd never forgotten it. Not when they'd come to get him out of his history classroom that rainy winter day, bundling him off to a room where grim strangers frowned at him and pretended to be concerned for him. Not when they'd told him everyone he loved was dead and his world was forever altered. Not when he'd realized that he must be next on the general's assassination list, no matter that the man's involvement was never officially confirmed, and no matter how many people told him that it had been an accident.

Not when he'd wondered, in his grief, if he should let the general exterminate him, too. It would have been so much easier than fighting.

He'd thought of the kingdom then.

"There's only the prince now," the woman had said on the news. She'd been a village woman from one of the most remote spots in the kingdom. He'd watched her from a guarded hotel room somewhere outside of Boston, while the authorities investigated his family's death. He hadn't been permitted to attend their funerals, but he'd watched his people mourn. "He's all that we have left of our history."

He'd served the kingdom then, and lived. Santa Domini's history—but ever unfit to lead. He'd made sure of it.

He thought of the kingdom now.

He thought of the general, dead at last with all the

blood of Cairo's family still there on his hands. And the things that roared in him then had sharp claws. They left deep marks that he knew, from experience, would never go away.

He thought of the woman who had called him magic, who had seen him as no one else in all the world had ever seen him. And no one else ever would. He told himself he didn't understand what it was that tugged so hard and so insistently at his heart then, leaving him bleak.

He had made himself unfit to be a king. He could not undo that now. He could not erase the things he'd done, nor allow the man who'd done them—the man his father would have loathed—to sit upon that throne.

Cairo had no choice but to gaze back at Ricardo blandly.

"Ready for what?" he asked, and, oh, what it cost him to sound so bored. So disengaged. "The funeral? I'm sure the general's men will give him a good show." He paused, as if something occurred to him. "You must know *I* cannot set foot on Santa Dominian soil, Ricardo. Not even all these years later, when no one could possibly care either way."

He saw the incredulity on his man's face, followed by a flash of something as close to pure rage as he'd ever seen a servant show in his presence. And if that made him feel sick, if he loathed himself as much as his father might have had he lived to see what his son had become, that was neither here nor there.

This wasn't about him. It never had been.

"Ricardo," he said gently, "what game do you think we've been playing here? The goal is to remind the world at every turn that I am not fit to lead. Has that changed?"

"I thought…" Ricardo looked lost. "Sire, that was a game you played, but now it's ended. I assumed we were merely biding our time."

"You know what they say about making assumptions, I am certain."

Ricardo put his coffee down as if he feared he might otherwise drop it. Cairo opened his mouth to say something else, to hammer in the man's low impression of him even harder and deeper, but heard the faintest sound from behind him.

Cairo knew what he'd see before he turned to confirm it. He'd grown accustomed to the sound of that particular light step. Those particular bare feet against the stones. He'd know her anywhere.

Brittany stood there in the wide-open entry to the lanai, in the deep shadows of the house. She'd thrown on a different dress, this one a bright riot of colors that cascaded from a neat bow around her neck all the way to the ground. Her hair fell in the careless abandon he found endlessly compelling here, copper and bright, but her hazel eyes were too dark and fixed on him.

He'd kept telling himself that he was scratching an itch. Week after week after week. That one of these mornings he would wake up and find himself as bored with Brittany as he'd always been with every other woman alive. But an entire month had passed, and all he felt was this ceaseless *hunger*.

Cairo wanted to know what she thought. About the book she was reading, about the weather, about what she'd had for her breakfast, about the cloud formations stacked in the sky. He wanted to see what she would say next, on any topic. He loved the stories she'd tell about her Mississippi childhood, the drawl that slipped into her speech and the evident affection she had for the grandmother she'd lost when she was only nine.

He hated not touching her. He hated that she stood across the lanai from him and didn't come any closer, which felt like a slap after all these weeks. And he felt something very much like shame that she'd seen him transform, so easily and so heedlessly, from the man she'd woken up with into Cairo Santa Domini, professional joke.

"Did you hear?" he asked her, and he thought he was the only one who'd be able to see the way she reacted to that smug, bored voice he used like the weapon it was. The faint widening of her eyes. The quick breath she took, then held. "Ricardo has come all this way to update me on events that cannot concern me in the least."

"Sire," Ricardo tried again. "The ministers are the ones most interested in these rumors of your death. They want to move fast and elect another regent while pretending they think you've abdicated."

"Then I should stay where I am," Cairo said, sounding even more bored than before. "I cannot imagine anything less amusing than a riot. Let them work it out amongst themselves, without my involvement."

"Don't be silly." Brittany's voice was cool, composed. As sharp as it had been so long ago now, in Monte Carlo. It made him as hard as he'd been then. But this time, it came with a pervasive sense of sorrow at everything they'd lost when that helicopter landed. At all the things that must happen now. They'd agreed on it long before the general had died. "Of course, you must return to Europe."

"He needs to take his rightful place," Ricardo said, turning to Brittany as if he expected her to agree with him.

But her eyes met Cairo's from a distance that seemed much, much farther than merely across the lanai. And he thought he could feel that pressure in his chest cracking into pieces and shattering all around him, so loud and harsh he was surprised no one else seemed to hear it.

"I think my husband's rightful place is in the tabloids," she said, and it slid between his ribs like steel. Like a killing blow. Like love, he thought, vicious and deadly.

Because she knew him best, this woman. She knew him better than anyone, his destiny and his heart alike. She knew exactly how best to hurt him, and she did it. It made him wonder how he'd hurt her, to make her respond like this. But then it hardly mattered as she kept going. "The more lurid, the better. That is, after all, how we make our money."

Brittany waited for Cairo outside his expansive master suite in the historic Parisian residence. The one she didn't share. The one he'd told her was his before locating her and her things far away from him, down two floors and all the way in the other wing of the grand old house.

It had been a very long handful of days since they'd flown back from the island.

Paris had welcomed them with a glum drizzle and packs of paparazzi, and Brittany had felt...off. She'd assumed it was the culture shock. She'd assumed it was the difficulty in transitioning from a life lived in a sarong and a hammock to all the appearances at parties and balls and charity events that were expected of her, all to be recorded in snide detail in the papers.

She'd assumed it was that little secret deep inside her that she'd still been pretending might be something other than what she'd known, on a deep, feminine level, it was.

"I can't imagine they think you'll discuss the lines of ascension here," she'd said that first night as their car inched closer to the red carpet outside some or other film festival Cairo had insisted they attend. The cameras were everywhere. Squat, grizzled men had poured over the cars like ants, and waiting her turn to be picked apart was making Brittany feel anxious and faintly queasy. "I wish they'd leave us alone."

"You had better hope they do not," Cairo had replied from his side of the seat, where he kept his face buried in the paper. "As that would render you obsolete and wholly useless to me."

He'd been about that charming the entire way back from Vanuatu.

Two nights ago, he'd swept a cutting glance over her when she'd met him in the grand foyer of his museum of a residence.

"You look tired," he'd said flatly.

"How flattering." She'd hated that she had to work so hard to sound crisp and unbothered. That she couldn't switch back into her old role as easily as he had. "That was, of course, my goal for the evening."

He'd looked impatient. "There is no need to look so tragic. I am thinking only of the photographs." He frowned faintly as he took in her exquisite gown and the jewelry he'd picked out himself. "Perhaps that shade of red is not your color."

It had been the precise shade of red as the dress she'd worn at their engagement dinner.

"Cairo." She'd wished she hadn't bothered when he'd stared back at her as if he hardly recognized her. As if she was nothing to him. She'd felt like nothing, and later, she'd imagined, she would lie awake in her lonely bed where no one could see her and if she cried a little bit about that, nobody need know. "There is no need for you be *quite* so brusque. People might mistake you for a Royal Jackass."

She'd thought she'd seen the Cairo she knew in there. Just the faintest glimpse of him, behind all that dark amber. It had made her foolish.

"I know this isn't you," she'd said.

"Do you?" he'd asked icily, dangerously. "Because I find I have no idea what awaits me in that mirror every morning. I was meant to be a king, but I made myself a clown. A disgrace to my name. I have no earthly idea who I am—but you think you do?"

She'd shaken at that, but she'd met his tortured gaze. "I know you are a good man."

"You know nothing of the sort," he'd said coldly, furiously. "What you know is that I am good in bed, as I told you I was when we met. Do not paint me with all your feverish little fantasies, Brittany. I am not a good man. I have only ever been a monster, and it hardly matters why."

"Cairo—"

"You are no use to me run-down and dragging," he'd said then, cutting her off. "My suggestion to you is that you see a doctor and sort yourself out, or leave. Your choice."

The bastard.

She'd only realized she'd said that out loud when his mouth had curved in a far icier smile than the ones she'd known and basked in on their island. It made her heart ache inside her chest.

"I am afraid I am distressingly legitimate," he'd replied. As if it hurt him. His mouth had been grim, his caramel gaze dark. "Therein lies the problem."

Yesterday, she'd summoned Cairo's private physician. She'd paged through articles on her phone while the brisk woman bustled around her and gave her the news, and she'd tried to imagine what it must feel like for Cairo with the general finally dead and a kingdom he'd made certain he couldn't claim clamoring for his return. She'd told herself to be calm, to be understanding, and if all of that failed, to be quiet.

Because she'd known going into this that it would hurt. Why was she surprised that, sure enough, it did—if in a different way than she'd anticipated?

"What are you doing here, Brittany?"

She jerked back into the present to find herself on the little upholstered bench in the hall outside Cairo's bedroom. He stood a few feet away, dressed in one of his three-piece bespoke suits and his hair a calculated mess, his expression as distant as if they'd never met.

Brittany told herself she should hate him. But she didn't.

She didn't. She couldn't.

I have only ever been a monster, he'd said, and that made her want nothing more than to prove him wrong. It made her want to do all kinds of foolish things, like tell him she loved him.

She didn't dare.

"It's lovely to see you, too," she gritted out.

He managed to look as if he was sighing heavily while not actually moving, a skill she might have admired under different circumstances.

"We do not have an appointment," he told her. "If we did, it would not be in my bedroom. I will see you this evening as planned, for the—"

"Will we just pretend that it never happened?" she demanded, and she was horrified to hear her voice crack. But she pushed on. "That whole month was nothing more than a dream, is that it? Have you truly convinced yourself of that?"

"The honeymoon is over." His voice was like steel. "It never should have happened in the first place. This was always a business arrangement. We should have kept it on that level."

"It's a bit late for that," she said, and couldn't help the laugh that bubbled up then. "Much too late."

Another look of impatience flashed over his beautiful face, and he shook his head at her.

"Do you know who I am, Brittany? Have you met me? Read about me in any tabloid?"

She had an inkling of where he was going, of what he might say, and it felt like a car crash. As if she'd spun out of control already and there was nothing she could do to stop it—all the while perfectly cognizant of the tree she was seconds away from smashing against.

"What," Cairo asked, ruthless and cold, "ever gave you the impression that sex with you would distinguish you in any way from the thousands of women who came before you?"

Everything inside of Brittany went horribly still, then. Frozen solid.

It occurred to her that was a blessing.

She stood, carefully. She smoothed her hands over the sleek line of the dress she wore. She remembered herself, at last. It had been so hard to pull her public persona back onto her and wrap herself up in it again—but look at that. He'd just made it remarkably easy.

"Calm yourself," she told him, from miles away. Her voice was crisp and cold, and the great thing about the way he'd yanked her heart from her body and crushed it on the floor beneath his shoe was that it couldn't hurt her any longer. It was simply gone. "I wasn't forming the queue for a chance in your bed. Been there, done that, thank you."

His harsh expression didn't change.

"Then as I said, I will see you tonight. We have a very precise plan, Brittany. I suggest you stick to it."

"With pleasure," she replied. Then smiled pure ice at him. "One small wrinkle in the plan, however. I'm pregnant."

One sentence and the world crumbled. Cairo knew that better than most.

He'd never thought it would happen again. It had already happened twice. He'd never imagined he would once more find his world divided so tidily into *before* and *after*.

"How?"

That hardly sounded like him.

Brittany looked smooth and perfect, which he'd come to hate. She was so different here in Paris. So far from his island lover she might as well have been a different woman. Her hair was pulled back in a sleek chignon. She wore a tailored dress and her usual impeccable shoes. She looked like a glossy photograph of herself. She looked untouchable, and no matter if she was slightly pale.

She made him ache. She made him wish he was a different man—a better one.

Her expression turned faintly pitying.

"You're the one with battalions of experience, as you are so happy to share with me and every tabloid reporter in Europe. Surely you can figure out *how*."

Cairo could only stare at her, the world he knew falling apart in great chunks all around him, though the hall was quiet. Deceptively peaceful.

"You cannot be pregnant," he told her.

Another cool smile. "Funny, that was what I told the doctor. Almost verbatim. Apparently, it's not up to me."

"You don't understand."

"I assume it was that first time, in the castle before our wedding," she continued, her voice as falsely merry as her eyes were hard. "How romantic, I'm sure you'll agree. I took the liberty of paging through our contract this morning and it seems there's no provision for pregnancy—"

"Of course there isn't." Dimly, he understood that he was raging. That he'd shouted that. "I am the last of the Santa Dominis, Brittany. It ends with me. There cannot be another."

Her composure cracked at that, and all the things he'd tried so hard to ward off and keep at bay swept over him then as her hands crept over her flat belly. As her mouth softened, even trembled.

He had always been so careful. How had he let this happen?

"Cairo." He had never heard her so tentative, and that tore at him. "Is it really so bad?"

"Do you think I spent my wasted life in the tabloids for fun?" he threw at her. "I did it for protection. The more irredeemable I was, the less likely anyone would ever see me as a king. The moment I became anything like a king, the general would have me killed."

Brittany shook her head, her eyes flashing. "The general is dead."

She had to understand. She had to see the danger.

He closed the distance between them, wrapping his hands around her shoulders and putting his face in hers.

"I cannot have a child." He heard the thickness in his voice, the decades of grief and pain. "I cannot condemn an innocent to this life. I have never been a good man. I have never lived up to a single expectation. But I will not be that kind of monster, selfish beyond imagining. I will not lock a baby in this prison with me."

He didn't know when tears had begun to fall from her eyes, only that they tracked down her face. And the hands he'd put on her shoulders to keep her at a distance curved to hold her instead.

"You don't have to do this alone, Cairo," she whispered. "Don't you understand? You're not alone in this any longer."

"We have a plan—" he started.

"I love you," she said, very distinctly.

Again, the world was cleaved in two. And again, he could do nothing about it but mourn the split—and the inevitability of what he had to do.

"No," he said, very clearly, so she could not possibly mistake the matter. "You do not."

"Of course I love you." She scowled at him. "You're the only man I've ever let touch me. I not only let you touch me, I threw myself into it without a single thought about the consequences. Please. I know exactly where babies come from, Cairo. I knew about condoms before I knew my own telephone number. None of these things are accidents."

"None of those things matter," he said. He shook his head, trying to clear it. Trying to think. "We will have to fabricate a lover and have him claim the child. It will be a huge scandal. The baby you tried to pass off as mine—"

"No."

She didn't scowl. She didn't shout. She simply stood there, her hand curved over her belly, her face pale, as if she was carved from marble, and as movable.

"No?" he echoed.

"No," she said again, even more firmly. "This is your baby. I am your wife. I'm done playing these games, Cairo."

"You already agreed to play them."

"I agreed to play tabloid tag with a man who doesn't exist," she said, and though her voice was still thick with emotion, she didn't waver. "But then I fell in love with you. The real you. The man who, deep down when everything is stripped away, is a king. The true king of Santa Domini, no matter what happened in the interim."

"The true king of Santa Domini died in a car crash years ago." Cairo's voice was harsh with the past. Bitter. "I am nothing but his embarrassing shadow."

"The general stole your country. He killed your family. He forced you into this terrible game and, worse than that, somehow got you to believe that the act you put on is who you really are."

"It is no act. How else can I tell you?"

But he couldn't bring himself to drop his hands, to step away.

"Is that what you want for this baby?" she asked him softly, her dark hazel eyes hard and beseeching at once.

"You want to condemn him to the same game? The same lie of a life in public, until it starts to feel real in private, too?"

"You have no idea what you're talking about." But he dropped his gaze to that belly of hers. "You have no idea what is involved."

"Here's what I know." And Brittany pulled herself away from his grasp, stepping back so he had no choice but to let her go. He saw the sheen of emotion in her eyes and the resolve, too. "Neither one of us had any choice. We did what we had to do, and our lives played out in a hundred different tabloids because of it. But our child deserves better."

"I agree," he said fiercely. "That is why no one must know it's mine."

She drew herself up to her full height and there was no pretending she was anything but regal. She had been from the start.

"I won't run. I won't hide and I won't lie. I am your queen and this baby is the heir to your kingdom. Don't you understand?"

She searched his gaze and he didn't want to hide from it any longer. From her. When he knew she was the only one who'd ever really seen him in years.

The only one who had ever known the man he'd hidden beneath a series of masks, each more elaborate than the next.

"It doesn't matter if you love me," she told him, and his heart twisted in his chest at the quiet resolve in the way she said that. "What matters is the future. The future you never had, but your child can. The general is dead. It's *your* throne, Cairo. All you have to do is claim it."

CHAPTER TEN

THIRTY YEARS AFTER escaping it in the middle of the night, His Serene Grace the Archduke Felipe Skander Cairo of Santa Domini walked back into the Royal Palace that his family had held for generations.

It had been remarkably easy to retrace his family's steps. Up into the mountains and over the border, then down through the farthest villages, making his way through the very heart of the alpine kingdom he had been born to protect.

And with every step, he knew. That this was right. That this was home. That even if what was left of the general's military executed him the moment he set foot in the palace, this was where he belonged.

In his country, with his people, taking back what was his so that no child of his blood would be forced to live as he had done all these miserable years.

The white-covered mountains were deep in his bones. The green hills, the crystal-blue lakes—they pumped in his blood. They made him who he was.

By the time he reached the palace gates, he had attracted followers and the inevitable press. But he didn't stop to read headlines or gauge public sentiment.

He didn't care what the papers said. This was right. Finally, he was doing what was right.

Ricardo stood proud at his side. Hundreds of loyalists stood at his back. The police had met them outside the capital city, but rather than arresting them all, had only escorted the procession along their route toward the palace.

"You are a movement, Sire," Ricardo told him.

Cairo knew better. He was a man. He was a mediocre husband and he was already well on his way to being a terrible father. He was famous for all the wrong reasons and he'd squandered the better part of his life in fear.

But none of that mattered, because one woman had looked straight into the monster in him and seen only the king.

Today, at long last, he would claim that crown.

He walked through the palace gates that the general's remaining cronies didn't dare close against the rightful heir to the Santa Domini throne. Not when he had made this so public. He climbed the ceremonial steps, as aware of the news helicopters buzzing overhead as he was of the brave men and women who walked with him, ushering him toward his uncertain future.

But he would walk to meet it with his head held high. As his father would have wanted him to do, he knew without question.

He hadn't been in the palace since he was five years old, but Cairo knew his way. He marched past the ancient canvases that depicted his ancestors, the frescoes and the marbled halls, to the grand throne room that he knew full well had not been used since his father had last sat there thirty years ago.

That was where they met him, a pack of fat, old men with soft hands and shifty-eyed guards.

Cairo did not wait for them to speak.

"Good afternoon, gentlemen," he said, stopping halfway across the polished floors and standing there beneath the statue of his grandfather, aware that there were cameras on him, as there were always cameras on him. Today he was grateful for it.

And he was aware that no matter what happened here, he would be remembered for this moment above all others in his life.

Better make it good.

"I am Cairo, the last of the Santa Dominis. I believe you have been waiting to execute me for the crime of possessing my father's blood for the past thirty years." He inclined his head, though his eyes glittered and he felt his rage inside him like a drum. "Here I am. Do with me as you will."

Brittany watched the dramatic reclamation of the Santa Domini throne with the rest of the dumbstruck world—on television, hidden away in a safe house in one of Cairo's lesser known properties in the remote Scottish highlands.

It had been part of the bargain they'd struck when Cairo told her what he planned to do, and what he needed her to do if he did not live through it.

It hadn't been lost on her that Cairo had not expected to survive. But it was one more thing she couldn't allow herself to examine too closely.

She and a Hollywood actor as well known for his collection of children by assorted famous mothers as for any actual acting waited out the march into Santa Domini together in the drafty old manor house. Meaning she had watched it live on the twenty-four-hour news channel in the cozy den while the blandly attractive, deeply boring man in question had done push-ups in the gallery and spent several hours on his mobile phone shouting at his agent.

"You don't have to stay any longer," she'd told him after Cairo walked into the palace. When the remaining ministers resigned on the spot and the bells of all the Santa Domini churches began to ring out across the land after lying dormant for thirty years.

Long Live the King! the news sites and the people cheered.

As if Cairo had never been scandalous in all his life.

Because he was the king, she understood. She was his scandal.

"I don't understand why I was here for this," the actor told her, annoyed. "Why would anyone pay that much money to have me just…sit around for a week?"

"Rich people are strange," Brittany said coolly. "Royals are worse."

Then she'd dismissed him and waited for the car to take her to the plane that would deliver her to her own fate.

She landed in Santa Domini the following morning.

Aides whisked her from the plane into a fleet of gleaming black cars with tinted windows, hurrying her into the palace as if they were trying to hide her from the public. She imagined that was exactly what they were doing. It was exactly what she'd expected they'd do.

Cairo might have been instantly forgiven his scandalous past by virtue of his being, in fact, a king. But she was a girl who'd taken her clothes off for a living and then married a few men for obvious practical reasons. There was no forgiveness for her. Especially when the king himself didn't love her.

She told herself it didn't hurt, because it shouldn't. This wasn't about her or her feelings or her battered heart. It was about the baby that grew inside her daily. It was about a different sort of love altogether.

She told herself that had to be enough.

Brittany didn't see Cairo again until they led her out onto the balcony high above the palace's famous square, where kings had addressed the nation for centuries. She had been dressed and styled by a pack of palace attendants, then brought here to wait for him with everyone else.

He strode from the great doors and did nothing more

than slide a swift, intense look her way on his way to his podium. She made herself smile. Because what mattered was that he claimed his throne and took back his kingdom so that his child would never have to hide as he'd done.

She smiled dutifully in her lovely silver gown, her hair sleek and sophisticated, as if she really was a queen. And then watched the man she'd never meant to fall in love with, the father of the baby she carried within her, take his rightful place before his people.

It didn't matter that he didn't love her, that no one could or ever had. What mattered, she told herself as he stood there so proud and tall and beautiful, was that she loved him. She hadn't known she could. She'd worried she'd been broken by her family, her squalid, public life. But she loved him, and that was a good thing, regardless of what happened next.

"I have been hiding in plain sight the whole of my adult life," Cairo told the huge, cheering crowd, and all the world. "I believed I served my country by disappointing it, day after day. By rendering myself the least likely king, I ensured not only that I survived, but that the vile enemies of this kingdom could not vent their spleen on any who supported me."

He stood there in the same sort of suit he'd always worn, the very height of male elegance and every inch of him royal. He was the same man he'd always been, so beautiful it almost hurt to look at him. But now, Brittany knew, the whole world saw what she'd always seen beneath all of that. The real man within him, brave and true, who had always been more than the role he'd played.

The man she loved desperately and totally, with every fiber of her being, but could never truly have as she had during those stolen weeks on the island.

He was the King of Santa Domini.

She was a jumped up stripper whose own mother was ashamed of her antics.

His voice was sure and true as he addressed his subjects. Brittany called on all her years of pretending, all the acting she'd done and all the situations she'd had to weather, and stood there smiling as if her world wasn't ending right there in front of her.

The pain of it would pass. Or fade, anyway. She was sure it would, some day. She would always be his footnote. And the mother of his child.

But because she loved him, she would step aside as soon as she could do so without causing him any further scandal, and let him marry the sort of woman fit for a king.

It wouldn't make her child any less his heir, and that, she told herself firmly, was the only thing that mattered. That and the life the child could live, a life not on the run, a life that Cairo hadn't had.

Out there in front of her, Cairo was still speaking. He talked of his parents. He talked of his sister, the lost princess, Magdalena. He mourned the dead and promised that he would see to it that any citizen of the kingdom who had suffered under the general's rule would meet with him if they wished, so he could personally see to it that their suffering was ended.

Brittany thought she'd never seen a man better suited to be a king.

That was why, when her phone had rung beside her while she'd been getting ready earlier, flashing her mother's number and promising the usual punishment, she'd ignored it.

She didn't need that abuse anymore. She didn't need to feel badly about herself to know who she was.

She would survive this. She would do more than merely survive this. She loved a man who loved his country, and she wasn't afraid of the sacrifices ahead of her, no matter that they might prove difficult. Life was often difficult. That didn't mean it wasn't good.

For the first time since she'd left that island, and since she'd found out she was pregnant, Brittany felt at peace.

And Cairo was still speaking, his voice ringing out over those famous palace steps, down into the fairy-tale courtyard, and all across the world that had always hung on his every word, but never so much as today.

"Some have asked, why now? What prompted me to find my way back to my people, my country, my life?" He shifted, and glanced over his shoulder, his caramel gaze grazing hers. It was a swift, quick glance, and yet it was as if he looked straight into her soul. Brittany found she was holding her breath. "It was not the ignominious fall of a vicious man who fancied himself a dictator, let me assure you. It was something far less noble than the urge to do my duty. I found myself a woman who wasn't the least bit impressed with me and I made her my queen."

That statement went through her like a lightning bolt. And it hurt.

She'd imagined he'd issue a tasteful statement, released quietly sometime after the world had grown used to the return of the king. Not…here, now. With so many people as witnesses.

Brittany had to remind herself that the whole world was watching. That this was not for her or even about her. This was about a kingdom that deserved better than a stripper queen. Better than an infamous woman who had only ever learned how to make money and headlines. She reminded herself that Cairo was not hers. That he had never been hers, not really, no matter that she carried their baby inside of her or wore the Heart of Santa Domini on her hand.

He belonged to his people. He had only ever been on loan.

But she cradled the precious ring with the fingers of

her other hand anyway, as if she thought someone might come and try to take it from her right there where she stood. She would give it back when asked, of course. She would do the right thing.

Until then, she'd pretend this was the fairy tale that deep down she'd always dreamed about, no matter how many times life kicked her in the teeth instead.

She lifted her chin. In front of her, Cairo smiled, then turned back to his subjects and all those cameras.

Brittany braced herself. And she smiled.

"I made her my queen and she made me a man," Cairo told the world. "And as I learned to be the kind of man who deserved such a queen as Brittany, kind and true, strong and brave, I understood what I owed not only to her, but to you, the people of Santa Domini. I did not know if I would claim my throne or lose my life when I returned here. I only knew that I could not live with myself if I stayed in hiding, forever on the run, forever a man unworthy of both his queen and his country."

He lifted his arm and raised it toward the crowd. "I pledge to you that I will always strive to be the king you deserve, and to serve this country with every breath and bone in my body."

Then he turned.

King Cairo, resplendent and fierce in the clear mountain air, with thousands of adoring subjects cheering him on from below.

Today, Brittany knew exactly what that glorious mouth of his tasted like, and how it felt against every part of her skin. She knew the heavy silk of his dark hair and how it felt to run her hands through it. She missed the careless scruff he'd shaved from his astonishingly handsome face, the better to show off that perfectly cut Santa Domini jaw.

And, oh, his eyes. They were caramel and they were

wicked and they were focused on her as if there was nothing else in all the world but the two of them.

He held her gaze for a moment.

Then the rightful king of Santa Domini dropped to his knees before her. Her heart stopped. Then pounded into her, wild against her ribs, so hard she almost toppled over.

"Brittany," he said, as if they were alone, though the microphone on his lapel transmitted his words around the globe, "I love you."

The crowd roared. And Brittany didn't have it in her to fight the tears that spilled over and poured down her cheeks.

"No," she told him, because she had to. Because he deserved a real queen. A good one, who was proper and good and had never been featured in a burlesque ensemble in a tabloid—much less on a reality television program. "You can't. You're a king."

"And you are a queen," he replied, the maddening man. "My queen."

And Brittany forgot the crowds, the cameras. She forgot where they were. They might as well have been back on their own private island, with nothing for miles in all directions but the deep blue sea.

Cairo held out his hands, then waited.

Brittany pulled in a breath, then let it out. She needed to walk away. She knew she needed to walk away. She knew she didn't deserve to be here, with him. She was supposed to be the joke he played on the world. She couldn't stay with him and let him become the joke because of her...

But she couldn't bring herself to do it.

She didn't *want* to walk away from him.

So instead she reached out and took his hands, feeling the heat of his instant, sure grip go through her, warming her like the sun.

"You married an exiled royal with a terrible reputation," he said, his voice low and sure and his eyes on her. "And you made him into a king. You wear the Heart of Santa Domini on your hand and you hold my own heart between your palms. I want you to marry me again, in the cathedral where generations of Santa Dominis have pledged their lives to each other, so I can make you the queen in my people's eyes that you have always been to me."

She opened her mouth to refuse him. To sacrifice the very thing she wanted most, the only man she'd ever loved and the only person she'd ever let get close to her—but she looked into Cairo's warm, steady gaze, and she found she couldn't do it. Not to him, not to their baby.

Not to herself.

The truth was simple. She didn't want to live without him.

Maybe, just maybe, he wasn't crazy. Maybe they could do this.

She knew she had to try.

"If you think I can be the queen you need," she said, and heard her voice echo back at her from all over the vast palace complex and the Santa Domini mountains that surrounded them, "then I promise you, I will do my best to live up to that honor every day of my life. I promise."

Cairo's smile broke across his face, brighter than the summer's day around him. He surged to his feet and he pulled her into his arms, and the whole of his kingdom cheered for them, loud and long.

So loud and so long that nobody could hear him when he leaned in closer, his gaze hard and hot and hungry on hers, just the way she liked it.

"I love you," he told her again, this time for only her. "I will never let you go, *tesorina*. Never."

"You'd better not, Your Maddening Majesty," she said. Then smiled back at him, hope and love and the whole of their future dancing there between them. "Just think of the headlines."

"I always do," Cairo replied, arrogant and sure.

And entirely hers, forever.

Then he bent her back over his arms, a dashing king and his Cinderella queen, and kissed her like a fairy tale come true.

Because, Brittany knew with a rock-deep certainty, it finally had.

* * * * *

Don't miss Caitlin Crews's next story,
book 4 of THE BILLIONAIRE'S LEGACY *series*
THE RETURN OF THE DI SIONE WIFE.
Coming soon!

In the meantime,
don't miss Lynne Graham's 100th book!
BOUGHT FOR THE GREEK'S REVENGE.
Also available this month.

Lynne Graham has sold 35 million books!

To settle a debt, she'll have to become his mistress…

Nikolai Drakos is determined to have his revenge against the man who destroyed his sister. So stealing his enemy's intended fiancé seems like the perfect solution! Until Nikolai discovers that woman is Ella Davies…

Read on for a tantalising excerpt from Lynne Graham's 100th book,

BOUGHT FOR THE GREEK'S REVENGE

'Mistress,' Nikolai slotted in cool as ice.

Shock had welded Ella's tongue to the roof of her mouth because he was sexually propositioning her and nothing could have prepared her for that. She wasn't drop-dead gorgeous… *he* was! Male heads didn't swivel when Ella walked down the street because she had neither the length of leg nor the curves usually deemed necessary to attract such attention. Why on earth could he be making *her* such an offer?

'But we don't even know each other,' she framed dazedly. 'You're a stranger…'

'If you live with me I won't be a stranger for long,' Nikolai pointed out with monumental calm. And the very sound of that inhuman calm and cool forced her to flip round and settle distraught eyes on his lean darkly handsome face.

'You can't be serious about this!'

'I assure you that I am deadly serious. Move in and I'll forget your family's debts.'

'But it's a *crazy* idea!' she gasped.

'It's not crazy to me,' Nikolai asserted. 'When I want anything, I go after it hard and fast.'

Her lashes dipped. Did he want her like that? Enough to track her down, buy up her father's debts, and try and buy rights to her and her body along with those debts? The very idea of that made her dizzy and plunged her brain into even greater turmoil. 'It's immoral… it's blackmail.'

'It's definitely *not* blackmail. I'm giving you the benefit of a choice you didn't have before I came through that door,' Nikolai Drakos fielded with a glittering cool. 'That choice is yours to make.'

'Like hell it is!' Ella fired back. 'It's a complete cheat of a supposed offer!'

Nikolai sent her a gleaming sideways glance. 'No the real cheat was you kissing me the way you did last year and then saying no and acting as if I had grossly insulted you,' he murmured with lethal quietness.

'You *did* insult me!' Ella flung back, her cheeks hot as fire while she wondered if her refusal that night had started off his whole chain reaction. What else could possibly be driving him?

Nikolai straightened lazily as he opened the door. 'If you take offence that easily, maybe it's just as well that the answer is no.'

MILLS & BOON®

Mills & Boon have been at the heart of romance since 1908… and while the fashions may have changed, one thing remains the same: from pulse-pounding passion to the gentlest caress, we're always known how to bring romance alive.

Now, we're delighted to present you with these irresistible illustrations, inspired by the vintage glamour of our covers. So indulge your wildest dreams and unleash your imagination as we present the most iconic Mills & Boon moments of the last century.

Visit **www.millsandboon.co.uk/ArtofRomance** to order yours!